THE
SINGING TREE

THE
SINGING TREE

An Alchymical Fable

A Novel by

Bruce Donehower

Cover Art: *Approaching Elowyn* by Marion Donehower

Library of Congress Number: 2003097175
ISBN :   Hardcover   1-4134-3343-X
                Softcover   1-4134-3342-1

This is a work of fiction. Names, characters, places and incidents either are the product of the author's imagination or are used fictitiously, and any resemblance to any actual persons, living or dead, events, or locales is entirely coincidental.

This book was printed in the United States of America.

A Publication of the *Novalis / Tieck Group for Fairy Tale, Mythology, and Culture.*

For information contact: www.NovalisTieckGroup.com

To order additional copies of this book, contact:
Xlibris Corporation
1-888-795-4274
www.Xlibris.com
Orders@Xlibris.com
21880

CONTENTS

PART ONE

PART TWO

BOOK EIGHT: THE RUINS OF HKAAR

BOOK NINE: THE SINGING TREE

Friends, the soil is poor. We must scatter abundant seed, if we are to reap even a middling harvest.

—Novalis

PART ONE

PRELUDE

The Departure

When Hannah was just a young girl, her father left her to discover the last unknown country in the world. Because he knew this journey might take a long time, he asked his brother Joseph to look after Hannah while he was gone.

At first Hannah was angry that her father didn't take her along. He told her that the journey was too dangerous and that even if he was successful and discovered the last unknown country in the world, there was no guarantee this country would be a good place for children. Hannah didn't consider herself a child anymore, but nothing she said could change her father's mind. He was a strong-willed and stubborn individual—a short, solid, muscular man with a peppery gray beard who much preferred red plaid shirts and always carried a useful knife upon his belt. Ever since Hannah could remember, he had earned his living as an adventurer and world explorer.

Hannah loved him very much, and she especially loved the way he laughed. Even in the most serious situations where no one else saw anything funny, Hannah's father often astonished everyone and caused his friends endless embarrassment by letting out one of his great, booming laughs. His laughter was so infectious that even someone very sad could not resist smiling when Hannah's father laughed. He was just that kind of person.

Needless to say, with such strange habits Hannah's father had a hard time fitting into society. Hannah often remembered the stories he had told her when she was young: tales of places he had visited long before she was born—strange countries way off beyond

China or somewhere deep south of the equator. Sometimes she suspected that he made those stories up. It's not that she thought her father was a liar—no, just that he sometimes let his imagination run wild. Yet, whenever she questioned him about some fantastic journey he claimed to have undertaken in his youth, her father never failed to produce some proof. Like the time he told her of his visit to the fabled ruby mines of Matagadask . . . *that* was a story she was certain he had spun, until he showed her a ruby, large as a robin's egg, which he'd kept balled up in a pair of old athletic socks inside a dresser drawer.

Seeing was believing, Hannah thought.

Even so, on the day that Hannah's father left to discover the last unknown country in the world, Hannah became very upset. And not without reason, for it is the opinion of today's most recognized brains that the world has been explored from bottom to top. Furthermore, if there were any spot on earth that hadn't been claimed, named, photographed, and charted, that spot must be a spot of dismal consequence, a spot no doubt well forgotten beneath some desolate snow drift in Antarctica or off beside a sand dune in some sub-Saharan waste. Certainly, Hannah argued, there were no more unknown *countries*, since countries were too large to overlook.

When Hannah's father heard these objections, he laughed. "How do you know there are no more unknown countries? If there were an unknown country, no one would know it—it's *unknown*."

Reluctantly, Hannah admitted that her father made some sense. Even Hannah's Uncle Joseph, a skeptical stay-at-home, admitted that his brother had a point. "I suppose it's not impossible," mused Joseph from the depths of their second-hand sofa, pulling on his ear lobe, as he always did when he thought hard. "Still, Charlie, you've got to admit, it's a long shot."

"I'll admit nothing," said Hannah's father, frowning. He preferred to be called by his proper name, Charles.

And Hannah, with a sinking of her stomach, saw that her father's decision was firm as rock.

"I'll write to you, Hannah," her father promised, "every day, or as often as I can. I'm sure I'll have a wonderful adventure."

"But suppose you get *lost?*" pleaded Hannah. She was barely six at the time. "Suppose something *terrible* happens?"

"In that case," said her father soberly, "your uncle will know what's to be done."

Joseph grunted, and Hannah did not feel reassured.

Uncle Joseph's greatest enjoyment was collecting second-hand books, and his greatest dislike was machines. He was a philosopher, and this, said Hannah's father, made him "odd." Unlike his brother Charles, who loved new territories and was always up and about, Uncle Joseph preferred to stay home. As her father had told Hannah many times, Joseph considered the world inside his head immeasurably more interesting than any place his feet might land him. Given the choice between a quiet weekend reading in his garden or tearing off to some unknown destination, Joseph preferred the life of settled habitation, hands down.

But Joseph's philosophical example did little to cheer his niece.

"Please, Papa, can't I come with you?" she persisted.

"No, Hannah. You may not."

"But when I'm older?"

Her father smiled. Although his tone made it clear that an argument was out of the question, his face soon softened with love. "We'll see," he told her, finally. "Now do this for me, Hannah, darling. Stay here; go to school. For you know, I promised your mother that I'd get you an education, no matter what. I'll be back from this trip before you know it."

"But my mother was a world explorer—you told me—before she died."

Hannah saw her father momentarily lose his smile, and his eyes took on a faraway, wistful look.

"Yes," he answered softly, "yes, she was . . . and one of the best. And you know, if your mother were living, she'd be the last one ever to permit you to come along."

Hannah knew that her mother had accompanied her father on trips all over the globe—so the situation felt especially unfair.

"Please, Papa, can't I come with you?"

Charles pulled his only daughter to his lap. His gray beard tickled her face.

"Now, now, don't worry, Hannah. You know I'll take you with me one day when you're really old enough to come along. There's a time for everything, and everything happens when it should."

"But suppose it doesn't? Suppose this really *is* my time to come along?"

Hannah's father frowned. "Well, it's not, and that's the way of it, I'm afraid. You'll have to stay home. Don't worry yourself a moment that I'll get lost or come to harm. I've been in this business long enough to find my way from there to back. Come on now, Hannah, perk up, you'll make it rain."

But Hannah, despite her father's laughter, just could not find a smile. She felt a great misgiving in her heart.

* * *

Since the day of that misgiving, seven years had come and gone. No one knew which way her father had traveled or how long his journey might last. No letters came to inform her; no telephones woke her late at night. Hannah grew older with her uncle, who kept to his books of philosophy and mused too much to worry about the time.

And then, one day, she received a mysterious summons . . .

BOOK ONE

Hannah's Gift

THE RUINED PARK

Until her thirteenth birthday, Hannah didn't even know if her father was still alive. On that day in early autumn, a day that started out like all the rest, two things happened that forever changed Hannah's life.

It was the kind of autumn weather that always made her miss him most of all: September, and the nights gone chill with creeping frost. Even in the city, she could sense the seasonal change; the smell of light was different—she could taste it. Was it the season or was it her birthday that made her sad? She guessed it was both—though a birthday, reasoned Hannah, could disturb even a philosopher's peace of mind.

How often Hannah cursed her annual fate! Her birthday was the one yearly festival that her otherwise philosophical and absent-minded uncle never forgot. They celebrated the event like clockwork, always the same way: with a cake baked and smothered with melting ice cream, pralines, fudge, and maraschino cherries— a disgusting mélange that no one but Joseph could have concocted—followed by a brief but ceremonious presentation of *The Gift*. Already six birthdays had passed since her father's departure, and now the seventh had come round. She had worried about it for days. So much so, that her sleep had been haunted with dreams and uneasy premonitions.

Her uncle only made the crisis worse.

Hannah knew that her uncle Joseph loved her, but each year as she became older she hoped he had forgotten she'd been born. Why couldn't the day just pass without their notice? (If birthdays passed unnoticed, perhaps your age never changed?) No such luck. On the morning of her thirteenth birthday, on the seventh year since her father had left her to discover the last unknown country in the world, Hannah knew at once upon awakening that as soon as she came home from school Joseph would have a birthday party neatly prepared—with cake, ice cream, present, and a card. At sunset, they'd light the thirteenth candle—*the unlucky one*, Hannah thought—and then Joseph would sing off-key, self-accompanied on his violin, his gray hair standing out like an electric halo—a pot-bellied Einstein—though Joseph had no aptitude for math at all. He had a Harvard degree, but Hannah never knew if this was something scandalous or fine. Joseph never mentioned his days as a student, and you'd never suspect a genius to see their cluttered house—what with yesteryear's Christmas tree still propped like a mummy in a corner, books piled everywhere, seedlings sprouting up on southern sills, tulip bulbs in the laundry, and the air a perpetual fog of shag tobacco from Joseph's pipe. (It was indeed a filthy habit—though not *the filthiest* of habits, Hannah judged.)

Birthdays always made the mess look worse. On birthdays, they'd observe the Neapolitan melt into a slush of turgid cream, with bits of cake, like stolid icebergs, floating gamely in the glump. At sunset, Joseph sang a sweet song and gave her a present—always a book that he found at the second-hand bookstore up the street, a book that invariably smelled of antiquity, to which he inscribed an uplifting quote: *To Hannah On Her Birthday, with loving regards* . . . Then followed a learned phrase or lines of poetry in a typically Horatian vein, often in a language such as Latin that no one but the over-educated understood.

Hannah knew he tried his best.

And she did try *her best* to appear appreciative of her uncle's wit and wisdom, but the book he gave her as a present usually ended up on one of their numerous dusty shelves, unread despite her best intentions.

She didn't want her birthdays ever to come round. So, this time, when the thirteenth birthday duly arrived, instead of going home right after school, as she often did, she went to the ruined arboretum a few blocks north of her house.

It was a good place to hide.

Hannah had gone to this park alone and moody many times, always to the same location, not minding the danger, for people never walked there anymore. They were afraid. Once the park, with its manicured lawns and graveled trails, its verdant glades and swan-swept ponds, its gazebos and memorial obelisks, had gleamed like the city's precious jewel. Now, punks and addicts and winos stalked its groves. The city had abandoned it—no taxes for things like trees.

Hannah found her way across the pot-holed avenue that ran beneath the screaming, elevated track, paused for a moment on the median, then leaped the graffiti-painted concrete wall that formed the old park's northwest boundary, careful to observe if she were free.

Indeed, she was.

The untrimmed trees reassured her. She greeted them solemnly, and quietly slipped beyond.

Once inside, she could forget herself—or at least, if not forget, she could *ignore* the everyday Hannah she had been before. She liked to think: *I am not who I seem to be. I am not just Hannah, I am . . . ?*

What?

She had trouble answering this question, but she knew that the question had to be faced, because, quite frankly, the person named Hannah who lived outside this park was not the real Hannah at all, she understood. Not in the least. The *real* Hannah, thought Hannah, was invisible. She was not the shy, awkward, twelve-year-old who lived with her crazy uncle, whose father had left her to discover the last unknown country in the world (whose father was maybe *dead*); she was not the orphan named Hannah who read too much, had trouble making friends, could not understand her teachers, and who wished she had been born in another place and time—no, no, thought Hannah, that person was not the *real* Hannah. The real Hannah was here, inside this park. The real Hannah, she told herself, was invisible. The *real* Hannah was on her way to becoming Hannah, but she hadn't quite figured out how.

Hannah had such thoughts quite often in this park. They often confused her. But sometimes, as she listened to the wind shushing the late summer boughs, she thought she heard an echo of her father's confident voice, cheering her up, consoling her, and urging her to soldier on, despite her doubts.

Then Hannah (whichever Hannah) brushed back her auburn hair, stood straighter, and squared her jaw.

A world explorer has to be resolved.

And this, she realized, sometimes meant doing just what you'd rather not.

In this case, her father once had told her, it meant that she could not come along.

Ah, whispered the wind; *suppose he's wrong?*

THE CHINESE PAVILION

On that Friday afternoon in early autumn, while walking alone inside the ruined park, Hannah made a remarkable discovery. It was the kind of discovery that you don't talk to many people about, the sort of discovery that happens only once—if at all—in a person's life. On that Friday afternoon in early autumn, seven years after her father left to discover the last unknown country in the world, six years, eleven months, and twenty-one days since her father's last postcard had arrived like a battered tomcat at her door, on that day of the celebration of her thirteenth birthday, Hannah met a fish that could talk.

It happened unexpectedly while Hannah washed her face in a reedy pond, a pond once noted for its ornate, shore-side gazebo— "the Chinese Pavilion," as it was called—a structure used for concerts, once upon a time—though now it just stood there . . . a graffiti-covered, termite-riddled hulk.

Hannah had just wiped her hands on the sleeve of her yellow sweatshirt when she noticed a fish watching her from the shallows, only an arm's length from the shore. It was a rather large fish, about the size of a football, and its skin shone emerald green and flecked with gold.

Hannah had never seen a fish so large or elegant in that pond. Minnows, yes, and frogs were there in abundance. But a fish of that size and beauty, well, it didn't quite add up. The pond was tiny and fed by a shallow stream, the run-off from a storm drain or a sewer. How could a fish so large ever have grown there—or was it just a carp that someone had flung away? Certainly not, Hannah thought. The fish looked as exotic as any fish from a tropical aquarium—like those fish you saw at pet stores. It was obviously not a local fish at all.

Strange and beautiful though it appeared, the fish looked rather friendly. And since it just swam there fluttering its fins, Hannah decided to say hello. "Hello, fish," she said, and that was that.

But the fish then made its reply. "Hi, girl. How are you?" Its words had a foreign twang.

Hannah blinked. It wasn't like the fish had actually spoken. No, its voice, as best Hannah could describe it, was more like a tickling inside her head, a kind of allergic discomfort that made her itch. She rubbed her eyes and ears and leaned over the pond, but the fish just floated placidly. It watched her and fluttered its fins.

"What'd you say?" Hannah asked.

"I said," said the fish, "*how are you?*"

Hannah rubbed her face. It was really a bit uncomfortable, this tickling inside her head. It made her sneeze. "Are you talking to me?"

"And who else is there?" said the fish. He swam a bit closer. "I know you quite well, even though we haven't met. You're Hannah, and you live with your Uncle Joseph on Banyan Street, and your father is Charles, the world explorer."

"That's right," said Hannah, marveling. "I guess you're a pretty smart fish."

"I am," said the fish, and his words, as Hannah felt them, were spoken with great dignity, assurance, and aplomb.

Hannah pulled up her sleeves and moved away. She squinted into the sun, low behind the ruined Chinese Pavilion.

"This is crazy," she told herself. "Fish can't talk."

"*Am* I talking?" the fish inquired.

Hannah wasn't so sure. She regarded the fish philosophically, as her uncle had taught her to do.

True, she noted, the fish's mouth had not moved. It floated beneath the water quite placidly. *If* it had spoken, it had spoken through the water, without moving its lips . . . perhaps by supersensible means. She suspected some rare species of telepathy.

"Who are you?" she demanded.

"*I am a Fish of Wisdom*," the fish replied. "I have many names and genders, but all that is too complicated for now. Since you ask, you may call me Walter, for Walter is one of my names. Now pay attention, Hannah, for there is an important reason we have met."

At once Hannah caught a tone of urgency in Walter's voice. "What is it?" she asked him nervously. "Is something wrong?"

"Yes and no," said the fish, swimming sideways. "What I have come to tell you must remain a little puzzling for a time. *Your life will completely change.*"

Hannah felt a tightness in her chest. High above the trees she heard the shrill, banshee motor of a jet.

"How will it change?" she asked him skeptically. "What do you mean?"

"I'm sorry," said Walter. "That's just the way of it, I'm afraid. When a tear from each of your eyes falls into my forest pond, then you'll learn more."

Hannah drew a breath. She had had her moments of sorrow; even so, she could not imagine how a tear from each of her eyes could ever fall in Walter's pond. Did Walter mean that something terrible was going to happen—something so awful he couldn't even tell her what it was?

Walter gazed at her with his two round fish eyes that never blinked. "Two tears, that is the condition—two tears, and then you'll learn more. But the tears must be *sincere.*"

Hannah pondered this answer and chewed on her lower lip. "Is it a riddle?"

"Yes," said the fish, "it is *a riddle.* Go home now, Hannah. We'll discuss this another time."

"But when?" demanded Hannah. "And how can I find you? Are you always here?"

"I am," said the fish, "unless I'm elsewhere." And he began to swim backwards, submerging in the emerald water of the pond.

Just before he disappeared, Hannah heard him speak again.

"*Guard the twig,*" said Walter. "*Guard the green and living twig and keep it sound.*"

"Twig?" repeated Hannah. She had not the slightest notion what he meant.

"*Try to remember,*" said Walter. And with that, he flicked his fins and swam away.

ELOWYN

It was nearly sunset by the time Hannah got home. When she arrived, Uncle Joseph had her birthday party ready, just as she had feared. She meant to tell him at once about her strange experience in the park, but as soon as she entered the kitchen, all thoughts of fish or prophecies fled her mind.

Two letters lay on the table. One open, the other not.

The open letter was from her school. Hannah recognized it at once.

But the *unopened* letter held her attention. She saw her name on the outer envelope.

Her uncle Joseph sat impatiently at the kitchen table. The tattered, unopened letter with Hannah's name on the envelope stood propped against the side of her chocolate birthday cake whose thirteen yellow candles had not been lit.

Joseph tapped his fingers nervously.

"Sit down, Hannah," he said to her, in a strained, unphilosophical tone of voice.

She had thought it was the letter from her school that made him nervous, for she already knew what *that letter* had to say. She had gotten those letters before. Quite a few of them, she winced. At the top of the letter, she saw the words: *Truancy Intervention*.

But it was the second, unopened letter that truly concerned her. This second letter, she observed, was far more strange.

"Read it," Uncle Joseph said to her impatiently. "I've been waiting all afternoon for you to get home."

She saw that her name had been written decisively in black India ink on the front of that brownish envelope. The paper was smudged and torn and faded; the stamps were unlike any Hannah had ever seen. The envelope bulged in an awkward way, and a dark stain of some unknown liquid had made a portion of her address nearly illegible. She saw that the letter had been forwarded many times, as though it had hop-scotched through the lost letter departments of several foreign post offices.

"I can't read where it's from," Joseph fretted. He nodded at the magnifying glass beside his arm. "The postmark's seven years old." His garden-booted feet tapped the linoleum.

Hannah could barely keep from tearing the brittle envelope apart. "*Seven years . . .*" she repeated. The words sounded pregnant with magic, as though this fragile envelope cast a spell that arrested the even and unnoticed pace of time. For at least *seven years* this message had been on its way to her, and perhaps even longer than that, like light from a distant star. She turned the letter over to check the return address, noting the many forwarding scrawls from the several foreign cities through which the letter had passed: Lanzhou, Loulan, Kashgar, Bokhara, Hamadan . . . *Elowyn,* someone had written in spidery script. "*Elowyn,*" she repeated—a sound like the sigh of wind inside a forest, a sound like the roll of ocean waves. "Open it," Joseph urged. He took out his Swiss Army knife and passed her its gleaming, serrated edge.

Carefully, Hannah slit the paper. A small, greenish twig, much like a clipping from a rose bush, fell from the open envelope into her hand. The envelope contained nothing else. She shook it to make certain.

"That's all?" said Joseph, disappointed. "No note? No letter? *Nothing?*"

Hannah didn't hear what else her uncle said. She stared at the twig.

There was nothing else in the envelope. Nothing at all.

Guard the twig, Walter had told her. *Guard the green and living twig and keep it sound.*

As the sun sank low to the western horizon, Hannah ran to the arboretum to look for Walter the fish. She carried the twig in her pocket.

Walter's pond, when Hannah reached it, was tranquil—gray and quiet and serene. No frog croaked from the grassy shallows; no bird flew from the shadowy, nearby trees. A slight mist had formed above the water, and the ruined Chinese Pavilion cast a melancholy pall upon the reeds.

Hannah hesitated, feeling a vague uncertainty, as though she had done something dangerous or wrong. She glanced at the darkening trees that crowded the pond's quiet waters. Nearly all their leaves had changed from green to gold. Now the gold had dimmed like a fading flame, though here and there, the higher branches sparked with a glimmer of sunlight. The air smelled richly of autumn and the threat of rain.

Hannah faced the pond and shouted: "Walter! Walter, where are you? It's me—*Hannah!* Walter, I need to talk!"

She waited but heard no answer—the only sound, a mosquito buzzing her ear. She shooed the bug away and called again. "Walter, it's me, Hannah—I found the twig!" She held it up—her mysterious gift. But the pond remained inscrutable. And no fish appeared.

Hoping that Walter could see her, Hannah squatted by the edge of the water, alert to the slightest movement. To her dismay, *nothing*. Strangely, the longer she knelt, the more uncomfortable she became, though she had never felt uneasy in these woods. She glanced around, afraid that someone lurked behind her, nervous because of the shadows that lengthened from the trees.

Scowling, she stood and brushed the dirt from her faded jeans, then she turned from the quiet water and started home. She felt angry that the fish had disappeared, or angry at herself for believing that a fish had spoken. Perhaps it was just a delusion; perhaps she was nuts. The fish had called itself a Fish of Wisdom, but a fish that spoke could tell you whatever it liked.

Guard the twig, the fish had told her. *But why?* And was this the twig that Walter meant? How had Walter known she would receive it?

Hannah had the twig in her pocket, and as she reached the edge of the arboretum, she took it out. The sound of the passing traffic made her feel somewhat safer, and she paused at the edge of the park, poised on the crumbling concrete wall that bordered the old arboretum. She shivered and drew a breath. A notion came to mind. She felt for a moment as though she were on the verge of remembering something vastly important. She could not quite imagine what it was.

The small, green twig looked frail and insignificant in her hand—and in the waning light of the sunset, a faint, yellowish aura seemed to shimmer along its bark.

Throw it away!

The voice that she heard came from somewhere distantly inside her.

Momentarily, she imagined how it would feel to hurl the leafless twig toward the forest, toward the dense darkness of those quiet, autumnal trees.

"*Throw it away!*" the voice commanded.

It was not *her* voice . . . no, it was someone else's.

"*Hanna'el . . .* "

Hannah shook herself as though awakening from a daze, as though recovering her self-remembrance. The twig lay securely in her hand. It looked so living-green—like a cutting ready for her uncle to transplant in their backyard garden. How could that be?

Guard the green and living twig, the fish had told her.

Quickly, she made up her mind. She pocketed the twig. *Better to keep it safe*, Hannah thought—*safe, until at least I know what Walter meant.*

She leaped from the wall and hurried through the traffic toward her home.

Near the wall where Hannah had stood a moment earlier, a shadow glided from the darkened trees. It moved in sinuous ripples to the concrete.

Briefly, it paused, as though observing the girl's retreat. Then, moving stealthily, it flowed through the deepening twilight and pursued her.

A Marvelous Book

When Hannah arrived home, she found that her uncle had fallen asleep on the living room sofa, a volume of eighteenth-century German philosophy spread open on his chest. He snored very loudly.

Hannah tiptoed to the kitchen where her birthday cake still awaited someone's fork. The thirteen candles had burned to pinkish stubs in the melted icing.

She did not feel hungry. On the table lay the torn envelope that had contained the tiny twig. Next to envelope lay the unopened birthday present Uncle Joseph had bought her; undoubtedly another book, Hannah guessed. The letter from her school lay beside it.

She threw the school's Truancy Intervention notice into the trash and took her uncle's birthday present upstairs to her tiny bedroom, whose ceiling sloped like an upside-down boat.

She did not feel tired, but she did not feel very well. Sitting cross-legged on her bed, she listened for several minutes as cars drove up and down her street. She stared at her quilted bedspread, lost in thought. Finally, for lack of anything better to do, she unwrapped her uncle's gift.

Hannah had already guessed that her uncle Joseph had purchased this present from the second-hand bookstore down the street, for that was his habit. A friend of his owned the shop: a curmudgeonly, ancient bibliophile named Mrs. Endicott. And, as Hannah tore free the brown paper wrapping, she saw that her intuition was correct. True to form, her uncle had given her a book for her thirteenth birthday: a small, antique volume bound in leather.

Hannah turned the book over and inspected it, displeased.

Surprisingly, she saw no title on its covers or spine. Bound in aged brown leather and embossed with a golden pattern of interweaving, serpentine vines, the book resembled a journal or a diary. And, like a diary, its covers were secured with a sturdy clasp. The book felt old—a hundred years old at least, Hannah reckoned . . . or maybe more; its leather cover was soiled and faded, as though it had weathered many a storm, passed from many a hand, through many a pocket, and had traveled with fortunate reprieve through the jaws of several near disasters.

She tried to open it but could not. The book was securely locked.

Curious, she searched through the wrapping paper for a key, but she could not find one.

Typical, she thought. *Just like my uncle.*

One year earlier, he had given her a Chinese fortune telling manual for her birthday—written in Chinese. This year, a book without a key.

Great.

Hannah pulled at the clasp and tried to break the book open, but the clasp, for all its apparent age, proved surprisingly robust. She could not dislodge it or make it budge, not even a centimeter. The book had been sealed so tightly, that even the edges could not be pried apart. It was indeed a nameless book without a key—as useless a present as anyone ever had ever received for a thirteenth birthday. Was this her uncle's attempt at scholarly mirth? She thought that perhaps it was, or perhaps he had found it at Mrs. Endicott's second-hand bookstore, christened the *Sphinx,* and had purchased it because he fancied its elaborate, antique binding. Who would know? Uncle Joseph often took a fancy to strange or misplaced things: antiquarian relics, hundred-year-old prints, post cards, porcelain figurines, maps, or romantic curios. Or maybe, thought Hannah, Mrs. Endicott, the second-hand bookstore's inscrutable ancient owner, had recommended the book for reasons entirely her own.

Hannah tossed the useless present to the foot of her bed.

For a moment, she considered waking Uncle Joseph to ask him

if he perhaps had forgotten to give her the key. But she realized
how soundly he slept, and the hour was late.

She yawned and settled herself down, taking out the twig that
had arrived so mysteriously—the twig that Walter had warned her
to protect.

What's wrong with me? she wondered.

She examined the twig again. Surely, she had imagined the
dialogue with the fish. But the twig, at least, was real.

A thought passed through her mind. *Did my father send it?*
And if he had, why and what did it mean?

Will he ever return? Will I ever see him again?

It seemed so long ago that her father had departed. Only seven
years had passed, but those seven years felt like seven centuries. So
much had changed. Sometimes she worried she would forget him—
that slowly, over time, what memories she had of him would slowly,
inexorably fade away.

She worried that someday the last of those distant memories
might flicker out.

What will happen to him then?

Hannah lay back and shut her eyes, trying her best to remember
everything about her father that she could: every detail, every
gesture, every smile or moment of time they had spent together.

But it was hard. She had been so young. Her memories felt as
vague as bodiless dreams. She could not hold on to them. And the
truth was that every day, every week, every month, there seemed
to be fewer and fewer of those precious memories left—and those
few that still remained felt less and less substantial. Sometimes it
even felt possible that she had imagined herself a father, when in
fact she was an orphan and had no father at all. Only her uncle
Joseph disproved this possibility. But Uncle Joseph was old, and if
he grew much older, as he surely would . . .

What is memory? Hannah wondered suddenly, sitting up.

The question had arisen so unexpectedly and clearly from amid
the turbid current of her thoughts, that it startled her. For a
moment, she had the impression that someone had spoken this
question inside her—someone else, but not herself. It was a woman's

voice. The sensation felt weirdly similar to the sensation she had
felt when Walter, the Fish of Wisdom, had greeted her from the
pond at the ruined Chinese Pavilion in the park. But the voice that
had spoken this question had not been Walter's.

It belonged to someone else.

Hannah yawned.

What is memory?

Such questions had no answers. Or else, the answer was as
sealed as the book that her uncle had given her as a present for her
thirteenth birthday. No one could understand memory; no one
had its key.

Tired, Hannah pulled her blue sleeping bag over her head.
The bedroom had grown chilly. Again, she thought of the quiet
waters near the ruined Chinese Pavilion and the fish that had spoken
from those depths.

Guard the twig, the fish named Walter had told her. *Guard the
green and living twig and keep it sound.*

AN IMPENDING STORM

Hannah awoke.

The sun streamed through her window, and the clock on her dresser told the time to be 12:00. "Noon!" she exclaimed, surprised (but not entirely disappointed) that she had overslept another day of school. Then she remembered. *Saturday!* Worse and worse. She never slept this late on a Saturday. Never.

For a moment, she lay still, trying to recall her scattered dreams. The pieces, as usual, made no sense. She could recall a feeling of panic, but the details had faded completely. She had only a vague sense of foreboding, as though the dreams had come as a warning of some future that did not yet exist . . . or of a past she could not recall.

Yawning, she rolled out of bed, and the book that her uncle had given her for her thirteenth birthday fell from the covers and on to the hardwood floor. Hannah picked it up.

Why can't Uncle Joseph give me something useful?

She pulled at the clasp then decided to ask her uncle for the key. Surely, he had it, or else (she decided) he must explain to her why he had given her such a vexing present as a locked, unreadable book.

Hannah struggled into a pair of faded blue jeans, found a T-shirt, tried it on, discarded it, found another sweatshirt under her bed, tried it on, liked it, changed her shirt, then tore apart her dresser drawer in a frantic search for socks. She found at the very bottom two wool socks that nearly matched and put them on.

Her room was very cold. Her window stood halfway open, and from outside she could hear Joseph whistling as he puttered about the backyard. Gardening, like philosophy, was one of the ways her uncle used his time. He liked to keep things green. And Saturday mornings were among his favorite times to dig.

Downstairs, in the kitchen, Hannah found some jelly and peanut butter and a loaf of that chewy wheat bread her uncle preferred. It would do. Crumbs of her half-eaten birthday cake lay strewn across the table, as well as an open book that her uncle had been reading the night before—*The Unconditional in Human Knowledge*, Hannah read.

She let it lie.

The kitchen was silent, and, except for the humming of her uncle out in the yard, her world felt silent, too.

It was all very odd. She felt strangely dislocated, saddened in a way she could not describe, as though she were outside herself, a distant observer.

Her birthday had passed, so it couldn't be her birthday that made her sad. Her *fourteenth* birthday (the eighth since her father had left her to discover the last unknown country in the world) would not arrive for another entire year. *Good news*, she told herself. But despite this good news, her odd feeling of dislocation would not pass. The longer she sat there, the stronger became her conviction that the day had started wrong. Something was lacking. But what could it be? It felt as though a part of *her* were missing, as though some vital piece of Hannah had gotten lost.

I'm missing, she told herself.

But that was silly, Hannah thought.

Scowling, she pushed the thought aside and browsed vacantly through the book of philosophy that her uncle had left on the kitchen table. So many words . . . As she fanned the closely printed pages, she became uncomfortably aware of a feeling that haunted her like an uncanny visitor, like the sweep of a ghostly shadow that hovered just at the periphery of her sight. It waited there and summoned her. But whenever she tried to direct the inner eye of her attention toward that shadowy feeling to understand it, the shadow shifted and momentarily disappeared.

Finally, she had enough. Rising, she walked back upstairs to her bedroom and sat on her unmade bed, thinking hard.

Her room looked just as it should: her books were all there: her maps and her pictures—her collection of stuffed animals, her antique dollhouse, and her desk (too small for her now). The walls were painted in the two colors, aqua and teal, that her uncle had criticized her for using when it was much easier, he had told her philosophically, to paint the whole thing white. She watched as her linen curtains fluttered in the cool autumn breeze, a breeze that smelled of dry, dead leaves burned in someone's yard. In the distance, she could hear the rumble of thunder.

Everything was just as it should be, but even so, something felt wrong. Her room, her familiar bedroom, felt cramped, as though—but this was impossible—as though the familiar things she looked upon had been kept for a person much younger than herself. They were no longer hers. *But it's my room*, she whispered; and after all, she had only turned thirteen.

On an impulse, she reached under her pillow and took out the greenish twig that she had put there the night before. The thought arose unbidden: *I should go to the Chinese Pavilion.* But why? Hadn't she already gone to Walter's pond? Hadn't she wasted an hour there, calling the fish's name?

The memory embarrassed her.

Holding the book and the twig, Hannah started for the hallway, but just as she reached the door, she stopped. Turning, she looked at the room, her childhood bedroom, and she felt gripped by a pang of sorrow that made her gasp. For a long moment, she stood there, puzzled and withdrawn, wondering what had happened. She felt as though she were leaving her bedroom forever, never to return. Even though it was midday, a part of her wanted to curl up in her bed and go to sleep. She had never had such feelings, and they frightened her. After a moment's doubt, she resolved to ignore them. Turning, she walked toward the doorway, and on an impulse, she grabbed a sweatshirt that hung on the knob, a blue, hooded sweatshirt heavier than the one she had on. The front of it said *Rutgers.* She put it on. And then, as she entered the hallway, she pulled shut her bedroom door.

The latch closed definitively with a snap.

THE LAST UNKNOWN
COUNTRY IN THE WORLD

Uncle Joseph was in the kitchen when she came down. Relieved, Hannah asked him whether the mailman had come, and Joseph, understanding her question, said that the mailman had already come and gone. There had been no more mail.

Hannah could tell that Uncle Joseph was as troubled by yesterday's mysterious letter as she, but he characteristically downplayed his emotions.

"Do you still have that twig?" he asked her.

Yes, she nodded. She could feel it inside her sweatshirt pocket. "What does it mean, Uncle Joseph?"

"I wish I knew," he answered, frowning. And the weight of his thought made him momentarily appear to be far older than his many years.

A thought flashed through Hannah's mind: *suppose Joseph died?*

She knew he would, someday. Everyone did. But until that moment, the thought of her uncle's death, and what it might mean to her, had been only a distant, abstract thought.

She shifted uncomfortably and took out the book that her uncle had given her for her thirteenth birthday.

Uncle Joseph, noticing her mood, smiled and shrugged. "It's locked," he admitted, "and I'm sorry, but I haven't got the key." He picked up the book and looked at it. "Feels *old*, doesn't it? Hmm . . . I liked the way it was bound. From the look, it must be something special—and it comes very highly recommended. Mrs. Endicott *insisted* it was just the item you should have for your thirteenth birthday. Don't ask me why. I'm afraid you'll just have to open it, one way or the other. Mrs. Endicott said she thought she could find the key. She said you should stop by and see her, when you have a chance." He weighed the book in his hand and stroked the cover. "I suppose we could break it open?"

Certainly not, Hannah thought. Aghast. She took it back.

"You do like the present, don't you, Hannah?" said her uncle. Hannah could not quite bring herself to hurt his feelings and say that she did not.

"It's very, mmm . . . *intriguing,*" she answered diplomatically, relieved that she could find the proper word.

Joseph smiled. He moved to the sink and began to wash the garden dirt from his callused hands. A pan of water simmered on the stove. The sink overflowed with carrots recently harvested, and a bowl of fresh-picked grapes had replaced yesterday's birthday cake, which, thankfully, had gone its way to the graveyard of discarded pastries.

Hannah popped a few fresh grapes in her mouth as Joseph found a kitchen towel.

"Looks like rain," he commented.

He pulled out a chair and sat down at the table, kicking off his black rubber gardening boots and removing a ratty stink-pipe from the pocket of his jeans. He took out a pouch of tobacco and began to stuff the bowl. Hannah had long since abandoned trying to get her uncle to give up his filthy habit.

"You're upset," he said to her in his awkward, friendly way.

Hannah nodded.

The afternoon light slanted through the blue curtains of the large picture window that faced their backyard. Hannah noted that her uncle had neglected to shave, and the bristle on his face reminded her of pictures of her father. Charles was heavier than his brother, a little older, but the two had similar eyes.

She reached in her shirt and took out the mysterious twig, the green and living twig that the fish Walter had mentioned—or at least she *thought* that the fish had mentioned, unless she had lost her mind. She held it up. "Uncle Joseph, do you think my father is still alive?"

Joseph nodded slowly, tugging his ear, as serious and kind and as well meaning as anyone Hannah had ever met. She wished he were a wizard who could just wave his hand to transform the world into a better place, but she knew he was only who he was.

"Yes," he answered slowly, softly and distantly, "yes, I do." He took the slender twig from her hand and examined it carefully. "I do believe he's alive, Hannah. In fact, I'm *certain.*"

Joseph rolled the small green twig between his fingers thoughtfully and then gave it back.

He said, "You must *remember.*"

Hannah looked at her uncle, confused.

Remember what?

For a moment, she thought that her familiar uncle reminded her of someone else. She could not say whom. He reminded her of someone very ancient.

But the idea felt silly, and she blinked.

She was on the verge of asking another question, when Joseph changed the subject abruptly.

"Go to the bookstore," he advised her. "Perhaps Mrs. Endicott has found the key that will open the book that I gave you for your birthday. She said she could. It may be helpful. You never know."

"Helpful? How?"

Joseph hesitated. "Well, it's like this," he explained thoughtfully. "Your father left to discover the last unknown country in the world. That's all very good, but you know as well I do that all the countries in the world have been discovered long ago. There are no more *unknown* countries . . . or if there are, we'll never find them . . . because they are *unknown.* Do you follow me, Hannah?"

"No," she answered, frowning, "I do not."

He tried again. "They're not unknown because they were overlooked. No, no, what I'm proposing is: they're unknown because by their very nature, there is nothing about them we can know."

Hannah shook her head. It made no sense.

"Then why did my father even try?"

"You're right," he told her, smiling. "I agree. But your father argued differently. I had this conversation with him years ago— when I tried to persuade him to stay home. None of my efforts made the least bit of difference. He decided . . . how shall I put this? . . . that it all came down to a problem of remembrance. That's what it hung upon, he believed—*memory*. Think of it this way, Hannah. If a country is unknown, there must be a good reason—don't you see? Either it's unknown because, by the very nature of the place, there's nothing about it we can know. Or else—and this was your father's point of view—it's unknown because we've *forgotten it*. In the first case, quite sensibly, things are hopeless. But in the second, there is clearly something we can do."

"What's that?" asked Hannah, suspiciously.

"*Remember*," said Joseph. And his features, as he spoke to her, again became for the briefest moment the features of a person she did not know.

"Oh Uncle Joseph," said Hannah, "my father is a person I could never, ever forget."

"That's good," her uncle nodded. "That's good news." He picked up the book that he had given her for her thirteenth birthday. "And perhaps this can help. I asked Mrs. Endicott for a journal, an aid to remembrance . . . something that would assist you, let us say." He tapped her book. "And this is what she recommended. Unfortunately, as you noticed, the book is locked. I don't have the key. Mrs. Endicott swore she could find it, and perhaps she already has. She is quite adept at conning that disaster she calls a bookstore. My advice: question her, if you have a chance. Who knows," he said, examining the mysterious book one final time, "it may be a consolation, if you can find a way to read what's written inside."

As he gave her this advice, Hannah heard a roll of thunder in the distance.

She did not think she needed consolation. Consolation just wouldn't do. She needed answers. Facts. But she saw that this was the best her uncle could offer.

It thundered again, and Joseph glanced out the kitchen window.

"There's a storm coming," he commented philosophically.

And if Hannah had been more attentive, she would have noticed that at this very moment her uncle's familiar features did indeed undergo a change. For a moment, the age-lines in his face deepened, as though the pull of gravity had increased. For a moment, he truly wasn't himself, but a person older and wiser, a distant stranger. But Hannah felt self-pity, and as she thought about Walter and her father and about herself, she failed to notice this change. Again, the thunder rumbled, this time a bit closer and more ominously.

"Try to find the key," her uncle advised. "Mrs. Endicott said she could locate it. Take an umbrella, in case it rains. And when you find the key, tell Mrs. Endicott to give me a call. I'm as curious to read in that book as you are."

Her uncle stood up, and Hannah followed him to the backyard door. From the porch, she could see dark clouds massing in the distance. The clouds looked like a threatening citadel perched atop dark columns of riven granite. The rumbles of thunder sounded like explosions from a distant battlefield, where unseen armies clashed.

"I don't like the looks of that," her uncle frowned. "Stay at the bookstore, if it starts to rain really hard."

Hannah promised him she would do so, and she left the kitchen as her uncle returned to the garden to gather up his collection of precious tools before it stormed.

INSIDE THE *SPHINX*

By the time Hannah arrived at Mrs. Endicott's second-hand bookstore about a half-mile from her home, the sky had become even darker and the first heavy drops of rain had begun to fall. Hannah entered the cramped bookstore breathless, and she found the owner busy with a box full of keys.

"Hello, Hannah," said Mrs. Endicott matter of factly, the tone of her voice suggesting that she had long been expecting Hannah to appear.

A bell that hung above the shop entrance, chimed as Hannah shut the door. Grumpy, Mrs. Endicott's bushy tomcat, who had only one eye, half a tail, and an ear raked ragged as a consequence of many alley fights, strolled over to say hello, happy when Hannah agreed to pick him up.

The shop, eighty or ninety years old at least, stood crowded from floor to ceiling with books. It had an odor of old books that Hannah could find nowhere else. The books, shelved in only the most marginally systematic order, were packed thick on pine board shelves, some of which sagged precariously beneath the weight. Woe to the person who entered Mrs. Endicott's bookstore expecting a snappy purchase. As Mrs. Endicott liked to say: "Nothing's to find; everything *must be discovered*"—meaning, she had long ago given up the Herculean task of imposing a semblance of order on this chaos. If one wanted a specific title, the bookstore remained as sealed as a hermetic tomb. But if one were willing to idle and abandon oneself to the order of this disorder, then the most curious and often enlightening discoveries might occur. (For this reason, Hannah's Uncle Joseph loved the used bookstore and thought of it as a second home.)

Somehow, Mrs. Endicott made a living from this Arcanum—

miraculously, since more books came into the store than ever went out. The books arrived by the box load, but they exited quite infrequently and often as solitary pilgrims, wrapped in brown paper, secured with twine. Nothing about Mrs. Endicott's business was understandable from the standpoint of common sense. The enterprise was as much a riddle as the Egyptian sphinx that someone long ago had painted on the wooden sign that hung above the shop's front entrance and which, over time, had given its venerable name to the establishment.

Rumor had it that Mrs. Endicott had purchased the store decades ago with the proceeds from the sale of a coffee plantation in East Africa. Others said that she had assumed the unlikely and pedestrian name Endicott to obscure her true identity—that in fact she was an exile from Czarist Russia, perhaps even a relative to the mythical Romanovs, and that she had inherited a fabulous fortune in rare art, jewelry, and precious Faberge eggs that she kept in a bank vault in Basel, Switzerland—or that she had betrayed the trust and love of a fabulously wealthy nobleman in the last great, tragic war. But Hannah thought these stories were fabrications, even though Mrs. Endicott did betray the slightest, unrecognizable foreign accent. No one knew the precise details of the old woman's past, and no one dared to ask—not even Uncle Joseph, who was perhaps the bookstore's most dedicated customer. Joseph was old—but Mrs. Endicott, Hannah realized by comparison, was even older. How old? Again, no one knew. But she was spry, with a mind as sharp as a hornet's sting, and tireless in the service to her trade. She lived above the store, in a cramped apartment with her cat, the indomitable Grumpy. This apartment, as Hannah once had glimpsed it, was filled with books. Years ago, a Gentlemen's Benevolence Society had used the store for its monthly meetings. But the swelling tide of books had crowded those odd fellows out. All that remained of their mysterious affairs was a dust-covered blackboard that stood propped behind Mrs. Endicott's cash register and on which had been inscribed years and years ago, in faded yellow chalk, a listing of accounts and several tantalizingly symbolic, occult-like sigils, beneath which were scratched the faded lines of what Hannah guessed to be an inspirational text, or perhaps a menu.

Mrs. Endicott was a tiny woman, not even as tall as Hannah, who was not by any means a giant for her thirteen years. The old woman had thin, sinewy limbs and iron gray hair that she chopped short severely at irregular intervals. Remarkably, given her age and line of work, her eyesight had remained nearly perfect; she seldom wore glasses, and her hearing was preternaturally acute.

Mrs. Endicott did not suffer fools to enter her store. Only serious book lovers could browse those shelves. Indeed, Hannah had once seen Mrs. Endicott insult a frivolous customer right out the door. For this reason, the bookstore's business was slow. Some would say glacial. People considered the old woman cantankerous, and in an age of friendly, fast convenience, no one could explain how she kept the shop in business year to year. Mrs. Endicott dressed the same from season to season, and at any moment, to look at her, one would think she hovered on the brink of impoverished dotage.

Uncle Joseph and Hannah liked her quite a bit, and Mrs. Endicott liked them also, but neither Hannah nor Joseph could say they knew her very well. She was a woman of many secrets and hidden paths.

After greeting Mrs. Endicott, Hannah gave Grumpy a few encouraging pats then put the bushy tomcat on the counter.

"You're here for the key," said Mrs. Endicott matter-of-factly.

The answer seemed self-evident, but before Hannah could respond, a loud clap of thunder rattled the store.

"Awful weather," said Mrs. Endicott. A strand of gray hair teased the right side of her face. She shooed it aside and returned to her sorting. "It's in here somewhere," she muttered, referring to the box of misplaced keys. "I've had that book that your uncle gave you for quite sometime. The man who sold it to me also sold me a key." Mrs. Endicott shot Hannah a curious, slantwise glance. "There were *two* keys once, he told me, but he only sold me one."

"What kind of book is it?" Hannah asked. "My uncle didn't know."

"Nor do I," said Mrs. Endicott. "It arrived one day in a trunk of old travel books—useless stuff, for the most part. It was down there at the bottom of the pile. I bought the lot of it from an agent at an estate auction years ago. I can't remember where, exactly. But when your uncle came searching for a gift, this book just seemed to show up right in front of him on the shelves. Books do that, you know, in case you haven't noticed—that is, if you're the sort person *they need*." She nodded at the shelves, which for a moment, Hannah thought, seemed less overstocked than freighted with some dim yet pregnant, conspiratorial intent. "Sometimes a book's invisible, and then, one day when you're really ready to read it, there it is— right in front of you," said Mrs. Endicott. "In this case, the book your uncle found for your thirteenth birthday seemed just the thing to give you, even though it's locked. Your uncle wanted to give you Gibbon. Humph. Why would a *child* of *this* century want to read Gibbon?"

Hannah bristled inwardly at this somewhat dismissive suggestion that a child—namely *she* (who did not consider herself *childlike* in any respect)—lacked the essential intellectual equipment to navigate the ocean of Gibbon (whoever that was), especially since long habitation with her eccentric uncle had schooled in the passage of perilous routes—known, unknown, or mythological.

But she kept her opinion to herself.

"The key's in one of these boxes somewhere," said Mrs. Endicott, "you can be sure. By the way, Hannah," she added off-handedly, "happy birthday. Many happy returns of the day."

"Thank you," said Hannah politely. For a moment, she wondered if she should share with Mrs. Endicott the story of her encounter with Walter the talking fish or the event of the arrival of the mysterious green twig, but somehow she thought the better of it. (She still felt miffed that the old woman dared characterize her as a child—and reported encounters with talking fish might confirm that characterization, Hannah feared.)

While Mrs. Endicott worked, Hannah took out the book that

Joseph had given her, and she eyed it with renewed curiosity and ambition.

"Well, it's not in this box," said Mrs. Endicott finally, shoving the old shoebox filled with keys back beneath the counter, next to a pair of gentleman's black galoshes. She took out another box, a metal tin, once used for Turkish tobacco, the label informed. This box, too, was brimful with keys. The old woman continued to sort them.

"How will you know if you find it?" Hannah asked quite sensibly. Nearly all the keys looked similar.

"I'll know because I'm the *owner*," said Mrs. Endicott archly. "That's my job. Are you here to help or to interfere?"

"To help, if I may," said Hannah pertly.

Again, it thundered.

Grumpy stretched. His fur looked bushy and electric.

Mrs. Endicott shoved the second box of keys toward Hannah. "Well, help then," she said.

Hannah sighed.

There must be at least three hundred in that box.

She began to sort.

"Bad weather," scowled Mrs. Endicott. And then, as though she had reached a decision that a moment's intuition swiftly confirmed, she added: "Take over, Hannah. I need to do an errand before it storms. Go through that box and see if one of those old keys does the trick. You'll have to try them all one by one, I'm afraid to say. It's a tedious business."

"Since I'm not the *owner*," Hannah added. She couldn't resist.

Mrs. Endicott frowned. "Precisely."

Grumpy jumped to the floor as Mrs. Endicott pulled a black umbrella from beneath the front counter. There seemed no end to the curious items stored beneath that counter, Hannah thought.

"If you finish with that box, I have another," the old woman added. "So many keys, where do they all *fit?*" She looked at Hannah's book, securely latched. And she nodded at the store with its overflowing shelves of books that appeared ready to collapse into the disorder of the ages. "Take your time," she advised Hannah soberly. "Be thorough. Be methodical. Go in the back. It's more comfortable to work. I doubt we'll see any customers on a day when the weather's this threatening. They only come when there's a sale."

Could this be a joke? Hannah wondered.

Mrs. Endicott fought open her umbrella and fetched her oilskin raincoat. "If anyone shows up, make him feel at home. Relax; take your time. You might be at this for a while."

"I hope not," said Hannah.

"Just stay until I get back," said Mrs. Endicott. "If you can't find the key in this bunch, I've got more. No need to get through them all today. If not today, tomorrow . . . the answer will arrive in the fullness of time. It always does."

Hannah picked one key at random and tried it on the lock. It didn't work. She tried another.

"Well, let's hope so, at least," Mrs. Endicott added. Her tone was less than reassuring.

The entry bell jingled, as Mrs. Endicott opened the front door.

Just before she left, she turned to Hannah and told her: "Hannah, I leave you *in charge*."

And then she left.

Hannah was alone.

After working a while, she took the box of keys to the rear of the store as Mrs. Endicott had suggested, and she sat down on the old, comfortable, overstuffed sofa that Mrs. Endicott kept there. Grumpy came along and purred beside her. He was a bit of a pest. An old space heater kept the musty room quite warm.

From outside came another loud crack of thunder. The wind had picked up.

It began to rain.

After pawing her leg suitably to make a nest, Grumpy curled up beside her and shut his eyes. He began to purr.

How many keys were there? Thousands!

She sorted through the box, key by key, discarding those that clearly didn't fit the book's diminutive lock, trying those that looked like they might. As her uncle had schooled her, it was important to be methodical, and Hannah was. Surprisingly, quite a few of the keys seemed likely to fit the tiny lock. Some even did. But none made the lock spring open. The book remained as sealed as a hermetic tomb.

Hannah thought of finding a pair of scissors and forcing the covers open, but for some reason she felt unable to take such drastic action. It just felt wrong.

Grumpy stretched beside her as another loud crack of thunder rattled the front windows of the store. It sounded as though the thunderstorm had settled right on top of them.

Hannah worked until she had gone through the entire box of keys. Mrs. Endicott had not yet returned. Maybe the storm had delayed her. Hannah, bored and cramped, looked about for the other box of keys that Mrs. Endicott had mentioned.

"Okay, Grumpy, where can it be?"

But Grumpy did not know.

He was a cat.

And then, in a pique of frustration or impatience that she really, in retrospect, could not explain, Hannah reached in her shirt pocket, took out the twig that Walter the talking fish had exhorted her to guard, and she put the tip of the twig in the book's brass keyhole, thinking only to amuse herself while she decided whether to wait for Mrs. Endicott to return . . .

When much to her amazement, the lock sprang open.

OPERIS PROCESSIO,
MULTUM NATURAE PLACET

Hannah was so startled, she dropped the twig and book to the bookstore floor.

Grumpy the cat, awakened by the sudden movement, leaped down and batted the twig with his paw. It spun beneath the sofa.

"Stop it," said Hannah.

She retrieved the book and opened it. Its paper was thick and cream colored, like fine old vellum; each page was a delight to touch.

Inside the book's leather cover, someone had written an inscription. She had never seen such lettering before.

Operis Processio,
Multum Naturae Placet.

It was the kind of inscription Uncle Joseph might have written, something from an ancient language to confuse, challenge, or educate her, as was his bent.

But Uncle Joseph had not written those inscrutable words.

Trembling, Hannah turned the page and saw, to her astonishment, her father's name, written in his own bold handwriting, in black India ink. And beneath it, in the same handwriting, she saw a note penned to her:

> *My dearest daughter Hannah:*
> *I am far from certain that you will ever receive this book. But if you do, and if you are now reading these words, it will mean that many years have passed since I last saw you. My darling Hannah, I miss you so very much! There is so much I wish to tell you, but so little time in which to write. Soon I must*

entrust this book to one of the Seven Friedrichs, who promises,
no matter what, to see that it comes safely into your hands. Who
knows how long that will take? I hope you still can remember
me when you read this!

My darling daughter Hannah, I must be brief. I am sending
you this document of my journey, along with another package,
which shall arrive by separate post. You will need them both . . .
that and much more. A far greater danger than what I have
ever faced . . .

But here, her father's writing abruptly stopped.

Frightened and upset, Hannah read the letter again, and then
leafed through the book's ancient pages, searching for more
information. She soon discovered that only the title page and her
father's inscription were in English.

The title page read:

The Monas Hieroglyphica.

Being A Manual of Exploration & A Catechism for the Dead; with
appended Testimonials and Observations, Advice, Diagrams &
Anagrammata; Magically, Caballistically, Anagogically Explained;
Assembled with due Diligence by an Editor Conversant with a
Varietie of Seasoned Travelers Who Seeke the Tree; for the Studie and
Improvement of Human Kinde; Herein a Translation from the
Original Ancient Script, with Annotations, Figures, and a Map.

Hannah turned to another page, surprised to see that in the
margins someone had scribbled notes. These, too, were not in her
father's handwriting. The faintly penciled words looked like an
attempt to translate the book's inscrutable foreign text, and the
graceful, delicate script of the writing suggested, strangely, a
woman's artistic hand, although Hannah could barely read the
smudged and faded letters. Perhaps whoever once had owned this
book had left these marks as a sign of her presence and passage.

Those who seek the Tree must attend to preliminary needs.
These words are merely seeds.

Hannah noticed that the words "husks" and "shells" had originally been written in place of the word "seeds" and that the writer had crossed out and changed the translation several times. She turned a few pages and saw that the graceful script became more childlike further into the book. She could still make out some sentences, but each sentence stood paddocked by question marks, as though the writer were trying to frame it, by exclusion— like a scientist working an experiment or an artist playing with color, shading, and line.

Those who seek the Tree must steal truth like a thief who can discriminate between wealth and value, who claims what she does not possess. Without such subtle understanding, the path forward cannot be discerned, for it hovers and cannot be fixed . . .

The way forward depends upon music.

No one completes the journey who has not encountered a Master of Forgetting and Recall.

You must learn to sleep and breathe.

This last sentence made Hannah pause, for she felt that she had read it somewhere before. Was it in another of her uncle's ancient books, or had she encountered it in a story? But no story that she could remember had mentioned such a thing as a Master of Forgetting and Recall. And everyone knew how to sleep and breathe.

She turned a few more pages, but the notes penciled in the margins became fewer and fewer, as though the person who had written them had abandoned the bothersome chore. One of the pages unfolded, and at the bottom, someone had written the word *Map*. But the page was blank.

What did it mean?

She flipped to the end.

On the last page of the unreadable volume, she found, to her astonishment, a final phrase. Those words, penciled firmly in the margin in a bold but childish hand, disturbed her greatly, for she realized she could have written those words herself.

Guard the green and leafless twig and keep it sound.

The Seven Friedrichs

Just as Hannah reached the last page of this mysterious journal, she became aware of a rhythmical tapping somewhere in the store. Grumpy bestirred himself and stretched. He hopped down from the chair in which he had been sleeping and strolled in leisurely fashion toward the front door.

Hannah put down the book. She could hear it again. Tap, tap, tap. And then a pause. Tap, tap, tap. And then another pause, quite regular.

Tap, tap, tap.

It sounded like someone knocking.

Cautiously, Hannah walked to the front of the store.

A man, dressed in a large, shapeless black rain cape and carrying an enormous black umbrella and wearing a floppy hat, stood at the store's front entrance, knocking and peering through the glass. His face, pressed closely to the door, was moonishly round, like the face of someone who knows how to enjoy a good meal. He peered through the window into the store, with one hand cupped to the side of his face, and he rapped upon the glass with the handle of his umbrella. Behind him, the rain fell hard. Terribly hard, thought Hannah, for a day that had begun so pleasantly serene.

She did not remember locking the door, and she did not know why the stranger did not simply enter. After all, the store was open for business, as the sign in the front window made perfectly clear.

"Hello?" she could hear him calling. "Sofia, are you there?"

Sofia, as Hannah knew, was Mrs. Endicott's first name, but in the years that Hannah had known the bookstore's irascible owner, no one, not even Uncle Joseph, had ever dared to address Mrs. Endicott in this way.

The stranger must have been myopic, as well as somewhat stupid, Hannah thought, for not only did he not try to open the door but he obviously did not see her standing there at the back of the store, watching him, even though the store was quite adequately lit.

As she waited to see what he would do, the wind gusted and blew his umbrella inside out. And it nearly snatched away the stranger's floppy hat.

"Oh bother!" she heard him curse. "Sofia, let me in! I beg you!"

Grumpy strolled forward and waited at the door, swishing his tail. He looked back at her, as though to say, "Well? Why don't you open it?"

But before she could decide what to do, the stranger apparently had a brainstorm and decided to try the door latch himself.

As expected, the door swung open. It wasn't locked. Anyone with the slightest curiosity or initiative would have discovered this sooner, since the lights were on and the sign in the front window said explicitly: *Open Saturdays, 10-4.*

The old pendulum clock on the wall behind the cash register put the hour at three o'clock.

As the front door opened, Grumpy leaped back. The stranger, fumbling with his enormous umbrella and losing his hat now entirely to a gust of wind, blew, more than stepped, past the threshold. He saw her at last.

"My goodness," he sputtered, "forgive me! I am here on urgent business to speak with Sofia. Is she here? The others are right behind me."

Hannah kept her distance as the stranger shed his black rain cape and fought to get his umbrella right-side out. It was indeed a hopeless chore. Beneath his cape, he wore a formal and rather odd-looking black and gray suit that might have been cut to fit the fashion of an earlier century. (The eighteenth century, Hannah thought.) Though its lines were severe, the man's portly figure softened the suit's accountant-like formality. The clothes, except for the rain cape (which was big enough for two gentlemen of his stature) were at least a size too small for his ample girth.

He was a young man, still under thirty, Hannah guessed, and when he took out a pair of wire-rimmed spectacles, he looked surprisingly like a portrait of the romantic composer Schubert that Hannah knew from her uncle's music books.

The stranger wiped off his spectacles on his coat sleeve, refastened them, and squinted at her critically.

"Who are *you*? What are *you* doing here? Where's *Sofia?*"

Hannah stood her ground. "I'm a friend," she informed him. "Mrs. Endicott's on an errand. She left me in charge. *Who are you?*"

Her tone of voice set him back. He became a bit flustered. "In charge? *You?* How is that possible?"

Hannah heard more knocking.

"Ah," said the stranger, "the others have arrived. They were right behind me."

With that, as though cued to entrance, Hannah saw five more strangers at the door. Each was dressed exactly like the fellow in the store. They all wore shapeless black rain capes and storm-tossed hats, and each one carried a battered umbrella. Adding to the awkward confusion, each one carried a parcel; a few carried several; and one or two held baskets on top of that. They crowded right up to the door, as the first had done, and rapped on it eagerly. They did not seem well acquainted with the use of doorknobs.

"I must let them in," said the stranger, shoving past her.

He opened the door, and one by one, the others entered. A gust of wet weather came along with them. It was really raining hard, like a monsoon.

"Friedrich!" exclaimed the strangers, each to the other. "Friedrich, how long it's been since last we met! How good to see you! Friedrich! How do you do?"

One by one, the six individuals (all apparently named Friedrich) shook hands with one another. They all looked so very similar that the whole process took quite some time, for no sooner had one shaken hands with the other but the entire greeting took place all over again. Invariably one of the six felt uncertain he had properly greeted his mate. It seemed an endless round of helloes, how-do-you-dos, and good-to-see-yous.

"Friedrich!"

"How have you been . . . "

"I thought you'd never get here . . . "

"It rained so hard . . . "

"I've missed you frightfully . . . "

Suddenly, Hannah remembered her father's letter that she had read just a moment before.

"Excuse me," she said, interrupting. "Are you *all* named Friedrich?"

"Yes," said all six of the similarly dressed gentlemen, almost with one voice. "Yes, we are."

She counted them again. There were only six.

Before she could frame a question, they shucked off their rain capes, flapping the water from the folds like geese spreading their feathers after a shower. The six black umbrellas went all into a corner, where they soon resembled a ring of mushrooms. The six odd Friedrichs then swung their hats on to the counter near Mrs. Endicott's antique cash register. Each one of them had long, unkempt hair. Without their outer gear, Hannah saw how very much alike they looked, so that unless she studied each one carefully it was really almost impossible to tell them apart. They were of slightly different ages, but aside from that, they might have been six identical siblings.

Now they picked up the parcels and bags and baskets that they had carried into the store. The one who had arrived first, who appeared to be the leader by default, motioned the other five to place everything on the large reading table in the middle of the bookstore and to move aside the books that the table already held.

"Excuse me," said Hannah. She did not feel comfortable watching them move those books. After all, Mrs. Endicott had left her in charge.

The sixth and oldest Friedrich (the first who had entered) paused to look at her, but the others kept busy and did not pay her any mind. Hannah saw that their parcels, bags, and baskets contained food. While the oldest Friedrich looked at her, the other five spread the food out across the table, and from the looks of things, there was enough bread and meats and cheeses and fruits and vegetables for at least a dozen Friedrichs to have feasted.

"Mrs. Endicott does not appreciate eating and drinking in this store," Hannah warned.

"That's not important," said the oldest Friedrich. He stepped close and scrutinized her. "My goodness. You're Hannah, aren't you? Hannah Kurtz?"

"I am," said Hannah, somewhat tentatively. She wondered how he knew.

At this announcement, the oldest Friedrich gave a smile of sheer relief. "And your father, Charles, is the explorer who left to discover the last unknown country in the world. Am I correct?"

"Yes," said Hannah. "But . . . "

"Then we are right where we should be," said the oldest Friedrich. "That's at least one modest accomplishment to our credit." He smiled and nodded at the other five, still busy dressing their feast. "Brothers," he said, "this is Hannah—*Hanna'el.*"

They all paused briefly, bowed to her, and said with one voice: "Pleased to meet you, *Hanna'el.* Walter speaks of you quite highly, to be sure."

"Walter?" said Hannah, confused by the strange way the Friedrichs had mispronounced her name. Perhaps they were foreigners. "Walter the Fish?"

"Walter *the Master of Memory,*" said the oldest Friedrich, as the others, bored by these pleasantries, returned to their eleemosynary chores.

Hannah did not know how to interpret this strange remark. She found the Friedrichs' tone and odd vocabulary quite baffling.

"Food's ready," one of them announced.

"But *are* you the *Seven* Friedrichs" Hannah asked them, remembering her father's letter.

"We are," they answered with one voice.

"But," she said, counting again just to make sure, "there are only *six* of you."

"Quite right," said the oldest Friedrich, the one who had first entered. He glanced at the large pendulum clock that stood on a shelf behind Mrs. Endicott's cash register. The clock, in turn, inspired a worrisome glance toward the outer storm.

"But if there are only *six* of you," Hannah persisted, "how can you call yourselves the *Seven* Friedrichs?"

The stranger shifted uncomfortably and then said to her in a very sober tone of voice: "We *are* the *Seven* Friedrichs, and the seventh will be here any moment, I would expect." But his worried expression, Hannah noticed, contradicted this assertion.

"*If* he survives the Zone of Night," one of the other Friedrichs muttered darkly.

"If he makes it here at all . . . "

"Let's have some discipline," said the oldest Friedrich.

The others fell back.

His voice softened, and he motioned Hannah toward the food that the others had placed on the table. "Come and sit with us, *Hanna'el*, and we'll do our best to explain. You'd better have some food, for it's not a certainty you'll have such a chance again." He nodded at the outer storm just as it thundered and lightning. "It follows hard upon us, I'm afraid."

Hannah scowled. It seemed that the Friedrichs enjoyed the deliberate mispronunciation of her name.

"*Hannah*," she corrected them.

The Friedrichs nodded most politely. "As you wish. Please sit down."

Hannah looked at the storm outside the bookstore. It raged quite fiercely. Fiercer, she thought, than any late summer storm she had ever seen. She looked at the oldest Friedrich, and at the other five.

She remembered the words in her father's letter.

"Do you know my father?" she asked.

"Yes," said the oldest Friedrich, "we did and *do* know him. We know him quite well. It is because of him that we are here. We've come to keep the promise that we made to your father long ago— and to satisfy the Master Walter's request. He sent us to find you." The Friedrich smiled in self-satisfaction as he said this. "And *you* must make good use of who we are, in what little time remains, before it comes."

"Before *what* comes?" asked Hannah. "The Seventh Friedrich?"

A terrible silence filled the bookstore, as all but the oldest Friedrich looked down, or away, or off to one side.

The five reticent Friedrichs stared at their feet.

"My god, is it possible she doesn't know?" one of them whispered.

"I thought that she said she was in charge . . . "

"She can't be in charge, if she doesn't *know*."

The oldest Friedrich summoned the courage to speak. "Sit down, Hannah. Sit down now, all of you," he said to his brothers. "We must first have our Ceremony. After that, she shall know everything. Walter would not have misled us. Surely not. If Walter sent us here, then surely she's the one. After all, she has the twig."

The twig, thought Hannah. She touched her sweatshirt.

The twig was gone!

Then she remembered that Grumpy the cat had batted the twig under Mrs. Endicott's old sofa, after she had used it to open the mysterious book.

"You do have the twig?" asked oldest Friedrich uneasily.

"Of course I do," said Hannah, lying. "I have it right here." She patted her shirt.

She did not have the presence of mind to inquire how he knew about it.

"You must never, *never, never* let it fall from your possession," the other five Friedrichs cautioned with one voice. "If it even for one moment should pass from out your hand . . . "

"I told you I have it," said Hannah testily.

"Let us see it," demanded the five Friedrichs.

The five gentlemen looked ready to storm her en masse, but the oldest Friedrich calmed them and held them back.

He seemed most sensible.

"Stay where you are," he warned them. "Remain calm, my brothers. Remember—*she is in charge.* If she says that she has it, she does! We must take things in proper turn, according to custom. Such is our bent."

"Custom and ceremony," the others assented, and they drew back.

The oldest Friedrich turned to Hannah, and with a sweeping gesture of aristocratic courtesy, invited her to join them at the table for their feast. *"Hanna'el,* I and my brothers would so very much appreciate if you would join us for some conversation and food."

"But we can't start without the seventh," the others objected. Outside the bookstore, the thunder rumbled again. It was even more threatening.

"Well, we can't wait for the Seventh Friedrich," said the sixth Friedrich anxiously. "Time will run out."

"Time has *never* run out," grumbled the others.

"In this case, it might."

"All the more reason to wait," argued the five. "The Seventh Friedrich must come. We are the *Seven* Friedrichs, and nothing can occur without the seventh. The Six shall do nothing without the Seventh. That is the law. We must stand by custom and ceremony."

"Custom and ceremony must be set aside," said the oldest Friedrich.

"Impossible," scoffed the other five.

The oldest Friedrich darkened at these words. "I tell you," he said again more harshly, tapping his foot, "we cannot wait. *We do not have time.*"

But before the five other Friedrichs could answer this challenge, their attention shifted to the rear of the bookstore, to the passageway just behind Hannah.

"Sofia!" they exclaimed with one astonished but delighted tone of voice.

To Hannah's surprise, the bookstore's inscrutable owner, Mrs. Endicott, had returned. She had arrived via the store's back entrance.

She stood there watching them. Hannah's twig and journal were in her hand.

CEREMONIOUS

"You dropped these, I believe," said Mrs. Endicott archly, to Hannah, as the others pressed forward to greet her. She handed Hannah the twig and journal that Hannah had left in the back of the store.

Hannah, blushing from embarrassment, slipped the precious twig inside her shirt. The six Friedrichs were so transported by Mrs. Endicott's sudden arrival that they somehow overlooked this smooth transaction. They were, as Hannah had begun to realize, by no means the smartest cohort she had met. Except for the oldest, whose personality somewhat stood out, the others struck her as a bit feeble minded or foolish.

They were certainly argumentative.

Mrs. Endicott greeted them as a group. She appeared to know them quite well and was not at all surprised to find them here in her bookstore. Nor did she appear surprised to discover that Hannah had somehow opened the journal that her uncle had given her for her thirteenth birthday.

And when Hannah began to explain and mumble apologies, the old woman cut her off.

"Not now," she said. And then, to the six eager Friedrichs, she quickly added: "Sit down, my dear friends, all of you. I've been expecting you for quite, quite some time."

"Sofia," said the sixth and oldest Friedrich, the first who had arrived, "I'm afraid that the Seventh Friedrich isn't here."

"I can see that for myself," snapped Mrs. Endicott.

"Well, he didn't make it," whispered the five.

"We don't know that for a fact . . . " corrected the sixth.

It was then that Hannah noticed that the lower part of Mrs. Endicott's dress was soaking wet.

Mrs. Endicott nodded at the journal that Hannah held. "You've opened it," she whispered. She sounded pleased.

"Sofia," said the oldest Friedrich, butting in, "we came as best we could, but as you see, it is becoming more and more difficult for us to navigate the *Zone of Night*. Even with Walter's help, we had the most awful passage. I don't know how or when we shall be able to return. We might be stranded."

"You probably are," said Mrs. Endicott. "But if that's the worst of it, count yourselves lucky."

The faces of the other five turned nervously toward the entry of the store. "How strong are these walls?" they inquired.

"Strong enough," said Mrs. Endicott. "At least for the time being . . ."

She flipped the latch to lock the front entry and turned the sign on the display window so that it now displayed the message: *Closed*. She nodded her head. Her face had an expression of firm and settled resolve. "Gentlemen, we must proceed with our Ceremony."

"Without the seventh, how can we?" answered the six, abashed.

"We must," said Mrs. Endicott. "Look at the clock."

Hannah had quite forgotten about the time. The book, the storm, and the arrival of the six Friedrichs had completely distracted her. Now she saw that the large pendulum clock behind the antique cash register told the hour at 9:00. *How could that be?* It was only 3:00 when Mrs. Endicott left her in charge to go do her errand. Six hours could not have passed.

Mrs. Endicott saw her confusion.

"Look at the clock again closely," she advised.

Hannah did. And now she noticed that the time was 8:59, and that, in fact, the hands of the clock—or the second hand at least—were moving backwards.

"It is a sign," whispered the Friedrichs.

The front door rattled.

Hannah stared at the clock. No doubt about it. The time was now 8:56. Not only were the hands moving backwards, time was running backwards more swiftly than it ran when it passed in the proper way.

"She has opened the book," said Mrs. Endicott. "And she has the twig as well. We must begin our Ceremony, and we must dispense with all but the most critical points of ritual."

"Begin the Ceremony? Without the Seventh? Amend the ritual? Impossible!" the six Friedrichs scoffed. "It cannot be done!"

"Yes, it can," said Mrs. Endicott. "It can, and it must! My friends, this is America. I shall be the Seventh," she told them forcefully.

Her announcement met with silence. The cohort did not look convinced. On the contrary, they appeared quite nonplussed.

Hannah concluded quickly that they were European.

"This may be America . . . " began one of the Friedrichs in a slow, apologetic tone of voice.

The others sighed.

"Here now, Sofia," said the sixth and oldest Friedrich, intervening, "let's get to the point. America or not, you know as well as I that we are creatures of order and habit—we can't simply *change*. Improvisation? Unthinkable. Perhaps with *six* we can manage a *minor* ritual—we've done that before," he nodded at the blackboard behind the front counter with its strange sigils and spidery script, "but a Ceremony . . . " He shook his head. "That would require an originality that the six of us plainly lack. We are not prepared . . . "

Hannah had an uneasy feeling about this conversation. She wanted to leave.

"Excuse me," she interrupted, "I'm sorry, but if you don't mind . . . "

It wasn't just that these strangers made her uncomfortable, for in fact she rather enjoyed the repartee, cryptic and allusive though it was—but as she stood there and listened to them argue, an image of her home and Uncle Joseph rose before her mind's inner eye, and that memory beckoned to her powerfully. She had the uneasy feeling that she needed to see if her uncle and her home were still all right.

"Ah, excuse me," she repeated. "Mrs. Endicott, I have to go."

Her statement met with looks of shocked incredulity from everyone, including the bookstore's owner.

"*Go?*" said the oldest Friedrich. "Go where?"

"Why home, of course," said Hannah. "It's getting late."

"Good gracious," said the sixth Friedrich.

But the others exclaimed less tactfully, and with one voice: "Sofia, this is impossible!"

Mrs. Endicott forcefully intervened.

"Hannah," she said fondly, in a motherly or grandmotherly tone of voice that Hannah had never heard her use before, "come to the table a moment and sit down."

The old woman's tone frightened her.

Hannah shook her head.

"No," she said. "I'd rather not. I have to leave."

But, as she moved toward her umbrella and the front door, the six Friedrichs assembled to block her exit.

"Let me out," said Hannah, squaring her shoulders.

Mrs. Endicott laid a gentle hand on Hannah's arm. "Hannah," she said, in the same strange motherly tone of voice, "if I tell you something now that's unpleasant, you must hear me out and try to understand me and be brave. You've opened the book—the journal that Joseph gave you for your thirteenth birthday. Do you know what that means?"

"It means I found a key. It means I got lucky. I don't know what it means *and I don't care*," said Hannah stubbornly. "Mrs. Endicott, I have to leave."

The six thoughtful Friedrichs shook their heads, as though they had just witnessed an unavoidable, tragic accident.

"Look at the book again," said Mrs. Endicott, in the same patient, motherly tone of voice that Hannah now found immensely disconcerting if not off key. "You wrote that book yourself. You wrote it, but you don't *remember*."

"That's impossible," said Hannah. She took out her father's letter. "My father wrote it. He said so right here. He sent me this book and the twig."

"Think again," said the old woman patiently. "How can that be? *Walter* sent you the twig. Without Walter's help, the book, your father's letter, and the twig would not be here."

"Can we hurry, please," said the sixth Friedrich petulantly. He nodded at the clock behind the register. It now said 6:13. The front door rattled. "You know I'm not a hasty man," he apologized. "We're incapable of haste in any case—we stand on ceremony. But in light of these extraordinary events . . . "

"Hannah," said Mrs. Endicott, "this book has come to you because your father is in desperate need. His journey has failed. You must continue it. This book belongs to you—it will teach you your way."

"But you told me you found it in a box of junk."

"I did," said Mrs. Endicott, "or rather, the book found me. We do not find books in any case, or at least not the best or truest that belong to us in a deeper sense . . . *we* belong to them and *they* find us. It's as I told you. A book is only a useless, speechless thing. It says nothing, unless it finds a voice—its destined reader, the one who can unlock its meaning with the proper key. Until you opened it, I had no way of knowing for certain that *this* was yours. I had my suspicions, of course—most especially when I recognized that it was the Seventh Friedrich who sold me that box of old books, long ago. But as I said, even the best book is useless unless it falls into the proper hands—and at just the proper moment. Too late or too soon, and all is for naught. The meeting must happen at the precise and exact destined moment. I've dedicated my life to making such meetings possible. But until Walter found you, the book could not be yours to own or read, no matter what I thought or did. You had to ask the question that would lead you to it. Do you know now what that question is?"

But Hannah did not remember asking any questions—either to Walter or anyone else. She shook her head angrily.

"My uncle gave me that book, and I didn't want it. Here, you can have it back!"

"No," cried the Friedrichs, horrified. "You have to keep it! You must! You have agreed!"

Mrs. Endicott did not change her tone.

"Hannah, try to understand me. After Walter met you, you were ready. The fact that you met him meant that the question was asked. *I gave the book to your uncle as a present for your thirteenth birthday, just as the Master wished. But the use of it had to wait until you discovered for yourself the proper key.*"

"But the book is unreadable!" Hannah exclaimed. "It's all stuff and nonsense!"

Stuff and nonsense? Under stress, it surprised her to hear a quaint phrase of her uncle Joseph's spring from her lips.

"You can't read it, yet," smiled Mrs. Endicott, in a steady and persistent tone of voice, "but you must try. Every book is like that, even these ordinary books that we see all around us all the time. They're all *stuff and nonsense*, every one. They're mute as stones until someone, and not just anyone, but just the right someone—finds the key and begins to read. And even then, the outcome is far from certain. It is a perilous journey through dangerous lands whose goal is uncertain and seldom achieved. At any moment, the slender strand of memory can snap. Worlds perish—but that is something the Master will need to explain. You met him once, you will meet him again, if you trust me and take the initiative. Your father did his best to help you begin this journey, but only you can determine how far and where the journey extends."

"Sofia," said the oldest Friedrich, tapping his foot anxiously, "you're only confusing her. Must you be so pedantic? She doesn't need to know these technical details. She's just a child."

"No longer," said the old woman. "And she certainly needs technique to survive against *that*." She emphasized this last word with a jut of her determined chin and pointed to the thunderstorm outside the store.

"I think if I could just borrow a raincoat and an umbrella . . . " Hannah began, edging away.

"You see, she is not yet in charge," muttered the other Friedrichs.

"Give her a chance," said Mrs. Endicott sternly.

But at this, the six Friedrichs fell into a heated debate.

"Too much is at risk."

"If she were really in charge, she would already be on her way. She would know what to do *intuitively*."

"Walter will help her."

"But where is Walter?"

"Even Walter could not make it here."

"Are you saying that Walter's powerless?"

"If Walter's unable to help her, no one can."

"Be quiet!" shouted Mrs. Endicott.

Hannah touched the twig inside her shirt. She had not understood much of what Mrs. Endicott had told her, but along with the urge to run home, another frightening image had arisen before her mind's inner eye.

"Mrs. Endicott, is my father all right? Is he in danger?"

This question, more so than the old woman's outburst, silenced the six Friedrichs and cast them down momentarily into a funk of introspective, silent gloom.

"Yes," said Mrs. Endicott. "Yes, Hannah. Indeed, I'm afraid that he—and for that matter, all of us—are in very serious danger . . . though very few have grasped the true nature of what has gone wrong."

Before Hannah could frame another question, the Six Friedrichs interrupted to say with one voice: "Sofia, we have argued long enough. *What shall we do?*"

Mrs. Endicott looked at Hannah. "The Friedrichs are right. Hannah, you must make a choice. You can go home—I can lend you a raincoat and galoshes—or you can stay here a bit longer and witness the Ceremony, as your father wished."

The mention of her father felt like an unfair tactic.

Nevertheless, Hannah hesitated.

"What ceremony?" she asked skeptically.

"You must *experience* to understand."

Suddenly, Hannah's attention shifted to the clock behind the front counter. She saw that the hands had reversed to 3:23.

Indeed, time was accelerating quite rapidly, but in reverse. She could see the clock's minute hand inch backward, while the second hand had begun a to circle counterclockwise in a hectic, Sufi dance.

The outer storm lashed the store. The front display windows

shook from the force of the wind. The door began to rattle, and the entry chime sounded faintly, as though someone had already entered, but no one had.

"It has begun," said the six Friedrichs soberly. "It is too late for our Ceremony."

"Not yet," said Mrs. Endicott. "There is still time. This store can withstand a little longer. *Hanna'el*, have you made up your mind?"

Hannah thought again of her father's letter that she had found in the mysterious book. She glanced at the raging storm.

"My father met Walter?"

"Yes."

"What is the Ceremony?" she asked Mrs. Endicott tentatively.

The old woman nodded.

The six Friedrichs began at once.

"Watch."

Working swiftly, as one unit, they cleared the table of all the food, and in place of a feast, they unpacked from a final basket a strange device.

It was a queer type of antique machine, such as Hannah once had glimpsed when she visited Thomas Edison's old laboratory in West Orange, where the light bulb had been invented in ancient times. The machine that the Friedrichs unpacked was built of polished wood—mahogany, walnut, cherry?—and foil and rods of a shiny metallic substance that Hannah could not identify. No plastic parts, no cheap dials and diodes, nothing glitzy—it all looked a bit Victorian, quality stuff. It stood about as high as a Tiffany table lamp and appeared to be just as delicate and expensive.

"What is it?" asked Hannah.

"This," said the eldest Friedrich proudly as his brothers assembled the queer contraption, "is a *Strader Machine*. It is the reason we are here."

His explanation meant nothing.

The storm wind struck again. It howled and raged outside the tiny bookstore.

"Watch and listen," said Mrs. Endicott to Hannah.

The six Friedrichs, with Mrs. Endicott as the designated seventh, sat down at the reading table, now cleared of food, and formed a rough circle with the curious machine as the center point in their midst.

They all joined hands. Their postures resembled an old time séance, and briefly, Hannah wondered if she might be privy to the communications of a spook.

But only for a moment did she have such frivolous thoughts. The clock had now reversed to 1:39.

She glanced away briefly then looked at it again. 1:17.

The strange machine began to rotate. It was like a little whirligig or windmill. No wires ran to it, and it had no visible source of power that Hannah could discern. The air in the room, despite the outer hurricane, remained quite still, so that not even a breeze was responsible for the machine's circuitous movement.

Is this the Ceremony? She wondered.

The others were now quite rapt, and the speed of the machine's rotation had gained intensity. It began to hum.

The clock now stood at 12:23.

Grumpy, the cat, meowed.

He had gone under the front counter for protection, but now he came out. His fur was all bristly and electric, and he faced the front door, as though he had seen something that frightened him.

Hannah put down the book and twig to pick him up.

But no sooner had she done so when suddenly the entrance to the store exploded open. A rolling gust of storm beat inside. Grumpy screeched.

Hannah saw what looked like a solid wall of black water rushing toward her. It came on with a roar like a jet plane accelerating for a take-off. She had never seen a sight so terrifying.

She tried to close the door, but the wind blew too strongly.

It blew her back.

What happened next took less than a few seconds.

In the well of rain and hail that blew in upon her from the outer storm, she saw a dark shape moving like a man. Its clothes flapped like rags about its body. Faceless and shadowy, it blew at her like debris.

The cat, Grumpy, reared up, its fur electric, and bared it fangs and claws.

At the same moment, from somewhere behind her, Hannah saw that the machine had become a whirling, singing sphere of bluish light. The light momentarily held back whatever creature threatened at the door. The blue light caused it pain.

The apparition howled.

At the same moment, Hannah heard a voice.

"Guard the twig. Guard the green and leafless twig and keep it sound!"

The voice was Mrs. Endicott's, and as she heard it, Hannah had a brief sensation of the old woman pressing the twig into her hand.

"Go," Mrs. Endicott commanded her. *"Find Walter!* Go quickly! Now! While you still can!"

Hannah clutched the twig and the mysterious book. Behind her, the strange machine began to dim. On the shelf behind the cash register, the hands of the pendulum clock came to rest at midnight.

ALONE

Hannah gasped and rubbed her head.

The lawn on which she sat looked vaguely familiar, as did the white clapboard house just beyond. She thought that she knew the person who lived there—perhaps a close acquaintance or a relative, though she could not remember any names. She tried to stand, but as soon as she moved, the world pulsed and swayed. She fell back to the ground with a grunt, hugging the dewy grass for reassurance, and for one sickening moment, the ground beneath her vibrated like the skin of a shaman's drum. The drum echoed deeply inside the earth. She could sense its tempo inside her bones, as though the entire planet were tuned to the drum's insistent rhythm.

Hannah scrunched tight her eyes, and her breath came in shallow, rapid gasps.

"I'm Hannah," she whispered. "*Hannah.*"

Her name was like a magic charm that stilled the throbbing drumbeats inside her head. Gradually, she felt the earth regain solidity; even so, she kept her eyes tightly shut. Her hands, too, had balled into fists. One hand held on to something precious: a tiny, leafless twig.

She did not know why.

A magpie scolded her loudly from the branches of a sycamore tree that grew at the edge of the lawn. Hearing that noise, Hannah opened her eyes and looked about.

She had once seen an illustration in a textbook that showed the black silhouettes of two women kissing. But when you looked at the picture long enough, it changed. Suddenly, the two kissing women became the outline of a goblet, and you realized that the goblet and the women were really just two ways of looking at one thing.

At that moment Hannah felt the same way she had felt when the picture of the two kissing women changed into a goblet. But instead of looking at a picture, she saw this happen to her world. She remembered she was at home. This lawn was *her* front lawn. This house was *her* house. And the magpie scolded her from the branches of a sycamore tree that *she* had helped Uncle Joseph tend. One of the trees ancient limbs lay storm-shattered in the street.

"I'm Hannah," she repeated. "*Hannah.*"

Just saying her name gave her strength. This time, she could sit up without feeling so terribly ill.

Once more, the magpie scolded, and then she saw it fly from its perch and swoop across the empty street. *Banyan Street, of course.* The street, the sidewalk, the trees, the neighboring houses—they all looked very familiar to her now. But they were deserted. *This is my home,* she repeated. And yet, the neighborhood looked so empty, lifeless, and still—like an old photograph that time had yellowed, a photograph without a future, from a past that no one remembered, in a present for which no one cared.

Slowly, she stood up. Her muscles ached. Her clothes and her hair were covered with dry leaves and grass clippings, and her jeans had a big tear across the right knee; her sneakers were muddy and wet.

Uncertain, she walked to her front door and tried to open it. The door was unlocked. She entered her living room and called for Uncle Joseph.

No answer.

Puzzled by the silence, she walked from the living room to the kitchen, noticing the freshly picked carrots in the sink, the ripe grapes in a bowl upon the table, the pipe that Joseph had been smoking, the aroma of its tobacco, and a book of philosophy still open to page 23. The kitchen faucet had been left on to rinse the carrots. She turned it off, then walked through the kitchen into the backyard garden—empty, just like the house.

Again, she called her uncle's name. She saw Joseph's tools and wheelbarrow in the garden, the sundial where his gloves lay, and the bed of vegetables he had left half-weeded. His straw garden hat lay on the ground next to his trowel. She picked it up and turned to face the house, empty and silent. Uncle Joseph and everyone else had disappeared.

Find Walter . . .

The voice that spoke was not her own.

Suddenly, a brief memory of Mrs. Endicott's bookstore flashed past her mind's inner eye. To see it that way was like watching a few frames of a grainy, silent movie. Weirdly, she had become both actor and audience, for she saw *herself* in those scenes. There were other actors, too, whom she didn't know.

The memory of the bookstore recalled her powerfully. A part of her wanted to go there, but when she looked across town in that direction, she saw a dark rain cloud hovering just where the bookstore should have been, and she considered it might be best to stay where things were dry.

Walter, said the inner voice again. *Find Walter. Go to the pond.*

This thought rose up inside her like a summons. It had replaced the insistent beat of the shaman's drum.

But how can I find him? The fish was gone . . .

Walter hadn't come the last time she called him. But surely, Hannah told herself, if she hurried to the Chinese Pavilion, he'd answer her desperate summons now.

All too soon, she discovered a hideous sight.

THE RUINED POND

At the park that she remembered and loved so well, all the trees had died. The entire forest had been cut and leveled flat. Where once tall hardwood trees had flourished, there now stood parked bulldozers, graders, dump trucks, and temporary toilets. Stumps of amputated trees littered the naked, muddy ground. The park looked like a battlefield after a slaughter. Instead of the quiet, wooded glades she remembered and loved so well, she saw a ravished wasteland. It was as if she had suddenly been transported to an alien world—a world where gluttonous monsters shaped like yellow bulldozers gobbled and digested everything green.

Hannah stumbled forward through the rain-filled, muddy ruts that crisscrossed the naked ground, dodging the jagged stumps and fallen branches that covered the earth on every side.

How could this be? No one could level all these trees in a single blow. No one, not even an army of bulldozers . . .

Quite soon, she stood gasping for breath. Panic coiled through her insides like a snake. *Was Walter dead?* How could anything survive this devastation?

Miraculously, the pond at the ruined Chinese Pavilion was still intact. The bulldozers had spared it. Two trees, a willow and an alder, had also been left alive, although the trees had yellow, plastic ribbons tied to their trunks.

The pond's once peaceful waters were slimed with oil. The Chinese Pavilion stood surrounded by a chain-link fence on which a large piece of plywood displayed a black, spray-painted warning:

NO TRESPASSING
CONDEMNED

Dumbfounded, Hannah staggered to the edge of the water and shouted as loudly as she could. "Walter! Walter! Where are you!" She hardly noticed the tears that fell from her eyes, tears that dissolved in the black, polluted water of the pond.

"Walter, where are you? You have to help me. I'm here—I'm all alone!"

But the fish did not reply.

Had he lied, or was his absence part of this terrible curse? Maybe, like Uncle Joseph, he had vanished—gone from the surface of the earth.

Find Walter . . . an inner voice repeated more insistently.

Hannah trembled and wept. She wanted to curl herself into a ball. More than anything, she wanted to sleep in her own bed. If only she could sneak into her bedroom, and then, when she awoke, everything would be as it had been and as she remembered it . . . as she wanted it to be until the ending of time.

Find Walter . . .

"No," she whispered, "no. There's no one here."

Despairing, she stumbled across the bulldozed acreage toward a highway that marked the northern boundary of the park. Her mind felt numb. Dumbly, automatically, her brain went through the motion of stringing thoughts together one by one, but her thoughts and her memories made no sense.

She shuffled onward like a sleepwalker. Outside the ruined park, she found herself following a ditch that ran along the highway, a ditch filled with garbage and junk. No cars zoomed past or honked at her. The strange emptiness of the highway felt like the emptiness inside her soul. "Keep walking," she repeated. "Just go on."

Find Walter . . . the inner voice insisted.

THE MASTER OF MEMORY

The sun had burned her face and her shoes had raised painful blisters on both feet when Hannah rounded a bend and saw a broken billboard.

WORLDWIDE DISMANTLERS
FAST FAIR FRIENDLY
ALL PARTS FOREIGN DOMESTIC
U PULL IT YOURSELF

Hannah didn't know what a worldwide dismantler was, but from the looks of things, it had something to do with junked cars. A long dirt road led from the highway to a vast automobile graveyard. The gate to this graveyard hung open (perhaps it had never been locked), and beyond the gate, rows and rows of stacked, ruined automobiles stretched for as far as she could see. Hannah had never imagined that so many cars could be collected in one place. The twisted, rusted hulks stood crammed next to one another and piled in some places five or six autos high.

All the cars were different, and yet, when massed together, they all looked numbingly alike. There were cars of every size and description, sorted by country and make. As she stumbled forward, she found herself standing in the section of ruined Fords, each Ford smashed and twisted and browned with layers of dust. On every side, the wreckage went on and on. The only thing visible besides the cars and the rickety gate that marked the junkyard's threshold, was a shack made of corrugated iron and spray-painted plywood that rose in a clearing of wreckage about one hundred yards from where she stood.

The shack, too, looked deserted. Gears, bolts, levers, and

mechanical contrivances lay strewn across the ground in front of it, as though some of the automobiles stacked nearby had exploded into a thousand pieces of junk.

As Hannah contemplated this disaster, a stranger stepped from the wreckage and tapped her shoulder.

Hannah jumped.

The stranger who faced her looked only a few years older than she. Dressed like a mechanic, he stood with his hands shoved into the pockets of his overalls. He had tousled brown hair that fell loose to his shoulders, and his slightly mocking grin showed a gap between his strong white teeth. His eyes, keen and lively, as though fired with restless amusement, sparkled at her ironically from beneath a broad and nobly formed brow.

His features looked very familiar. But as she tried to remember where she had seen this stranger before (perhaps in a portrait from a book in her uncle's library), he spoke a friendly greeting.

"So, *Hanna'el*. You have found your way here at last."

Hannah's heart beat fast. As she ransacked her memories to discover who this young stranger might be, two ravens flew down from the roof of the corrugated shack and settled on his shoulders, one on each side. He did not flinch. "Do not be afraid," he told her. "I'm here to help. My name is Fritz. I'm Walter's apprentice. Walter told me you were coming, and he warned me you'd be confused."

"Walter? *Walter the fish?* Is Walter *here?*"

"Walter, the *Master of Memory*," the young stranger replied. He smiled at her. "Yes, he is." And with that, he took out a key and unlocked the padlock on the door of the corrugated shack, allowing her to see inside. "Please enter. He's expecting you."

Hannah looked inside. There she a large aquarium supported by a workbench in the middle of an empty room.

And inside the aquarium, serenely observant, floated Walter the talking fish.

WALTER SPEAKS

Walter, the Fish of Wisdom, floated in his tank and watched her with round, unblinking eyes. Confined to that aquarium, he looked even larger and more exotic than he had in the forest pond. He fluttered his fins in a stately, undulating rhythm while the tank's electric motor pumped and hummed. A concealed nozzle emitted a stream of spiraling bubbles into the tank.

"Hello, my friend Hannah. So there you are at last."

Just as before, Walter's soundless speech tickled her head. She scrunched her nose and squinted, afraid that she might sneeze.

Her anger prevented her.

"Walter, why did you leave me all alone? You promised to help me, and then you disappeared! What happened to Uncle Joseph? What happened to the bookstore? Why didn't you help me like you said?"

Walter ruffled his fins and waited for her to calm down. When at last she fell silent, he spoke again. "Hannah, you're not speaking wisely. You're not quite yourself. Do you remember the Seven Friedrichs? Have you kept the precious twig?"

His words confused her. Dimly, a picture rose up before her mind's inner eye—a picture of six eccentric gentlemen and Mrs. Endicott, the seventh, seated in a circle whose center point consisted of a strange, whirligig sort of device. And at the same time that she glimpsed this memory, a sound like mighty waters cascading over a cataract made her flinch.

Frightened, her hand shot instinctively to her pocket, digging deep. She took out the twig and held it for Walter to see. A fish must swim sideways to use its eyes.

"Oh yes," said Walter, "that is just the twig I meant. Good

that you have it! Do you have the book as well? Without that twig to protect you, you wouldn't even exist."

Briefly, a memory of Mrs. Endicott's bookstore flashed into her awareness, like a meteor plummeting through a darkened autumn sky. She saw seven individuals huddled in a circle at a table in the midst of which glowed what looked like an ancient electric light bulb, while outside the bookstore a terrible rainstorm raged. The memory faded.

For a long moment, Walter floated serenely, and in the silence, Hannah fingered the small, green, leafless twig that lay in her palm, and she pondered it.

I was in that bookstore once.

Another memory dawned: *the six Friedrichs and Mrs. Endicott . . . the storm wind that had crashed open the front door of the store . . .*

She remembered how all her thoughts had felt scattered as though by a raging wind, a wind that had threatened to destroy her. She remembered a terrible drumming. And she remembered how her hand had instinctively clutched at Walter's twig, and how as soon as she had touched it the roaring wind and drumming inside her head had suddenly stopped. Had the twig saved her life? What had happened at the bookstore? What had happened to Walter's pond? Why was she here?

"The twig sustains memory," said Walter gently. "It was cut from the Tree, the Singing Tree of Remembrance that grows on the shores of Elowyn."

"*Elowyn*," repeated Hannah. She had read that word on an envelope long ago. And suddenly, Hannah heard herself ask, "*But Walter, what is memory?*"

Walter, the Master of Memory, flicked his fins. "Ah Hannah, that is indeed the most difficult question you can ask. Come here, step closer to my tank."

Hannah walked hesitantly toward the aquarium where Walter swam. Her legs felt rubbery and weak.

"Watch," said the fish.

Suddenly, as she stared into the clear water, Walter emitted a large blue bubble from his mouth. *Fish do not breathe air*, thought

Hannah—*how can a bubble be formed?* The bubble grew in size until it looked as large as a tennis ball. Then it floated free and slowly rose.

All her attention focused on that perfect, translucent sphere. The bubble glowed with serene, crystalline, inner light. It glowed and shimmered and ever so gently pulsed. She wished that she could embrace that perfect, self-illuminating sphere, and no sooner did this wish awaken but she felt herself drawn forward and away. At the very same moment, the bubble swelled to enormous size, and she saw that within this bubble were many other spheres. Each sphere pulsed and hummed. She felt that she floated amid a galaxy of living stars—each star a sphere alive and singing, each star a full and perfect world. The spheres, the stars, were all distinct and separate, and yet they were one harmonious whole. She could hover between these spheres as though she were swimming or floating, until she realized that all these spheres in all their movements and interactions wove a current of light and song that formed her awareness of herself. The "I" of this awareness hovered everywhere and nowhere at once, completely dispersed, yet freely reforming within that current as a single sphere of luminous self-awareness wherever her attention lingered momentarily or dwelled.

Then she discovered something else: each of these hovering spheres revealed a tale. By listening and by swimming on the currents of their song, she could understand them. She felt awake inside a dream, awake and able to experience any memory she desired or summoned forth. She thought of her father, and immediately a glowing sphere drew close to her and swelled. It opened like a morning glory. She saw her father, alone on a barren plain. He walked with his head down, leaning into a howling wind. "Father!" she exclaimed, but the scene altered shape. She could not maintain it. Another appeared instead. Still amid that desert landscape, she saw a barren hillock crowned with a ring of bone. Inside that ring of bone, blasted and destitute, stood the trunk of an ancient, weathered tree. Many of the tree's leafless branches had died and fallen. They littered the ground. The tree stood alone and solitary in the light of a pitiless, desert sun.

Hannah felt drawn to this barren hillock, and yet, at the same time, she felt gripped by an icy fear. "Turn back, turn back," she heard a voice command her. And she did.

At once, the many sparkling bubbles reappeared, and she hovered amid them. "Where do you wish to be?" a familiar voice questioned her. Without a moment's hesitation, she said that she wished to be home.

And home became a sphere. Only, the sphere was now completely an image of her remembrance; it had transformed.

She found herself in her kitchen eating wheat bread with peanut butter, watching the TV and thumbing through a weekly magazine. A man came on the tube to tell her she needed to buy a car. *I've heard this before*, she remembered. A cascade of images flashed through her mind, moving rapidly like a speeded up video. Despite this rapid movement, she could see every image in great detail. The images showed what would happen to her next: how she would leave the kitchen, go to her bedroom, return and speak to her uncle. For a moment, nothing changed. And then . . .

The kitchen door slammed shut with a startling bang. Uncle Joseph, wearing his familiar garden jacket and rubber boots, walked in and said hello. He took off his gardening gloves and tossed them on the counter. Then, drawing a glass of water from the leaky faucet at the sink, he turned off the chattering boob tube and sat down.

"You Must Find the Tree!"

Uncle Joseph sat with his arms crossed akimbo and his head cocked curiously to the side. His eyes twinkled as though he enjoyed a private joke.

At first, Hannah wanted more than anything to leap forward and hug him—she was so overjoyed to find him again—but with a magisterial motion of reserve, Uncle Joseph restrained her.

"Stay where you are, Hannah," he cautioned. "You may think I'm Uncle Joseph, but I'm not. I've borrowed Joseph's image from your remembrance."

Hannah quite consciously closed her mouth. "You're Walter," she said. It wasn't a hunch. The truth just formed inside her, like a poem.

"Stay with me, Hannah, and listen very carefully to what I say. You asked me what memory is, and I have shown you. Have you *understood?*"

Hannah shook her head in disbelief. Was she really in her kitchen? She touched the table in front of her and tapped the red linoleum floor. Yes, it was certainly *her* kitchen. Why did she doubt?

Walter, the Master of Memory, nodded twice. "Try to understand . . . People take their memories for granted, but they shouldn't, really, because memory is not a part of them at all. Your memories are like separate, living things. Memory can flourish, or it can die. Its health depends on a subtle balance—let us call it a balance of shadow and light. If this balance becomes over weighted, if the forces of shadow or light become too strong, then memory weakens; its leaves and branches wither, like a plant. When that happens, spheres of remembrance are lost, and those spheres are not just separate memories, they are worlds."

"*Worlds?*" said Hannah. She had trouble comprehending her

uncle's words. Each time he paused, the room seemed to rubber out of shape.

"*Beings*," Walter said to her. For a moment, the Master's eyes glowed with a fierce inward light. Hannah felt as though she stood in many places at once, and she saw once more those serene, pulsating spheres. The spheres danced and sang in Walter's eyes. The Master contained them. The spheres swelled and diminished, afloat on currents of song. "Stay with me, *Hanna'el*," said Walter. "You must *remember and act . . .* "

Hannah's head throbbed with a terrible ache.

Did Uncle Joseph forget my name?

Again, the kitchen swayed and blurred, and for a brief moment became a junkyard. Hannah saw herself standing before an aquarium, staring at a large, gold and emerald-green fish. This image faded, and the vision of a desert hillock took its place. A lone, barren tree stood before her. Its empty branches swayed in the shrieking wind.

She squinted and rubbed her forehead very hard. As she did, the kitchen came back into focus, and the dancing, weaving spheres faded away.

Walter, or Uncle Joseph, leaned across the table and took her hands. His palms felt dry and callused from the garden, and his voice throbbed insistently like a drum.

"Do you remember the park where we first met? Do you remember how that park has been destroyed? It is an image of what lies before you. The Singing Tree of Remembrance has fallen silent, and because it is silent, worlds fade into the frozen darkness of the *Zone of Night*. These worlds do not fade at once, nor does everyone notice their slow disappearance, but those who are drawn to Elowyn feel the disappearance as an unceasing sorrow in their hearts, as a melancholic ache that's always present. Often they cannot explain the reason for their sadness, or they blame it on lesser things. They lose themselves in distractions, seeking solace. But while they keep busy, the unmaking darkness grows and spreads."

"Stop," said Hannah, "stop. Uncle Joseph . . . Walter . . . I don't want to hear this . . . "

But the Master of Memory would not.

"The loss of the Tree's healing music grieves them like a wound that never heals, like the death or absence of someone they dearly love, but the reason for their sadness eludes them. They look at the changes in themselves or in the world and feel grief for the loss of something they do not understand or cannot recall—beauty or innocence, culture or civility . . . they have many names for it, each according to his bent—but it is *memory* that has weakened. The Tree no longer sings; and because it is silent, memories fade into the *Zone of Night*. Each disappearance, slight though it may seem, is significant for the destiny of everyone; those small effects gain consequence over time. This is the cause for your despair, the reason you have lost your home and those you loved. Unless you heal the Tree, unless you find your way to its dying roots and face the one who dwells there, unless you plant the twig that can restore the Tree to health, in time you shall lack the power to recall even yourself, at last becoming so powerless that your soul returns to the unmaking darkness beyond recall."

A terrible vision seized Hannah: a vision of herself drowning in a blackened sea. She cried out for help, but no one heard her. All around her, on the surface of that freezing ocean, scattered wreckage bobbed and floated. She saw that there were many corpses floating, too. Her head kept passing beneath the icy waves. Each time she sank, she struggled to rise again, gasping for breath, coughing and spitting, while far, far above her, the nighttime sky shone clear with countless stars.

She saw the constellation that her uncle once had taught her to name Orion.

"Walter, Uncle Joseph, let me go!" Hannah pleaded. She did not want to hear what the Master said. She felt frightened and dreadfully tired. She wanted to sleep.

Uncle Joseph, or Walter, released his grip. His voice, though soft and kindly, had an urgent edge.

"*You must find the Tree.* According to a destiny none can foretell, the Tree summons those who bear it love. It knows of you from your father, who sought it also. Now the summons has passed to you. You must find it—*now, this very moment—do not refuse!* Go while I can protect you, while you still have the strength. When you find the Seventh Friedrich, ask for his help. The Seventh Friedrich will teach you to hover. He will help you find the others, who in turn will help you on your way. But this above all, *Hanna'el*: *Guard the green and living twig and keep it sound.*"

A great, age-heavy weariness settled upon Hannah as Walter spoke. She felt as though she were struggling between sleep and wakefulness, oppressed by a weight of slumber she neither could withstand nor shake off.

She felt herself sinking. The abyss felt very deep—so bottomless and vast, that light and time and being were swallowed up.

"Walter," she stammered, "Walter!"

But Walter, the Master of Memory, had gone.

BOOK TWO

Aeron's Caer

THE SHEPHERD'S TENT

Hannah bolted upright and drew a ragged breath. Her sweat-damp hair fell loose across her shoulders. Her head throbbed wickedly.

"A dream," she whispered tensely, "I've had a dream . . . "

But the dream had felt so real, more real than this shepherd's tent in which she had paused to rest during her long journey westward to the mountains—a journey, she recalled with nervous certainty, nearly done.

She rubbed her eyes and brushed aside her long, black hair, noticing as she did the silver bracelets on her arms. She had seen them a thousand times; why did they look so unusual? Her father had given her this jewelry long ago, before she could wear it, when she was still a small girl. The bracelets had once belonged to her mother, who had received them from her mother, and so on down through time. She slipped one off her wrist and held it for a moment, tracing the pattern engraved upon its surface, a decoration of swirling vines that entwined into intricate whorls.

I dreamed of the Singing Tree . . .

A sudden cascade of memories rushed through her mind. A man had appeared whose name was Walter, or perhaps Joseph . . . odd names, like none she knew, though the man had looked much like her familiar guardian and tutor, Thomas, who waited outside the tent. The dream had felt so very urgent, but of course, she reasoned, that was understandable. She had cause for urgency and fear.

She swung her legs off the sheepskin-covered cot. Her feet touched a floor of pounded earth. Feeling dizzy, she cradled her head in her hands, breathing deeply, as the tent spun round. *Father, why did you leave me?* Waves of remembrance and sadness washed over her. Mingled with them, like strains of fading melody, came brief recollections of her dream. She drew a sharp breath and straightened up. The tent, plain and familiar, felt wrong. She saw that it was a herdsman's tent no different from many she had visited or lived in. But no, it *was* somehow different.

She saw that her mentor, Brother Thomas, had placed a silver basin of water near her cot. She leaned over to wash her face. The polished basin mirrored her features dimly: dark hair lush and thick, skin browned by prairie winds and sun, eyes that slanted in the manner of her clan: the people of Arcatus, her distant homeland. She touched her young womanly features, wondering why she felt puzzled, why something felt wrong. Strands of her raven hair fell across the basin, and her image vanished in rippled water.

A dream. It was all just a dream. I'm tired from the journey, that's all. That's what her guardian Thomas had told her. And Thomas knew as well as anyone that now she had no choice but to be strong. Much depended on this journey, on what she did or failed to do. Not only for herself but for others also.

"Hannah . . . "

The voice that she heard startled her. Looking around the narrow tent of hides, she saw no one. The voice had come like a whisper, a brief pulse of breath.

She rose and walked to the entrance. Light filtered through a frayed blanket, and from outside came the sound of men in conversation. Laughter, curses, and boasts.

Perhaps I've fallen ill . . .

She pulled aside the entrance blanket, and looked out . . .

*　　*　　*

A broad meadow of yellow-sunlit wild flowers stretched before her, broken in the distance by groves of greening trees. Here and there along the sparkling banks of a rushing stream, horses stood tethered, while men bearing swords and bows strolled about or lay napping on patches of bright green grass. A group of these men, seeing her appear, rose and nodded respectfully. The men—short, sturdy riders—wore furs and coarse, felted clothing; many of their brown faces had scars. Their eyes slanted like hers, as though from long exposure to wind and sun.

A sudden wave of nausea overcame her. She swayed in the narrow door.

"Send for Thomas!" someone shouted. For a moment, the words rang incomprehensible to her ears—musical, foreign, and frightening.

Gasping, she sagged backward into the tent. Her head spun and her heart beat as fast as though she had run several miles. She staggered to the sheepskins, clutching the tight collar of her clothing—felted wool and leather.

A thin, gray-haired man clad in a robe of brown fabric entered the tent. He hurried to her side.

"*Hanna'el,* what's wrong? Are you ill?"

She shook her head.

The man knelt by her side and felt her brow. She looked up into his eyes. They were kind and gentle, edged with wrinkles and deeply set in a face framed by gray hair and a beard.

"I'll send for help. We're scarcely a day's ride from Aeron's Caer," she heard him tell her.

"No," she answered sharply, drawing a breath.

The words *Aeron's Caer* echoed inside her, familiar and strange at once. She felt drawn to the vortex of a mystery.

She frowned and refused the old man's help.

She remembered his name. *Brother Thomas . . .*

"Hanna'el, what's wrong?" he asked her anxiously.

"Let me stand. I must go out." She felt an urgent need to stay busy, to move, to ride—anything to forget this inner confusion—as though if she sat still for even a moment the disturbing dream would return to plague and haunt her . . .

*   *   *

Outside the tent, armed men leaped from the grass where
they lay resting. Her presence galvanized them. It both startled
and pleased her that this was so. Curious and eager, yet frightened
at the same time, she gripped the tent tightly and held herself
upright, feeling warm sun and wind upon her face. She inhaled it
proudly.

Thomas stood behind. She could feel him watching. She could
sense his unspoken concern.

She did not acknowledge it.

Instead, she faced the landscape ahead.

The tent had been pitched in the shelter of rolling hills. Waves
of lush grasses, like folds of an ocean prairie, billowed in the light,
sun-golden breeze that blew softly out of the east behind her until
this golden-green sea of grassland merged with a distant blue
horizon. She knew with a feeling of homesickness that she had
ridden from that direction. To the east lay safety and freedom;
behind her, to the west—unseen but dimly remembered—rising
hills extended to a range of high, granite mountains—a rocky,
wooded upland.

Aeron's Caer.

"Hanna'el?"

"Leave me a moment," she told the old man tensely.

Brother Thomas stepped away.

I am Hannah, a voice inside her whispered. Desperate and alone.
She could remember herself now. *At least a bit more of me.* Her
dream had faded. But other thoughts and memories reappeared.

She had come this far with her escort to approach the ancient
fortress long known as the Guir-Caer'oq—to confront its lord and
ruler, Aeron, who once had been her father's closest friend.

More than a friend, she remembered. Aeron had been like a
brother to her father, in those distant times.

But why? Who am I? What is this place?

The day shone clear and unclouded, as beautiful a day as she had ever scene. Like a scene from a picture magazine . . . a view of Montana. The air bore the scent of damp soil and eager horses. Its taste was a rare delight. She inhaled deeply, as though parched for renewal. The grass, the trees, and the gray-purple mountains rising in the distance had a sharpness to their outlines that she had never noticed so clearly before, as though the world stood closer to creation. She shivered as someone misspoke her name.

"*Hannah!*"

Turning, she saw a shepherd standing near. He was a young man no older than twenty, with tousled brown hair that fell loose to his shoulders and a kind but ironic smile that showed a gap between his strong white teeth. His dark eyes, keen and lively with restless amusement, watched her from beneath a broad and nobly formed brow. As she looked at him, he came forward in a familiar, friendly way. He reached in his jerkin and handed her a brown, deerskin pouch. To her amazement, she quickly accepted it, as though she had expected this gift.

"Keep it with you always," said the shepherd. "Walter says to wear it about your neck. You must *never* lose it."

"*Walter* . . . " The name sounded familiar, though she could not place it with any face she could recall. The pouch that the shepherd had given her felt light and trivial. And yet, some inner voice whispered it was vastly important.

"We'll meet again," the young shepherd told her, before she could speak. "I will wait for you at the Chinese Pavilion at Walter's pond, at the edge of the *Zone of Night* . . . "

She stared at him blankly as he nodded and stepped away.

"Wait . . . " she began. "Who are you?"

"Not now. Not here. I cannot stay with you," the young man smiled. "You know who I am."

His strangely accented words made little sense.

"Stay here! Let me talk to you!"

"Not now. Not here. The others need you. There are things you must do. You will soon find your way."

She knew what he meant, and yet she did not. She could not

understand why she felt this overwhelming need to ask him questions. A part of her felt alien and helpless—though she stood there angry and proud.

"I will wait for you," the stranger repeated, smiling in a knowing and familiar way. His familiarity taunted her. "You can find me whenever you need me. I will wait at Walter's pond."

He backed away.

"Wait. Stop! I order you to tell me . . . What's your name?"

"Try to remember . . . " he answered.

And then, the tall grass concealed him. He had vanished into the steppe.

"Mistress!" someone shouted. It was Brother Thomas.

She felt a sudden impulse to plunge after the shepherd in pursuit. Instead, she stood still, holding the leather pouch that he had given her and hearing on every side the loud preparations for departure.

Quickly, she undid the pouch's leather tie. Inside, attached to a braided cord, was a green and leafless twig.

It looked alive.

For a moment, she felt as though something vast and important was about to become clear. But then, the feeling passed.

She turned and faced the camp. As she started down the hill to join the men who awaited her, she heard the shepherd's voice a final time. It spoke from a place well hidden deeply inside her.

"Guard the green and living twig, and keep it sound . . . "

INSIDE THE STORM

Wind chimes and a steady patter of rain . . .

Hannah felt the firm pressure of damp plywood against her back. She shivered as a cool breeze touched her face.

Gasping, she drew herself up, knees pressed tightly to her chest, feeling the familiar stretch of her hooded sweatshirt.

"Walter?"

She saw that she sat alone on the floor of a small, ramshackle, circular building made of wood. Through an unglassed window, she could see a pond on which rain fell heavily, blown by a stormy wind. Three ducks floated disconsolately.

Walter's pond . . .

And this, *the ruined Chinese Pavilion* . . .

She touched the familiar plywood walls.

Beyond the pond stood the arboretum where she remembered she once had loved to roam. Its rolling hills were veiled with windblown rain. The trees were gone. Someone had destroyed them. Past the chain-link fence that ringed the pond, she saw yellow bulldozers parked in muddy rivulets where grass and trees and shrubbery had grown. The bulldozers loomed like sleeping dinosaurs.

How did I get here?

How did I lose my way?

She remembered a junkyard, and inside the junkyard, a shed in which she had seen Walter, the Fish of Wisdom, floating in a tank. Walter had spoken to her in the strange way that Fish of Wisdom speak, and he had told her something about memory . . .

The green and living twig . . . *Walter's gift* . . . hung from a golden string about her neck. She touched it gently.

Someone spoke her name.

*   *   *

Hannah turned in surprise, and for a moment she recalled a distant, grassy hillside where a young woman stood alone. "Calm down," said a voice reassuringly. "This is how it feels when you begin to *hover.*"

She remembered something else: there had been someone with her in that foreign, grassy place—a young man—*was he a shepherd?* The young shepherd had told her what to do. He had given her a gift. But she could not remember his words. She could only recall the *feeling* of what he had said. The feeling came first, to guide her.

"I will wait for you in the Pavilion at Walter's pond, at the edge of the Zone of Night . . . "

Hannah blinked.

A young man sat with her in the ruined Chinese Pavilion. She recognized him as the young man who had met her in the junkyard long ago. The young man, she could recall, was Walter's apprentice. That's what he had told her. He had called himself Fritz. An unlikely name for an apprentice, Hannah thought.

Fritz smiled. The cheerful, brown-haired apprentice, placid as a Buddha, sat cross-legged on the floor of the ruined Chinese Pavilion, leaning against a wall. She remembered him in the junkyard with ravens on his shoulders, one on each side. He had seemed quite familiar with those birds.

"Here," said Fritz, opening a thermos that he took from a leather knapsack at his side. "Drink this. The tea will steady you. I made it myself. Walter asked me to meet you here. He knew you'd be confused. You're afloat now—I call it *hovering.* It will take you a while to adjust. It took me several lifetimes." He shrugged good-naturedly as he managed to pour some steaming tea into the metal cup of the thermos bottle. "It is difficult to find one's way between the spheres," Fritz apologized. "Until you can master the art of hovering, you will not be able to discriminate between imagination and remembrance. I know—I had the same problem.

Here, drink some tea. Would you like a peanut butter and jelly sandwich? I have some. I made them just for you. Walter said they were what you liked to eat."

He smiled and offered her the food and drink.

Hannah shook her head. She stared at him numbly, too baffled to know what question to ask first.

She looked through a window of the ruined Chinese Pavilion at the rainstorm that raged outside, and she recalled that the Fish of Wisdom had spoken of a journey—something to do with her father's absence. *Something to do with a tree.*

Again, Fritz offered her tea. "Please," he urged, "drink some. It will steady you. Small but familiar sensations—the taste of green tea or a peanut butter sandwich—will anchor you until you find your way. Please try. You'll find that it's a splendidly refreshing experience."

Hannah touched the slender twig about her neck.

"Where am I? What happened?"

Fritz laughed. "You're right where you were and right where you need to be. It's always that way—nothing changes; you simply *shift*. Your attention *hovers.*"

Hannah touched the familiar walls of the ruined Chinese Pavilion. They felt quite solid. The rain drummed loudly on the roof. Drops of water broke through the cracks and splattered her face. She recalled cascading spheres of light . . . and Walter's voice.

"Is it real?" she asked him.

Fritz put down her tea. He made a serious face, then laughed and tapped the dampened floor. "Yes and no. It is and is not. When was memory ever *exactly* like the thing recalled? You must overcome what you think you know. You still believe that memory is *reflection*, a finished picture that you somehow present to yourself. *Viola!* It may seem that way at first, but only until you've mastered the art of hovering. Hovering is the key. When you master that art, then you will understand that memory is pure creation of the thing itself. It is absolute thetic capacity. The secret lies in the stories you choose to tell, and how you choose to tell them, and why, and for whom. That's all that it really means . . . it's very simple, really, when you get down to it. But I admit, it sounds like magic when you first begin." Again, he handed her the cup of tea with a fond and apologetic shrug. "All beginnings are magical, aren't they, Hannah? Please sip this tea. It's delicious. It's from Japan."

Hannah shut her eyes, closing him out. She had no idea what he was saying. His words were just sound. She cinched her eyes and saw for a brief moment, like a memory bobbing to surface on the smooth mirror of untroubled water, an expanse of waving grassland, a group of riders, a distant range of granite mountains, and a young shepherd who smiled fondly and held out to her Walter's gift.

She opened her eyes.

"Who are you?" she confronted him.

Fritz put down the tea and reached in his knapsack. "Let's talk about something else for the time being, shall we? Look here, I brought you your book. You forgot it in all that rushing about."

The apprentice held out an old book. With a tremor of recollection, Hannah recognized it as the book that Uncle Joseph had given her for her thirteenth birthday. The book had been locked; now it lay open. *Of course,* she remembered, *I opened it with the twig in Mrs. Endicott's bookstore.* As though greeting a friend, the scene of that past discovery replayed itself through her mind. She recalled that she had not been able to read the book's foreign script, though now, as she glanced at it, the writing felt very familiar, like a face dimly recognized from the past.

"*This is the journal of your remembrance,*" Fritz explained, speaking slowly, as though to a very young child. "The book writes and rewrites itself each time you use it. The language is *yours.* Look, the story begins wherever, however you like. We all get such a book when we begin. Reading your way into it is the first exercise you need to master, if you wish to hover and not just sit here in the rain."

He tapped the walls of the ruined Chinese Pavilion to underscore his point. The pavilion was a wreck. The storm wind blew droplets of rain through the window and through the hundred cracks in the broken wallboards. Except for a dripping tent, she couldn't imagine a worse shelter. The rain outside the pavilion fell in a never-ending, ceaseless, time-effacing flood. It reminded her of the Bible. To north, south, east, and west the storm extended, like a dark wavering monsoon of forgetfullness . . . a *Zone of Night*. It appeared that her world had drowned completely.

Hannah took the book from Fritz's hand, and she leafed through it slowly. The apprentice watched her with a slight cat-like twist of his inquisitive head.

"The book is yours," he repeated. "Whatever is written there, however strange, is there because you wrote it." He watched as she turned to the many empty pages. "The pages are blank until you use them. You must make the effort on your own."

Hannah slammed it shut. "I don't like it here," she told him. "I want to leave."

"Of course, you do. Who wouldn't?"

"I want to go home."

He seemed to expect her to say something else. She did not know what. Instead of answering, she looked at her book again, the one that her uncle had given her for her thirteenth birthday—the one that Fritz had called her Journal of Remembrance. She started to read.

Operis Processio,
Multum Naturae Placet

The strange inscription inside the book's leather cover had changed. Earlier, the meaning had eluded her. But now she could understand it perfectly well, as though the inscrutable script had changed to English. It required a little effort to make it so.

The Progress of the Work
Pleases Nature Greatly

"More tea?" asked Fritz agreeably. "Are you sure you don't want a sandwich?"

She turned a few pages more. The effort to read those blank pages felt almost physical, as though she were pushing through some dense, almost watery substance—a mixture of water, air, and light—that parted as she exerted her attention but closed in upon her darkly as soon as her attention lapsed.

"That's it," said Fritz approvingly. "You'll get the hang of it. You must do it all on your own."

"There was a letter in here," said Hannah, remembering. "A letter from my father."

"You'll find it again," said Fritz. "Nothing's lost."

The rain fell monotonously. Hannah looked at the book again, studying the foreign script, whose meaning had eluded her once upon a time. Now, as she studied it, it seemed as though the words transformed into glowing spheres, like the spheres that had danced in Walter's eyes. As they slid into her understanding, they seemed to change their shapes. She could join them and make them dance. She had that ability.

"That's it," said Fritz. "*Try*. You'll get the hang of it. Confidence makes it easier. Enthusiasm breeds success."

Clichés, thought Hannah dismissively.

Fritz's words merged with the floating spheres. She could feel herself hover between them. She could join them, slipping free from one sphere to the other, in and out. She wove between. As soon as she turned her attention to one sphere or the next, she became the glowing object she beheld.

"Wait," said Fritz, "you should stay here a bit longer. Don't go so fast. You need to understand what is required. You'll lose yourself again. Stay here a little longer in the pavilion. Time is not the problem. No need to rush."

A part of her wanted to listen, but she felt willful. And then the Chinese Pavilion washed away.

THE INCIDENT AT THE BRIDGE

"We'll soon see a stand of trees beside the river—oak and beech and alder. They call it the Sighing Wood. The river is narrow but flows strongly this time of year—brown and swelled. We'll come to a bridge of stone built by the Guir, those ancient folk who built the Caer. Some say they were more than human."

She heard the words as though she were far away. The person who spoke, Brother Thomas, turned to her. She saw concern and worry on his face. She saw him reach out to steady her. Perhaps he thought she would tumble from her saddle.

Bryhs, the old warrior who led the cohort, rode closer to her side, his back unbending straight. "Did you hear what I said?"

She nodded, forcing a smile, but she could not recall a single thing that Bryhs had told her.

Again, the man named Thomas frowned.

What's wrong with me?

She saw her panicked question in their eyes.

Somewhere she heard rain, pounding rain, ceaseless driving rain. But here, from horseback, the sky was clear.

"*Hanna'el?* Are you all right?"

Just as in the shepherd's tent . . . a feeling, nearly overwhelming, that she was not herself . . . that someone else looked out upon these riders and this forest and listened to a language she did not know and yet somehow understood. She swallowed and fought down a feeling of nausea. She forced herself to breathe slowly.

Stay in control.

But even her mare felt strange. She had ridden horses almost from the day she had taken her first steps. She knew horses as well as some persons know their families. She could never fall from this

95

saddle . . . *never* . . . and certainly not at a pace as slow as this. Why did the ground look so threatening and hard?

"I'm fine," she muttered.

To forestall more questions, she rode forward alone.

*   *   *

Aeron's Caer stood at the end of a mountain valley carved by a glacier ages past. A stream, swelled by the melting snow-pack in the mountains, flowed noisily through the valley's midst. On either side, sheer granite cliffs soared upwards two thousand feet. Spumes of water coursed from the heights of these cliffs, vaporous falls that caught the sunlight and refracted it into a hundred shifting rainbows.

The valley, unlike the meadows they had recently traversed, grew thick with hardwoods—maple, oak, ash, beech, and elm. Each tree stood green with the first flush of spring. The valley narrowed as they reached the river crossing. Above, heights of sun-swept granite and feldspar shimmered brightly in the afternoon sunlight. Here and there, she saw patches of melting snow that sparkled like polished crystals. The breeze blew colder, scented with the smoke of distant fires.

True to Bryhs' prediction, they soon saw a bridge.

A clan of herdsmen, driving cattle, blocked the way. One of the wagons, a great ox cart bearing hay and wood, had broken an axle, and the mishap had pitched the cart's contents across the road. Wood and hay lay scattered everywhere. Cattle stood before and behind the broken wagon, lowing disconsolately. Four drovers argued with the soldiers posted to meet her. Their captain, a young man with thick black hair cut short so that it bristled on his head like the quills of a frightened porcupine, shook his fist in the herdsmen's faces. He bellowed orders to hurl the broken wagon over the railing, and at once the herdsmen baulked. Adding to the mayhem, cattle broke loose from the dogs that nipped at their

shanks. Three other carts waited in line to cross the bridge, and
these held families. Mothers clutched sobbing infants to their
breasts while dusty, barefoot children scampered over and under
the stonework. She watched as several desperate soldiers forced
their way through the throng and began to hurl the fallen firewood
into the stream.

A louder argument erupted.

Bryhs scowled. "See what comes of haste."

She was about to follow his lead and order her riders to push
through this unruly crowd, when a voice said quite distinctly:
"*Wait. Pay attention. This concerns you . . .* "

She looked at Bryhs, startled.

"What did you say?"

The old warrior shrugged, not noticing the confusion in her
voice. He nodded dourly at the broken cart that stood in their way
and at the throng that swarmed it. "You see what comes of haste,"
he said dispassionately.

She smiled, shaking off her sense of confusion, and was about
to say something humorous, when the voice spoke again:

"*Watch. Pay attention. This concerns you . . .* "

On the bridge, the soldiers won the argument. Using their
weapons, they forced the herdsmen off and began to heave the
wreckage into the stream.

Confusion erupted as the bulk of the massive wagon hit the
raging water with a splash. Everyone rushed to see the destruction
as the current swept the wagon toward some rocks. Men cursed
and fretted, and one of the louder herdsmen, a dark-haired,
impetuous youth slightly younger than Hanna'el, rushed forward
and seized one of the soldiers by the neck, apparently meaning to
hurl him off the bridge.

At once, the guards beat the young man down. They kicked
and pummeled him, and his cries diverted everyone's attention
from the wagon, which crashed into a jutting rock and split in
two.

From her vantage point near the bridge, Hanna'el saw the captain draw a blade and hold it to the young man's neck. Suddenly, without any thought of what she meant to do, and contrary to her intention to remain aloof, she urged her mare forward.

"Stop," she ordered loudly. "Let him go!" She shouted at the captain of the guards, who stood incredulous. The edge of his weapon poised at a hand's width from the fallen herdsman's throat. Caught between surprise and anger, the soldier hesitated, dumbfounded by her loud command.

"Do as I say! Step away from him!"

Once more, but only faintly, she had the dizzy sensation of watching herself from a distance, but the feeling quickly passed. It felt good to act and to speak commands.

Bowing swiftly, the captain of the guard put up his sword.

"Chase these cattle off the bridge! Quickly! Hurry!" she commanded.

Her orders caused fear and haste. The others hurried to obey. Even her own riders looked shocked that she had spoken.

She did not know what had prompted her to act.

"Move these people out of my way!" she heard herself shout again.

Only one person did not obey.

The young herdsman, whose life she had saved, clutched his bruised ribs and struggled to stand. Gasping for breath, he stared at her defiantly. His face, despite the bruising, had handsome, intelligent features and black hair like hers, though his complexion was much lighter. For a moment, she felt certain that she had seen the young drover before and that she knew him in some other circumstance, perhaps when she was younger. As their eyes briefly met, she felt shocked by a distant but electric sense of recognition, as though she had turned down a corner on a dark street she thought to be empty but instead had run head first into an acquaintance she intimately knew. *You . . . here . . .* She felt seized by a strong desire to speak to him, but she fought this impulse down.

"Kit!"

A young woman clutching a baby ran to the drover's side. Ignoring everyone else, she berated him in a shrill and abusive tone of voice. Hanna'el could barely understand the woman's dialect, but she judged by her mood and gestures that this was his wife. The woman pressed forward, clutching her husband's arm, while the baby at her breast screamed shrilly. Hanna'el saw an ugly frown come over the young man's face. He turned to the woman and shouted something in the dialect of his clan. His fists had clenched.

Hanna'el did not wait to see what happened next. Bryhs directed her attention to the bridge, nodding that they should proceed. She rode ahead, but as she started, the young man broke free from his wife to accuse her. "It's your fault," he screamed. "It's your fault this happened!" He pointed at the ruined wagon in the stream.

Hanna'el halted, appalled that the drover dared to address her in this familiar way. Had he no shame? Without her merciful interference, he'd be dead.

At once, the captain on the bridge drew his sword, ready to kill this young man for his insolence.

"Stop!" she commanded.

Kit, the young drover, had not moved. He stared at her fixedly.

"You did this!" he accused her.

"Pay him for the damaged wagon," she ordered Bryhs. She saw how this offer surprised him. *Good. Let them wonder at my moods. Let them respect me.*

She had trouble forcing herself to return the young man's defiant stare. Her heart beat strongly; her face grew warm.

The old warrior Bryhs looked at her dumbly.

"Pay him!" she shouted.

She wanted only to be done with this and leave.

Bryhs took a single coin from his pouch.

"No," said Hanna'el, "give him three gold coins." She forced herself to face him as she spoke, head high and back straight. She saw the effect of her words. The crowd fell silent—dumbfounded. Those coins were worth ten times their scrawny cattle. Briefly, a shadow of uncertainty softened the young drover's expression. But only for moment. His face hardened with pride. He spoke again. "Keep your coins. I don't want them."

"You fool!"

Before Hanna'el or anyone else could intervene, the young drover's wife rushed forward and seized the coins from Bryhs. She thrust them in her bodice. "You fool!" she screamed. "Have you lost your senses?"

The young man, to everyone's astonishment, spun and attacked his wife. In the middle of the bridge, they wrestled for the coins. "No! Mine!" she shouted. "We need that money!"

Everyone laughed as the two fell to the stones. In a moment, the young man had torn his wife's dress and taken back the payment. He was by far the stronger of the two and more determined. Rising to his feet, he shook his fist at Hanna'el while thrusting aside his screaming wife with the other arm. Then, in a gesture that shocked everyone, he threw the three gold coins into the raging stream.

With a cry like a woman giving birth, his distraught young wife flung herself on him again. "You fool! You idiot! What have you done!" Three brawny neighbors dragged her off. The young man's face bled from her attack.

He did not acknowledge his wife's insults at all. "I don't want your gifts! I despise you," he shouted instead at Hanna'el.

Bryhs' hand leapt to his sword, but again she restrained him. "Ride on," she ordered loudly.

Flushed with anger and outrage, her cohort obeyed.

As she and her cohort left the bridge and entered the mountainous forest, two ravens, which rested on a pine tree, spread their darkened wings and flew behind them.

ELOWYN

Hannah closed the book and confronted Fritz. The apprentice had said not a word. It appeared, from his expression, that he found it hard to keep silent. Conversation seemed his natural bent. But he sipped a cup of tea and watched her quizzically, quite composed. The way he watched her reminded her of a cat. Outside the Chinese Pavilion, the rain continued endlessly. It rained and rained. The hot tea gave off steam.

Hannah touched her world. True, this Chinese Pavilion felt solid enough, and the rain pounded loudly on its roof—but how did she know that any of this was real? She traced her memories backwards, one by one. It took effort, and she often felt lost. But time didn't seem to matter so she just kept trying again and again. Sometimes she could hold her attention steady. Sometimes not. Maybe Fritz could help, but she just let Fritz the apprentice sit there as she willed herself to think backwards, patiently, moment by moment, step by step, like puzzling a move in a game of chess.

She thought herself back until she stood in Mrs. Endicott's bookstore. And there her memories stopped.

"Where's Mrs. Endicott?" Hannah asked.

Her question surprised him. "I'm not sure where she is . . . *at the moment*," Fritz answered tentatively.

Hannah scowled and looked out the window of the ruined Chinese Pavilion. This rain just wouldn't quit. The rain fell so heavily; it looked like it would wash away the world.

How do I know that I'm not in a coma in a hospital with Uncle Joseph sitting next to me pressing my hand while precious bodily fluids seep through a needle into my arm? How do I know I'm not dead?

She turned to Fritz angrily. "What happened to Uncle Joseph? What happened to the bookstore? Where are the Seven Friedrichs?"

101

The apprentice remained unperturbed. It was clearly an accomplishment of his training.

"It's all where it was," said Fritz patiently. He nodded at the outer storm. "It's all where it should be. Nothing's lost."

The pavilion, Fritz, the book, Walter's twig . . . *these all might be hallucinations,* Hannah thought. How did she know that this person who called herself Hannah wasn't an imagined character in a dream or just a phantom in the book that Fritz called her journal of recollection—or, for that matter, maybe someone else was reading that journal, or writing in it, and this was the crazy result. Who could tell? Was she Hannah and all those other memories at once? *You're Hanna'el . . .*

She recalled what Walter had shown her when she asked him about memory. Or rather, she recalled the feeling that his answer had conjured forth, for the vision of those singing spheres afloat on a river of light was not really an experience that she could put into language. In that moment of recollection she had been everywhere and nowhere at once, the center *and* the periphery of each envisioned sphere, freely moving in and out of those floating, ephemeral worlds as they formed and reformed, arose and perished . . . endlessly.

She wished she had asked Walter another question: *if what he had shown her was memory, then what was the difference between imagination and remembrance? Were memories real? Was it possible for an imagination to become a memory . . . and how did one discriminate between the two?*

Ideas were purely imaginary . . . were they not? No one could touch them. Where was the touchstone?

Certainly, she decided, on some level *memories* had to be real. Things happened, and you remembered them. But once things happened, memories changed. Were *imagined* memories real? And if you forgot that something happened, had it ever really happened at all?

She looked at Fritz, afraid that he might have vanished, but there he sat, sipping his green tea and eating crackers, smiling in his Cheshire way. Patient and polite, but rather dumb, she suspected. He *had* done his best to restrain his tendency to talk. Maybe if she tried she could think him out of existence. But no one could will herself to forget. While she knew she could will herself to remember, forgetting seemed to happen for reasons over which she had no discernable control.

What did it *mean?*

She looked at the outer storm.

If I lose my memories, thought Hannah, *do I lose myself? How many selves are there?*

Who am I now?

She stared out of the Chinese Pavilion at the rain-pocked pond. It rained just as hard as ever. (People said *it* was raining; they never said *it* was remembering . . . though perhaps, thought Hannah, they should.) She remembered the eerie silence that had followed her after the storm, after that moment of terror in Mrs. Endicott's bookstore, as she had walked all alone to the junkyard, as though everyone in the world had disappeared.

Was the bookstore still there? Did the Sphinx exist?

And surely if everyone had vanished, their memories had vanished, too . . . Worlds might perish.

A horrible consequence.

It was all so torturously complex.

Keep thinking, she told herself, remembering her uncle's sober, philosophic advice. Just follow your thinking like walking down a path, he once had told her. One thought, one step, and then another. *Step by step, breath by breath, patiently, in time.* In that way, she came to Walter, the Fish of Wisdom, or Walter the Master of Memory, as Fritz called him. Walter, certainly, must remember her, so perhaps that was why she hadn't disappeared in a poof of smoke. She touched the tiny twig about her neck.

Do my memories belong to me at all?

This question stopped her like a wall.

She had followed her thinking as far as she could go, and all she had were thoughts: thoughts about thinking as she thought them. It seemed like an endless circle, like a snake that has swallowed its own tail. It didn't resolve the problem of this storm or explain how she had come to this ruined Chinese Pavilion. It didn't explain Fritz.

It just left her nowhere.

Hannah's head throbbed terribly, and she leaned against the wall. She lifted her face, allowing cool drops of rainwater to run down her forehead. The water felt alive and refreshing. She could taste it. It had to be real.

She recalled Walter's words:

"People take their memories for granted, but they shouldn't, really, because memory is not a part of them at all; it is a separate, living thing. Memory can flourish or it can die. Its health depends on a subtle balance—let us call it a balance of shadow and light. If this balance becomes over weighted, if the forces of shadow or light become too strong, then memory weakens; it withers, like a plant. When that happens, spheres of remembrance are lost, and those spheres are not just memories, they are worlds."

"Wouldn't you like some tea or something to eat?" Fritz interrupted. She looked at him angrily.

"Why are you always offering me food? I told you I'm not hungry."

Fritz shrugged, unabashed. "I thought you were hungry. I'd be *very* hungry, if I were you. Eating is a sensible habit."

"I don't want to eat. I want to go home."

"And where do you think home is?"

"I don't know, but it isn't *here*."

"Oh no?" said Fritz. He tapped the wooden floor.

"*No.*"

"Then what are you doing here?"

"Talking to you."

"Fine," said Fritz. He leaned back and crossed his arms. "Go on then. Talk."

She felt fed up with his evasive answers. Walter had certainly dipped the bottom of the barrel to find an apprentice like him. She guessed he'd be at his apprenticeship pretty damn long.

"I can leave right now," she threatened.

"Yes, you can."

"I don't have to sit here in the cold—talking to *you*."

"That's right, you don't. You can be silent."

"That's not what I meant."

"Oh really?"

"I don't even like you."

Fritz shrugged. "Like or dislike—it's quite irrelevant. What's important is that you *understand*."

She felt totally fed up with all his riddles.

"I'm leaving," she said. "And you can't stop me."

Fritz nodded. He uncrossed his arms. "You can go wherever you like, any time you like, however you like. *It's up to you*."

His answer seemed to imply more than was said. And she thought she heard some hesitation in his voice.

Fritz smiled. "Just don't lose the twig—the green and living twig that Walter gave you. Sooner or later, you'll have to seek the Tree."

There it was again . . . *that word*.

"Let me get this straight," she said to Fritz. "I'm supposed to carry this twig to a dying tree in a place called Elowyn and replant it. Right?"

Fritz nodded. "Correct."

"And what will that do? Will it grow?"

"Not precisely . . . but yes, in a manner of speaking, *it must*."

"*How* can it grow?" said Hannah. "It's not a seed."

Fritz sat silently for a moment, as though the complexities of this predicament had never quite presented themselves so clearly to him before. He made some kind of vague, gardening-like motion with his hand, as though digging with a trowel.

"I'm not sure exactly how you do it," said the apprentice thoughtfully. "That's something only you can figure out. Each person has to do it on her own. U PULL IT YOURSELF— remember what the sign said?"

She scowled at him blackly. "That isn't funny."

"Sorry. I was only trying to help."

"Help what?"

"Help *you*, of course, to go where you need to go."

"And where am I going?"

"That's easy," he smiled at her, satisfied that they had found some common ground. "*Always toward home.*"

"You don't know what you're talking about," said Hannah. "You're just repeating what someone else said."

This last remark annoyed him, Hannah observed. Fritz frowned. "Well, if you have a better explanation, let me hear it. I don't have *all* the answers. I told you I'm just an apprentice. But I'm doing the best I can. Take all the time you need to decide what to do. We've got nothing but time—and plenty of that."

"And suppose I just stay here?"

"You have that choice."

Hannah rolled her eyes. "I mean," she persisted, "suppose I just take this twig and throw it out the window of this Pavilion. What then?"

Fritz thought for a moment. At last, he excused himself and fished a leather notebook out of his knapsack. Hannah watched him flip the brown pages. They were covered top to bottom with fragments of notes. He wrote with a very close, flowing, and old-fashioned script. Not an inch of paper had been wasted.

She felt proud she had stumped him.

"Don't you know *anything*?"

"Of course I do," said Fritz, testily. "I know plenty. I'm not like you. I am a *very advanced order of life*. I just need to review what Walter told me. It's important I get it right. You're a *human* being, after all."

"And I suppose you're *not*?" said Hannah scornfully.

"I am. But you're from New Jersey."

Hannah rolled her eyes. "What's that got to do with it?"

"Ah, here it is," said Fritz suddenly, before she could argue. He opened his notebook and spoke as he read the page. "Actually, as far as you're concerned, nothing too serious will happen if you throw the twig away. It says here that the twig is safe, whether you wear it *here* or not. Walter saw to that. But your world, I'm afraid, has no substance." He tapped the ramshackle wall of the Chinese Pavilion. "It's all just a phantom of its former self. And worse, it says here that your world is fading. Not that this will happen all at once. No, according to Walter, things will persist as appearance for quite some time. They might even fool most people. Nevertheless, inevitably things will fade. Or perhaps a better way to put it: *they'll wash away.*" He nodded at the outer storm. "What you see here is the end result of a process that's been happening for quite a long time—for what you would call centuries. Little by little, remembrance has leeched from your world, although almost no one noticed. Or, if they noticed, I guess no one cared." He shrugged and tapped the pavilion again. "If you stay here and do nothing, then, like the old song says, you'll slowly, inexorably fade away— right along with the rest of your world, such as it is." Fritz closed the leather notebook with a clap. "That's it. That's the best I can tell you. You must find the Tree. You really must. You must begin your journey to Elowyn as soon as possible."

Hannah looked at the rain. Endless. She assumed from Fritz's comments that Elowyn was somewhere else. It certainly wasn't here, inside this soggy arboretum, and probably it wasn't on any continent she could recall. It wasn't just out there in the maelstrom.

"Give me that notebook," she said to him.

Fritz drew back. "I'm afraid I can't do that. It belongs to me. I wrote it, on my own initiative. *You* have to write your own. But even if I did give you my notebook, you couldn't read it—or if you did, you wouldn't *understand* . . . just like I can't read your journal . . . I mean the book your uncle gave you. Only *you* can read it. That's how it works. If you want to know what I wrote here, you have to write it yourself."

To demonstrate his point, Fritz opened his notebook and showed her a page. It was true; she could not make heads or tails of it. The notebook was written in some foreign language, like maybe one of those languages Uncle Joseph could understand.

"Is Elowyn the last unknown country in the world?" Hannah asked.

"You can say so, if it helps you decide what to do."

"Suppose I don't say so?"

"You have that option."

"I can go back to Mrs. Endicott's bookstore."

"You could."

"I could find the Seventh Friedrich."

Fritz smiled. "You could do that, too."

Annoyed, she challenged him: "Is there anyone out there at all in this rainstorm?"

"Besides you and me?" He hesitated thoughtfully. "Well, it all depends."

"On what?

"On what you *do*. Didn't I say that? On what you remember. On who you are." He nodded at the book that her uncle had given her for her thirteenth birthday. "It depends on the stories you choose to tell. I told you that before. The rules don't change. Everything depends on stories; that's really all you need to know."

"That's dumb," said Hannah.

She wondered what would happen if she just waited and did nothing—if she stayed in the ruined Chinese Pavilion and refused to do anything. Suppose she just kept silent—*would things really fade? Would her world just vanish?*

"Take all the time you want," said Fritz amiably.

Ignoring his agreeable comments, Hannah turned away. As the rain continued heavily, she opened her journal and began to read again...

AERON

Lord Aeron of the Caer was angry. He slapped the broad, wooden table that stood before him and allowed the sound to echo in the large, stony room in which he stood. He wore a heavy, fur-lined cloak, and he kept this cloak pulled tightly about him, despite the room's warmth. Scowling from beneath his dark, untended hair, he scanned his frightened counselors.

"How dare she ride here with her miserable escort and petition me like one of my sworn chieftains!"

All but one of Aeron's four advisors looked away. The oldest of the four, Et'elred, met Aeron's angry gaze. "You ignore a point of obvious importance," Et'elred said. "This young woman, Hanna'el, is the only child of Carlon, your foster brother and former ally. And," he added pointedly, "he was once your friend."

At these words, Aeron turned with sudden vehemence and gazed out the open window to the stone courtyard fifty feet below. His jaw moved tensely behind his graying beard.

"Carlon's dead. He betrayed me . . . "

Et'elred was calm. Methodically, as though schooling a wayward pupil, he continued. "Nevertheless, there remains the matter of your oath. You swore to protect Carlon's lands and only child. You know as well as I that Carlon's memory is revered. There are many of your chieftains who chafe under your rule. Fear keeps them from rebellion, but fear of one another more than you. Each chieftain distrusts his neighbor, and this mutual hatred is your strength. Had they a leader or cause to unite their discontent . . . "

Aeron scoffed. "You think that Carlon's daughter could be such a leader? Can she challenge *me?*"

Et'elred paused. He began again. "Why exert yourself when you can use the strength of others? Receive Carlon's daughter and treat her as your guest. She is young, true—but by right, she should inherit her father's lands. You must woo her and bend her to your will."

Aeron showed pleasure. But he waved his hand in brusque dismissal. "Get out. I need to think."

"As you wish. How shall I speak your instructions?"

"As soon as she arrives, confine her to the Caer. But do this in a way that disguises my intentions. Make certain she is isolated from her cohort. Go now, I want to be alone."

Et'elred and the other counselors bowed and departed. Then, as a servant prepared to close the chamber doors, Aeron spoke again. "Send me my physician."

As the servant hurried to obey, Aeron eased himself into a chair by the chamber's hearth. His lips moved silently as his eyes caught the sparkle of the flames. "Damn you, Carlon," he muttered, wincing from the pain below his ribs. "Damn you, and damn your daughter."

A knock on the chamber door forced Aeron to turn.

A cloaked figure stood within the doorway.

Aeron shuddered. He could not overcome the chill that always afflicted him in the presence of the physician he called Azael.

THE PHYSICIAN AZAEL

Azael entered the room softly, robed in the austere habit of his guild. He did not remove his cowl. His face, thin, hawkish, and intelligent, shone whitened in the dimly lit room like the moon that glows through drifting wisps of cloud. He inclined his head ever so slightly in a posture of humble respect. "Has your old affliction grown more troublesome, Lord Aeron? May I assist you?"

Aeron shivered. He had never accustomed himself to that voice. Sometimes, in the midst of a sound night's sleep, Azael's thin, icy tone pierced his dreams like a ghostly summons, bolting him upright. Many a time Aeron had observed some animal—a cat or dog—leave the room when Azael appeared. After sixteen years of residence, the physician had no friends within the Caer.

He wanted to say no. But he could not. His need and his pain were too great.

Azael already knew.

The physician watched Aeron carefully, like a man deciphering a text.

"Relax," he said, "your pain is momentary. It will pass. I will help you. Haven't I always stood by to help?"

Briefly, like a star shooting swiftly through a moonless night, Aeron possessed the thought: *There was a time when I could have resisted, when I was younger, when I was whole . . . I didn't need him . . .*

"I have seen her approach the bridge," Azael said quietly. "She is young and beautiful, Carlon's daughter. I warned you of this danger many times. You did not listen. Carlon betrayed you, and here is your chance to have revenge. Carlon lives through his daughter—*you must destroy her before she remembers her quest.*"

Aeron muttered a curse and turned away. He approached a door above which had been carved a single glyph and below that a name.

At'theira

Softly, he traced the glyph.

The physician Azael followed him like a shadow. "Aeron," he whispered, "do not fail me. I have served you well. I was here for you always, whenever you needed me, day or night. No one else consoled you when you were in pain. No one stood by when you suffered in your solitude. No one could help. The time is at hand to repay me as we agreed."

The door that Aeron approached was a slag of granite, set in place without hinges or handle. Aeron placed his hand in the middle of this portal. He waited until the stone moved aside, set in motion by an unseen mechanism.

Behind the portal, a narrow, curving stairwell descended into darkness.

Azael pointed down.

"Go to her," said the physician.

But Aeron stood still. "Swear that you will help me."

"I have always helped you. It is my nature to help. But before I help, you must renew your vow. Carlon's quest must fail."

"Carlon's dead. He has already failed."

"Then make certain he is truly dead."

"How?"

"Carlon's memories must perish. To do that, you must destroy his daughter. Her arrival is a sign. Already, she remembers. The Tree will summon her. I cannot let that happen. You must destroy her first."

"Destroy her yourself—you have the skill! Use your art—all humans are weak."

The physician smiled. "I can only employ my arts if the patient asks."

Aeron paused at the height of the spiraling staircase that led downward into the depths of the Caer.

"As I asked?" he muttered.

The physician pressed close. He whispered tensely.

"Carlon loved your queen—he stole her from you—and with

her, your only son. Can you forgive such treachery? Can you endure that pain? Have you forgotten so soon the agony he made you suffer? Your wound is raw. Let me assuage it."

"Carlon's dead," said Aeron. "His quest was a failure. I punished Carlon—I punished *her*. I will deal with Carlon's daughter another way."

"There is only *one* way," said the physician. "You know my terms."

Aeron groaned and turned aside, avoiding the physician's cold, unblinking eyes.

For moment, Aeron seemed ready to descend the darkened stairwell, but the distant sound of bells caught his attention.

Thrusting the physician aside, the Lord of the Caer staggered from the darkened stairwell to the window that overlooked the outer courtyard. From here he could observe the main, torch-lit entrance to the fortress.

Loud confusion had arisen at the gate. A group of itinerant players had arrived, and with them a Singer and his imp.

The bells were around the imp's neck.

"See there," said Aeron, surprised and momentarily distracted by this arrival. It was not so common for a Singer to visit the Caer. He had not seen one since childhood. The arrival revived pleasant memories.

But the physician, when he saw the object of Aeron's gaze, withdrew silently from the chamber, departing so quickly that Aeron did not have time to question him further about his plans.

HANNA'EL

After leaving the bridge, the ravens followed Hanna'el until nightfall. Then, as the sky darkened and storm clouds gathered from the north, the two birds disappeared. One flew toward the escarpments of the valley; the other remained near the forest, close to the road that led upward to the Caer.

Hanna'el had kept silent since the crossing of the bridge, for she could not put the incident with the young drover out of her mind. The drover's angry words burned in her memory, and she imagined a dozen ways she should have responded. Surely, her authority had been compromised, and news of her embarrassment would travel quickly to Aeron. As she rode the trail up the mountainside, she imagined dealing with the impudent youth as he deserved: leaping from her horse and hurling him off the bridge. *Let him fish those coins from the river—let him drown!* She pitied the poor woman who bore his brat.

Thomas rode beside her and observed her furious mood. He coughed diplomatically and urged his gelding closer to her side.

Hanna'el scowled. Her black hair swirled in the cool mountain breeze like a shadow of the rage inside her. She had in her looks something of the wildness of the steppes, though beneath her dark hair, her paler complexion gave sign of her mother's northern blood.

Uncertain what to say, Thomas nervously pulled at his left ear lobe, a usual habit. "When we arrive at Aeron's Caer . . . " he began uncertainly.

But Hanna'el cut him short. "What would Aeron say if I confronted him directly instead of pretending to be his friend?"

Thomas frowned.

Patiently, dispassionately, he began to guide her thoughts to a calmer course. "I don't think Aeron would look generously upon an offer of friendship . . . "

"I'll spit in his face. I'll have him whipped!"

The old scholar went pale. He stammered, shocked by what he heard her say.

Hanna'el saw his expression. "Not *Aeron*, you fool," she told him crossly. "I mean the idiot who challenged me at the bridge."

Drawing a breath and wishing he had a flask of wine to dull his overwrought nerves, Thomas did his best to laugh at her boast, and his starved attempt made her grin.

She relaxed and gathered her loose hair together with a cord. The clop of the horse's hooves on the stony roadway fell as a soothing complement to her humor.

"I suppose you'd perish of fright if I said that," she said to him teasingly. "Don't be afraid. I haven't ridden all this way and bruised my backside to destroy myself with a single hasty remark." And then she added in a musing tone of voice: "Tell me again of my father's friendship with Aeron."

Thomas sighed, relieved to speak of matters he knew better than a young woman's changeable moods. "As you know," he began, "your father and Aeron grew up together. The Caer was once Carlon's home. From the age of seven, Carlon and Aeron were closest friends. I recall the stories Carlon told—how Aeron and he hunted, fished, and roamed this valley side by side—like brothers. Your father spent thirteen years of his childhood at the Caer—such was the custom."

"But if they were friends, why won't Aeron support my claim to rule Arcatus?"

"That's why we've come," repeated Thomas. "To obtain his consent."

Hannah scowled. "Tell me again what you know of my father's departure."

Thomas sighed. Somehow, the recitation of this story felt inauspicious now that they stood nearly within eyesight of the fabled Caer. Nevertheless, he continued patiently. It was his duty.

"Queen At'theira, Lord Aeron's wife, perished giving birth to

Lord Aeron's only son, the lost Prince Raemond. You were only a stammering child when this occurred. Aeron was inconsolable upon the death of his wife, and your father, grieved to see such suffering, swore to a quest. He swore to travel westward to Elowyn to pluck from the fabled Tree that grows upon those shores a blossom whose fragrance can restore the dead to life."

"The Tree that he hoped to find, is it also called the Tree of Life?"

Thomas hesitated. "Yes, it is called that by some, and by others it is called the Tree of All Remembrance. I have heard it called by other names as well. In the ancient legends of Urd, which your father trusted, it is called the Singing Tree. I do not know why those ancient legends name it in that way. I do not understand why they say the Tree must sing. The ancient folk of Urd had many customs that they say were given to them by the gods, the founders of civilization. But the cities of Urd have vanished, and with them all the wisdom that the folk who dwelled there once preserved. Carlon knew faint echoes of those ancient legends, and he often spoke of Urd. But no mortal can cross the Karakala, the river that lies between our lands. The land of Urd is impassable. Its ruins are cursed."

"Why?" asked Hanna'el stubbornly.

Thomas shrugged. "You ask me questions I am not schooled to answer. All that I know of Urd I know second hand, for as I said, no man has gone there and returned. Perhaps the dead can speak of those vast ruins. Perhaps only the dead understand the legends of the Singing Tree. But your father believed in it . . . "

Hanna'el shivered. Thomas saw her reach inside her collar to touch a small leather pouch that hung from her neck. He had never seen that pouch before.

Her tone became more wistful. "Thomas, answer me truthfully . . . is it possible that the Tree sings this world into existence, as legends say?"

"Where did you hear such legends?" he asked her, surprised.

She stared straight ahead, as though listening inwardly.

"I do not know . . . I just remember . . . "

Thomas did not like her mood. To break the uncomfortable tension, he laughed. "There are many tales to explain these riddles. But what is truth? Your father believed that blossoms of the Singing Tree could summon the dead to life. He believed in this so completely that he gave up everything else—you and all of Arcatus—all for the sake of his quest. He wanted to revive Aeron's queen."

"But why?" she asked him. "Why did my father care so much for her? How can a single blossom restore to life a woman who's been dead for sixteen years? And if there were such miraculous blossoms, why didn't he seek them for my mother when she died?"

Thomas shook his head. He did not know how to answer her question. Indeed, he had often pondered this question as well.

He saw her hand unconsciously move to her neck, and she touched the string that hung there.

"What do you have?"

"Nothing," she said. "A talisman. A shepherd gave it to me at the tent, where I rested earlier."

Surprised, Thomas said suspiciously, "A shepherd? What was his name? What kind of gift did he give you? Let me see it."

With one quick movement of annoyance, Hanna'el slipped the string free from her neck. "Here, if you're so curious . . . you can have it. It's only a twig."

Thomas shook the green and leafless twig out the leather pouch. Puzzled, he shook his head.

"A *shepherd* gave you this?"

"Yes," she nodded. She described the lad—his nut brown hair that fell loose to his shoulders, his high, noble forehead, eager eyes and ready smile.   ·

But Thomas could recall no such youth among the shepherds. He fingered the twig and smelled it as Hanna'el had done. He, too, could not identify the plant from which it had sprung.

"May I keep it?"

Hanna'el hesitated.

"You don't need this kind of luck," Thomas chided her, shaking his head at the rustic talisman. "Luck has nothing to do with what lies ahead for us. And you can't wear something so homely at Aeron's court. A shepherd gave it to you? What was his name?"

"I can't remember . . . "

She reached to take back the twig, but Thomas swiftly put the pouch inside his garment.

"Trust yourself, Hanna'el," said Thomas. "What happens will depend on who you are and on the strategies we discussed. Your cause is just. Aeron will see that and agree. The memory of your father will protect you."

After pausing for a moment with hand outstretched, Hanna'el nodded, and they rode on.

HANNAH'S QUESTION

"Why did you stop reading? Is something wrong?"
The voice of Fritz the apprentice dispersed the swirling images in her mind. She felt cool wind and rain upon her face. The Chinese Pavilion vibrated as a storm-blast shook its flimsy walls. Fritz rubbed his arms and clapped his hands. He had only an old varsity sweater for warmth.

"Hannah?"

"She lost the twig," said Hannah, more to herself than to the apprentice. "She gave it to Thomas . . ."

As she spoke, her hand went to her neck. She felt for the string that had hung there and on that string, the green and leafless twig that Walter had given her. The twig was gone.

"You must lead her to it," said Fritz gently. "It's up to you."

She touched her neck where she remembered she had hung the shepherd's gift.

But no . . . that had happened to someone else . . . To a stranger . . . It was just a story . . .

Fritz saw her confusion. "Yes," he said, "the twig is gone. The scholar has it. His name is Thomas. He took it because you couldn't remember what to do. *You* gave it to him."

"But it wasn't *me*," said Hannah. "It was someone else. It happened in a story. I only read about it."

"Are you so sure? Is the Pavilion real? Am I real? Are you? Look at the pages of your book."

She took her journal out of its plastic bag and opened it to the page she had been reading when the young woman, *Hanna'el*, gave the twig away. From that page onward, the rest of the pages were blank.

"Your home is not out there," said Fritz gently, nodding at the storm. "Your home is forward, into the journal, toward remembrance. I tried to warn you. Walter warned you, too. We told you not to lose the twig. You did it once already, but Mrs. Endicott helped you. Now you've lost it again. It must be something you really needed to do. No one can stop you from being the person you are. But now you must accept it. You must go deeper into your remembrance. It will seem quite confusing, but only at first. *You must find the Tree.*"

"Why?" she demanded. "And even if I did, what good would it do? What would I find there?"

"That depends on you," said the apprentice. "If a Master of Memory journeyed to Elowyn, he would find the source of remembrance, for that is his bent. Each person drawn to Elowyn carries a question in her heart. The question determines who we *are*, who we *were*, and what we will *become*. The question determines everything. It is our story. Sometimes it appears we have many questions, many stories . . . in fact, so many that the way forward appears fractured like a mirror that has shattered into a million shimmering fragments. But as you learn the art of remembrance, as you learn to *hover*, you will understand that behind those many fragments you have only *one story*. It is this one story or question that draws you onward, no matter what. It is this one story that will lead you to the Tree. *You must feel it before you can begin.*"

She looked down at her book again as the rain beat hard upon the ruined Chinese Pavilion.

She felt so cold and tired, homesick and lost.

"I don't know my question," she sighed. "I don't know my story. I'm *sick* of reading stories. I want to go home."

"I understand."

"No you don't!" said Hannah angrily. "What can you understand? You don't know me! You're just some kind of freak!"

"Please," said Fritz, "don't be mad. I'm just trying to help. You can rest right here, until you're ready to try again."

"I don't want to stay *here*," said Hannah. "This pavilion leaks. It's falling apart. This whole miserable world is washing away. I want to rest where I feel safe and warm and comfortable. I want to go home."

Hannah put her journal on the floor.

"What are you doing now?" said Fritz, alarmed.

"I told you . . . I'm going *home*."

"No," said Fritz. "You can't."

"You said I could do anything I want."

"Yes, but . . ."

"*Whatever I want* means *anything*. Am I a prisoner, or can I go?"

"You can do whatever you want. I told you that. It is the truth."

"Good. Then I'm going home. You can follow me, or you can stay here. Suit yourself. I'm going home. And then I'm going back to the bookstore where all this started. I'm going to find Mrs. Endicott, and I'm going to make this stop."

Fritz shook his head. "On no, that's not a good idea. The bookstore is right at the center of the *Zone*."

"What *Zone*?" said Hannah. "And anyway, don't answer, I don't care. I'm leaving. See you. Bye."

And she was gone.

Fritz the apprentice sat on the floor of the ruined Chinese Pavilion and stared at the open doorway in disbelief.

He watched the rain falling hard.

The girl he knew as Hannah had faded into the *Zone of Night*.

Impossible, Fritz thought. *Why didn't Walter warn me?*

The girl had run off without the book and without the twig and had left him sitting here—quite, quite alone and abandoned. He had only one obligation in all eternity, and she was it.

I blew it, Fritz thought.

The thought made him sick.

She was the reason he'd been sent here, and he'd gone to so much trouble to make sure he'd come prepared to take care of her, no matter what—with tea and sandwiches and all sorts of other equipment—all things she should have liked and needed—everything that was useful for her to succeed.

She needed him . . . but even more importantly, as Walter had told him, *he needed her.*

Fritz shook his head.

The girl had made the decision he least expected her to make. She had made absolutely the stupidest and most dangerous decision he could imagine.

All right, he sighed, *so be it.*

Humans did what they chose to do. There was no reason or argument—no way to predict—and nothing to do but go after her, despite the *Zone of Night.* And if she made it to Sofia's bookstore . . . well, what then?

Perhaps she would meet the Privy Counselor.

The apprentice sighed.

He admired the Privy Counselor, but in recent times the two of them had not really seen things eye to eye.

Perhaps she will learn who I really am.

The apprentice put Hannah's journal carefully in his knapsack and prepared to enter the *Zone.*

One thing for sure that he'd forgotten to tell her, and now it was too late: the journey continued, whether she bothered with it or not. And everything she did changed the journey's outcome, whether she knew about it or not.

Not choosing was not an excuse.

Sooner or later (Fritz muttered) the girl would remember that *not choosing* was only another choice.

All right. So be it. So it goes . . .

Shouldering his canvas knapsack, the apprentice Fritz stepped out of the Chinese Pavilion and into the furious storm of the *Zone of Night.*

BOOK THREE

The Imprisoned Queen

KIT

On the bridge below the Caer, the herdsmen reassembled their cattle and reloaded the wagons. The young man whom Hanna'el had confronted stood alone in the midst of this activity. After his wife cursed him for throwing away the three gold coins, the rest of his relatives took their turns. His father, an aged drover still powerful in his shoulders, cuffed his impudent son across the cheek. "Idiot! Ass! Do you know what those coins were worth! A year's hard labor—the chance to live like men instead of swine! All you've ever given me is trouble. Here's your wife and brat, and how will you feed them? How will you feed the next child and the next? I curse the day I took you in."

The youth, nicknamed Kit, stood with his jaw rigid and his fists clenched. He stared at his father defiantly, while inside he felt poisoned with disgust. When he looked at his young wife and recalled how she had hurled herself upon him and fought for the precious coins, he jammed his nails so tightly into his palms that the skin broke and bled. His father's words burned like acid, and every glance felt like an arrow embedded in his heart.

The soldiers who had thrown the broken wagon into the stream stood by the edge of the bridge and traded jokes. Kit looked at them like a stray dog eyeing a pack. They saw his expression and laughed, daring him to respond. To them he was just a cattle-hand—a stupid, unlettered drudge. *Damn them all*, swore Kit.

Hadn't he nearly broken the neck of one of these smirking bastards? *Cowards!* They had attacked him all at once—he had fought them bare fisted—where was the honor in that? What a fight he could have given if the odds had been fair; he knew that blood would have flowed.

Once more, the face of the black-haired princess rose in his mind. *Hanna'el!* He could not forget those dark, flashing eyes. He remembered the way she had looked at him when he threw her coins into the stream. He felt thrilled by his defiance. "Yes," he muttered, "I am the better of any man on this bridge—only let me prove it." He saw his wife and cringed, remembering how he had been forced into this marriage. His father—he called him father, but in truth he was not his father (his real parents were dead)— this father had arranged his marriage to seal a trade for a cow, a pig, some water rights, and a field. *Why should my life become a commodity that a fat, greedy drover can buy and sell?* Birth and circumstance had trapped him as a lowly herdsman while she, the dark-haired princess who sat so haughty on her mare and showered golden coins like rain, *she* was highborn and suited to wed a noble lord. He hated her for all that he lacked. He detested her charity, and he loathed the expression of pity he had seen on her patronizing face. It was a hatred so unreasoning and self-certain, he could feel it grow dense inside him like a tumor.

The sounds of barking dogs and squealing children filled the air, rising above the constant uproar of the stream.

"Kit!" someone shouted.

He saw his wife climb into a wagon with her sisters. She stuck out her tongue, a gesture typical of her intelligence, Kit thought. He felt no love for this wife . . . nor for that mewling brat she had given birth to, six months after they were married. His wife seemed the very symbol of his fate: cattle boy, swineherd, drover, peasant, slave—these were the titles *he* had inherited, while others, others less worthy, *they* had been born as rich lords and chieftains of the realm. Where was the justice in that? In his heart, he knew himself cheated. Born for higher things, somehow the gods had played a cruel, practical joke at his expense. Silently, he swore for the thousandth time that he would defy those capricious gods. Someday, somehow, he would escape this life of servitude and become the lord and master he knew himself to be. Then let the others be astonished; let them regret how they had treated him when he was low. He would not forgive a one of them—*no, not one.* They all would repay him for their abuse; each scornful look, each insult, he would avenge.

And that dark-haired princess who mocked me on the bridge—she, most of all.

*   *   *

It was dark by the time the noisy caravan reached the second bridge that crossed the ravine to the Caer. Torches flared from the rails and on the blackened ramparts of the fortress. Kit hunched his shoulders against the cold damp wind that blew from the north. Even before he saw the clouds at sunset, he could smell the rain in the air. No moon or stars tonight. By the way the cattle fretted, he judged the storm would be severe.

Kit had been to the Caer before, for his people often drove animals there for slaughter, at Aeron's request. While the drovers dickered with the solders that manned the Caer's main gate, arguing about the bribe they'd need to pay to gain admittance after sundown, Kit walked close to a group of men who sat throwing dice by a small, smoky fire near the wall. The men already had downed several crocks of bitter ale, and their voices were loud, slurred, and abusive. Even at a distance, they reeked of garlic and mutton. Kit was about to walk away when he heard one of them mention the arrogant, black-haired princess from the steppes. "Carlon's daughter. She's come to plead for her lands." The soldiers laughed harshly, exchanged profanities, and said what they thought of her chances. All agreed that Aeron should take her lands, and one wagered that Carlon's daughter would never again leave the Caer, joking that he'd buy her from Aeron's dungeon, once Aeron had had his pleasure. "And what'd you do with her?" Before the man could answer, another soldier claimed that he'd heard plans to invade the steppes. "Aeron sent Carlon westward to his doom. Now that Carlon's dead, he'll take his land and horses." "Dead," said another, "that's not certain."

Hoots of derision greeted this comment.

Kit scowled and turned away. The drovers and the gate wardens had at last agreed on a price, and the wagons rattled forwards.

Past the gate, in the inner courtyard, other travelers had arrived. Kit saw several wagons bearing food and firewood, while off to one side of this hubbub stood a solitary traveler next to what Kit first took to be a small child. When the stranger moved forward into torchlight, Kit saw that this tall, lanky man with braided black hair and tattooed forearms was a Singer. The child that stood beside him was an imp.

Curious, Kit moved forward to have a better look. He had never met one of these roaming Singers, though he had heard tales of their mysterious talents—their ability to foretell or even mold the patterns of time. The man looked strange, but the freakish imp especially caught Kit's attention. No taller than Kit's waist, it resembled an idiot child. Around its neck, the Singer had placed a tight collar of silver bells, which chimed merrily each time the imp made one of its darting motions. Kit also observed what appeared to be an amulet made of lead. The imp had straw-colored hair as disheveled as a cornfield after a thunderstorm and restless eyes that were continually in motion. Kit tried to get closer to have a better view, but before he succeeded the Singer and imp passed through a narrow doorway into the Caer.

Mindful of the dung that littered the way, Kit followed the leading wagon. Once through the archway he paused as the drovers unhitched their teams and herded the cattle into pens. Force of habit made Kit step forward to help, but seeing his wife, he turned aside quickly. Silent, moody, and unobserved, he slipped away to the wall like a shadow.

There, an old man spitting sunflower seed hulls sat hunched by a broken axle-tree, and Kit, distracted by anger and thoughts of revenge, nearly tripped over the vagrant's outstretched legs.

"Damn you," he swore.

The old man laughed. He did not move aside. "Lost, young master?"

"Get out of my way."

The old man didn't budge. His eyes fixed on Kit coldly.

"I know you," said the old man.

"That's impossible."

The stranger spat more hulls. He muttered to himself softly.

"I know you. And I've been waiting. You arrived together—as you must."

"Bah," said Kit. "What are you talking about?"

He turned to rejoin his folk.

"Wait," said the old man. "If you wish to enter the Caer, go that way, through the kitchen. The door leads inside. I know what you're seeking."

Kit paused. Curious, he tried to see the old man's face, but the shadows had grown too thick and the old stranger wore a hood.

"That door leads inside—to the kitchen. Go quickly, before you're noticed." The old man's voice, Kit noted, bore the faintest edge of mockery.

"Who are you?"

"A friend," said the stranger. "One who knows you—better than you know yourself."

"Tell me your name."

The old man spat more hulls and lowered his head, and at that moment, Kit heard his wife summon him loudly.

"This is your chance," said the stranger. "Take it. You will not get another. The door over there is unwatched. It leads to the kitchen. Go quickly, before they see you. If you hesitate, you will never find her."

"Find who?"

"You know the one I mean."

A feeling suddenly possessed Kit that this was not a man at all, but only the semblance of a man, a talking shadow.

"Go quickly, young master," said the old man again. "This is your chance to change your destiny. Two worlds exist for you. Which do you choose?"

"What are you talking about? Why should I believe you?"

"Believe me or not. It is your free choice. Two worlds exist; and you must choose."

The old stranger spat more sunflower seed hulls. His face remained in shadow. He laughed softly.

Kit swore again. Back at the wagons, they called for him more loudly. "Kit!"

"Go," said the stranger.

Moving purposefully, Kit crossed the busy courtyard to the door. No one saw him as he slipped inside the Caer.

THE GREAT HALL

The smell of food greeted Kit at once. He had not had a full meal all day, only some stale bread and cheese at noontime, and his stomach growled.

Just as the old man had said, the corridor, narrow and cramped, led to a kitchen. Baskets stood loosely piled along one wall, creating a barrier. Kit sidled forward, noticing that one of the baskets held cabbages, another unshelled walnuts, a third some withered apples. He took a handful of nuts and cracked them against the stony wall, chewing slowly as he considered what to do.

The kitchen was a chaos of activity. The hiss and crackle of roasting flesh and the mouth-watering aroma of basting juices mingled with the clatter and slop of pots, and workers slipped and slid on a floor made treacherous with grease. The master cook, red faced and sweating, showed no pity for those under his command. His thick hands rained blows on the heads and shoulders of his assistants, who in turn hurled abuse at sooty children.

"You there! Stop gaping—get the stewards. Ask how soon they need the fowls."

At first Kit did not realize these words were hurled at him. He stood with a blank expression until a wet, greasy rag struck his cheek.

"Wake up! Get busy, you blockhead!"

Only the press of servants kept Kit from striding forward to fight the cook. He looked for something to hurl at the man who had insulted him but was distracted by a sharp tug on his sleeve.

A crone, her face daubed white with flour, grinned at him like a ghost. "Get moving," she told him sharply, hissing her words past toothless gums.

Kit shied away, but the crone kept a tight grip on his arm.

"That way," she urged him. She pointed one crooked finger, and before Kit could ask any questions, she released his sleeve and hobbled off.

Kit passed through the kitchen and at once saw two of Aeron's guards. He stiffened, but the men pushed by and did not even look at him. Other servants hurried past, moving with laden trays or sloshing pitchers. No one paid him any mind, as indifferent as though he were a shadow. Continuing, he reached the end of the corridor and found that he had come to the central hall.

He had heard many descriptions of the Caer's great hall and had visualized it many times in his imagination. Even so, the first sight of it made him gasp. Domed and circular, the great hall looked like a vast cavern. Rows of torches burned along the curved walls, and fires blazed in a dozen hearths. Everywhere, the stones had been carved in the weird and intricate patterns of the Guir, shapes that swirled in the weaving shadows cast by firelight. Long rows of columns extended on either side, giving the illusion of a forest.

As he wondered what to do or why he had come here, Kit noticed a small, wooden door about twenty yards distant. Acting with the same impulsiveness that had brought him this far, Kit crossed the open space to the door, grasped the handle, and stepped over the threshold.

He found himself in a passageway much narrower than the one he'd left. As he wondered whether to follow it, a guard appeared behind him and shook his shoulder. "You there, boy! Take this to the guests." The man thrust a heavy basket into his hand. "Hurry up. That way!" He pointed and gave Kit a shove.

He thinks I'm a servant.

"Get going. Hurry!"

Kit silently obeyed. As a precaution, he took a cloth hat from his pocket and put it on, pulling the brim low to his eyes. He walked in the direction that the guard had shoved him, carrying the basket at his side. He decided to continue until he thought no one could see him and then find a quiet corner to eat the food himself. But the corridor offered no place to rest or hide.

As he wondered which way to go, another guard appeared and looked at him suspiciously. At once Kit asked where he might find the guests, and the guard, an older man with a large reddish nose swollen from too much beer, checked Kit's basket before he answered. He stole a biscuit and hunk of cheese and then grunted with his mouth full and pointed to a narrow set of stairs.

These, too, led to a stone corridor. Kit was just about to turn and go back when two soldiers hailed him.

"You there, hurry up. Take the food inside. Set it on the table near the fire."

"Wait," said the second soldier.

He examined the basket carefully, as though searching for a weapon. He found a ripe apple to eat instead.

"It's safe. Let him pass."

Kit nodded his agreement to obey their orders, but as the door opened to admit him to the chamber, he saw he had made a dangerous mistake.

Before him sat the arrogant, dark-haired princess, Carlon's daughter, whom he had confronted on the bridge. She waited in the room with one of her attendants.

AERON'S GIFT

Hanna'el did not notice Kit. If she saw anything when the door to her room opened, it was only a nervous servant with a basket of fruit who hesitated at the entrance. Her mind was on Aeron and what must happen tonight, when she confronted the lord of the Caer.

Brother Thomas sat beside her and spoke in a subdued tone of voice. His thin scholar's face had grown even more haggard since arrival. He, too, paid no attention to the servant bearing food.

"Lord Aeron's health is as bad as I feared," Thomas whispered. "I've done my best to gather information. Many of the older servants remember your father fondly. They were glad to assist me."

Hanna'el cut him short. "I knew this already. Thomas, what else can you tell me? Will Aeron acknowledge my claim to Arcatus?"

"There are stories—you have heard some yourself—that Aeron never recovered from the death of his wife, the Queen At'theira. Many say that grief has overmastered him. Aeron has for his advisor a physician named Azael. No one knows why Aeron has come to trust this physician so completely. I could learn nothing of Azael's background, only that he arrived here at the time of Queen At'theira's death."

"But that was years ago," said Hanna'el impatiently. "What good does this do me?"

Thomas shook his head. "I do not know. I cannot explain. I wish we knew more about the physician."

Hanna'el rose and poured herself a drink from a silver carafe. She pointed to an ebony box on the table.

"Look here," she said to Thomas, "Aeron sent this. It arrived just before you came. What do you think of it? Lord Aeron wants me to wear it to the feast."

Thomas opened the box and lifted out its contents: a gold necklace of exquisite craftsmanship that held as its pendant jewel a brilliant tourmaline gemstone.

"The stone comes from the mines of At'hanor," said Hanna'el. "The design is Urdish. The jewel was once presented as a gift by my father, Carlon, to At'theira, Aeron's queen."

"How do you know this?"

"Aeron's messenger told me, when he brought the gift."

Thomas marveled at the costly necklace. "Your father gave this to Aeron's queen? *But why?*"

"I hoped *you* would know."

She paused, catching sight of the servant who had entered the room nervously, pushed forward by a soldier. The young man carried a basket of bread, cheese, and fruit. He wore a hat pulled low to his eyes.

The soldier gave him another shove. "Put the basket on the table and freshen the fire," Hanna'el heard the man growl.

For a moment, her eyes lingered on the servant who held the basket, for she felt there was something familiar in his stance. She glanced at his face, but the clumsy hat fell low across his brow, obscuring his features, and the room was poorly lit.

"We haven't much time," said Thomas impatiently, seizing her attention. "You must decide what you will say and do."

But in fact, she did not know.

After laying down his basket, the young servant hurried to the hearth and began to rake the coals. He kept his back toward Hanna'el.

Brother Thomas again drew her attention to Aeron's gift. He lifted the beautiful necklace and held it to her throat.

"I think you should wear it. Perhaps Aeron intends this as a sign of friendship—a promise that all will go well. If you don't wear it, he may be insulted. We cannot risk his anger or disfavor."

Reluctantly, Hanna'el allowed Brother Thomas to hang the necklace about her neck. She adjusted the tourmaline so that it rested near her heart.

"It suits you," said Brother Thomas.

But Hanna'el felt otherwise.

The necklace belonged to a dead woman, Aeron's queen. The jewelry felt cold and heavy at her throat, like an enemy's fingers. "I don't like it," she said to the scholar uneasily. "I won't wear it. Take it off."

"No," said Thomas. "You must wear it. Aeron means to test you." Before she could protest, the soldier who guarded her room announced that it was time to escort her to the great hall.

"Be wary tonight," Thomas urged her. "Remember what I told you."

"I will do my best." Hanna'el came close and kissed the scholar's cheek. "I'm scared, Thomas . . . " she whispered.

"You'll do fine," he said, patting her hand. "You look quite lovely. You must trust yourself."

But there was something else she needed to say.

"Where is the pouch that I gave you earlier? The pouch that the shepherd told me I should keep."

Thomas looked surprised, and it took him a moment to understand what she meant. He searched his robe and found the leather pouch stuffed in a pocket. Taking it out, he untied it and showed her the small, leafless twig that it held.

"Is this what you mean? Why do you ask? It has no significance."

Hanna'el paused for a moment, trying to recall what the shepherd had said. He had said so much, but she felt there hadn't been time for so many words. The memory confused her. "He called it a charm. I'm not sure why . . . He mentioned the name *Walter* . . . "

Thomas frowned. "I do not know that name." He wound the golden cord about his finger and held the simple twig to Hanna'el's neck. The gift indeed looked insignificant, particularly next to the finely wrought necklace, Lord Aeron's gift.

"Go," Thomas urged her, pressing her hand. "Aeron will respect you. He must. Remind him of his friendship to your father. Do not be afraid. Speak cautiously, but do not fear to argue your cause. Much depends on the outcome—for you and our people. Surely, the gift of this necklace is a sign that all will go well."

Hanna'el smiled and kissed Thomas on the cheek. "Wait for me," she told him. And with that she followed the guard who had come to summon her.

Thomas waited until she had gone, then looked at the servant, still busy at the fire. Smiling, he replaced the shepherd's twig in its leather pouch and placed the pouch on the table where Hanna'el would find it when she returned. "Lay in another log," he ordered the servant. The night felt cold, and by midnight they expected heavy rain.

Drawing his cloak about him, Thomas left the room, determined to learn more about the Caer and Aeron's physician, Azael.

As soon as Thomas left, Kit stood and wiped his hands. He grinned.

Here was good luck. She did not even recognize me!

Kit pulled off the hat that had concealed his features and looked about the empty room, relishing the feeling of power this moment gave him.

In a fit of pride and anger, he had thrown the three coins into the stream. The gesture had been spiteful—and he still savored that petty moment of revenge. Even so, he wasn't stupid. Unless he brought some offering to his father and his wife, he knew that his next meals would be scarce.

Damn her, thought Kit.

Alone in her chamber, he looked for something he could steal, something of equal value to the coins he had tossed away. Something that would allow him to buy back his clan's good will.

He saw the shepherd's gift, the leather pouch that Thomas had left on the table, and he picked it up. The pouch was light, but just the size of a small coin purse. Thomas had tied the pouch securely, and the string would not yield quickly to Kit's impatient fingers. It did not feel very valuable. He threw it down and searched for something else to steal, but Hanna'el traveled lightly. She had few possessions.

"Damn her."

Seizing the leather pouch again, he gnawed loose the string that bound it and emptied out the contents into his hand: a string tied to a silly, useless stick.

Scowling, Kit hung the worthless string about his neck and stuffed the slender twig inside his shirt. He did not know why he bothered to keep it.

There was nothing else at hand that he could take.

Just then, he heard footsteps in the outer hallway. The guards had returned. Kit moved to the door.

Before he left the room, he tossed the empty leather pouch into the fireplace, pleased with at least this small gesture of revenge.

ET'ELRED

Almost at once, after she left Brother Thomas, Hanna'el understood how wrong she had been to ignore her misgivings about Aeron's gift. As she approached the great hall, the necklace that Aeron had sent her pressed like cold steel against her skin. The jewel felt fantastically heavy.

Pluck it off! a voice inside her urged.

But her hands refused. Each step made her feel more helpless.

Dully, she allowed the guards to guide her. As she entered the Caer's great hall, only a few of the assembled guests noticed her. Laughter and loud voices washed over her in waves.

"Good evening, Hanna'el . . . "

An older man—gray-haired, with narrow intelligent features and a sharp, aquiline nose—stepped near and observed her closely. She forced herself to speak, but at once the strange sensation that she had felt earlier in the shepherd's tent overcame her with a sudden, unexpected and fresh intensity. She felt as though she were two persons at once—two souls in a single body.

This is not real. It isn't you. It is remembrance . . .

"Are you not well?" the old man asked her, one gray brow slightly cocked.

There was something queerly familiar about this old man, though Hanna'el could not place him. She struggled to orient herself and to suppress the panic that the weight of Aeron's necklace somehow made worse. She breathed in shortened gasps as her face beaded with cold sweat.

"Are you ill?" the old man asked.

Remove the necklace!

But she could not. Instead, she stood there helplessly and stared at the old man who smiled at her.

"I am Et'elred," he said, "Aeron's advisor. Perhaps you remember me. I knew your father—and I knew you as a child." He examined her like a jeweler observing a precious gem. "I hope that your long journey from Arcatus has not exhausted you."

A scene rose before her inner eye. She saw a child at play in Arcatus—her father was still at home. She remembered a man—younger than this one . . . a young man with features similar to the old man who spoke to her now—a man who had come to stay with them for a season. He had liked to fish. He had taught her the lore of fishing. Together they had fished on the banks of her father's streams. She remembered the smoky taste of the trout that he had caught in the fast-running waters. She remembered the gleaming scales of the largest trout that swam away. He had taught her a rhyme to lure strong trout to his cunning hook—a rhyme that she still knew by heart. Was this the same man?

"*Uncle?*" she repeated. Her voice caught in her throat. "*Uncle?*" She used the word politely, though her tone said more than she wished to reveal.

Et'elred glanced down as the people to either side of them spoke loudly, indifferent to their exchange. The meal had yet to be served. Aeron's seat at the head of the great table stood empty. She heard dogs growling for scraps, women laughing, men cursing and boasting and swapping toasts.

Again, a voice inside her seemed to say: *This is not real. It isn't you. It is remembrance . . .*

The necklace, Lord Aeron's gift, had weakened her so terribly. The necklace hung like a noose about her neck and called forth from deep inside her all the dark emotions of her childhood; it enlivened feelings she had taught herself to forget. She felt like a powerless child, as powerless as when she found herself abandoned years ago, caught in a torrent of grief and confused recollection.

"Help me," she said to the old man. Her voice was not her own.

Et'elred looked at her strangely. For a moment, a harsh, unfeeling mask obscured the face of the fisherman she recalled.

The sight of this indifference chilled her even more than the hateful necklace at her throat.

Et'elred looked away, prepared to ignore her, but Hanna'el knew she must speak. She had only this chance. Her words came with great effort, for the necklace froze her speech. "Uncle, you knew my father. He was your friend. If you loved him—if you love me—please, I beg you, help me . . . "

Et'elred hesitated. "I know this necklace," he said, as though to himself, his voice quite low. "Your father gave it as a wedding gift to Aeron's queen. At'theira wore it the night she married Aeron."

The words floated between them like snow blown over a grave. She remembered cold nights on the steppes of Arcatus, crying into her pillow as a child. Those memories reached toward her like black fingers from the rocks of this black fortress. Her words stopped frozen in her heart.

"Uncle, take it off me, please . . . " Hanna'el gasped.

She saw how the sudden directness of her request confused him. How calm and utterly rational he had always been—a patient angler. Clearly, he would ignore her.

"*Do this for the sake of the Tree*," she heard herself whisper.

It was all that she could force herself to say.

She did not know why she spoke in this way. She did not know what she meant. The words came from her as though someone else had spoken. Again, she felt that another person lived inside her and that this stranger had seized her will.

"*For the sake of the Tree, I beg you . . . Uncle, please . . . *"

Et'elred startled as though slapped. He glanced fearfully at the empty seat where Aeron would sit, as though her words made him feel ashamed. Hanna'el felt the last of her self-possession leech away. The necklace was even more hateful than she had imagined. Aeron's gift was choking her. She felt numbed by the jewel at her throat, as cold as if this room were a frozen grotto. Her breathing slowed, and her fingers stiffened. Her chest felt crushed.

Et'elred's face had lost all its distant composure, and he looked at her like a man who contemplates a ghost. Then, with a sudden motion that made her cry out with startled pain, he gripped the necklace and tore it free with a forceful tug. The clasp bit the back of her neck, leaving a wound that bled in a thin trickle. Where the jewel had lain, the skin of her throat had turned a shade of blue, as though the flesh had been bruised or deadened or frozen.

"May this deed of treason clear me of the debt I owe your father," Et'elred said in a hoarse, quavering voice. He held the necklace before him as though it were a serpent, then thrust it away. "I am condemned for what I have done."

Hanna'el gasped like a person nearly drowned. "Thank you," she whispered, touching her throat.

"Beware the physician Azael," Et'elred whispered.

Before Hanna'el could question him, Lord Aeron entered the hall.

THE SINGER'S HARP

The Lord of the Caer looked grayer than she had remembered. Though Aeron and her father had shared their childhood, spending those years together like two brothers, she knew Aeron mostly from second-hand reports. She had met him scarcely half a dozen times. She recalled him as a man quick to anger and thoughtless in his speech, but she also recalled the times he had laughed. Lord Aeron had a simple, earthy humor that preferred practical jokes. Once when she was quite young, Aeron had come to join her father for a hunt. Early on the morning of their departure, Hanna'el had awakened to watch them ride forth. As they mounted their horses, the girth on one of the saddles gave way, sending one of Aeron's men sprawling in the courtyard. The man had landed awkwardly and broken his leg—ever after walking with a limp—and Aeron, observing this misfortune, had nearly fallen from his stallion with laughter. Later, her father offhandedly told her that Aeron had loosened the saddle girth himself. He had said that this was a trick Aeron and he had often secretly played when they were boys, and that Aeron had played this prank out of fondness for their childhood. And though this incident had happened years ago, she still remembered that her father had smiled as he told her this story, enjoying the joke.

Hanna'el watched as Aeron took his seat at the center of the foremost table. She watched as he raised his silver goblet in a ceremonial toast to begin the meal. She, too, raised her cup, eager not to offend the local customs.

To her surprise, Aeron turned his glance directly upon her. His dark eyes caught her unprepared, and she found herself unable to look away. They were thirty feet distant, the length of two great tables, and yet, in that moment before Aeron spoke, she feared that he might reach out and touch her. Again, she felt the numbing sting of the necklace that had bruised her flesh, and involuntarily she gasped. Above, in the shadowed dome that encompassed the hall, she saw for the briefest moment a shadowy movement, as though a dark bird flitted amid the rafters.

Lord Aeron smiled. "My friends—a toast. To the ancestors, the Caar'oq Hyme. May we dwell in their approval."

Throughout the length of the hall, conversation ceased. Hanna'el saw rows of goblets rise high, and voices echoed Aeron's blessing.

"To the ancient kings of the Caar'oq Hyme—may their spirits prosper!"

"To the spirits who guard the stones—to the dead who defend us."

"Aye, aye," cried voices from every side, slurred and boisterous. Many had already eaten and drunk too much.

"To the kingdoms beyond the realms of men—to Urd, Karakaat, and At'hanor—to the Aeneaid of the western ocean."

"All honor!" shouted Aeron, his voice overmastering them. "And to the one sacred Tree that grows for all—and to him who seeks it!"

The cup that Hanna'el had lifted hung in midair. Despite the noise on every side, she heard the gray advisor Et'elred draw a breath. She felt illumined by a burst of sunlight. All faces in the hall turned toward her. Lord Aeron grinned.

"*To Carlon*," she repeated, surprised at how loud her words sounded. Could anyone see that she cringed? Could Aeron see the bruise upon her neck?

But before her thoughts could be gathered or sorted to speech, a brightly clad stranger entered the hall through its eastern door. He held in his hands a wooden harp. Behind him, close upon his footsteps like a spaniel, cavorting and leaping from side to side in merriment came an imp.

The imp, clad only in a deerskin loincloth, stood no higher than a three-year-old child. Its hair, as Hanna'el had often heard described, shone white like the full moon in autumn, and its skin, unblemished and smooth, had the faintest greenish tinge.

Puckish in its merriment, the imp somersaulted twice and feigned affection for the ladies. Each time it bounded for a table, the finely dressed women screamed in mock terror and surprise. The men laughed loudly, as though a hare had gotten loose, and Hanna'el realized that most of them had seen such a creature before. With a whistle and a touch of the harp, the Singer recalled the mischievous imp to his side.

Those nearest to the portal raised a shout, and the Singer, with a courteous bow, struck another chord.

"Hail, Lord Aeron! All blessing to you and to your court."

Hanna'el saw how a shadow of surprise and anger passed briefly over Aeron's face and how his eyes, so firm a second earlier, momentarily showed confusion and hesitation. She saw the startled soldiers who guarded the hall's east entrance face one another like men awakened from a daze, as though the Singer had passed by them while they slept. She saw as well how Aeron briefly glanced to the dome of the hall. And there, amid the shadows, she saw once more the flitting, darkened outline of a bird.

"I claim the hospitality of the Caer," the Singer declared loudly. "I claim the ancient welcome of the hall."

Suddenly, Hanna'el saw a raven swoop down from the vaulted dome. The bird plummeted so quickly that she spilled a drop of crimson wine upon her dress in surprise. The raven shrieked, dropping like a stone at the Singer's head. Its sharp claws grazed his brow, leaving a blood streak.

But the Singer only grinned. As the shrill raven mounted high toward the rafters, the Singer raised his harp in a gesture of mock respect. "And greetings to you, Master Raven—and to all that creeps or crawls amid these stones."

Hanna'el saw the bird wheel and dive again. The Singer ducked, but just as he moved, the imp by his side changed its shape. Somersaulting spryly, the imp transformed itself into a black tomcat as the angry bird drew nearest to the ground. The cat clawed at the raven and gave it a blow to the wing. Three feathers fluttered loose, and the bird, shrieking angrily, flew away through an open casement.

"Well parried!" someone laughed. Hanna'el saw that Et'elred had dropped his goblet. The blood red wine stained the floor.

The Singer received applause with a gracious bow and lifted up the three fallen black feathers. But his imp did not change again. Still in the shape of a cat, it darted quickly away through the legs of a startled warrior.

"Forgive my imp's manners," said the Singer, speaking now to Aeron, who stood in angry silence. Aeron had turned to view the raven's flight. His face was ashen.

The Singer, striding closer, called out to her. "Hanna'el of Arcatus, Lord Carlon's daughter!" He spoke her name formally, and as he did, she could see Lord Aeron tense.

Now the Singer stood close, his harp cradled to his chest. To her surprise, she could not determine his age. From a distance, the Singer had looked young. But now that he came near, she saw that she was wrong; he was much older. He had bound his hair into two long braids decorated with shells, ribbons, and bones in the manner of his craft. She seldom noticed the color of a person's eyes, but the Singer's eyes were dark obsidian, like his hair. Though he spoke in an even tone of voice, his every word resonated. Neither tall nor powerful, his body radiated a calm and warming strength, and she noticed that no one dared to check his words or movements. She had heard of such Singers but had never seen one; men of this sort seldom visited the steppes. Nor had she ever witnessed a fabled imp.

Unconsciously, her hand went to her throat, feeling for the necklace that no longer hung there.

"I greet you, Hanna'el," said the Singer. "What news from your father, Carlon? Is he well?"

At first she could not speak. When her mouth began to utter sounds, she heard herself say only the most conventional, mannered lies. "He is well," she answered.

"Aye," said Lord Aeron, seizing this moment of hesitation to take command. "And what of Carlon's quest? What news of *that*?"

Suddenly, Hanna'el knew that her moment of destiny had come.

Aeron turned to her, shouting down the Singer's greeting and turning the eyes of the court back to the power of his throne. He had said what everyone thought: *What news of Carlon? Is he alive? And what shall we make of you, Lord Carlon's daughter?*

Hanna'el stiffened, and her breath came quick. Beads of cold perspiration collected on her forehead. She felt the floor sway beneath her, but she forced herself to speak in even tones.

"There is no news . . . "

"No news?" said Aeron archly, cutting her short. His tone was one of mock sympathy and disbelief. "Haven't sixteen years passed since his departure? And still no news?"

Hanna'el nodded. *Yes*, she responded. *Sixteen years.* She did not know how to answer any better, but the conversation shaped itself.

"And tell me," said Aeron stiffly, "what need has brought you to the Caer, *Hanna'el of Arcatus?*"

Swallowing, she spoke the words that she and Thomas had rehearsed, words that Aeron surely expected, for they said only what he well knew: that her lands had been held in trust till she was of an age to receive them. She said that she had grown old enough to rule them herself.

To her surprise, Aeron did not answer her at once. She had expected anger. She had expected anything but what happened next.

Aeron grew pensive, as though she had reminded him of a duty long ignored. She looked to the Singer, hoping that he might say something on her behalf. But the Singer remained silent, the slightest smile upon his lips. How she wished that Thomas had accompanied her! She looked to her left and saw Et'elred watching her closely.

Lord Aeron cleared his throat. "Your request has shamed me. I have been remiss in my duty and friendship toward your father. I have not been sufficiently mindful of your needs." He smiled as he said this, and Hanna'el suddenly recalled the story her father had told: how Aeron delighted in cruelties, how he relished a practical joke. She shivered as though struck by a wintry draft. "Very well," said Aeron, drawing himself tall. He addressed the entire court. "Know all who are present and absent: full right to the lands of Carlon, Lord of Arcatus, passes by decree to his only daughter. I, Lord Aeron, declare it."

Hanna'el staggered. Beside her, Et'elred reached out and touched her arm. His touch was firm, and the pressure reassured her. All around, she heard the swell of voices. This was all that she had hoped for. She had won!

But Aeron spoke again. "I declare it upon one condition," she heard him say. "The condition is this: that she marry and forthwith name a husband."

Now the hall exploded into a fury of conversations. Hanna'el heard him, but the words had made no sense. *Marry?* Whom could she marry? What did he mean?

"What is your response?" said Aeron harshly.

She could not answer. She did not know what to say. Indeed, she felt as though she had awakened inside a dream. Lord Aeron's words were meaningless.

Marry? Marry what?

Too late, she saw Aeron's trap.

"Very well," he said to the entire hall, smiling at her confusion. "You have heard Carlon's daughter decline by her silence the right to choose a mate. In the absence of her father, and by right as the custodian of her lands, I, Aeron, shall resolve the matter for her. It is a duty I fulfill on her father's behalf.

"The lands of Carlon shall pass to his only daughter and through her, by right of marriage, shall become the lawful property of her husband. As she declines to choose, I, her appointed guardian, claim her as my queen!"

Like waters released from a dam, waves of loud voices overwhelmed her. Hanna'el clutched the table, her face gone white.

Suddenly the Singer struck his harp. With surprising harshness, the music swelled through the hall. "Wait," he cried. "You must listen!"

Aeron turned, his face livid. Once more, the Singer's hands were at his strings, and the harp cried out in hectic grief.

A blinding lance of light struck the Singer, piercing the hall like rays of the midday sun. Those closest to the Singer cringed and shied away, dazzled by the spectacle. Hanna'el, too, shielded her face, unable to look directly at such radiance.

"Hear," cried the Singer. A wild cascade of notes resounded loudly, silenced suddenly by the touch of the Singer's palm. All shuddered as from that silence a voice came forth.

Carlon, Hanna'el's father, spoke from the Singer's harp.

Lord Aeron, check your wrath. Do not take vengeance on my daughter. I, Carlon, speak to you. I live and keep my quest for the sacred Tree

The brief words hung like incense in the stunned silence of the hall. Men and women fell to their knees. Aeron shook but remained unbowed.

"Marry her I shall," he swore again loudly. "A dead man shall not stop me."

"*But I shall!*" came a cry. "Challenge me, Lord Aeron, before you claim Hanna'el for your bride!"

All present turned toward the one who had spoken.

Bryhs, the aged chieftain from Arcatus, had forced his way into the hall. He stood with his hand on his sword.

The court raised a sudden clamor of outrage: no one dared enter this chamber armed to challenge its lord. They looked to Aeron, expecting wrath.

But Aeron stood silent.

"The challenge stands!" cried the Singer. "Lord Aeron, you must meet it!"

Hanna'el stood frozen; her father's ghostly words echoed inside her. All around she felt the press of bodies, but her spirit felt plunged into a darkened void. She could not move. Dumbly, she allowed herself to be guided by Et'elred's steady hand. Bryhs strode forward to support her by the waist.

And in the confusion of this moment, no one noticed that the Singer had withdrawn.

THE PATH TO REMEMBRANCE

Bryhs carried Hanna'el to her chamber and placed her on the bed that Thomas had prepared. Hanna'el's room had grown hot from the blazing fire in the hearth. The young servant who had been there earlier had stoked it too high. Thomas forced open a window. Outside, hard rain had begun. A wild wind blew from the north, splattering drops of water onto the wooden sill of the casement. No guards stood watch at Hanna'el's door; the recent events had thrown the Caer into confusion.

Hanna'el struggled to sit up. "Let me go ... my father ... " But Bryhs placed his hand on her shoulder and forced her to rest.

Thomas prepared a concoction to calm her nerves. He stirred the potent herbs in a bowl of sweet red wine and held the fragrant mixture to her lips.

All had happened so rapidly that her mind had not yet sorted out the events. She remembered only that her father had spoken from the Singer's harp—or seemed to have spoken. So many years had passed since Carlon's departure that she could not say for sure that it was his voice.

Perhaps this was the Singer's trick—she had heard of men who could disguise and throw their voices, making it appear as though inanimate objects could speak. Still, the Singer had not seemed that sort of trickster, and she desperately wanted to believe that the voice had belonged to her father.

"Drink," said Thomas. "Drink this and rest." His tone was so persuasive and kind. He had always been close at times of crisis, ever since she was a child. A longing for those simpler times came over her, and she accepted the bowl, drinking the wine in one long gulp.

The potent draught quickly took effect. Hanna'el fell back upon the pillows. Her eyelids fluttered. "Leave the window open. The room is so hot. Thomas, I must have air . . . "

Thomas turned to Bryhs and spoke in a whisper. "It is best if she sleeps. Have our men watch the door. If Aeron's guards return, they must be challenged."

Bryhs nodded, glad that the occasion for action had come at last.

Thomas covered Hanna'el with a coverlet. A cool wind rustled the blue curtains of the casement, and the sound of constant rain fell soothingly on her ears. She wanted to sleep, as Thomas suggested, and yet, there was still so much she needed to know. Had her father really spoken? How did the Singer know her? And why had Aeron chosen her for his bride?

This last question troubled her most deeply.

"I'll leave you now," said Thomas. "Try to sleep."

"I can't," she mumbled. Her words were slurred. "Please, Thomas, stay with me . . . "

Thomas smiled, trusting in the draught. He looked at Bryhs.

"I gave her more than she needs," said Thomas softly. "Enough so that she'll sleep very soundly."

Bryhs frowned. "Are you sure that's wise? We must leave this place. She'll need a clear head."

Thomas shooed him back.

"I know what's best. Aeron wouldn't dare to harm her now— not after what happened. She will be safe. It is best that she sleeps. Go and see to the others."

As Bryhs went out, Thomas surveyed the room once more, making certain that all had been readied for the night. The fire had burned lower since they entered, and his gaze rested on the blackened, half-charred remains of a leather pouch lying before the hearth. He walked forward and fetched it.

"Thomas . . . " said Hanna'el. "What is it? What have you found?"

"Nothing," he said to her. "Don't trouble yourself. Go to sleep." He held the charred pouch where Hanna'el could not see it.

"You have something. Show me," she insisted.

Thomas frowned. "It's nothing. Just a trinket. See, it is the pouch that that held the shepherd's tiny gift."

Hanna'el became alarmed. She did not know why. "Is it burned? Let me see it."

"You mustn't trouble yourself. You need to sleep."

The draught made her words slurred and heavy, but she fought to stay awake.

"Let me see it," she said again.

"Well here, if you insist. See for yourself," he answered testily. "It's a useless thing. You see; it's barely harmed. I don't know how it fell into the fire. I left it on the desk when I left the room."

"Give it to me," said Hanna'el. Her fingers fumbled with charred leather. "Open it. Is the twig inside? Did it burn?"

Thomas scowled and shook his head. Carefully, he pried the pouch open, but the thin, greenish twig had vanished. "Gone," he answered ruefully. "Are you sure it was there?"

Hanna'el fumbled with the empty pouch. "I'm sure it was. Walter gave it to me . . . "

"Walter?" said Thomas. "You told me you received this from a shepherd."

Hanna'el stared at him, momentarily unable to speak. "Yes . . . of course. That's what I meant."

Thomas took advantage of her confusion to remove the pouch from her hand. Hanna'el sank back.

Thomas said, "You really must sleep. Don't fret any longer. This was only a rustic trinket, and now it's gone. Perhaps Aeron's guards are responsible. From now on I shall not leave your room unwatched."

"Thomas . . . sit with me . . . I feel so very tired and confused . . . There are so many questions . . . Thomas, I'm scared."

"You must sleep now," he urged her.

"I wish I were still in Arcatus. I wish I was home."

Her dark hair spread across the white linen covering of her pillow, and she pressed her eyes with her hand.

"Sleep," said Thomas gently.

He laid the half burned pouch upon the table and walked softly out of the room. The door closed gently, and the latch fell in place with a heavy snap.

Alone, Hanna'el fought against the tide of slumber. She could hear the patter of rain and the crackle of the fire. Her mind echoed with the sounds of the feast, with the wild, hectic chords of the Singer's harp, with Aeron's mocking words, and with the hollow-sounding voice that had claimed to be her father.

She knew that she had never doubted her father lived. And yet, if he were living and had really spoken from the harp, why had he not told her anything else? Why had he not spoken to reassure her? Why had he sent her no message all these years?

If he loved me, why did he leave me all alone?

A flood of guilt and sadness overcame her. Hanna'el bit her lips to stifle a sob. She seldom gave in to her emotions; she had never wanted anyone to accuse her of self-pity or to feel anyone's sorrow for her plight. She had always tried to be strong and self-sufficient, as she imagined her father must have been, but now all her discipline fled. She felt exhausted, lonely, and depressed— surrounded by enemies and far from home, with no way to return to the world she had left far behind her.

She did not have the strength to continue. Her decision to visit the Caer had been a terrible mistake. She recalled the reasons that had prompted this journey, but when she examined those reasons one by one, they had no weight. It all felt like a insubstantial dream or fairy tale . . . something that Sylvia, her old childhood nurse, might have told her long ago to while away the boredom of a long winter's night . . . the sort of tale that her sober guardian Brother Thomas would have scoffed at.

What shall I do?

She felt lost in the shifting currents of past and future, no longer able to tell what was memory, imagination, or thought.

"*Walter,*" she whispered, "*help me . . .* " She did not even notice she had spoken this name.

The way forward depends upon music . . . You must learn to sleep and breathe.

The feelings she had had earlier in the shepherd's hut came back with startling force. She felt as though her identity had fractured, and the face of the young shepherd, who had given her the twig, appeared with startling clarity, as though he were with her in this room.

QUEEN AT'THEIRA

Something touched the covers of her bed. Hanna'el gasped, fully awakened by a sudden pressure on her legs.

She sat up swiftly and stared into the green eyes of a purring cat.

She recognized the creature at once. It was the imp who had accompanied the Singer. Still in the shape of a black tomcat, the imp had entered her room through the open casement. She saw that its fur was damp and its paws wet and muddy and that a tiny leaden amulet hung from a collar on its neck. It eyed her calmly, unthreateningly, and though she had seen it change its shape, she could not resist stroking its silky, rain-damp fur. The cat purred loudly and rubbed against her hand, biting her finger playfully. She sat up and saw that its wet paws had left the faintest track across the floor. The track meandered from the window to her bed.

"What do you want? Who are you?"

The cat looked at her and said nothing. An imp, she knew from legends, could not talk. It knew no human language. She wished she had listened more closely when the old women of Arcatus had told their tales, but she had never expected to meet such a creature. Why had it come here?

Almost as soon as she had this thought, the cat jumped off the bed and scampered to the door. It clawed the wood, meowing to get out. She wondered why it did not change its shape and open the door itself, but perhaps the imp had exhausted its powers.

"I'll let you out," she said, surprised that Thomas' concoction no longer fogged her mind.

Because of the open window, the room had grown much cooler, and she took a gray shawl from the chair next to her bed. Outside her window, the rain fell very loudly; the storm had increased.

Perhaps hers was the first open window the imp had seen. Maybe it wanted to find its master, the mysterious Singer.

She opened the door, and the cat slid out. To her surprise, the corridor in front of her room was empty.

Alarmed, she wrapped the shawl more tightly about her shoulders, slipped on a pair of sandals, and ventured out. The cat stood waiting in the hall, purring loudly enough for her to hear it at a distance. Its green eyes watched her intensely, as though beckoning.

She chose a direction and walked, and the cat remained in front of her, strutting with its tail proudly erect. For a moment she had the feeling that the cat wanted to lead her somewhere, and to test that feeling she deliberately turned down a smaller corridor to her left. The cat, however, followed her and serenely loped ahead. It seemed not at all troubled by her choice of this new direction, and still it walked before her in its proud and haughty way.

Candles lit this corridor at irregular intervals. The hallway felt quiet and still—unusually still, as though the Caer were deserted, but Hanna'el did not pause to wonder why this was so.

At the end of the corridor, a set of stairs appeared, and when she neared them the cat leaped up several, paused, and licked its paws.

Puzzled, she began to climb the stairs, and with each step the cat, too, climbed higher, pausing each time she stopped, continuing each time she continued.

The stairs ended at a broad corridor that led to a set of open double doors. Beyond these doors, she saw a large apartment in which a fire blazed behind a large table. The cat scampered ahead. No guards challenged her. No one appeared. Distantly, she could hear the sounds of the banquet, still in progress.

She entered the chamber, expecting at any moment to be accosted. Though the danger felt very near, she could ignore it, as though her body walked by itself while she, the self-aware "I" that should guide that body, stood aside distantly and only watched.

"Kitty, kitty, kitty," she whispered, advancing to a curtain that partially concealed the adjacent hall.

Beyond, the cat sat resting in front of a stone wall. The wall had been inscribed with letters that Hanna'el recognized as Guirish runes. Just above the cat, at a height she could just reach, Hanna'el saw a strangely familiar glyph carved into the stone, though she could not recall where she had seen this glyph before—perhaps in one of Brother Thomas' books—and beneath that glyph a name: At'theira.

The glyph summoned her. As she drew near to it, the cat rubbed itself against her legs. She paused and traced each line of the strangely familiar sigil with her finger, and as her finger traced the last curve, she felt the stone upon which it was carved begin to tremble. Gasping, she leaped backward, nearly stepping on the cat, as a portion of the wall swung back to reveal descending stairs. A rush of cool wind rose from the depths of this narrow stairwell. In the draft, Hanna'el heard the faintest voice. It was a woman's voice, and it called her.

At once, the cat leaped away from her and descended the spiraling staircase.

She had no light except for a candle that burned on a nearby table. Using its feeble glow, she peered into the stairwell, straining to catch a glimpse of the cat and wondering if her ears had played tricks.

The stones of this stairwell were different from those of the Caer. They looked older and more massive, and moss grew in cracks along their surfaces. The air smelled musty and damp, and far below, in the darkness, she thought she heard the steady drip of water.

Again, she heard the faint meow of the cat.

"Kitty, kitty, kitty," she called, feeling very stupid when she heard her own voice.

Wait, she told herself; *I'm not some child who needs to worry about a cat. I'll send a man to fetch it. Let the Singer watch out for it himself.*

But beneath these thoughts, another voice, more insistent, urged her forward.

Slowly, she began to descend the spiraling stairs, shielding the candle lest the upward draft extinguish it and plunge her into darkness. After many steps, the stairs ended at a wooden door. The door stood warped on a set of iron hinges, its boards joined carelessly with the studs of rusted nail-heads sticking out. Water dripped steadily, for the dark entryway lay deep within the mountain.

Clearly, the cat had eluded her on the stairs, but the way had been so narrow that she knew she could not have overlooked it, even in this feeble light. How had it gotten through this door? Had the imp disappeared or changed its shape? She paused and prepared to ascend the stairwell, when again she heard a woman call her name. The woman's sad voice came from beyond the ruined door.

"Hannah, come to me . . . "

Was it she or someone else the woman called?

Hanna'el tipped her candle to spill the melted wax. "Who's there," she challenged, putting authority into her voice in the manner that Thomas had coaxed her. From behind the canted door, the sorrowful voice urged her on.

She gripped the bolt that held shut the ancient door. The metal, cool and rusted, moved reluctantly at her touch. She pushed against the door and heard it groan, surprised that a light shone from inside to guide her.

Cautiously, she entered a circular chamber whose floor lay covered with straw. In the middle of this room, on a stool near a lamp that burned fitfully, a woman sat with her head bowed low. Except for this stool and a broken bench propped in one corner, the room contained no furniture. It might be a dungeon, Hanna'el thought; the cell looked too filthy and cramped for anyone to inhabit. The air smelled musty, damp, and cold, and water dripped steadily down the walls.

As Hanna'el stood watching, the woman looked up. "Come in; do not be frightened."

The woman's face, though sad and aged and battered, had a glow of inward beauty. She sat with her naked feet amidst the straw; a linen shift, more like a stitched assemblage of rags, draped her thin body and spread across her lap, while her hair, gray and tangled, flecked with stubble and no doubt infested with vermin, fell disheveled down her back and across her face. How long had she been here? With a gasp, Hanna'el saw that a rusted chain bound the woman's right ankle to the floor. The manacle had chaffed the skin raw, and her bare, dusty feet had a bluish tinge.

Slowly, hesitantly, Hanna'el entered the room, not noticing that her tiny candle had flickered out. For a moment, she felt that this scene might dissolve. Had she fallen into another trance like the one that had befallen her in the shepherd's tent? "Who are you?" she asked uncertainly. "Are you a prisoner?"

"Sit down," said the woman. "The time that we share is precious."

Hanna'el felt compelled to do as the woman asked. She settled by the feeble lamp, gathering her legs beneath her. She felt curious and horrified at once.

"Where is the green and living twig the shepherd gave you?" the woman asked, looking keenly into Hanna'el's face. And when Hanna'el blinked and said that she had lost the shepherd's gift, the woman moaned. She turned to the wall, and the chain on her ankle rattled pitifully.

"Lost the shepherd's gift? Then another has claimed it. Why was that precious token entrusted to a child!"

I'm not a child . . . Hanna'el wanted to say, but she paused for a moment, as though pondering her own meanings.

The strange woman's fingers nervously braided two pieces of straw . . . braided and unbraided them continuously. There were many such straws at the woman's feet.

"Do not speak," the woman said sharply. Her tone was bitter. "You must learn from me—you must listen. What a fool you were to lose the shepherd's gift! What can a girl do against enemies who are so ruthless, cruel, and resolved? Better that Carlon's daughter should have hidden herself in the vast grasslands of distant Arcatus where at least she might have lived out her days in ignorant peace. Child, what vanity possessed you to challenge Aeron?"

The woman's accusing tone angered Hanna'el. She had not come here to challenge Aeron—she had come to claim the lands that were rightfully hers. Her father was to blame for this dilemma, not she! Had he not abandoned her, she would never have ventured from her homeland.

It's his fault, not mine! she wanted to shout.

Grief and hatred mingled in the woman's woeful expression. She clutched at another braid of straw.

"You move within a dream, Hanna'el of Arcatus. The past haunts you, but you refuse to hear it or understand. You have blocked your ears to the truth of your own remembrance, but that which you ignore will destroy you unless you pay heed. Listen, Hanna'el, hear me well. It is the Singer's art that brought you here and which briefly lifts the curse under which I suffer. Hear me in the brief moment we can share."

The woman stretched forth her bony hand and touched Hanna'el's forehead. The icy touch sent tremors of horror through Hanna'el's body. She staggered back.

The woman laughed.

"I, too, once was proud. I, too, was beautiful. Look at me now. I had rather be damned to hell than continue this existence—I am lost between heaven and earth. Do not make my mistake. You must awaken! Do not forget who you are."

"What do you mean?"

The woman smiled. "I am what you will become—unless you act. Know, then, the reason Aeron wishes to harm you: how Carlon, your father, once the most trusted of Aeron's lords—Aeron's foster brother, his dearest friend—loved secretly Aeron's queen, and how Queen At'theira returned your father's love. Aeron, guileless and deceived, never knew of their passion until a child, the lost Prince Raemond, was conceived.

"One moment's passion—and all was changed forever. If only

your father had accepted the truth of that moment—but Carlon could never obey his gods. He was too good, too pure—his sense of honor tortured him. He wanted to confess to Lord Aeron, to my husband, but before he could do so a spy, an evil minister, intervened. This grim physician has become the hidden power in the Caer. It is he who poisoned Aeron and encouraged him to turn against himself and those he loved. It is he who plotted Queen At'theira's death—and he who stole Prince Raemond from the Caer.

"Hear, Hanna'el of Arcatus, how Aeron, advised by his physician, used the physician's arts to hold his queen in thrall—to imprison her between life and death. He confined her to a lead coffin. There her body lies, neither dead nor living, while her spirit wanders between the worlds, unable to perish, unable to live—unable to forget what once it was.

"For At'theira's sake, your father swore to his quest. Carlon seeks the Tree whose branches bear a power against this evil and against the intrigues of Aeron's minister, the physician Azael. Few believe that the Tree exists—so feeble and weak have the powers of remembrance become. *But the Singing Tree lives!*—it grows by the western ocean, in the land that the ancients called Elowyn, beyond the kingdom of Urd. The Tree is the source of memory; its blossoms have power to lift the physician's curse. Yet, the one whose evil medicines poisoned Aeron's heart will not see your father's quest succeed, *and he desires this fate for you.*"

Hanna'el felt numbed by this revelation. Shock and grief contorted her features, and she shook her head in panicked disbelief. "It's not true!" she shouted. "My father never loved Lord Aeron's queen!"

The woman put down the straw she had been braiding and unbraiding and touched Hanna'el's raven hair with tender astonishment. She spoke quite gently.

"No, Hanna'el, it is true what I have told you, every word. I know because I am that woman. I am Queen At'theira—and my child, the lost Prince Raemond, is your half-brother, your father's son. I am your step-mother, Hanna'el."

All strength deserted her. Hanna'el sagged to the straw-covered floor and stared at the woman with an expression of horror, disbelief, and dread.

"Neither dead nor living," the woman said, as though repeating a litany. "Neither forgotten nor remembered. After Aeron discovered my love for Carlon, after Prince Raemond's birth, Lord Aeron locked me in this cell as punishment. Here I remained in utter darkness and solitude, frantic with despair. I beat at the door; I howled; I implored Aeron to free me and to let me see my son. See where my bloody fingers scored the wood—see where the iron manacle tore at my leg until the flesh bled and festered. Aeron would not relent. His physician would not allow him. The child I bore did not die in childbirth, as many say; Prince Raemond vanished as a babe, stolen from the nurse whom Aeron made his guardian. On the day of the child's abduction, Aeron came to this cell in a rage. He told me the child had vanished and blamed me for the loss. I denied it—I implored him—but Aeron, already under the physician's care, had only a heart for revenge. He struck me, and when I would not plead for mercy or confess, he struck me again." She pulled aside her lengths of graying hair. "See what he's done. My silence enraged him, but I would not submit. *I can not—I never shall! I never harmed my son.* Each time Aeron struck me, I turned to receive another blow. *Where is my son?* he cried. His anger and grief had maddened him. He did not want the truth, and at last, I screamed at him: *ask the physician!* And so, he struck me again, this time even harder, and the world went black. While I lay unconscious, Aeron's physician Azael came to my cell at Aeron's bidding and employed his subtle art. Now I am lost, suspended between life and death. You see me as once I was. My spirit repines in this abandoned cell, where I mourn for my lost child, my husband and lover."

Shocked and horrified, Hanna'el struggled to raise herself from the floor, but her legs felt powerless. She shook her head from side to side in wild denial. "My father never loved you. He would never do such a hateful thing!"

But Queen At'theira answered even more forcefully, and her eyes shone fiercely. "*Carlon loved me—and I loved him. I love him still!*

Child, were it possible, he would have married me, and you would then be my stepdaughter." She laughed, and her laughter echoed weirdly from the stones. Her laughter fell on Hanna'el like the sharp blows of a hammer. "How greatly Carlon suffered to conceal our love. I urged him to challenge Aeron, but he would not. He could easily have ruled the Caer—the fool! He was too weak! Now see what he has lost! Carlon would not act, and his weakness and guilt destroyed me. It destroys us all . . . His guilt and weakness haunts you—as it haunts my son! Woe that you ever came to this hateful Caer!"

Hanna'el, crawling backwards, drew herself away from the harridan queen. She felt imprisoned in some adamantine web, a web so finely spun, it hung invisible.

"Listen," said the hag, "you must obey me. You are my hope. You must travel westward in pursuit of your father. Follow his steps. He traveled to Urd. There is a passage out of the Caer; the door is concealed in this cell, behind that stone. Go through and down; you will find a hidden river and a boat. It will bear you through the caverns of the Guir. This is your fate, to follow your father Carlon. To undo the curse. At the frontiers of Urd, you will find an ally, someone to guide you. Accept that help. To one who's begun the quest, nothing is strange."

"No," said Hanna'el. "Stay away from me! I hate you!"

But the woman would not relent. "You must continue your father's journey to the roots of the dying Tree. The Tree alone has power to absolve and to heal. The Tree recalls you—surely, you know that—you feel it, you hear it—you have received the shepherd's gift. The green and living twig was meant to protect you and guide your steps. Though you have lost it, you may yet find your way. Take this as a gift in its place."

So said, At'theira removed a necklace of braided hair. Hanna'el saw that the necklace held the severed fragment of a golden ring. "Take it," said At'theira. "It was a gift to me from your father, a token of love. Aeron split it with an axe. You will find the matching half when memory recalls you to your goal—when you meet the one you fear above all others—in the place where the two become one. His name is also *Azael.*"

Hanna'el trembled and would not accept the broken ring, but Queen At'theira hastily pressed it into her hand. Her touch felt freezing cold.

"You're lying," Hanna'el muttered. "It's all untrue. My father never loved you. You're as evil as the Caer."

Queen At'theira laughed again. "Perhaps I am. There's no one who is innocent. May you travel well and fast, Carlon's daughter. *You must find the Tree.*"

Something in the woman's challenging tone gave Hanna'el courage. She looked into At'theira's reddened, sorrowful eyes, and for a moment, she saw the woman's face change to that of an older man.

"*Walter!*" she exclaimed.

She did not know why that name sprang so suddenly from her lips.

Queen At'theira smiled—a woman once again—and she placed her icy hand on Hanna'el's cheek. Her touch was more gentle and motherly. "Do not deny me, *Hannah.* Do not refuse. You must find the Tree. Do this for your own sake as much as for your father's sake or mine—do it for the sake of that other you do not know. Find the Tree, my daughter. Find it, if you would be whole."

Escape From the Caer

"Wake up," cried an urgent voice, "we are betrayed!"

Raising his head from the table where he had fallen asleep after leaving Hanna'el, Thomas blinked.

A young man, wide-eyed and breathless, stood in the door. His words came out in a rush that Thomas could scarcely grasp. "Who is betrayed?" he muttered, annoyed and embarrassed that the younger man should see him so befuddled.

"Lord Aeron has imprisoned Bryhs. His men came upon us by surprise."

Thomas saw that the man who stood before him had been wounded beneath his left arm.

How can this be?

He still felt half asleep.

"Old man, don't you hear me? *Aeron has betrayed us*—our men are cut down! Save yourself—Carlon's daughter is dead!"

This news alone had power to clear Thomas' brain. He lurched to his feet, throwing backward the chair on which he had been sleeping, his arms a riot of discomfort as the blood flowed freely once again.

"Hanna'el! Have you seen her? Where is she? What happened?"

The messenger, weakening, glanced with fear and uncertainty toward the door. He clutched his wound.

"Speak to me!" Thomas shouted. "Where is she!"

"Dead or wounded or imprisoned—every one of them—even Bryhs. They came upon us in force. Bryhs fought them in the yard. Hanna'el must be dead—they surely found her. Old man, they'll kill you, too!"

The messenger staggered, but Thomas seized him and held him upright. He could hear the sounds of fighting from the courtyard below his room. He glanced toward the open doorway. "Dead—but did you see her? Did you see them kill her? "

Numbly, the warrior shook his head. "I did not see her. Her room was empty. The men who watched her were cut down."

Thomas heard voices echoing through the corridor that led to his room. The man he held freed himself and staggered backwards. "Go," he whispered. "Save yourself. I'll meet them here."

Thomas had no weapon. Allowing the wounded messenger to slump in a chair, he hastened to the doorway; his long brown robes swished against his legs. The corridor outside his room stood empty, but he could hear loud voices and footsteps on the stairs.

"Go," said the soldier. "Hurry. I'll hold them here!"

The scene at Hanna'el's chamber was just as the messenger had described. The three men posted to guard her lay dead in a pool of blood, their bodies hacked and mangled. Thomas' hands trembled uncontrollably as he entered Hanna'el's room, and for a moment his brain refused to interpret what he saw.

The room had been savaged. It looked as though a storm had destroyed it. The bed, the furniture, the benches and the small table where he had sat the night before had all been overturned and smashed. All of Hanna'el's possessions—everything she had brought from Arcatus—had been hurled in disarray throughout the room, cut to shreds and torn. Even her books, what few he had made her bring along, her grammars and ancient histories, the poetry he had made her commit to heart, these texts had all their pages torn apart. The white pages lay like fallen leaves upon the floor.

Where had they taken her?

Moaning, Thomas turned and stepped from the doorway, slipping in the blood that coated the floor. He fell, crying out as his knee painfully struck the stone.

Fear drove him to his feet. He stood and began to limp away, his sore knee protesting every step.

"That way," came a shout. "I see his footprints."

Thomas turned down the nearest passage. This smaller corridor soon divided again. He turned to the left and then to the left once more, grateful that the Guir, those ancient builders, had constructed the Caer as such a labyrinth. His breath came in great panting gasps. Try as he might, he could not control the sound of his own breathing, and he feared that his pursuers might track him by sound alone.

He came to another corridor and did not know which way to run. *What was the use?* Sooner of later they would find him. Hopeless and exhausted, he sagged against a wall.

As he panted and caught his breath, a figure appeared at the far end of the corridor. To his surprise, he saw that it was a woman. He had met no women in this place. The woman, pale and dressed in white, raised her hand as though beckoning him.

"Hanna'el?"

But it wasn't Hanna'el. Thomas saw that the woman had gray hair. Perhaps it was one of the older servants who remembered Carlon.

He rose and followed her. The woman stayed far enough in front of him that she always turned a corner before he could get a closer view. She appeared to be ancient and walked as though her feet and legs were sore. Thomas saw blood upon her ankles, and her feet left damp marks of blood upon the stones.

"Wait," he shouted, gasping again for breath.

He saw ahead a set of double doors that led to a suite of rooms, the foremost of which had a table behind which burned a fire in the hearth.

"Come, hurry," a voice spoke softly.

He saw her again. The old woman stood inside the chambers, toward the rearmost wall. Hesitantly, Thomas obeyed. He saw that she stood beneath a stone wall carved with a variety of Guirish runes, and above he saw a glyph that he knew well from his studies of ancient lore.

The woman turned and touched this carved symbol, and at once, the stone wall revealed itself as a door. She entered the darkness beyond.

"Wait!" cried Thomas.

He had no choice but to follow. The voices behind had grown too loud. Thomas passed into the stairwell, and at once the stone door swung shut, sealing him in darkness. He could do nothing else but feel his way down.

As he descended the spiraling staircase, light filtered dimly toward him. It grew brighter the deeper he went, until he saw that the light came from a chamber at the bottom of the stairs. He hurried down to it.

The pale, greenish light came from a crypt. The light glowed from a lead sarcophagus that stood in the middle of the tomb.

Thomas entered and viewed the body that lay inside. At first he feared that he'd find Hanna'el, but it was the body of a young woman he did not know. Then he heard another moan and saw, stretched in a darkened corner of this crypt, the one he sought.

Hanna'el lay unconscious along the wall. Flecks of straw—some braided—covered her hair and clothing, though Thomas saw no straw inside the tomb. Hanna'el lay with her head cradled on her arm, as though resting.

She did not awaken, even when he shook her.

"Oh Hanna'el, Hanna'el, what will we do?"

Thomas felt the brush of fur against his leg.

A black tomcat had somehow entered this tomb. It sat beside them.

WITHIN THE TOMB

Thomas bent to Hanna'el's face and felt her pulse. Her hands and face were cold, so cold they felt nearly lifeless—and yet, she breathed. He smoothed back her raven hair and caressed her cheek, inspecting her as best he could in the pale light that glowed from the sarcophagus.

"Hanna'el," he pleaded, "wake up."

He saw that her hands clutched tight some brownish object. It was a book, a small diary sealed with a clasp. Pressed tightly to the cover of this book, twined between her fingers, was a single braided circlet of human hair. Her other hand, the left one, was also clenched, and as he moved her a crescent of gold fell to the wooden floor. Thomas saw that it was half a golden ring. He picked it up quickly and stuffed it in his pocket.

"Hanna'el, wake up!"

Had she been injured? Was she ill? Or was this some strange enchantment? Suddenly, as he tried to lift Hanna'el from the floor, the cat that sat nearby leaped forward and scratched his hand. Thomas screamed, more from tension than pain, and clumsily shook her. The sudden motion aroused Hanna'el from her swoon. She sat up quickly, exclaiming his name and dropping the small book that she had clutched. The cat, which had attacked Thomas only a few seconds before, looked satisfied at this recovery. It rubbed itself against Hanna'el as she groaned and felt her head.

Thomas took no time to question her, nor did he dare to tell her that the cohort had been overcome. Already his ears caught the sound of footsteps on the stairs that led to the crypt. He glanced about for some weapon, but the room was empty. He saw no defense.

Suddenly, the cat leaped from Hanna'el's side and ran to the stone behind her. It clawed the wall and meowed.

Hanna'el understood. Crawling forward, she touched the stone and ran her fingers along its edges.

"Thomas," she ordered, "come here. Help me."

He saw no reason to hope, but long habit had made him obedient.

"This stone slides free," she said. "The Queen told me. It will open to a passageway. Help me search."

"Queen?"

He did not know what she meant.

Nervously, Thomas glanced at the door, judging that in a few more seconds Aeron's men would be upon them.

"Thomas, hurry!" Hanna'el shouted. "Help me move this!"

He pried his fingers into the cracks at the stone's edge, breaking his nails with the effort. The stone seemed a massive weight well set in place and immovable, but to Thomas' surprise it swung backward once his fingers were in place. It slid on some mechanism he could not see, opening to reveal a chute. A narrow metal ladder had been set into the stones on the other side.

"Climb down," said Hanna'el, "and pull the stone back into place." She had already started to descend; the black tomcat perched upon her shoulders.

Thomas waited only until her head was out of the way, then squeezed through the opening and started down. As his shoulders came level to the floor, he reached back and seized a small handle that had been set in the center of the massive stone. He gave this handle a violent pull, and the stone, balanced by its mechanism, slid with a whoosh into place. It settled into the grooves that had been carved for it, sealing itself like a lid screwed tight to a jar.

When Aeron and his men entered the crypt, they found nothing but the body of Queen At'theira, entombed within its sarcophagus, as it had been for sixteen years.

The Descent to the Grotto

Downward they climbed in a chute of darkness. Thomas could not even see the stone in front of his face. "Talk to me, Hanna'el," he pleaded, for heights were something he had always detested, and he feared that he might lose his grip on the cold, wet rungs to which he clung.

"I hear water," said Hanna'el, breathless. "Go slowly, I'm right below you. Don't step on my head."

He felt better hearing her voice and better for the darkness that pressed them close. He didn't dare to think what lay at the bottom of this passage, and his arm and leg muscles trembled with fatigue.

Now the sound of rushing water came loudly to his ears. Had the chute become a well? The air, cold and damp, smelled strongly of mold and decay. Suppose the ladder simply ended? Suppose there was nowhere they could go? He knew he lacked the strength to climb back out.

But Hanna'el, farther down than he, raised another warning.

"Thomas, my foot's on something. It feels like wood. It must be . . . yes, it's a boat. She told me I'd find it! How far are you above me?"

"How can I tell?" answered Thomas, speaking into the dark, though he judged by the sound of water that he was no more than thirty feet away. He bit his lip and continued on. "Is there any solid ground?"

"None," she answered. "Only a boat. Come further. We'll have to trust to the current to bear us out."

"Out to where?" Thomas muttered, shivering. This subterranean river might bear them to their doom. Yet, if the water flowed only underground, why had a boat been placed here for someone to find? Was it a trap?

Distracted by these thoughts, he paid less attention to his footing and nearly fell. The fright gave him a surge of energy, enough to keep him hanging until at last he felt Hanna'el touch his leg.

"The boat is very narrow," she warned him. "Be careful! I've found the rope that holds it to the wall."

Like a man treading carefully on ice, Thomas slowly trusted his weight to the bobbing craft. Once he was sure of his footing, he released the ladder and collapsed. He could not remember ever feeling so exhausted. The muscles in his arms ached and twitched.

"Untie the rope," he muttered. "Untie it. I could never climb that ladder again."

He felt the brush of fur against his face and startled before realizing the black tomcat stood near him. The cat allowed itself to be gathered to the scholar's lap, and Thomas felt glad for its warmth and friendship.

"We're free," he heard Hanna'el exclaim; her excited voice echoed in the pitch darkness. "Crouch down, stay low. We don't know where this flows or how narrow this passage might become."

Thomas did as she instructed, crouching low with his head pressed to the wood. The sound of water felt marvelously soothing after a time. They floated in total blindness, a sensation like being freed from one's body, Thomas thought. He expected the boat to crash upon unseen rocks, and he braced himself, but the tiny craft touched nothing. It glided along so serenely that except for the sound of the current they might have been afloat on a languid midnight sea.

In the cold darkness, Hanna'el sat close to him. Neither spoke. The cat lay purring at their feet. After a time, Thomas could not tell if he slept or woke. If sleeping, then he dreamt, or if waking, then the boat slowly drifted into a cavern stranger than any dream.

Only later did he recall what he beheld. The impenetrable darkness gave way to a faint glow that appeared to rise from the depths of the water over which they floated, and he saw that they had traveled through a tunnel to emerge onto the surface of a vast underground lake whose cold, placid depths glowed with a subtle blue-green radiance. This light illumined the enormous cavern evenly in all directions, though Thomas could perceive neither ceiling nor walls, so vast was its expanse. The boat moved of its own accord, drawn by some power that Thomas could not comprehend. Time passed unnoticed, and language felt lost to him.

He saw at last a shore and on it what looked to be the shapes of men. But as the boat passed closer Thomas realized these were statues or else the weird growths of minerals that mocked the proportions of humankind. The shapes increased in size and variety as they drifted closer past the shore, and he saw what looked to be an entire petrified forest, uncanny formations of rock and crystal that swayed like flowers, bushes, and trees in the blue-green shimmering luminescence of the lake. This mineralized forest gave way to an open rocky vista that stretched into the shadowed depths of the cavern, and in the gloom Thomas could just make out what appeared to be buildings and towers carved from rock and encrusted with multicolored gemstones, a dark and silent city devoid of life; or, if any creatures dwelt there, they flitted unseen like spiders amid the looming shadows of the walls. The boat changed course and drifted away from the dimly lit shore, until it passed between small islands. On every island, Thomas saw piles of bone. The piles rose like whitened pyramids. "The catacombs of the Guir," Thomas whispered. He looked downward into the illumined lake and saw a weaving, swaying grassland, a kaleidoscope of intermingled colors and ever changing shapes. It seemed that amid these weaving forms he could see buildings, as though an entire city had vanished beneath the waters, drowned long ages past. He heard water falling, and soon on every side of them cascades of green shimmering waters tumbled from hidden fissures. The sound of the cataracts, loud and louder, echoed in the darkness like music inside a shell, and in the roaring Thomas heard what easily he imagined to be voices, the voices of the dead who had taken refuge in this sunless world.

"*Westward,*" they whispered. "*Do not stop. Follow these waters to the Karakala and beyond that river to the sun burnt ruins of ancient Urd. Follow to the Singer. Follow to the roots of the dying Tree.*"

Thomas touched Hanna'el to see if she, too, heard these whispering voices, but she did not move. For a moment, Thomas panicked. Unable to see Hanna'el's face where she lay against the boat's shadowed hull, he suddenly felt seized by the conviction that this was not Hanna'el but a stranger that had taken her place. Perhaps a child.

A splash at the gunwale turned his attention to the water. He looked into the shimmering depths and saw a flash of green and gold. It was a fish. The fish swam at arm's length below the surface, near the bow of their tiny boat, as though it were leading them. For a moment, Thomas believed that the fish was the source of the mysterious power that guided them through this hidden, subterranean realm, but then the fish deserted them. With a flick of its emerald golden fins, it dove into the lake's unseen depths and disappeared. Suddenly, Thomas understood why. Their boat had drifted to the end of a vast cavern. Here, the current gained speed. He saw that the lake drained through an opening in the rocks that loomed before them. A whirlpool marked the place where the waters rushed from the cavern and deeper underground. The vortex had already trapped them. Their boat began to circle faster and faster, as the swiftly draining water drew them down.

"Help me!" shouted Thomas.

His frightened voice awakened Hanna'el.

Understanding all at once that their lives were in danger, Hanna'el cried out: "Walter!" And she clutched the scholar's hand.

Thomas did not know what she meant.

Just as he felt her hand inside his own, the whirlpool overcame them and it was night.

BOOK FOUR

The Seventh Friedrich

HANNAH'S GARDEN

In her dream, the old man came to her and spoke encouraging words. She met him in a green and pleasant place, a place with which she was quite familiar—a place that she remembered she had loved. She realized, almost lazily, where it was. She had come home. She was in her old backyard.

This old man, whose name was Walter, knew her well. He told her that he was her godfather, though really, Hannah chuckled, she had never had such a thing. *Godfather*, she scoffed, please be serious; she had no time for these jokes. She had to get on with her journey; she had to awaken Thomas; she had to . . . *what?*

"Just what is it, Hannah, that you think you have to do?" Walter asked.

And she found that she could not answer his smiling question. Whatever it was that had bothered her, she found that she could not put the concern into words. The effort tired her. Rather than struggle, it felt so much easier to accept things as they were.

At least I'm home.

"Home?" said Walter, quizzically.

His question made her doubt. Her doubt felt dangerous. Hannah frowned.

"Home," she repeated. This was, after all, *her* backyard.

"*Hanna'el*," she heard Walter say. His voice sounded nostalgic.

"That's not my name," she told him crossly.

Walter stepped away, merging with the green and scented background of the garden in which they stood, his form as insubstantial as the aroma of blooming lilac. She watched him submerge in the green-golden foliage of the garden. She felt she should follow him, but she could not or did not know how.

"Wait," she exclaimed, strangely panicked. "Where are you going? Walter, don't leave me. Am I a ghost?"

This last question sprang from her lips quite unexpectedly. She did not know why. She did not feel like a ghost. She felt quite alive, to be perfectly honest.

Walter laughed. She could see him shimmering, fishlike, in a veil of trembling sunlight that rippled on the delicate surfaces of the leaves.

"No, Hannah," he answered patiently, "you are not a ghost. You're real enough. You are, however, adrift. You've lost the thread of remembrance that bound you to your world. Your world is fading. Slowly but surely, your world is fading away. Its memories are vanishing."

"But Walter, what is memory?"

She imagined him answering: "Ah Hannah, that is indeed the most difficult question a human can ask . . . " But instead, his voice became wistful, his tone more musical and profound, and as she watched him shimmer in the green-golden sunlight of the garden, he appeared to swim deeper, until his outline, man or fish, hovered just at the vanishing threshold of her vision.

She understood why this happened: *It's because I've lost the twig. I did what Fritz warned me not to do . . . I tried to go home.*

But she glanced at the house that stood behind her and the foliage of her familiar backyard, and instead of questioning she said defiantly: "But I am home. My name is Hannah. Why is that wrong?"

Immediately, almost before the words were spoken, Walter answered her gently, as though he were swimming inside her thoughts. "Find the Tree," he reminded her.

Guard the green and living twig and keep it sound.

"What tree? What twig?"

She felt frantic now, abandoned and utterly alone. An unexpected, heart-pounding anxiety swept through her young body, as though the ground she stood upon had yawned apart to reveal a calamitous abyss.

Earthquake! some small, reasoning part of herself pronounced. And yet, that was impossible. There were no earthquakes in her backyard.

You must find the Tree . . .

She felt as though a wind roared through her brain, as though a great equinoctial storm had swept her up. This raging storm wanted to blot her out, to scatter her thoughts and memories like pieces of straw. It wanted to destroy her.

And worse, although she did not understand what Walter meant, she felt that she *ought* to understand or even that she *once* had understood but now could not. It was a sensation as awful as forgetting the name of your best friend—or even more terrible than that, she quickly decided. A ghostly resonance of remembrance hovered at the penumbra of this absence. It felt like a cavity in her soul.

Twig? Tree?

"Walter, help me, please!" Hannah cried desperately. She could feel the place inside her where understanding once had lived—she called it memory—but the place was like this garden, silent, suggestive, and deserted.

She knew that she was alone. Moreover, as soon as she knew this, she understood something else. She knew that she had needed to be alone, but she did not know why.

Solitude is the reason I am here.

Somehow, this understanding gave her hope.

She allowed Walter's voice to touch her gently.

Walter's words, a steady mantra, were also part of her solitude. They echoed inside her and without. How long would she live in that resonance? How long would this solitude endure? She didn't know . . . she didn't care.

Walter, the Master of Memory, had disappeared.

He was, she again decided, a most annoying fish.

THE ENDLESS SPRING

It did not take Hannah long to confirm what she suspected: she was alone. What surprised her was how quickly she accepted her solitude. Of course, she had the cat—*whose cat was it?*—though the cat was independent and loved to roam. She wished that she could train it to stay put.

She spent most of her days in the garden, the garden that her uncle had planted, for that was where she lived. Though no one tended the garden, it had never looked so blossoming green. She especially loved the carrots—rows and rows of bushy carrots, perfectly sweet. No matter how many carrots she ate, their number was not diminished. Certainly, she decided, these were among the best carrots in the world, which clearly said something marvelous about the soil, since, as Uncle Joseph often told her, you could always judge a garden by its carrots. If the carrots were sweet and tender, the soil was good. You could also tell by feeling the dirt and smelling it, but Hannah hadn't the knack. She confined herself to nibbling, and she ate so many carrots that her skin had a carroty tinge. The cat never chewed on them at all.

She had come here—well, just how had she come? *That* was a great mystery, Hannah thought—but only one of many, and by no means the greatest mystery of them all. Why was she alone? And even more puzzling, why didn't she worry about it?

At first, she counted the days since her arrival, dutifully penciling their passage on the complimentary real estate calendar that hung in her kitchen by the phone, which had no dial tone. She started counting on May 2. When she reached the end of May, she just kept going. But the weather never changed. On the calendar, June merged with July and July with August, August with September and so on and so forth, but as far as she could tell, nature had slipped a cog. Outside, in the garden of her backyard, the place she most liked to spend her time, the trees, the flowers, and the vegetables looked just as they had on May 2, the day that she had arrived, the day that she called her Homecoming. Flowers bloomed but never wilted. Vegetables plumped but never ran to seed. The trees were green but never summery heavy. And each day dawned with exactly the same weather: each day an exact copy of the splendid day before, each day a glorious day in middle spring.

She lost count of the days and let the calendar fall from the wall. What surprised her was how little this loss of printed time really mattered and how little she felt bothered by living alone. Of course, she had the cat, but the cat wouldn't talk. He liked to sit in a tree, watching magpies, and at night, he went off prowling heaven-only-knew-where. She doubted he found any friends.

Of course, there was more to keep her busy than the cat. She could roam the house at will and read whatever she liked—all the books that her uncle had left behind in his enormous library. The TV was broken; she hardly missed it. She had tried that gummy portable the very first day she arrived. Nothing but static. The phone was broken, too—the radio also. Lights worked, but only the lights in her house, and those were dimming. At night when the moon rose as a silvery crescent—and the moon was always a silvery crescent—only her house stood illumined. All the other houses were dark—and empty as well. The streetlamps were dark, the stoplights were dark, power lawn mowers didn't operate, and batteries had lost their juice. What did it matter anyway, Hannah thought; no one lived here. She had to admit: the world had become a bit thin, like a person hooked on dieting who had lost too much weight—things just weren't so very present any more. The only things still present were the stars.

She tried to put the problem out of mind. Most days she sat in her garden with a book, often volumes of philosophy or poetry, which in homelier times would have bored her. She had no trouble reading them now, except (and this was troubling) when she finished an hour or two (or three?) of careful reading, she'd glance up to discover she had almost no recollection of what she had read. Reading, she soon discovered, had taken on the qualities of sleep. Try though she might to stay present while she read, she had very little success. It was like trying to stay awake while one dreamed—an impossible paradox, Hannah thought. But this paradox seemed related somehow intimately to the riddle of her backyard—and to those greater, sphinx-like riddles of who she was, what had happened, why she was here. If she knew the answer to just one of those riddles, she'd know the answer to another, for the one determined the other, like endless reflections in a mirror, Hannah thought. But the procession of those reflections made her dizzy. There were just two many—just like each night there were just too many stars. If only she could find a way to contemplate just *one* question—for example, *why am I here?* But to do so, she needed a place to stand, a bit of solid ground, some secure foundation of memory from which an industrious self-reflection could spin its dependent webs. Unfortunately, she couldn't find such common ground.

And so, the days flowed by.

Occasionally, and just for variety, Hannah put on some comfortable sneakers and went for a walk. World explorers had to keep in shape, Hannah thought, though in fact she found little to explore. The town was completely empty—no one lived here—but all the buildings were furnished and ready to use.

Everything was just as she remembered—with a few rare exceptions that she only noticed after a very long time. When she walked into the Speedee Market, all the food was right on the shelf. The registers sat with money in the drawers. All the checkout magazines stood ready on their racks—each cover dated May 2. In the frozen food section, even though the electricity had gone off, the ice cream sat perfectly frozen, like mammoths caught in a blizzard. How this could be, she had no idea. Some things just defy the human intelligence.

She often took a quart of ice cream and ate it outside on the curb—there were no flies; flies and gnats and mosquitoes had left with the people. In the beginning, before she got used to abundance, she ate as much ice cream as she wanted and threw the rest away. But after awhile, even though the supply looked nowhere near to giving out, she began to feel bad about wasting food, and she only took as much as she could eat, leaving the rest to stay frozen in the freezers forever. If she wanted something different, she took pretzels or soda from the shelves. After eating, she carefully sealed up the bags and closed the bottles, tucking the surplus away for later use. The soda never lost its tingly fizz. It was sometimes just downright depressing.

Was this silly? Well, she told herself, so what? She could do as she pleased and no one bothered her. Not that there was much she wanted to do. That was the most frustrating part. As she walked through the center of town, the black tomcat at her heels, and looked at all the shops and stores that held all the items she had always wished for but couldn't afford, she realized that now that she had the chance to take whatever she wanted, she didn't want anything at all. To be honest, she was content and discontent at once. Even though she had everything, she felt this tremendous *lack. What was it,* she asked . . . *what was missing?* Perhaps it was time. Without time, nothing mattered; everything just happened as a matter of course. Today or tomorrow, now or never, it made no difference. Without time, there was no aging, without aging, there were no wants—no needs, no desires, no urgencies, no loss or gain. Life had become two-dimensional. Even the snacks that she stole from the Speedee Market, she didn't really *need.* She soon discovered that if she got too engrossed in a book and forgot to have a meal, it didn't matter, because she never felt *really* hungry. She had the permanent sensation of being just between two good meals—the way one felt four hours after a Thanksgiving feast, when the leftovers were still in the kitchen. Just as an experiment, quite early after her Homecoming, before the calendar fell off the wall, Hannah tried fasting. The sun rose three times, but she never felt hungry. She believed that she didn't need to eat at all—a feeling like seeing a best friend move to Biloxi.

Likewise, she found she didn't need to sleep, although what sleep she enjoyed was always deep and dreamless and serene. Moreover, she could fall asleep whenever she wanted and wake up whenever she wanted and if she stayed up all night reading it didn't matter because the next day she felt like she had slept ten hours straight. She could also stand on her head and whistle shrilly, tricks she had never been able to perform. And if it weren't for the clasp on her diary, she might have been content.

The clasp was locked and she couldn't find the key. Maybe she never had one in the first place. She called the book her diary, but really, it wasn't hers. For all she knew, it wasn't even a diary; it just looked like one. She had found it on the sundial in the garden just after she arrived. Someone must have lost it or placed it there—it might have been her—who could tell? The brown leather cover had a gold symbol on the front and above it a strange inscription.

Operis Processio,
Multum Naturae Placet

She knew that the words were Latin, but it took a bit of hunting to track down their sense. She had to ransack her uncle's library to finally discover what they meant. At last, in an old volume devoted to the quaint habits, customs, and lore of medieval miners, she found the reference she sought:

The Progress of the Work
Pleases Nature Greatly.

It was not much help. Disappointed, Hannah laid the book aside.

What did it mean?

She had hoped that the golden inscription would teach her a magic spell: a charm to turn cats into people, a hex to turn people into cats—so that her vagrant tomcat could become occasionally human, for example, to keep her company, when she felt in a sociable mood.

But the inscription seemed more ponderous than that.

She needed a key.

The book felt old and special, and she cursed that she couldn't read it. Why not simply cut the leather clasp? That would solve the problem, but she just couldn't bring herself to damage the fine old leather. Instead, since the lock wouldn't budge, she tried to peep in at the edges, reading parts of sentences here and there. That's why she decided it was a diary; she saw her name written inside it several times.

Hannah cherished that diary; indeed, it was the only true vexation she had left. Without it, her life might have passed like the calmly sustained tone of a meditative chant. But because of it, she had a problem.

Like the speck of sand in an oyster's shell, the book's intractable silence wore upon her day after day. Annoyed and discomforted, she played games with her imagination—it was the only way, short of violence, that she could respond. Without a key to open it, imagination or violence were the only methods she could think of that could pry her into that text. And since, by nature, she was not a violent person, she began the game of imagining what might happen on the Day of the Breaking of the Seal.

Day of the Breaking of the Seal!

How wonderful that phrase sounded on her lips.

She said the words often. Over time, the phrase assumed a marvelously melodramatic if not biblical self-importance. She said the phrase as often as she could, and slowly, over time, she invented a modest ceremony to accompany this litany of frustration. Since time felt negotiable, the ceremony took on a free-form spontaneity that seemed to Hannah more appropriate to the worship of this mystery than some dreary ritual performed with rhythmic regularity in a church. She allowed her moods to dictate what would happen. And although her moods were at first admittedly rare, practice improved them. Her moods, she soon discovered, were not merely disturbances in the unvaried weather of her soul, they were eruptions of chance and opportunity, brief out-runners of chaos whose swift passage through her inner landscape shocked the flat two dimensions of her existence into perspective and gave her, she soon discovered, a precious something: a goal.

It happened modestly at first. Sometimes for amusement (for she really didn't need to find it), she conducted searches for the book's mysterious key—at first, but unsuccessfully, through her house, and then, since keys could be anywhere, throughout the entire town. In this way, she at last discovered two things.

The first thing she discovered was that her world wasn't as large as she had thought. In fact, her world of things appeared to be fading. The farther she roamed, the thinner things became, like a tablet slowly dissolving in water, edges first. As she moved to the town's periphery, objects became less substantial. They first became ghostly, and then they disappeared. She realized that whole swatches of the world had faded like a vanishing mist. She could walk in any direction from her garden, and sooner or later, the world just faded out. Worse, she discovered that she could not remember what had faded; she merely guessed these parts had faded because she knew from her education that the world was supposed to be a very, very large. Well, if it had been large, reasoned Hannah, it wasn't large any longer. It was now exceedingly small—only the size of her memories, Hannah realized—only the scope of what she could recollect. Beyond what she could remember, there wasn't a world at all. And perhaps just as puzzling, she observed that all the mirrors in her world had vanished. They had not broken; they were gone, every last one of them, as far as she could tell.

This was her first discovery, and the second was just as strange. She discovered the *Zone of Night*.

BEFORE THE FLOOD

Zone of Night! The very phrase had a shivery importance. She was proud that she could think of such a thing.

Because the calendar had long since fallen off the wall, she couldn't say exactly *when* she discovered the *Zone of Night*. Three months? Four months? Ten months? More than a year? Such measurements had no meaning, since all the days resembled May 2. That was probably why she could overlook something so anomalous for so long.

Except for the fading away of *things* (which, when she thought about it, didn't bother her all that much), the *Zone of Night* was the one truly troubling aspect in an otherwise implacable universe. The *Zone*, for that was what she called it, began at the border of her town, toward the north. At first when she discovered it, she thought that her eyes had played her tricks. From the distance, the *Zone* looked like a tremendous thunderstorm: black ponderous clouds and massing rain. She had gone walking farther than usual on the day that she discovered the *Zone of Night*, following the road that led to the ruined arboretum where once, she recalled, she had spoken to a fish. She had no desire to speak to that fish again; in fact, she was glad to avoid it. But she remembered that a park had been destroyed there, and she wondered, now that the world bloomed so harmoniously, if the park and the pond had been restored.

She recalled that it normally took her twenty minutes to reach the arboretum—ten if she took the shortest cuts. Most of the short cuts went through people's backyards, and since no one lived here except her, there was no reason to avoid them. Besides, she had long since realized that nothing green or living could be damaged. If she broke the stalk of a daffodil or crushed a budding crocus underfoot, those plants soon sprouted again. Nature took care of itself, Hannah saw—a remarkable improvement, since people had the habit of damaging living things. She found it a great relief to feel no longer responsible for the non-human world.

On the day that she discovered the *Zone of Night*, she also discovered that walking became more arduous the farther that she traveled toward the *Zone*. The twenty minutes that it once took her to go from her front yard to the park lengthened to what seemed hours before she even saw the park appear.

She soon discovered the truth.

The park had been destroyed. All the trees she had loved had been cut down. The lawns had been plowed with bulldozers, and the pond where Walter the Fish of Wisdom had greeted her was dry. The Chinese Pavilion, where once she had waited out a storm with Walter's apprentice, stood surrounded by a chain link fence.

She wanted to get closer to the Chinese Pavilion, but the last part of her journey proved the most arduous. The cat also looked fatigued. He always followed behind her when she explored, his black tail proudly erect like a jaunty banner. As they came closer to the ruined arboretum, his tail sagged low, a sign that he had lost his enthusiasm, Hannah surmised. She certainly had lost most of hers.

What was it like to approach the *Zone of Night*? Well, to begin with, she didn't even suspect that the *Zone* was there. That discovery came later. The signs of its approach were in her limbs. She felt like she was walking on a treadmill, one of those silly exercise machines that her uncle Joseph ridiculed. Walking wasn't hard; it just went nowhere. Or rather, she saw herself progressing, but the goal toward which she traveled never appeared. A most frustrating sensation, Hannah thought. Were she not so stubborn, were the weather not so splendid, were she not troubled by pangs of hunger or aches of thirst, were the cat not dutifully walking at her side, she might have turned around and given up. After all, what did it matter? Everything she needed lay at hand. But she had always been stubborn, and this absence of arrival annoyed her. She kept on walking despite the useless strides, and after what seemed an immeasurable length of time she saw a dense, black veil of night appear in front of her like a sudden dimming of the horizon.

As noted, it looked like a monster storm. Massive thunderheads reared high and the air had an electric charge that made the cat's fur bushy and full. Rain felt imminent—the kind of pelting rain mixed with hail that no one wants to endure. A low rumble of thunder hummed in her bones, and snarls of lightning harried the outer darkness. From where she stood, peering forward to the darkened, deep horizon, Hannah could imagine that this wasn't merely a storm but rather a tremendous battle. Some vast expanse of conflict swept in front of her, and the bursts of lightning and explosions of thunder were not the mere atmospherics of bad weather—they portended war. The longer she contemplated the black, swirling thunderheads, the more keenly she could discern in their billowing mists the assembled ranks of armies, the grim shadows of armored warriors (some moving through the air and some on ground), and the sabre-toothed machineries of death. A great, if not cosmic, battle appeared to be joined. And as she contemplated this imagination, she began to comprehend that the storm—the *Zone of Night*—surrounded her entirely and that she dwelt on a small island of dappled sunlit remembrance in its midst.

Behind her, the sun shone pleasantly—a glorious May 2. Ahead, all the fountains of hell looked broken loose.

That day (and for many after it), Hannah turned back. She returned to her garden, and not without relief.

As she had expected, returning was easier than going out: like finding your way through a telescope, one direction made things closer while the other made things appear farther away. Going home was the closer direction, and it felt a whole lot better in her heart. She walked to the Speedee Market and stole a quart of ice cream. Sitting on the curb, she shared some with her cat, who always tried anything once, and she thought about her journey to the *Zone*. Of course, she didn't call it the *Zone* right away. That came later. How much later, she couldn't really tell, since time had a way of passing unremarked. She ate the ice cream, which never melted, and reflected on what she should do. *Nothing*, she decided. And uncounted days passed before she changed her mind.

It was remembrance that finally prompted her to act.

She *remembered* there had been a bookstore only a half-mile or so from her house. Mrs. Endicott owned it, she recalled.

Strange. Despite all the days of exploration, she had not come upon that bookstore yet. Where had it gone?

Months went by, as she pondered this enigma. Quite often, she unexpectedly found herself pondering the enigma on the edge of that terrible storm.

But at last, following some inward rhythm and spurred by the persistent lack of a key to her mysterious book, Hannah decided to conduct an expedition. After all, she told herself, world explorers had to be resolved. No need to make preparations, she was ready for anything any time. Just to be on the safe side, however, she took along a raincoat and several peanut butter and bologna sandwiches in case the trip took longer than she planned.

She had decided to enter the *Zone of Night.*

Inside the *Sphinx*

The cat came, too.

To test an idea that had been growing in her mind, she did not go the same way she had gone before. Her first glimpse of the *Zone of Night* had suggested that the mysterious black thunderstorm extended like a curving dome about her town. It appeared to start at just that boundary where the world began to fade, which, when she thought about it, coincided with the extent of her remembrance. She walked until the scenery began to feel vague. She had come to a part of her environment she had never before visited or perhaps had forgotten. Sure enough, at just this point the world became thin and thinner, at last vanishing into a haze which, with a few more steps of effort, merged with the stormy darkness of the *Zone*. To continue took effort, and she recognized how much her progress actually depended on finding some affinity with the past. She set her jaw and forged ahead.

The journey felt like days, though the sun never changed its position. Again, after walking what seemed like an endless path, the dark mass of thunderheads reared up. They all were just suddenly there. One moment blue sky surrounded her like the enveloping shell of an egg—next moment: thunder, lightning, and the threat of pelting rain.

Hannah hunched into the yellow hood of her raincoat and looked at her cat, who now walked quite slowly. She wondered if she should carry him. If it rained, the cat would get drenched. "Come here, kitty," she beckoned, but the cat would not come. He seemed to know what she wanted, and he seemed to be warning her back.

But Hannah felt determined to press on. As she approached that wall of cloud, a strange presentiment awoke inside her. She felt like she was walking toward herself. Each step that brought her closer to the storm clouds made this feeling stronger. She turned and looked for the cat. The poor, devoted feline had fallen behind, already several paces to the rear. He usually stayed at her heels. She saw the tranquil sunlight of the endless May 2 illumine the tomcat's fur like the halo of an angel, and for a moment, she stood in doubt. She could hear the rainfall now; the downpour started perhaps only twenty yards ahead. Her feet were still playing tricks. Now that she had found the infamous Zone, it seemed to draw her forward like the undertow of a powerful ocean wave. Space and time contracted, just as, a moment earlier, space and time had stretched like rubber bands. She turned and faced the massive, swirling darkness, which felt alive. And she heard and saw once more the turmoil of battle and war.

After a few short steps, she met the rain. The rain fell with the stunning impact of a mountain cataract. It knocked her to her knees. As she struggled to her feet and fought for balance, she saw that there were shapes inside the water. They looked like floating spheres—though she could not see them very well. She kept her balance and wiped at her eyes, staggering forward and breathing despite the torrent; she did not know how.

"Kitty, kitty, kitty," she called to her only friend. But the cat trembled behind her in the sunlight, paused at the edge of the downpour, and stared at her as though she were nuts.

Maybe I am.

She knew that she could try this anytime. *Why hurry—why do it now?* But instead of answering, she touched the cascading water. The rain felt warm—warm like a summery shower, though her ears rang from the constant thunder that rolled from the clouds. Her raincoat was useless in this storm. Better to leave it behind, Hannah thought . . . and well she might have, except that she remembered her mysterious book—the precious book that she had wrapped in a plastic sandwich bag stuffed deep inside her raincoat's inner pocket. She could feel its reassuring bulge.

Just to make certain the diary was still intact, she took it out. To her amazement, she saw through the plastic bag that the diary's stubborn lock had opened. It must have undone itself, just like that. Amazed and eager to read what the book had to say, she pulled it out of the plastic bag, disregarding the rain, and opened to a page. Too late, she understood her mistake. The rain overwhelmed her and soaked the pages. She tried to shield the pages by pulling her raincoat around the book like a protective shield, but somehow the water moistened the ink despite her best efforts to keep the pages dry. The words ran and faded more quickly than she could read them, so that the entire diary began to dissolve in a watery stream of ink.

All she could see was the symbol on its cover.

She felt confused now, uncertain, and utterly, utterly alone.

The destruction of the book was more than she had reckoned on. Suddenly, she felt like a swimmer who entrusts herself too carelessly to the waves only to discover that the current has silently sucked her far out to sea.

"Walter, help me!"

She looked backwards and caught a final glimpse of her cat, now terribly distant. The cat had become incandescent. It shone through the raging rainstorm like a lighthouse on a wave-battered rock—her very last beacon of hope. As long as she could see him, she could return. She could pilot her way to safety and dwell in the harbor of her familiar backyard forever, endlessly content. No one would miss her, but even more enticingly, *she* would never miss herself.

And then, suddenly, as she sputtered and struggled to keep herself upright against the storm, a sign appeared.

Sphinx

Dimly, Hannah remembered what this meant. It had to do with a bookstore where she often had gone to browse. Where was the bookstore now? *Why have I forgotten it?*

The memory of this lost location hovered just in front of her like the bobbing hope of a life preserver. She could almost grasp it. She could almost make out the bookstore's friendly lights. She saw those lights glimmer through the torrential downpour of the storm. With every ounce of strength and courage left in her body, Hannah struggled toward them. It took all her concentration to keep those lights in view. Waves of paralyzing water threatened to drown her, but she swam on. She found that if she could hold the bookstore firmly in her attention, the lights of its shop windows glowed more brightly still.

But just when she thought she had reached the safety of her goal, a tremendous current thrust her back. She screamed desperately—a shrill, inward cry of despair and exhaustion.

"Please, someone, anyone, help!"

Turn back . . . a voice from somewhere in the storm waters whispered.

But she would not.

Instead, she hunched her shoulders and soldiered forward until the rain fell so heavily she could see nothing in front of her at all. The world had become uniformly black and empty, without shape or texture, entirely wet. The cold rain stung her face. It lashed at her. She could feel herself eroding, washing away like soil in a heavy downpour. There would soon be nothing left.

Just as she feared she could not press forward another step, she bumped into something solid. She reached out her hand and touched a flat, slippery surface that felt like glass. Running her wet hand along it like a blind woman, she bumped a familiar object: a door latch. She tried to open it, but the door was locked. She knocked upon it frantically: "Hello, hello . . . is someone there? Anyone? Help!"

But no one answered.

Desperate, Hannah threw her shoulder against the glass. The door remained locked. She tried a second time.

On the third and last attempt, the door sprang open. Before she could respond, a strong hand seized her arm.

The grip was so firm, that Hannah winced with pain, but the pain forced back the floodtide of darkness that threatened to drown her. She blinked in sudden light, and for a moment, she had a clear, penetrating glimpse of a man's face poised in front of her own.

"Walter!" she exclaimed.

But the man shook his head. He had large, magisterial eyes whose alert self-possession filled her with courage.

"Swim to me, Hannah!" he commanded.

And with the last bit of her strength, Hannah tried.

Hannah's only friend, her patient tomcat, sat at the edge of the *Zone* and licked his fur. He had watched with disapproval as the girl named Hannah swam and floated away. The *Zone of Night* was especially tempestuous. The cat had no wish to soak himself in that torrent. *Not again.* Besides, he knew from experience that humans changed their minds. The girl, for whatever reason, might remember to come back. Humans changed their minds at the strangest moments, even when they knew their choice was wrong. And Hannah had good reasons to turn back. What could she meet but herself on the farther side?—a self she could neither recognize nor remember. *She had lost the green and living twig.*

The cat waited patiently. It knew that it could wait for a million years, or even longer if necessary. *I have my orders.* But at last, after thoroughly cleaning its glossy fur and resolving that there was nothing else realistically that it could do—even if it waited for an eternity—the cat stretched and meowed. It changed its shape.

Turning a quick somersault, the imp dove into the rainstorm as a fish.

SURPRISED!

Hannah paused.

The sound of the rain outside the bookstore and the heat from the room's tiny space heater made her sleepy. Slowly, she remembered why she was here. Her uncle had given her a journal—a locked and unreadable journal for her thirteenth birthday—and she had come here to Mrs. Endicott's bookstore to fetch the key. Mrs. Endicott had left, and now she was alone—alone, except for a cat (*was it Grumpy? Mrs. Endicott's cat?*) who slept curled beside her on the battered, second-hand sofa, his paws resting on a half-sorted box of oddly shaped keys.

Hannah sat up and rubbed her eyes. At once, she noticed something strange. Her hair was completely wet. Her clothes were dry, but her hair was wringing wet, as though she had just stepped out of the shower. Her wet hair had left a dark mark on the sofa pillow where she briefly had rested her head. The cat was also damp. As she puzzled the reason for this dampness and looked about the bookstore's familiar backroom, Grumpy regarded her with serene disapproval. And then he yawned.

At the moment Grumpy yawned, Hannah heard something else: someone was snoring loudly in the *Sphinx*.

THE PRIVY COUNSELOR

In the front of Mrs. Endicott's store, near the cash register, Hannah saw a large, reclining aluminum beach chair. Sprawled on this recliner, asleep beneath a frayed Afghan blanket, lay a man. He was middle-aged and somewhat on the plump side—rather thick in his torso in proportion to his legs. He wore a turban-like hat that fell low over his eyes as he slept. His mouth was open, hence the snores. A book lay on his stomach, and one arm dangled from the beach recliner to the floor. The old blanket only partially covered him, and Hannah saw that he wore what she first took to be a theatrical costume but in a moment decided must be a suit of extremely old-fashioned clothes: he had on lime green pants of the sort that fastened high up on the calves and a lemon yellow frock coat made of the same material with curiously robust and over-sized antique buttons. His voluminous shirt was made of linen. He had kicked off his shoes, and his blue socks, which had holes near the toes, were made of wool. From the way those socks ballooned about his feet, Hannah decided they were clearly hand knitted.

The bookstore had changed, too . . . or, at least, she didn't remember it looking the way it looked now. Several artist easels had been set up near the front bookshelves. Upon these easels, Hannah saw several water colors in various degrees of completion— color studies and landscapes, mostly, though some featured what looked like scenes of ancient Greek or Roman ruins in a landscape that reminded her of California, or maybe Italy. On another table, near the front window, through which she caught sight of a torrential downpour, Hannah saw a varied collection of objects. These included shells, bones, plants, bugs, butterflies, crystals, bits of bark, leaves, fossils, shark's teeth, bear claws, pine cones, skulls, bird nests, and a variety of quaintly constructed scientific instruments, such as weighing scales, calipers, prisms, water clocks, bell jars, journals, and a collection of assorted quill pens stuffed in a large beer stein that stood next to several bottles of jet black India ink. There were also three open wine bottles. It looked as though someone, no doubt the middle aged gentleman who lay snoring contentedly on the beach chair, had been industriously at work cataloging and evaluating a variety of natural objects and had entered the results of this scientific scrutiny in a densely copied, minutely annotated journal that Hannah saw propped open on the table and held in place with what she took to be a slag of gunnery lead. Behind the journal, a small gas burner emitted a constant blue flame that heated a black teakettle whose steam had just begun to rise.

But these were not the only changes Hannah noted.

On the main reading table, stood an odd machine. The machine, no larger than a reading lamp, reminded her of a miniature carousel. With no source of energy that she could discern, the machine twirled at an amazing rate of speed, emitting as it spun a constant purple/blue light and all the while humming pleasantly. Surrounding this machine, Hannah saw the remains of a partly eaten meal, and in the corner of the bookstore, near the front door, she observed a collection of seven, wet, black umbrellas. They all stood open. Mrs. Endicott was nowhere in sight, and outside the store, as Hannah could see quite plainly through the front window, rain, mixed with hail and shot through with sudden illuminations of lightning, descended in a mighty cataract, while in the distance low rumbles of thunder shook the display glass. It sounded like the drumming for a battle.

Suddenly, the teakettle that stood on a rack above the gas flame on the specimen table began to whistle. The man on the beach recliner broke his snores and shifted. He had not yet woken up, and Hannah moved forward nervously to silence the noisy kettle. As she did, Grumpy the cat, who had preceded her into the room, gave a hop and landed on the sleeper's stomach.

"Hoopla!" he exclaimed.

Hannah froze.

The man woke at once, with hardly a moment to transition from full slumber, and then he saw her.

"Ah, there you are! Back at last!"

He smiled. His words (slightly accented) were so focused and cheerfully spoken that Hannah turned to see if Mrs. Endicott perhaps had returned to the bookstore and stood behind her. Hannah greatly regretted the old woman's absence, since Mrs. Endicott, more than anyone, seemed somehow knowledgeable and in charge. After all, hadn't Mrs. Endicott enticed Uncle Joseph to give her that locked and unreadable book for her thirteenth birthday . . . the book (she now remembered) that she had somehow misfortunately misplaced, along with the mysterious twig that had opened it—Walter's gift? But Hannah and the reclining stranger were all alone.

"Here now," said the stranger, gently shooing Grumpy to the floor. He struggled to sit up in the wobbly beach recliner, which thankfully did not overbalance. In the process, his headgear slipped free momentarily to reveal a bald spot and thinning brown hair. The man deftly and swiftly bound the turban back in place. He tossed aside the wool blanket that had covered him while he slept and closed the book he had been reading, after marking his place with an ivory-handled paper cutter. He then stood up carefully and ceremoniously adjusted his strangely old fashioned clothes, even buttoning the front of his frock coat so that when he completed his wardrobe he stood before her in a curiously formal, courtly exotic pose. He looked like the inhabitant of an earlier century . . . *perhaps the eighteenth century*, Hannah judged. He did not wear the whitened periwigs that her imagination associated with that time, but his clothes generally reminded her of pictures she had seen of classical composers—Mozart, Haydn, and Beethoven, for example—pictures that Uncle Joseph had kept about the house.

She decided on the spot that there was something aristocratic and refined about the stranger's proud and somewhat rounded features. His impressively large eyes were clear and discerning. They reminded her of two dark pools. She could easily imagine him at work in the bookstore or hunched with scholarly diligence over a microscope in close study of the diverse and sundry natural objects that lay strewn upon the specimen table behind him, although his scientist eyes were tempered with a clear, persuasive light that suggested the sensitivities of a person at ease with inner landscapes—a scientist of the soul, Hannah deemed. The shaggy cut of his thinning hair, which, Hannah noticed, fell to the bottom of his ear lobes, (in addition to the somewhat bohemian ease of his attire . . . old fashioned though it might be)—added to the impression of a free and active spirit used to having its way. And the slightly flirtatious sparkle of his eyes told her he was a gentleman attuned to the graces of society—in particular, *women.*

All this, Hannah discerned in a split second flash, comprehending every significant detail intuitively as the stranger rose with slightly ironic courtesy and pronounced old world grace from the impromptu divan of a beach recliner to greet her. And although it would take her years to articulate all the subtleties of this first impression, everything she later thought about him was contained microcosmically in those very first few moments of their acquaintance.

Years later, she would come to appreciate how very much she owed to this event.

Hannah regarded the stranger suspiciously as Mrs. Endicott's cat Grumpy rubbed his leg.

"How do you do," he said to her formally. As he spoke, he fished from his frock coat pocket a rather ostentatious medal, which he pinned on the front of his coat above his heart with an air of gratified pomposity.

Hannah just stared.

Amused, the stranger bent down to pick up the cat. From the way he handled Grumpy, and from the fact that Grumpy didn't claw him right away, Hannah judged he had an affinity for small critters.

"Where's Mrs. Endicott?" she demanded.

"Ah," smiled the stranger, "you're quick to the point. That's good—that's excellent! What else can you remember, *Hanna'el?*"

For a moment, it felt like a cold draft from the outer storm had invaded the cozy room. Hannah shivered. At the same time, she thought that the stranger had mispronounced her name.

Before she could respond, the odd gentleman walked with the cat to the bookstore's front counter and carefully put Grumpy down. Hannah glanced past him to the rainstorm outside the store, and she looked at the collection of seven wet umbrellas near the store's front entrance.

The sight of those drying umbrellas prompted another memory to bubble unexpectedly into her mind.

The Seven Friedrichs . . .

She saw that behind the counter and bookstore's cash register, the old blackboard that the Gentleman's Benevolence Society had abandoned here long ago stood covered with freshly chalked calculations and a variety of obtuse symbols. It was a hodge podge of rune-like squibs, Hannah noted—parts resembled the seal script of the very ancient Chinese, parts seemed mathematical, parts looked hieroglyphic or alchemic, and parts resembled the fragments of a poem or shopping list. For example:

> *The pinecone, as a prehistoric emblem,*
> *Suggests obscure delineation*
> *To the fossil life about it: in Winter,*
> *All things turn to dust. Secure*
> *In their delicate reformation,*
> *These perfect seedlings caution yet . . .*
> *Such manners might resuscitate*
> *Declensions of Spinoza.*

If this were a poem, it was by far the strangest poem she had ever read, Hannah judged, although she could not deny that its meanings felt somehow troubling and familiar.

She frowned and suppressed this vagrant thought.

Suddenly, she had an idea.

"Are you the *Seventh Friedrich*?"

It was her father, she recalled, who had mentioned the Seventh Friedrich in a letter, long ago.

The stranger smiled, a bit startled and obviously flattered by the question. But, sadly, he shook his head. "No," he replied, pleased and disappointed at once, "I am not. But it is excellent that you can remember so much so soon." He nodded again at the torrent of rain outside the store. "You've traveled a very long way."

"The *Zone*," said Hannah, more to herself than to him. "*The Zone of Night.*"

The stranger scowled. "Is that what you call it?"

"What do *you* call it?"

"I call it . . . " and he said something in a language that Hannah did not understand.

While Hannah pondered this response and wondered how much she should share of her confusion or personal information, the stranger's attention shifted. He seemed to possess the sort of keen, restless intelligence that quickly tired of routine. In this case, Hannah realized, her tentative conversation bored him.

"Take a moment to think it over," he advised her sensibly. "No one's going anywhere right away."

And, turning aside from her perplexed expression, he picked up a paintbrush that lay near one of the easels and added a few strokes of watercolor to a scene he had started earlier. It was a picture of Roman ruins set in a natural landscape of cypresses and open meadows, with sheep and a scampy shepherd in the foreground. The shepherd was in pursuit of a shepherdess, who fled from him with tantalizing grace.

The stranger, Hannah noticed, had shifted with remarkable ease from their conversation to his art. He at once became completely involved in this other task, and for a moment, he simply tuned her out, as though she were of even less consequence than Grumpy the cat, who had sprawled with self-satisfied languor on the front counter to lick his forepaws. As the stranger carefully layered some colorful veil of detail onto his painting, he hummed to himself a melody that Hannah, thanks to her uncle's pedagogical influence, recognized as an aria from Mozart's *Magic Flute*. Her uncle, she remembered, had often unsuccessfully attempted various tunes from that opera on his violin. It was, Hannah remembered, a torture to hear Joseph play that instrument, for despite long years of effort he had yet to master the elementary requirement of fingering the strings in tune. The notes were frequently a nerve-torturing, quarter tone off pitch, and though the imprecision did not dampen Uncle Joseph's musical enthusiasm, it drove children, sensitive elders, cats, dogs, and just about anyone else who was not tone deaf into exile, or else (and this was terrible from the standpoint of Joseph's musical self-esteem) it doubled them over in laughter.

"*Excuse me?*" interrupted Hannah testily. She felt miffed at the quaintly dressed stranger's odd behavior and the uncanny way he now ignored her. "*Excuse me!*" she repeated more forcefully, "who are you and what are you doing here?" And then she remembered and added: "Mrs. Endicott left me in charge."

"Hmm," said the stranger, still puttering with his brushes and not even turning around to face her as he spoke. "Did she? Well, I might ask the same of you. What do *you* think you are doing here, *Hanna'el?* Or for that matter, where do you think we are?"

"My name is *Hannah*," she told him sharply. "And anyway, it's obvious where I am. We're in the bookstore. Mrs. Endicott's bookstore. It's called the *Sphinx*."

"Oh really?"

"Yes."

"Indeed?"

The stranger wiped his hands on a multi-colored paint rag and turned toward her again, smiling pleasantly. He nodded at the outer storm.

"I'm here to be your teacher. Walter sent me. I had quite a time to get here, let me tell you. And you did, too. It is no small testament to your abilities, *Hanna'el*, that you managed to get here in spite of *that*."

Again, he mispronounced her name. At the same time, he nodded at the rainstorm that battered the front windows of the store.

As she pondered what to say, he moved to the table on which the teakettle whistled strenuously.

"I'll tell you what, why don't you sit down, maybe over there at the reading table, and let's have some tea and something to eat, and then we'll chat and get acquainted. I'm quite brilliant at conversation, by the way, and my impression is that you have some talents in that direction also."

Hannah glanced at the reading table, and at the strange machine that stood in the center of it. She stubbornly repeated her earlier question: "*Are* you the Seventh Friedrich?"

The stranger laughed and shook his head. "I'm sorry, no. But that's not to imply I can't help. Why don't you sit down? I can tell you're a bit confused."

He raised one eyebrow.

"Help with what?" Hannah challenged him.

The stranger sighed. "Well, as a place to start, I can help you understand what's going on. You see, this isn't quite the bookstore that your memory tells you it ought to be. It's more like . . . well, how shall I put this . . . it's more like *Noah's Ark* . . . " He frowned. "Hmm, you do know what I mean by Noah's Ark, don't you? I can never be sure, with people of your century, what allusions we still have in common. So much has fallen into the . . . what did you call it? . . . the *Zone of Night*. I am referring to the old Hebrew Sumerian tale of Noah and the flood . . . You know that story, don't you? You've read your so-called Bible? Or, if that's not the case, maybe you've seen the story of Noah's flood in . . . what do you call those things that destroy the imaginations of pre-adolescents? . . . *cartoons?*"

"I *know* the story of Noah's ark," said Hannah archly. She was losing her patience with his verbose, circuitous manner of speech.

The stranger smiled. "From your religious studies, possibly?"

"I'm not religious," Hannah informed him. "I never went to church." She felt greatly annoyed by his segue into a patronizing, pedagogical tone of voice, and she fully gave vent to her anger. "Uncle Joseph never went to church; *I* never went to church; I don't like church; I don't like people who go to churches; I don't like priests; we don't have *religious* studies; and I barely even made it to school . . . on a regular basis, I mean . . . when I did go to it."

"Excellent!" said the stranger, genuinely pleased. "Then there's hope for you. Did your uncle tutor you at home? What was his name? Johannes?"

"Joseph."

"Ah yes, of course. *Joseph*. Well, your uncle had the right idea. What good are *facts* if they don't give birth to *ideals*? So, you've *read* the story of Noah and the flood. Well, well, that's excellent, excellent. Two thousand years of western culture have certainly not gone to waste. We have at least some common ground. And what better place than a bookstore to lodge an anchor against the flood, eh? . . . if you permit me the extended metaphor. Tea? Milk and sugar?" He picked up the kettle and a cup.

Grumpy leaped to the specimen table just as the stranger asked this question. He appeared interested in the tin of almond cookies that the stranger produced from the hip pocket of his blue frock coat.

"Black tea," said Hannah critically.

"Something to eat with it?"

"Thank you very much."

"Nothing to thank," he said politely. "Excuse me just one more moment."

And he poured some heavy cream into in a saucer for the cat, adding some crumbs of almond cookie to the top, which Grumpy greatly appreciated.

"Tell me," said the stranger, "are you interested in botany, as well as the book of Genesis?" He nodded at the large notebook that lay open next to cat's saucer.

Hannah saw that he had covered the pages of this book with large and small sketches of plants.

"Not particularly. No," she told him frankly. But to be polite, she added, "Did you do these drawings yourself?"

"Yes, I did." He seemed genuinely flattered by her interest.

Hannah had tried her hand at sketching, and she saw that the stranger had a good deal of skill, in addition to his talents as a watercolorist. "You're a very good artist."

"I'm a poet, actually," he corrected her. "All this," and he gestured at the table and the easels, "is what I do as an avocation, in my free time."

Hannah knew quite a bit about poetry from her uncle, so she quite sensibly asked him: "What sort of poetry do you write? Can you support yourself?"

"Yes, actually, I can. I've written in quite a variety of metrical styles, as well as plays and novels." He nodded at the table behind him. "I like to keep busy, as you might suspect."

And he added three cubes of sugar to his tea.

"But enough about me," he said. "Thank you for asking. Shall we sit down?" He gestured toward the table in the middle of which sat the mysterious, revolving machine.

But Hannah had had enough.

"*Who are you?*" she confronted him.

Her bluff question did not faze the stranger at all. He pulled out a chair for her to sit upon and then sat down himself, crossing his legs, left on right. "Think of me as a friend or a distant uncle. Or maybe as someone quite close to your family, in an unrelated way, like someone you might choose to call your *Uncle Bob*."

Uncle Bob seemed like a terrible choice of names for the eccentric stranger.

"Well, perhaps it is," he admitted, when she protested the choice. "Would it be better to call me Uncle Hans?"

"You're not my uncle."

He sighed. "No, I'm certainly not. Actually, the old-fashioned term for what I do is Privy Counselor. And in fact, you might say I'm here in that capacity, as Privy Counselor, to advise you privately, *Hanna'el.*" He smiled, pleased with his bon mot. "My name's not particularly important . . . I doubt that you've heard of me, even if you have done some eccentric reading in the course of your brief life, as I gather your Uncle Joseph prompted you to do. No, no, think of me as a Privy Counselor, a closet advisor, your secret friend—an associate of the Seven Friedrichs who's here in this ark of the flood to help you through some difficult times. You've had a rough go of it, obviously, haven't you?"

Hannah twitched. Had he misspoken her name again, or did she misunderstand him? Was he deliberately teasing her?

"What did you call me?"

"Excuse me," he apologized. "I used your other name. Your powers of remembrance aren't quite strong enough yet to comprehend me, are they, *Hanna'el?*"

Again, a slight chill passed through her as she heard this mispronunciation, as though a ghostly presence had entered the room.

"My name is *Hannah,*" she told him slowly, looking him directly in the eye.

"Oh yes, I know," he answered pleasantly. "Just keep saying so, if you like." He pointed to the middle of the reading table on which the odd whirligig machine continued to revolve. His expression had become quite thoughtful. "Let's see . . . how I can put this . . . How shall we thread this needle? Hmm, perhaps we should start with the experience of things as they are."

"Excuse me?"

"Look at the machine. What do you *see?*"

Hannah complied. She looked at the whirligig device, and she observed that its curious rotations seemed to require no obvious source of energy at all. (Simultaneously with this observation, the thought came into her mind: *there's no electricity in this bookstore.* Sure enough, the light bulbs that hung from the bookstore's ceiling were all unlit, and yet the store was uniformly illumined by a diffuse and soothing light whose source she could not identify and which, she noted with astonishment, cast no shadows.) This lack of electricity felt like a mighty clue, somehow, Hannah thought.

And suddenly, she remembered something else. In her garden and the home she had left behind, there had been no shadows either—and the mirrors had all disappeared.

The Privy Counselor smiled. "Now we're getting somewhere, aren't we?"

For a moment, Hannah had the weird sensation of being outside and *inside* her own body at once. Everything felt questionable.

"Where am I?"

"In the bookstore."

"Where am I going?"

"Always toward home."

For a moment, an eternal moment, the store felt completely still. The only sound was the constant, reassuring hum of the whirling device. And in that moment of silent contemplation, another memory rose into Hannah's thoughts.

Guard the green and living twig and keep it sound.

"But I lost it," she exclaimed suddenly, with horror. "I lost Walter's twig!"

The Privy Counselor smiled. "Yes, you did. I know it. 'Its a pity."

He sipped his tea.

"How do you know?"

"The Walter told me."

"Walter? Do you know Walter? Where is he?"

The Privy Counselor gestured at the storm. "He's out there somewhere, I suspect . . . in the—what do you call it?—the *Zone of Night.*"

Hannah felt suddenly quite dizzy, as though someone had taken all her thoughts and memories and had shaken them into a disordered chaos of imaginings.

"Oh god . . . " she muttered, holding her head. "Where is Brother Thomas?"

The stranger steadied her.

"There, there, *Hanna'el.* Take a deep breath. Sip some tea."

"That's not my name," she protested weakly. But she felt less sure.

Again, the Privy Counselor nodded at the revolving machine. "Concentrate. Try to remember. Only *you* can decide how to resolve these questions, but maybe I can help. That's why I'm here. I can certainly try. I am not one of the Seven Friedrichs, but I am a particularly close friend of Mrs. Endicott—Sofia—and that is the reason, I suppose, that Walter summoned me. The Seven Friedrichs are philosophers. I am not. Granted," he added proudly, "I have a philosophical bent, but I'm a natural scientist and, as I mentioned, a poet, first and foremost. I'm here to help you while the *six* Friedrichs and Sofia take care of that device."

He pointed to the whirling machine.

She had the impression that he meant that the Friedrichs and Mrs. Endicott somehow powered that mysterious instrument in its dervish dance.

"Please don't touch it," he advised her.

Hannah drew back her hand.

"The device keeps you safe for the time being. Like I said, you might think of this tiny bookstore as an *ark*."

And he nodded at the front window of the store.

The terrible rainstorm had engulfed them. The store was like a tiny bubble of light and safety submerged in that raging torrent, Hannah understood. Her comprehension came as a sudden and convincing flash of inspiration.

"What you see out there," he told her, "is the storm that has drowned nearly all the memories in your former world—*your world and mine*. The rainstorm is not really a rainstorm. It is your *imagination* of what has happened and is happening . . . the imagination of a thirteen year-old confused and frightened by that change . . . the imagination of a child who hasn't yet had time or enough experience to relate what has happened to concepts matured with age—and so, you've made sense of it as best you can. Don't feel badly. Don't think you've done anything wrong. You can just as well imagine that rainstorm as the flood at the end of time. It's happening to you, but it is also happening generally. Different people explain it in different ways. The *what-it-is* is not important; it's *how* we explain the *what-it-is* to ourselves that really counts. I'm talking about the stories we choose to tell, those tales that will determine our individual and collective destinies. It's our only human freedom; don't you know? Your life, if you choose to call it that, is nothing but story, reminiscence, and poem. Do you follow me, *Hannah?* Can you understand? This is what your uncle tried to teach you, once upon a time. Your father attempted, too. And the one you refer to as Walter. They told you: there are only stories, constantly told. We participate in them, and *they participate in us*. Some of those stories are individual—unique to an individual's destiny—some are collective. But, as Walter told you long ago, just as an individual's memory and imagination can weaken and grow ill, so can the memory and the imagination of the macrocosmic individual, the Human Being, in whom our single destinies are jointly found. You can't grasp this yet, I know. But trust me, some day you will understand. You must—you're Walter's pupil. And because you've begun the journey to the Tree, I know you have at least an intuition that what I am saying is true."

And then he winked.

What is truth? Hannah wanted to ask.

But the stranger immediately answered: "Oh don't fall into the silly trap of asking: *what is truth?* That sort of tired questioning won't help you at all. Leave that to the stodgy accountants. Better to ask: *how is truth?* Grapple with that, why don't you, and then we might get somewhere."

Hannah felt dizzy. She could not make the room remain in focus. The feeling of being two persons at once—or maybe more than two, maybe thousands—overwhelmed her momentarily, and she struggled to thrust this feeling away. For a moment, just holding to her remembrance of this bookstore felt like a desperate, physical act. She saw herself clutching tight to a granite boulder in the midst of raging rapids. If she relaxed her grip for even a brief moment, the current would tear her loose and drown her.

The Privy Counselor nodded at the outer storm. He seemed able to understand her every thought.

"It all began in what you might be able to recall as the fifteenth century," he told her, referring to the outer storm. "In my day, it already had the intensity it has now, though fewer individuals felt threatened—or at least, not in a conscious way—not like you. Poets, scientists, and philosophers were aware of what you call the *Zone of Night*, but most others felt the disturbance in only the most dreamlike, childish way. But for you, and many others like you, *Hanna'el*, the experience cannot remain a dream. No, for you and many others, that storm has become an unavoidable fact of life, a fact as real as this bookstore." He rapped on the reading table with his knuckles, to make his point. "A fact as real as who you are. You can't ignore it; you have to respond; you have no choice. To be aware of it, as you are, means that something must be done. Walter tried to explain this to you once. Can you remember his words?"

"I don't need to know this," said Hannah stubbornly. "I want to go home. I never asked to come here. I never agreed."

"We don't have to *agree*," he reprimanded her. He spoke sternly now, like a schoolmaster. "And yes, you *did* ask to come here, whether you asked explicitly or not. And you did agree—long ago. Do not blame Walter. Walter is not the one in control. You are, *Hanna'el*. And everything that's happened is a result of something you've remembered, imagined, or done."

His tone steadied her. And into that moment of inner quietude, a picture appeared: Walter afloat in his glass aquarium . . . and with that picture, the remembrance of the question she had asked the Master long ago: *Walter, what is memory?*

The stranger seemed to understand. He could follow her thoughts. "Very good, now you are learning. The line between imagination and memory is very musical and hard to discern. Only a Master can trace that boundary in utter certainly. You must learn to sleep and breathe. Others can learn the art, but it takes time. We call it the art of *hovering* . . . "

She had heard that word before. She did not know where.

"Am I hovering now?" she asked him simply.

The Privy Counselor shook his head. "Not yet, I'm afraid . . . or only partially. You might say, you are *wavering*. *Wavering* and *hovering* are similar, but even though they are similar, they are not alike—you must not confuse them. *Wavering* means that you have taken the first tentative steps. You found your way back to the bookstore, for example . . . and that's to your credit . . . even though I had to help you. Even so, there is still so very much more that you need to learn."

The Counselor's mature advice depressed and angered her.

"Walter lied to me!" Hannah exclaimed. "I came to him for help. He promised to help me. He promised he would help me if my tears ever fell in his stupid pond. He lied. He wasn't there! I never asked for this to happen. I never asked for his stupid twig! Never! I wish I had never been born!"

The Counselor's voice remained calm. "That isn't true. Think back. Everything that happened has happened because you desired it in some way. And nothing *can* happen that your desire or your questioning hasn't prepared. If you hadn't asked, Walter could never have found you, and the green and living twig would never have been yours to cherish or lose. That's why you're here. I had to employ considerable exertion to guide you into this bookstore, although much of the journey you accomplished on your own, despite the mistakes you've made, and there have been many. It is just as I've told you: this bookstore is a kind of Noah's Ark. Mrs. Endicott furnished it. But instead of all the animals two by two, male and female—as the older tale relates—Sofia has filled this ark with books. Look around you, *Hanna'el*. Contemplate these shelves. What do you see?"

Hannah allowed her glance to take in the cluttered confusion of the store.

"Books," she responded wearily. *Obviously.*

"*No*," said the Privy Counselor, "that's not so. What you are really experiencing are memories. How large is this bookstore, *Hanna'el*? Have you ever *really* explored it? Think back. The times that you visited this bookstore with Uncle Joseph—did you ever find your way to the very last shelf? How many books do you think are in here? Thousands? Millions? *Not at all.* The Sphinx is a palace of memory. There are as many books in this bookstore as there are memories in your world. They are countless as the stars in the Milky Way. From this one bookstore, entire universes spring into existence. But it all depends on something you no longer possess."

Hannah's thoughts raced ahead, as though she had already heard the stranger's words. She knew what he meant. She knew what was lacking—and she feared it.

"Walter's twig . . . "

He nodded. "Yes. *The green and living twig* that the Master gave you—*you must return it to the Singing Tree.* Only then will you find your way home. Only then will you learn to *hover*."

"But I lost it," she told him in despair. "Someone stole it."

"That's not true. The twig was stolen because you let it slip from your attention. You allowed yourself the temptation to forget. Another claimed it. But *you* must get it back. Where have you been these many days?" he asked her accusingly.

"I was at home."

"Was *home* as you remembered it?"

"Yes," she nodded. "No! I'm . . . I wasn't sure! There was no one else but me. I was all alone!"

And suddenly, it occurred to her how utterly impossible that situation had been.

"Try to remember, *Hanna'el* . . . "

"Why do you call me that? My name is Hannah!"

"Try to recall . . . "

"It wasn't *really* my home," she added, groping for recollection. "I was there all alone. Where were the others? What happened to Uncle Joseph?"

The stranger nodded, professorial and stern, although his tone of voice remained compassionate.

"The storm that began in our fifteenth century is now a raging flood. Someday you will learn of this, when you are older. We shall meet again. But for now, *Hanna'el*, you must understand your immediate task. Stop indulging in the comfort of your childhood, stop dreaming dreams of fantasy, and press onward with the quest you so haltingly began. It is . . . hmm, how shall I put this? . . . like learning to awaken inside a dream. It is like having a lengthened awareness of that moment between falling asleep and lying awake, when you hover between two worlds, two states of mind. This split that you feel—the two selves, *Hannah / Hanna'el*—the two are one. You have many names and selves; the "I" is boundless. *Names change; the I remains.* Once you grasp this, once you understand how to put the art of *hovering* to proper use, you will understand what you must do. This is the reason that Walter sent you the twig—this is the reason for your father's long absence. It is a gift. Through *hovering*, you will learn to sleep and breathe. You will find your way back to the quest that you interrupted. Ideally, the Seventh Friedrich should be the one to tutor you. He is the greatest human master of the art of *hovering* that ever lived. But the storm has grown so much worse. And so very quickly! The Seventh Friedrich is needed elsewhere. Perhaps you will meet him in that place. Concentrate, *Hanna'el!* Feel how the storm wind batters our tiny ark. The darkness extends in all directions. Only here are we safe and sheltered for the moment. Only here can we speak the Master's word. How long that moment will last, no one can predict. *You must find the Tree.*"

Hannah glanced at the whirling machine. She now could discern along its periphery seven tiny shadows that looked like human beings. With a little more effort that did not by any means involve focusing her eyes, she further discerned that the seven tiny shadows in fact consisted of the Six Friedrichs and Mrs. Endicott. The seven sat with hands clasped, each to the other, as though in a séance. Together, they ringed the whirling machine in a circle of quiet, purposive contemplation.

The Privy Counselor nodded. He approved of her diligence.

"Very good, *Hanna'el.* Now you have begun to understand. The Six Friedrichs and Sofia keep this ark afloat. It is what they promised to do. It is their gift. You remember what happened just before your journey began?" He nodded at the outer rainstorm. "Without their help, the floodtide would overwhelm you. It had nearly swept you away. Only a Master of Memory, such as Walter, can navigate those currents. Humans, even the most exceptional, such as myself, have no chance against beings so strong, *unless they learn the Singer's art.*"

His use of the word Singer momentarily confused her. She did not recall him using this term before. She did not recall ever hearing it, and she did not like it. The word *Singer* seemed to beckon her back to a place of discomfort, where she felt tired, abandoned, and confused.

"The art of *hovering?*" she asked him, attempting to focus. The bookstore walls felt very thin. Paper thin, she decided. *Japanese.*

"Yes," she heard him answer.

She could not turn back.

As much as she would have preferred to stop her ears or to

bury her head under the pillow on the sofa in Mrs. Endicott's cozy backroom, a part of her yearned to hear what the Privy Counselor had to say. It was the part of her that he had addressed as *Hanna'el*. She could feel that older person in herself, watching and observing silently—but unable to act. Somehow, she and that woman were one. But it was she, *Hannah*, who had to choose which way to go. The woman could not. For some reason, this woman, this other self, this *Hanna'el*, was lost without her help. She needed her. They needed each other. And it all began with the book that Hannah had lost—and with her story.

The Privy Counselor's words merged with her remembrance of the Master Walter. "Listen to me, Hanna'el," the Counselor said. "The Tree no longer sings. The Singing Tree of All Remembrance has fallen silent. And because it no longer sings, worlds vanish into the forgotteness of endless night. Only the human can help. If one human being were to complete the journey to the dying tree and return to its roots the green and living twig that the Masters cherish, the balance of remembrance would shift. Your father tried, but he could not do it. And now the twig has been lost. And the book that your uncle gave you—the Book of All Remembrance that only you can write—is gone as well. You cannot read it; you've lost the key. But unless you complete the journey to the Tree and confront what dwells there, the outer storm will increase. If you fail, not even the Seventh Friedrich can hold back the flood. The *Zone of Night* will drown your remembrance for eons."

Though she could not comprehend with daylight logic exactly what the Privy Counselor meant, the prospect of doom that the Counselor's words conjured forth chilled her with a feeling of panicked, unreasoned dread.

"Please," she said, "help me. What must I do?"

To her surprise, from the pocket of his yellow frock coat, the Privy Counselor drew forth the book he had been reading earlier, the one that Hannah briefly had observed spread open on his stomach when she first came into the room and saw him asleep. With a shock, she understood that this was *her* book, the book that Uncle Joseph had given her as a present on her thirteenth birthday, the book that she thought she had lost in the terrible storm. On its cover she could read the familiar words, which now made complete sense to her, where once before they had seemed a random arrangement of letters and symbols. Inside, too, as the Counselor opened the pages, she saw that the writing had reappeared. It was just the opposite to what had happened earlier on, when the pelting rain of the storm had threatened to turn the pages into a soggy, illegible pulp. Somehow, the book had dried. It was not only legible, but it was filled with characters and illustrations that she had never seen before.

Amazingly, she now could read it.

"Wait," said the Privy Counselor, "there is one more thing. I must caution you—do not allow your fantasy to guide you. You must awaken inside your dream. That is what it means to hover. You must learn to be as skillful as a scientist with what you imagine. If not, your fears and desires will overwhelm you."

Hannah barely heard him. Excited, she eagerly reached to take her journal from the Privy Counselor's hand. But he was not the Privy Counselor any longer. The entire bookstore had shifted. She found herself squatting in the ruined Chinese Pavilion, just where she once had been, while outside the dripping walls, the cold rain continued its eternal lament.

Fritz, the Master Walter's young apprentice, sat in front of her. He smiled at her quite fondly, pleased and delighted she had returned. His face looked radiant with love and agreeable acceptance.

There was nothing she needed to say and no reason to be surprised. She could shift her attention and see quite easily beyond him a textured landscape whose threads of probability and perspective extended from infinity to herself. She could move in any direction she desired along those threads. And it all felt completely natural, unified, and whole.

She smiled at Fritz.

Apprentice! The very idea made her laugh.

"I know you," she said. "*You* are the Seventh Friedrich. You're Walter's friend. You were with me all along."

Fritz said nothing, neither yea nor nay. But he smiled, and at once she completely relaxed, allowing the last bit of her hesitancy and anxiety to fall away.

"I'm *hovering* now, aren't I?"

Fritz nodded.

Yes . . .

And, thrilled by a sense of freedom that the ruined Chinese Pavilion could in no way suppress or contain, Hannah opened her journal.

She began to read it again.

PART TWO

BOOK FIVE

The El'ohyme

FLOATING

When at last Hanna'el stirred from her dreamless sleep, she saw a dense canopy of blazing stars. On the wide and silent expanse of the flowing river, the moonless sky made the stars look especially close. Hanna'el gazed up at them, lulled by the sound of water against the wooden hull of the boat that had carried her from the caverns below the Caer. She knew she had slept and that the journey through the darkness of the mountain had been long. The river, broad and soundless, extended to either side, so wide and dark that she could not discern the shores. The river seemed to mirror the river-way of stars high above her.

Hanna'el stretched. All her muscles felt cramped and painful. As she moved, the boat tipped precariously to one side, and Thomas, sleeping cramped in the boat's stern, groaned but did not awaken. She let him sleep, while her attention soon discovered a small leather-bound book afloat in a shallow pool of water that sloshed at her feet. The book lay with its covers open flat. She lifted it from the water, but its pages had already drowned. All the ink had run; the paper was sodden. Only the golden words embossed inside its cover were legible, and these were in a language she had never seen.

Operis Processio,
Multum Naturae Placet

Something else soon puzzled her. In the largest pocket of her dress, wrapped in a clear, stretchy paper that crackled when she unfolded it, lay a hunk of exotic food. Two pieces of pearl white, cake-like bread held between them what looked to be a perfectly circular piece of gray meat. The meat smelled vaguely like ham. It had been cut very thin, as thin as shoe leather, and whatever butcher had trimmed it had done a masterful job. Smeared on top of this meat was a pale brown and sticky substance that had a sweet, nutlike odor. She licked it—surprised that it tasted familiar, though her tongue could not tell her what it was. The paste had little chunks of nuts mixed into it, unlike any she had ever eaten. The food looked disgusting, but the taste, she soon discovered, was not unpleasant. She ate half the meal and saved the other half for Thomas. As she ate, she played with the queer, transparent paper in which the food had been wrapped. To her surprise, she found that it repelled water.

How had she escaped the Caer?

She remembered following a cat down the winding stairs into a dungeon where a woman had greeted her; the woman had been a prisoner in that cell. The strange woman had told her many things. But Hanna'el could only remember the feeling of that encounter. The woman's words had disappeared, as though hiding shyly and afraid to show themselves.

And there were other strange feelings as well. These, too, were like the first dim out runners of clear memories that would not draw near enough for her to befriend. One of those memories concerned a garden and a child. But that memory did not seem part of her own life. It felt more like the memory of a story or a dream. Try though she might, Hanna'el could not relate that memory to any other memory from her childhood, nor could she explain the sense of uneasy nostalgia that overcame her when she contemplated the book she had found afloat in the water at the bottom of the tiny boat. Where had this book come from? Why did she feel that the blank, waterlogged pages somehow challenged her to explain their silence?

Unable to answer these questions and nervous because she

could not, Hanna'el gently shook Brother Thomas' shoulder until he awoke.

"Thomas, where are we? What's happened?"

Thomas sat up groggily, a look of amazement on his face.

"Where is the cavern? How did we survive the whirlpool? Hanna'el, are you all right? I thought we would drown."

"What whirlpool?" she asked him. But then, another shy memory revealed itself to her attention.

Find the Tree, Hanna'el. Find it, if you would be whole.

It was a woman's voice that spoke, and as she pondered it, a question sprang to her lips.

"Where is the severed ring?" she asked Thomas. "The woman at the Caer gave it to me."

Her statement confused him. "I found you in a tomb," he told her softly, holding tight to the gunwale as he spoke. "You lay on the stones behind a lead coffin. I saw no one else but a corpse."

She did not remember finding a coffin, but it was hard to fix the details.

"Wait," said Brother Thomas. He quickly searched his robe, surprised when his hand removed from his robe's inner pocket the severed half of a golden ring.

"Is this what you mean?"

Hanna'el nodded.

The scholar shook his head. "These gifts and your visions are troubling. The ring, and before that, the shepherd's twig . . . "

"And this as well," said Hanna'el. She handed him the unfamiliar food she had found in her dress pocket.

Thomas touched with wonder the marvelous, clear paper. He, too, had never seen such curious wrapping.

"I dreamed I was someone else—a child . . . " Hanna'el told him softly, gathering more of her scattered memories. Again she felt overcome by a sensation that her body was not her own—a feeling that had seized her once before in the shepherd's hut. She remembered a garden and an empty kitchen, a pond and a ramshackle hut that barely kept out the driving rain, a calendar, a sundial, and a marvelous, golden fish . . .

"Where's the cat?" she suddenly asked Brother Thomas. "Where's Fritz?" She did not know why she called the Singer's imp by that silly name.

Thomas looked about the tiny boat in which they floated. He saw no cat. Perhaps it had drowned.

"Oh, Fritz!" Hanna'el exclaimed.

The loss of the Singer's imp, who had helped her escape the Caer, felt like an ill omen.

"There, there," began Brother Thomas.

But Hanna'el drew away. "You don't understand." She gazed at the broken ring, straining to recall the words she had heard the woman speak. She could not find them; those memories felt distant and blurred. All she could feel was a sense of anguish, and she recalled the woman's sad, insistent voice.

"I must find the Tree," said Hanna'el, surpised by this sudden conviction.

As soon as she spoke, she had the feeling: *I'm here, I have come back. I have found you . . .*

Brother Thomas put down the food he been chewing and placed his hand on her arm. His eyes glistened like the starlight, and his voice became even more thoughtful and soothing. He frowned. "Hanna'el, you must understand that the Tree is merely a legend. We have discussed this before. You had best count yourself lucky to be alive. We've escaped Aeron's Caer. That in itself is a miracle. We must put behind us any regrets and misgivings and find our way home to Arcatus as soon as possible. You will be needed there soon enough."

"But my father believed in it. He believed that the Tree had power to bring the dead back to life. There must be some truth to the legend."

Brother Thomas paused for a long moment before responding in a calm, pedagogical tone of voice. "Hanna'el, whatever happened at the Caer, it could not have been your father's voice that spoke from the Singer's harp. Singers are no better than actors, tricksters, or magicians. They are men with no fixed loyalties or convictions— artists and entertainers. They live in disregard for the rules that give sense and order to our lives. You know that as well as I. Men like that are dangerous. They are tempters. They have the skill to manipulate and mislead our hopes and dreams—to distract us from our duties and from the anchored, common sense routine of our daily lives. Do not be tempted. You're a woman now, a princess . . . no longer a child who delights in trickery and tall tales. Whatever power a Singer appears to have, he has because you unwittingly lend him your belief. Dead men cannot speak, much as we might wish it. You must not allow your hopes to mislead reason."

"It was not a deception," she insisted. "My father spoke to me. I heard him. You were not there."

Thomas frowned.

"This is a minor accomplishment that any skilled performer can master. I have seen statues appear to speak and move. It is a trick. You wanted to hear; you needed to hear—and all that the Singer had to do was allow the illusion to appear. You willed it to be so. Your own hope and desire has misled you."

"But the imp . . . the others saw and heard it, too. The imp changed its shape."

Thomas scoffed. "They heard and saw something . . . but what? Did you have time to compare objectively what you think you saw and heard? Singers play upon our passions; that's why they are artists. You cannot trust them."

"But how do you explain what happened?" She gestured at the wide expanse of river on either side, and at the sky brilliant with stars. "How did we get here?"

Thomas shrugged. "We were lucky. Luck and coincidence are not to be denied. But a healthy mind accepts good fortune with humility, knowing that chance and the mere random play of events can also lead to disaster. Can you explain our escape in any better way?"

"Not yet . . . No. I can't remember."

"Accept this good fortune for what it is."

"But it was more than chance," Hanna'el insisted. "I know it. I am sure. My father spoke from the Singer's harp. He believed the ancient legends. He believed in the Singing Tree. *Walter told me.*"

Thomas raised one eyebrow. "Who is this Walter you've mentioned several times?"

But Hanna'el could not answer this question either. She realized she either did not remember or did not know.

"Very well," said Thomas, when she remained silent. "It is best not to complain. We're lucky to be alive, as I said. Let's take our bearings and get ashore. Once on land, we can work our way homeward to Arcatus."

"No," said Hanna'el stubbornly. "I cannot go back. I must go on."

"On?" said Thomas. "But how? Why? We have no food; we have no weapons, no soldiers to protect us. We have no map or understanding of this land. Returning home will require another miracle." He gestured at the river on either side. "One miracle is enough. Don't challenge fate."

"No," she said, "you're not listening. You don't understand."

"I understand that you are exhausted," said Thomas. "I am, too. And this is not the time to come to a decision. What's best to do will reveal itself when we're ashore."

"But I must go on. I have to."

Thomas sighed and reached within his robe, shifting his shoulder blades as though scratching at a flea. He took out a leather pouch. "Look here," he told her, dumping a handful of golden coins from the leather bag into his hand. "I carried these coins for an emergency. It is enough wealth to buy us horses and food. We can use them to hire a guide and protector who can lead us home. Let's talk no more about the impossible. The possible is difficulty enough."

Hanna'el did not answer. She set her mind instead toward the first difficulty, which was to pilot the boat ashore.

DAOSHIN

The boat had a set of oars, though neither Thomas nor she had any experience at rowing. Thomas felt too ill and sore to do much work, so Hanna'el rowed as best she could. They made little progress, for the boat had floated to the middle of the river, which, as they discovered, flowed swiftly and stretched more than a mile wide.

As the light brightened in the east, they caught their first glimpses of the shore. Arbitrarily, Hanna'el pulled to the left; she had no idea which way might serve them better.

The sun had risen quite high by the time they set about landing their tiny craft. At this stretch, the river flowed through a semi-forested land. The trees grew close to the water, and the current near the forest churned fast and treacherously. Several times Hanna'el attempted to bring them in, and twice they nearly capsized. Thomas could not swim. This and her awkward rowing kept them adrift far longer than she liked.

At last, they saw near them a broad field of ripening corn that grew upon a bluff. The corn stood tall, green and golden, swaying in the gentle breeze of the afternoon. Just downstream, behind a copse of trees, smoke rose to the sky—smoke that they thought came from a chimney—while ahead they heard the growl of angry waters.

"Rapids!" Thomas exclaimed. He lurched forward and nearly capsized the boat.

Hanna'el shouted him back to his seat. She seized the oars and bent her back to the labor. Her hands, blistered by the morning's work, ached and protested as she pulled; each stroke made her muscles tremble. The current had increased, and as they drew near the open meadow, the water became shallow and roiled. Unless they made a landing they would sweep past the meadow and into the swifter current ahead, and Hanna'el feared that even the smallest collision would upset them.

"Crouch down," she ordered. "I'm going for that beach."

Thomas, pale and wide-eyed, said nothing.

Hanna'el dipped in her oars and pulled as forcefully as her painful muscles would allow, but just as she started rowing, the bow struck a hidden boulder. The collision spun them around, and Hanna'el could not control their drift. She saw the meadow rapidly passing—soon it would be too late to land.

Another rock struck the hull, and the force of this impact startled her so much that she lost her grip. One oar came loose from the oarlock and floated away. She cursed and used the other as best she could.

She saw that the current now swept them from the shore. They were only twenty feet from land, but twenty feet of water might as well be twenty miles. Thomas crouched and moaned. "Hold on," she warned him. As the boat drifted past another rock, she thrust out her oar and gave them a push. The lunge did nothing to alter their course, but the movement toppled her off balance. She fell into the river, screaming, and Thomas, horrified by this accident, leaped to his feet. His sudden movement capsized the boat.

The current ran fast, but it took Hanna'el only a moment to realize she could stand. The water came to her waist, but each time she tried to catch her balance on the slippery river rocks, the swift current bowled her down. She saw Thomas hit the water, and she lunged to seize him. The old scholar coughed and thrashed, probably not even realizing he could touch bottom, and his desperate efforts overwhelmed her. His wool robe weighted them both like an anchor. Repeatedly, her head passed under water, but she held on to him somehow and struggled to stand.

Then the current hurled her against a fallen cottonwood whose trunk jutted from the shore. The tree saved her life, for it gave her the stability she needed to stand up. She yelled for Thomas to come to his senses, and the scholar, thankfully, had enough strength left to obey. Thrust against the tree, he found his footing, and the two waded awkwardly to shore.

Thomas reached the grasses first and collapsed, coughing as though his lungs would turn inside out. Their clothes hung sodden, and the weight pulled them heavily to the ground. Hanna'el's dark hair lay plastered to her muddy face. She flung it back and knelt next to the scholar, slapping him on the back to help him breathe.

The sound of barking dogs drew her up. For a moment, she wondered whether her ears had played her some trick, then she heard the barking again, louder and frantic. Desperate, she glanced about for a weapon, though all she saw was a single, egg-sized stone.

Like a sudden gust of wind, two dogs burst over the edge of the bluff, tumbling down a trail that led to the water. Hanna'el didn't have time to fight or even scream. The dogs leaped at her, knocking her down, but it didn't take her long to realize they meant no harm. Barking with excitement and wagging their tails, they licked and fawned upon her. Thomas, too, received a welcome. He had never liked dogs, and he shouted with disgust as his face became wet from their friendly slobber.

"Down! Get down!" a loud voice shouted, and the dogs at once fell back.

Hanna'el wiped the hair and dust from her eyes and looked up to see a short, barrel-chested man staring at her from the edge of the river bluff.

Round and sturdy like a stump, the stranger had a face tanned and wrinkled from the sun and eyes that shone brightly through slanted lids. He laughed when he saw her, resting his weight on a staff that he carried for walking. The long beard that grew from his chin reminded her of elders she had known in her homeland. Moving with surprising ease, the stranger leaped from the overhang and scampered down the path to her side. "Here now," he said, offering his hand, "I saw your boat approach and how you steered it. That was as clumsy a landing as any I've seen. It takes some skill to drown in two feet of water."

His hand, as Hanna'el took it, felt solid as oak. One pull of his arm nearly lifted her off the ground.

He seemed three times her age or older; his hair, dark as her own, had been pulled tightly back into a topknot to keep it from his face. He stood only a hand's breadth taller than she, shorter than Thomas, whose lanky height made him walk with a perpetual scholar's stoop.

The stranger laughed. "Little sister, you look frightful. My name's Daoshin, and these are my forests and pastures. Do not be afraid, I am El'ohyme. Come with me to my home, I'll make you comfortable. My wife, Maea, will dry you out."

Hanna'el saw no choice but to agree. Brother Thomas looked pale and very weak and had not said a word. She knew he needed shelter.

"My name is Hanna'el of Arcatus," she answered, doing her best to put authority into her voice. "This is Thomas, my companion and tutor."

But Daoshin silenced her with a shake of his hand. "Don't talk until we meet Maea. Whatever you say, you'll have to say again if Maea doesn't hear. Come on, *Hanna'el of Arcatus*," he said teasingly. "Bring your companion and follow me. I'll keep an easy pace."

With the dogs wagging their tails, Daoshin turned left to a trail that climbed the bluff, not bothering to see if she had obeyed. Walking close to Thomas lest he stumble, Hanna'el came along.

THE EL'OHYME

Daoshin's lands extended along the shore where Hanna'el and Thomas had nearly drowned. She soon discovered that he had built his wooden house into a steep hillside that overlooked a bluff that bordered the river. As Hanna'el approached, she could see the smoke that rose from the house's chimney, and she soon saw also the outer barn that housed the animals. The barn's roof was thatched and its walls a mixture of timber, straw, and river clay. Pens for sheep and pigs surrounded the barn, and chickens roamed freely in the yard. Behind the house, in a clearing, she saw fields of rice, barley, and wheat.

Daoshin strode quickly over his fields, keeping a pace hard but not impossible for his tired visitors to follow. As they approached the yard of his farm, Hanna'el saw a woman appear on the green hillside to greet them. She had the same facial features as her husband but none of Daoshin's squatness, although she stood no taller than Hanna'el. She wore her dark, silky hair pulled back and gathered together, and her clothes were simple wool: a blue skirt and yellow blouse fastened at her hips by a cloth belt of many colors. Unpretentious though she looked, she possessed an authority, inner grace, and beauty that Hanna'el felt at once. Daoshin introduced her as his wife.

The woman smiled—her name was Maea—and spoke a greeting in an accent thick as her husband's. Instead of asking questions, as Hanna'el had expected her to do, she clapped her hands and ordered them all into the farmhouse, bowing graciously as they entered.

"Sit by the fire. Daoshin, get the old gentleman out of his dripping clothes. He can change behind the screen. Here's a blanket to wrap him with. We'll dry his robes outside in the afternoon sun."

The room to which she led them stretched lengthwise along the hill. The outermost wall faced south, so that the room was well lit. The light, thought Hanna'el, had a green and wavering charm, as though the grass upon the hillside had softened it. The walls had been paneled in pine that had yellowed with the years to a soothing tone of amber. The furnishings were simple—only enough to serve the couple's daily needs, Hanna'el guessed, with straw mats near the window for sitting and conversation—and from the looks of things Hanna'el concluded that Daoshin and Maea lived alone. Judging by Daoshin's age and friendly disposition, she had expected to meet some children.

The woman, Maea, dished a hot broth from a kettle that hung simmering above coals in an open cookpit, and she offered it to Hanna'el in a wooden bowl. "Eat," she said simply. It was not an invitation, but an order that left room for no argument. While Hanna'el ate, Maea found her some clothes. "Mine will do," she said, "though you're too skinny to fill them out properly. Poor little rabbit, you look half-drowned. Where'd you come from? Daoshin says you can't be river-born—not if you swim so badly."

And she laughed.

Hanna'el took another long sip of the broth and felt its warmth with gratitude. She answered that she came from the steppes of Arcatus, though she hesitated to tell much more than her proper name.

Maea seemed not to mind.

While Thomas stood changing behind the screen, assisted by Daoshin, Maea pulled off Hanna'el's wet and clinging clothes. She did not ask permission, but Hanna'el gladly submitted to her care. It felt good to be doted upon.

"You have the look of the eastern steppes in your face," agreed Maea. She paused and gazed at Hanna'el, as though judging her character. The look was deep and penetrating, but at the same time Maea's gentle authority felt oddly comforting. "Wherever you come from, *Hanna'el*, whatever you fear, the El'ohyme will give you shelter and help. This is *our* country. You are safe here."

Hanna'el blushed, not knowing what to say and feeling

suddenly helpless and awkward now that she stood half undressed. "You don't even know me."

"A person's character's plain enough," said Maea sharply. "Take this towel to your dripping hair. Use this brush. I imagine you're very pretty once you're clean."

Thomas, coughing and sniffling, shyly emerged from behind the screen. His long, skinny white legs stuck out from a gray blanket and made him resemble a sad and ungainly bird. He looked red-eyed and exhausted and he had no energy for talking, except to mutter that he was grateful for their help and for his life. When Maea suggested he lie down, he did not protest. Hanna'el encouraged him with a look that told him she felt safe and comfortable in this house, and Thomas, nodding slightly, shuffled stoop-shouldered after Daoshin to a tiny bedroom. In a moment, Daoshin returned laughing, saying that the scholar had fallen asleep almost as soon as his body touched the mat.

"And what's this?" said Maea, turning out the pocket of Hanna'el's dress.

To her surprise, Maea held up a severed ring, the ring that Hanna'el had placed there for safekeeping—the ring that the woman in the Caer had given her. *What was her name?* Miraculously, the severed ring had not fallen out of her dress pocket when Hanna'el had thrashed and floundered in the river.

"That's mine!" was all that Hanna'el managed to respond.

Maea held out the severed ring, but before Hanna'el could take the golden fragment from the woman's thumb and forefinger, Daoshin seized it. He held it in his palm long enough for Hanna'el to see, then made a fist, and when he opened his hand, the severed ring was gone.

"Where did it go! Give it back to me! It's mine!" exclaimed Hanna'el.

Daoshin laughed, and, like a magician, he swiftly passed his hand behind her ear and fetched the trinket back, handing it to her before she could jerk away.

"Now," he said, winking, "suppose while the old gentleman slumbers you tell us how you escaped from Aeron's Caer?"

And Hanna'el, despite her resolve to be cautious, flushed as she self-consciously shut her mouth. She had said nothing that might have hinted they had come from the Caer. Reflexively, she began to speak denials, but Maea came close and took her hand. She patted Hanna'el's cheek like a fond aunt or mother.

"My dear, you're safe in our country. Didn't I tell you? We're El'ohyme. You can be yourself here. You can relax. No one will harm you. We're a modest folk, but we have powers that others respect."

"The river told me everything about you," Daoshin explained, growing serious. "I was on my way to help you land your boat, but before I could get there you fell in. Maea, you should have seen the old scholar thrash and scream."

Maea frowned at her husband's laughter while offering another bowl of steaming soup to Hanna'el. "*You're Hanna'el of Arcatus, Carlon's daughter,*" she said as she passed Hanna'el the bowl. "The river told us. The river recalls."

Daoshin lit his pipe.

"It was years ago that Carlon of Arcatus, your father, passed this way. He spoke of you often."

"My father?" Hanna'el repeated in astonishment. "You knew him? My father was here?"

"He was our guest," said Daoshin, nodding, "just like you. Carlon followed the land route; you came by water. The water route is more difficult—and less direct. Carlon stayed with us for many seasons. We taught him the ways of the El'ohyme. He seemed quite content here, but then, one day, he at last resolved to resume his quest."

Hanna'el trembled at these words. Tentatively, she voiced a question. "His quest for the Tree of All Remembrance?"

Daoshin smiled. "Yes. That is its name. Carlon chose to follow the Crystal Highway to the border of Urd. He could not be detained. He sought the fabled Tree that sings on the shore of the western ocean, in a place that the legends call Elowyn." Daoshin paused for a moment as thick blue smoke filled the room. His wife remained silent while he puffed. Daoshin looked at Hanna'el knowingly and raised his left eyebrow as though inviting her to speak or question him. "And now, *Hanna'el of Arcatus*, you, too, have sworn a quest to find him . . . "

His sentence remained floating.

Hanna'el's thoughts were racing. "Did my father stay with you? Where is he now?"

"He stayed with others," said Daoshin calmly. "But we knew him. He visited here." He paused and looked at his wife. They seemed to converse silently. "The river flows to Urd, but it's hard to get news from that direction. The ruins of Urd have been impassable for generations. No one knows what happened to your father when he entered that ancient land. Those humans who attempt to travel through Urd seldom return—I know of no one who's come back. Thus it's been since time beyond recall."

"But is my father still alive? He must be alive. The Singer told me."

Daoshin and Maea again exchanged looks.

"Your father came to the El'ohyme and asked for our help. I heard that he spoke with the Elders in Wushan, a district north of here. I am told that the Elders advised him and aided his quest, and that a Singer once visited them—though what was said or where this Singer went when he left our country, no one can tell. For myself, I do not believe that the Singer visited Wushan, for the Elders there are not so free with their speech—they guard their wisdom jealously and are difficult to find. The Elders of Wushan have no interest in Singers—they are students of those whom they call the Masters of Forgetting and Recall."

"Who are these Elders? I must speak with them," said Hanna'el eagerly.

Maea cleared her throat. She looked at her husband sternly. "Daoshin, it's not right to raise her hopes too far."

Daoshin nodded. "The Elders are no longer in Wushan. They have dispersed. But even if you found one or two of them, they are helpless without the others. They must gather together in one place to access their wisdom. That is the way of things. But the Elders seldom gather any longer, I have heard. Their time lies in the past."

"How many Elders are there?"

"Seven. But some say there are nine."

"Some say twelve," Maea added.

Her husband frowned. "I think that is wrong. There are only seven."

"Where have they gone?" Hanna'el asked.

"Here and there, throughout the world, until the currents of time reassemble them. They were last in Wushan when your father began his quest, or so I have heard. The Elders of Wushan serve the Singing Tree and its Masters. They are known by other names as well."

Daoshin leaned back in his chair and glanced out a window that overlooked the swaying, sunlit branches of a chestnut tree. He spoke with a musing tone, his eyes fixed on the chestnut's mingled green and gold. "Once I would have followed Carlon gladly, but that was years ago. The Tree of All Remembrance grows in the land of Elowyn, but the path to its branches leads through Urd. Your father surely crossed that border, but what befell him in Urd is unknown to any living man. Urd is a deserted wasteland; no human being lives there."

As though hearing someone else speak inside her, Hanna'el interrupted Daoshin with an urgent question, using words that felt foreign when she spoke. "But does the Singing Tree really exist?"

Daoshin closed his eyes. He answered guardedly, weighing each word. "Some swear that it does. Some swear that in better times human beings could glimpse the Tree's broad branches in the glow of the rising or setting sun. Its music is different at sunset than at dawn. They say that faint echoes of the Tree's singing overcome human beings as they fall sleep. You can hear it, some claim, in the moment between wakefulness and slumber. Others deny that this is possible any longer. They say that the Tree has sickened, or even died. Others claim that the Tree still sings as it always must, but that humans have grown too coarsened to hear its subtle music. They lack the sensitivity."

At once Hanna'el startled, for she remembered something from her dream. She saw again the young shepherd who had given her the green and living twig. She recalled what he had said. "Keep it with you," he had warned her. "Walter says to wear it about your neck." And later, hadn't the sad-face woman warned her again? She could almost recall that woman's name. *You have lost the shepherd's gift—another has claimed it. You will find your way much harder for its loss.* What had she meant? Who was she? And why did her words summon such uneasy feelings?

For a moment, Hanna'el felt that her sense of self and identity was about to splinter, but Daoshin's voice drew her back.

She saw him watching her.

Daoshin nodded as though he had followed her recollection. As he spoke, she had the sense that he did not intend his words for her at all, but that he spoke through her or around her, as though to an unseen visitor who had entered the room.

Daoshin said: "The Lords of Memory who serve the Singing Tree are older than the race of men—older than the folk of the Karakala, older than Urd, older than the Guir—perhaps as old as the fabled Tree itself. The Makers created them—those whom we honor as Masters. Once, perhaps, those Masters were human, but their humanity lies ages in the past. Now they are Masters—beings of wisdom and splendor—for they tend the eternal currents of forgetting and recall, and the Tree is their foremost treasure."

For a moment, just a moment, Hanna'el felt herself drawn from the narrow, homely farmhouse. She remembered her recent dream: the strange old man who had met her in that green and blossoming place. She remembered his name—*it had been Walter!*— but in the dream she had not been the person she was now. She had been someone else. A child. Not yet a woman.

Surprised, she found herself speaking, as though speech might distract these troubling thoughts, and with halting words she recounted the events at Aeron's Caer. Daoshin listened but made no comment; his face had furrowed with consideration. But then he smiled.

"You should rest," said Maea. "After you rest, we shall talk this through. You're safe here; no one will find you. You may stay here as long as you like."

Hanna'el nodded gratefully. She did feel frightfully exhausted, though not because of her swim. She felt wearied by this conversation and by her efforts to recall. She smiled at Maea and gratefully allowed the woman to lead her to a bed. *Later,* she thought, *later we will talk this over.* Later she might find the strength to remember more.

MAEA

Hanna'el awoke to the patter of heavy rain. For a moment, she thought that she floated on the river, resting in the boat that had carried her from Aeron's Caer. This thought transformed into an image of a ramshackle hut where she saw herself resting in the midst of a driving rainstorm. The ruined hut stood by the shores of a shallow pond, and she saw that she shared the hut with someone else—was it the shepherd who had given her the mysterious twig? She remembered a name—*Hannah*—a name like her own.

Surprised, she raised her head. A small, yellow candle flickered near the mat where she slept. Its feeble light barely filled the simple room of the farmhouse. She heard snoring and guessed that it was Daoshin or Brother Thomas—the old scholar had always slept restlessly. *What time is it*, she wondered. *Already past midnight?* She had tossed aside her coverlet in her sleep; perhaps that was why she had awakened. As she reached to retrieve the blanket, she heard footsteps on the broad, uneven floorboards outside her room.

Maea, wearing a blue nightgown and carrying a candle, her dark hair ungathered and loose about her shoulders, came into the narrow room where Hanna'el slept. Smiling, Maea asked if she could rest and talk, and Hanna'el nodded. The woman knelt gracefully.

The rain fell more loudly outside.

"I heard you stir and wondered if you might be unwell," Maea said. "A fall into the river can chill a person to the bone."

Hanna'el nodded, glad for the woman's attention and kindness. Something in her manner felt so familiar, especially in the candle-lit shadows. She thought of Sylvia, the nurse who had raised her as a child. How long it had been since she had recalled her—but no,

235

that wasn't so. She had thought of her often while living in Arcatus. But she had left those thoughts behind when she rode to Aeron's Caer. So much had changed in so short a span of time. It felt as though years had passed since she had left her home on the steppes. She felt so very distant from those memories of her childhood.

The remembrance of Sylvia made her sad. Sylvia had died when she was seven, and since that time Hanna'el had not known another woman she loved so much. Brother Thomas was her friend, advisor, and confidant—more like an elderly uncle than a teacher—but there were thoughts she could never share with him, Hanna'el knew—feelings and emotions that she had never been able to voice.

Maea saw Hanna'el's troubled glance. "You may stay here as long as you like," she said again gently, stroking her hair. Maea's warm hand felt reassuring. "Perhaps your enemies will search for you when they learn you escaped the Caer, but they will not be able to find you. No evil can come here. We are El'ohyme. Later, if you wish to return to Arcatus, Daoshin and I will help. There are tracks to your homeland that go far around the Caer. Routes that evil men do not know and will never discover."

Hanna'el yielded to the woman's gentle touch and wanted to do nothing more than lay back and be comforted, but she recalled her conversation with Daoshin.

"The Elders of Wushan that Daoshin mentioned . . . they may know something of my father's quest. Can I speak to them?"

Maea frowned. "It is as my husband Daoshin told you. Even the El'ohyme cannot summon the Elders at will. Here or there, if you are lucky, one or two of the Elders might be found, but unless all seven of them assemble with good will, you can learn nothing of what they know, for individually they are quite helpless and even stupid. It is useless to seek the Elders of Wushan; *they must find you.* Haven't you had enough trouble in your life? Fix your attention on the present. It is far better that you rest with us in safety. Every journey has its season; you must learn to abide the tempo of your quest. Learning to trust that tempo is like learning to sleep and breathe."

Hanna'el swallowed and fell silent, feeling a strange chill as

Maea spoke. Her words felt strangely familiar, as though she had dreamt them. For a moment, she felt as though two souls inhabited her body. One slept; the other watched.

"Sleep," said Maea, casting a glance toward the shadowed interior of the farmhouse and nodding at the sound of snores that came from the adjoining rooms. "My husband and I will help you, no matter what."

Unable to explain herself, Hanna'el said good night. But long after Maea had left, she still considered the woman's words. She thought again of her old nurse Sylvia and of the years she had spent under Sylvia's care. She remembered Sylvia's voice and habits, the stories she had told her and the way the nurse had sung her to sleep when she lay ill or troubled. Even now, she could recall those songs, whose words were in a dialect of the steppes. She hummed one now. The melody felt as fresh and new as the very first evening she had heard it.

The rain continued steadily until morning. Its insistent, soothing rhythm soon became a backdrop to her dreams.

REPOSE

That same night Thomas fell ill with fever and was not able to stir from his bed for many weeks. During the time he lay ill, Hanna'el kept herself busy about the farmstead, helping Maea and Daoshin do the chores that they ordinarily tended alone. She took care of Thomas and cheered him as best she could, fearing at first that the old scholar might have permanently damaged his health. Maea, who had seen such illness before, assured her all would be well if only he rested, but Hanna'el remained skeptical until the fever finally broke. Thereafter she left Thomas to rest in the room that had become his private quarters, and she did not trouble him with talk of what they were to do, for each time she mentioned these questions, the scholar complained of weakness and fragile health.

Indeed, she did not know herself what action was best. On the night that Maea had visited her, she had felt certain that she should leave this place of safety as soon as possible. Thomas' illness broke the momentum of this resolve, and her hosts did little to remind her of her purpose. She sometimes wondered if Daoshin and Maea conspired to keep her in their home; and yet, she had to admit, she greatly enjoyed her days and nights in the grassy house by the flowing river. When she questioned Daoshin about the country to the west or if, when Thomas recovered, they might buy ponies to continue their journey—or, as she worked near Maea in the garden, when she asked again if she might with Daoshin's help at least try to find the mysterious Elders in Wushan to learn more of her father's quest for the fabled Tree—neither Daoshin nor Maea gave her clear answers. She wondered where the other El'ohyme dwelt, for she saw no one except Daoshin and Maea, who appeared quite content and self-sufficient. Their peaceful farm by the river was like a small, well-tended island or oasis of well-being and friendship. Time lengthened unnoticed within its boundaries. Even Thomas, when he recovered enough strength to move about, said nothing about leaving. He no longer spoke of Arcatus. This settled, orderly life suited his scholar's temperament, and Daoshin kept a library—a small collection of histories, legends, and poetry—which he invited Thomas to use whenever he liked. The scholar soon spent hours in quiet contemplation, abandoning Hanna'el to Daoshin and Maea, whose solitude enveloped her irresistibly.

At first, it surprised Hanna'el that she felt so content. But as weeks and months went by, she blended with harmonious ease into the companionable rhythm of this experience.

As the days flowed by, she found less and less occasion to disrupt this rhythm.

Sometimes she tried to draw Daoshin into conversations concerning the lands that lay to the west or the legend of the fabled Singing Tree, but each time she spoke of these subjects, Daoshin grew reticent, or else, with good humor and tact, he changed the subject. His wife was the same. "Stay with us," Maea once said on an afternoon that the two of them had spent pleasantly baking bread. "We've always lived alone with no child to brighten our lives. You can be as a daughter to us. The river wanted to bring you here—that's what Daoshin believes, and I think he's right. What's the use in journeying west? The lands to the west are dangerous, plagued with outlaws, unsafe for a young woman and an old man. You'd need an armed escort to travel safely, and even then, you'd risk attack. Then, too, lately we hear the river whisper news from the Caer. There's been a struggle for power, though the details remain vague. It is whispered that Aeron's only son, the lost Prince Raemond, has returned. They thought he was dead, but in fact, he matured in exile, ignorant of his identity until he came of age to seize the throne. It is whispered that this Raemond has wrestled rulership from his father and that with the help of Aeron's physician he has become a dread warrior sworn to vengeance on all whom he deems an enemy. Aeron has been deposed. Aeron's son, Prince Raemond, occupies the ancient Caer, and he has set armies in motion to attack any country he believes to threaten him or the interests of his kingdom. They march to the east, west, north, and south—so the river whispers—and wherever Raemond perceives a threat or challenge, he strikes first and piteously to destroy the least contender. His weapons are always at readiness, driven by fear. I do not advise you to leave this protected place. The river whispers that even the peaceful grasslands of Arcatus are threatened."

Hanna'el nodded, knowing that Maea meant her well. Even so—and despite her growing affection for the woman—a part of her stood distant and reserved. Though it seemed that each day this distant and reserved second self grew less insistent, it never fell silent entirely. Always, if she allowed attention to this other self, she heard it whisper a warning that she must leave. She heard this voice most clearly at night as she hovered between wakefulness and sleep, and hearing it, she then lay awake for hours trying to piece together her jumbled memories and thoughts. She often wished that her cat had not disappeared. The cat, who was really the Singer's imp, had been sent to guide and help her, she was sure. He had been with her in the Caer, for she had carried him on her shoulders down the ladder to the boat. And in her dream, he had been with her in the mysterious, dreamlike garden that increasingly came to remind her of a distant, abandoned home.

THE VOICES AT THE RIVER

Many, many weeks after Thomas had fully recovered from his illness, Hanna'el decided to accompany him on one of his leisurely, contemplative riverside walks. She had tried several times to speak to Thomas privately, away from the keen ears of Maea and Daoshin, yet each time she had sought an opportunity, events somehow conspired to distract her and keep them apart.

A decision had to be made to leave or stay, Hanna'el saw; and unless she made it soon, she feared she would never make that decision.

This long delay with the El'ohyme bothered her, but not enough to make her desperate, she admitted. In moments of candor, she confessed to herself that she enjoyed this seemingly timeless sojourn with Daoshin and Maea. Months had passed since her arrival, and still no date had been set for her departure. Whenever the late evening conversation flowed to the subject of her quest, she found her journey discussed in the way one might discuss or retell a very old and familiar legend, a legend whose only purpose was to entertain.

Hanna'el felt worried and in doubt. In the weeks that had passed, she had seen the plum trees blossom and had watched as their downy white flowers, swarming with bees, had mingled with the budding leaves, and then she had seen those delicate flowers wash away in the pelting rains of early spring and had waited each day as the plum leaves, tinged reddish gold, grew large on the gnarled branches, sheltering the fruit that slowly ripened for the harvest. By now, the light had changed, and the air had become much cooler in the morning and at night. In only a few more weeks, the first frost of autumn would overtake them. She knew she had to act soon, if she were to act at all. To delay into autumn meant lingering through winter. And by next spring she feared she would be so much at home with the El'ohyme that she would never find the inner discontent to leave this settled farmland.

Thomas kept silent as they walked together across a golden meadow, recently cut, following the same path that Daoshin had used when he met them on the riverbank the day they had arrived. Whenever the subject of their conversations threatened to stray toward a decision to leave or stay, the old scholar became taciturn and moody.

Hanna'el spoke haltingly, often starting her sentences several times. At last, she arrived exhausted at the wall of the scholar's stubborn silence.

She did not know how to proceed. She had run out of words. Lately, she had found it increasingly difficult to argue with Thomas. Worse, and even more disturbing, was the thought that her passion to argue had diminished. The settled life with Daoshin and Maea had changed her. She could feel that inner fire of restlessness had subsided to a modest flame. Each night she fell asleep with greater ease. Each day it felt harder and harder to contemplate moving on. As the weeks flowed past she no longer dreamed of her father, her father's quest, or the mysterious garden—and worse, the prospect of travel had begun to feel too much like the wearisome and frightening ordeal. She felt she had to act soon or not at all.

"Thomas, you're not understanding what I mean. Please, if you felt as I do . . . "

"That's just the problem, isn't it?" Thomas challenged her. "If I *felt* instead of speaking to the facts, we'd meet disaster."

Hanna'el drew a breath and kept her tone patient, for the scholar did not react well to confrontation. Again, she explained that she had made a plan. Aeron—or whoever had replaced him— would watch the roads leading eastward to Arcatus, since that was the logical route for them to take. Instead, she argued, they should travel westward on the highway to Urd by stealth and in disguise. It was the route that her father had taken years ago.

Thomas laughed, and his voice took on a sarcastic edge. "Disguised? Disguised as what? As outlaws? You've heard Daoshin's tales; the highway's too dangerous—and especially dangerous for folk such as us who travel unprotected. We'd likely lose our lives. Hanna'el, you must be reasonable. I'm old and you're a young woman. We have no way to defend ourselves—none at all. I beg you; be reasonable. When you announced your plan to ride to Aeron's Caer from Arcatus, I did not oppose you, though I judged the plan risky enough. Still, I was willing to take that risk, because when I weighed the advantages and dangers there always seemed a chance you might prevail. Your mission was just; your appeal to Aeron had the weight of tradition and civility behind it. What you now propose to do is nothing like that earlier choice. Then you had men behind you, armed warriors. Not enough, as it turned out, but more than we have now. Now we have nothing, Hanna'el. No strength, no options—no choice but to remain here where it is safe. Were your father still alive to advise you, I am certain he would tell you the same. I owe it to his memory to speak plainly. Your plan is foolish."

They had climbed a gentle slope, and from the hilltop, they could look down upon Daoshin's pleasant farm. The land, awakened by recent showers and a warming sun, appeared lush and fertile and inviting. Rooks and butterflies darted above the grasses, rising and falling like waves of visible wind, and late season wild flowers of many colors enlivened the rolling hills. Hanna'el realized that already she had begun to think of this place as home. She turned to Thomas and saw him frowning darkly. She saw that he loved this homeland, too.

"Hanna'el," he said slowly, softening, "if I thought that there was the slightest chance that your father was still alive, I would endorse your decision entirely. But reason argues against it. Think it through. What proof do you have that Carlon's alive? Only the assurance of a vagrant Singer. Only a legend that an adult would recite to pacify a moody child."

He pulled at his left ear lobe as he spoke, as he often did when he became thoughtful or anxious.

Frowning, Hanna'el saw that Thomas had misunderstood her, and she impatiently cut him short.

"It's not for my father's sake . . . "

"Then why?" asked Thomas sharply. "Hanna'el, there is no point in traveling westward; nor do I believe it is safe to return to Arcatus. Fate has directed us to the El'ohyme; we should remain here, perhaps indefinitely. What will you gain beyond this place but grief, despair, and eventual death? I know how bitter it is to admit defeat, but the Tree, if ever it existed, is surely dead—or else, as I have argued, it is a parable meant to instruct us. It is a *metaphor*, nothing real. Men mistake words for actual things—it is the common failing of human knowledge. Look at these gentle lands and the people who live here. Isn't this a homeland worthy of the name? The Singing Tree is not a *thing* or a *place*, it is, as you say, a *feeling*, and it grows where the heart feels best content and at peace. Carlon, your father, was a fool to believe those ancient legends—and his own inner restlessness destroyed him. You should learn from your father's mistake and not repeat it."

Hanna'el colored, for Thomas seldom spoke to her so sharply. She knew that his fears and cautions were sincere, and for a moment she felt uncertain. His last words, especially, hurt. Had she allowed her emotions to deceive her? She feared Thomas' challenge and looked aside, allowing her eyes to roam the green horizon to the east, the direction home. Far above, mingling with the fleecy clouds that drifted toward them, she saw a hawk gliding on currents of air. The hawk appeared so distant and so removed from her human world—she wished that she could live with such serene spiritual detachment and inner certainty.

But she could not.

Instead, she touched the severed ring inside her pocket, the ring she had taken from the Caer. Even if she had imagined that encounter with the nameless woman—even if the Tree grew only in a legend that children or sentimental adults mistook for fact—she could not doubt the touch of that severed ring. It reminded her of a mystery whose missing half promised an answer that she dreaded but had to understand. *Why did my father leave me?* The answer lay to the west—through the ancient land of Urd—not here, with the peaceful El'ohyme. She knew she might be deceived. The Singing Tree might exist only as legend, as the scholar argued, but what did that matter? The Tree had less importance than her doubts and questions—it was *these* that she could trust, for they were real, as real as the missing half of the severed ring. Thomas had misunderstood the matter entirely. His self-certain, scholarly knowledge, his pedantry, had made him deaf and blind. Whether the Tree existed or had ever existed, whether it lived only in the minds of poets or grew in a land she might discover someday somehow—this was not the important thing. Her search did not depend on the *Tree's* existence; it depended on who *she* was. The Tree might be real or it might not; it did not matter, Hanna'el saw. What mattered was the honesty with which she sensed the loss of its fabled song, and the story that she told to heal this loss.

"I'll go to Urd myself—you needn't come," she announced to Thomas. "If the journey seems too dangerous, I release you from your pledge. You may remain here with my blessing. I'll travel alone."

But the scholar became even more agitated when he heard this decision, and he swore that he would never allow her to travel alone.

"Hanna'el, that's not fair. You mustn't threaten me."

Hanna'el knew that only a direct command could resolve this argument, but she hesitated to assert her will. She tried to equivocate, for she valued his free choice.

"How much money do we still have?" she asked.

Thomas frowned. "Enough to purchase ponies, if that's your thought. If Daoshin consents to sell us any at all."

Hanna'el nodded. "Very well. If they will sell me ponies, good; if not, I shall leave this place on foot."

"Then you're certain?" said Thomas doubtfully, crestfallen. And when she nodded, he sighed in resignation.

"Thomas, you needn't come with me," she told him gently. "You can stay here. I mean that. I will not make you go."

But the old scholar sadly shook his head. "No, Hanna'el, I

must follow you. Our paths cannot separate now. I gave you my word, and I will keep it—no matter what fate confronts us."

As he answered, the old scholar took her hand.

Together, she and Thomas walked down the hill, no longer speaking, until at a fork in the trail she asked Thomas to continue alone. She told him that she needed a moment of solitude to prepare for the arguments Daoshin and Maea would surely make. But in fact, she had decided on a plan.

Walking alone to the bank of the river, Hanna'el followed the shore upstream to a small, sandy beach where branches of ragged alders and graceful poplars overhung the river in a shady bower. She found a rock and made herself comfortable, watching the current that flowed so smoothly at this stretch. The river ran onward to the west, Daoshin had told her, to the border of Urd. Only those who knew the river's currents and who were skilled at running the rapids that appeared farther downstream could navigate this route. She knew she did not have that skill.

But that was not why she had come to the riverbank alone.

Before leaving the farmhouse, Hanna'el had taken a pair of scissors from Maea's sewing basket. The plan that she had decided upon had long been forming in her mind, for she knew that Thomas' words of caution were correct: as soon as they left the El'ohyme, they would expose themselves to terrible risk. A young woman and an aging scholar were easy prey on the open highway; and no matter how cautiously they traveled, danger would find them.

From the folds of her dress, Hanna'el took out the shiny scissors that she had borrowed from Maea and she held them for a moment in her hand. She had decided to cut off her hair. She had not told Thomas of her decision, for she knew that he would protest. Well then, she thought, let him confront the consequences: by then it would be too late for another argument, and she hoped that this gesture would prove her determination to continue, no matter what.

But the deed was far more difficult than she had planned.

Carefully, she separated several strands of her raven hair and held the silvery scissors to their length. She drew a quick breath, grimaced, and cut. The strands fell free, but as soon as she caught them, she heard faint laughter.

Quickly, she spun around; angered that someone had followed her to this place. But the path along the river lay empty, and though she waited for a long moment, scarcely breathing, she heard nothing more.

She hesitated, gathering courage to act again. Once more, she cut, and again, as the strands fell free, she heard the faint, mocking laughter of many tiny voices.

Hanna'el flushed and bolted to her feet. "Who's there? Show yourself!"

As soon as she stood, the severed strands of her hair fell from her lap to the gray river rocks that dotted the shore. Hanna'el saw them drop, and as they touched the stones she leaped backward in astonishment, for all along those rocks, appearing at just that boundary where the water overlapped the sand, a host of tiny, human-like creatures observed her, and they laughed with delight to touch her severed hair. Each creature stood no taller than a blade of grass.

Frightened, Hanna'el stepped away. But seeing the small creatures vanish as she retreated, she knelt again by the water and cut another strand of hair. Again, the creatures reappeared to observe her, and again their lilting laughter rose above the sound of wind and water.

She tried to touch those creatures but could not. Each time she leaned forward or drew away, the tiny creatures vanished. They only reappeared to watch her cut. Fascinated, she continued her work with the scissors, and now she noticed something else as well. With every length of raven hair that she clipped from her head, several of the tiny creatures faded from view, their number seemingly decreasing by just the amount of hair that she cut free.

"Who are you?" Hanna'el asked. But the tiny people were much too nervous to respond.

Entranced by their laughter, she continued to trim her hair, laying each severed length on the rocks before her and watching in astonishment as the tiny, mercurial folk darted forward to caress the severed strands. *"Ah, ah,"* they repeated, and their small bodies vibrated like the silvered wings of hummingbirds.

Hanna'el became so fascinated that she began to cut her hair more quickly in order to observe how the creatures performed, even though with each snip of the glistening shears more and more of the tiny folk faded from view. At last, all her long hair had been trimmed to a length well above her shoulders and there remained amid the rocks only a dozen of the laughing sprites. One of these, much larger than the others, ventured close to Hanna'el's knees, but as she bent low to have a better look, it shivered and vanished.

Hanna'el knelt alone, her hair piled before her in a careful heap and weighted with a rock against the breeze. She shook her head and combed her fingers through her shortened hair, and as she did, she heard a voice address her in a clear yet whispering sing-song tone.

We've always been with you and always shall—no longer will you see us.

For a moment, she again had the uncanny feeling that she wasn't alone. Someone else abided with her, someone younger than she—a person on the borderline between childhood and adult—but neither understood the other's speech.

"Where are you?" she shouted at the trees that lined the shore. And then, more gently, "Please, let me see you. I won't harm you."

She felt certain that the shy, childlike stranger would appear, if only she could coax her from concealment.

But now, the lilting laughter of the small creatures that had gathered her falling hair rose again from the river. Their laughter mingled with the music of the current.

In the chime of their musical speech, she caught the sound of a name much like her own: *"Hannah . . . "*

And at once she stood up, feeling a sudden sense of panic, embarrassment, and confusion much like the feeling that had disturbed her many months ago when she awoke in the shepherd's tent.

Agitated, she glanced at the passing water in the hope of seeing her own reflection. She wished that she had brought a mirror. The loss of her hair made her feel suddenly lightheaded and very much younger, exposed and naked, and for a moment she felt a cold panic for what she had done. Her decision left no doubt—*I must go on.*

Hurriedly, she swept her lap and gathered as best as she could all the strands of hair that she had cut away. Wrapping them up in a cloth that she had brought for this purpose, she pocketed Maea's scissors and walked quickly toward the farm.

DAOSHIN

To her surprise, Daoshin laughed when he saw her.

She met him as she emerged from the tall grasses of the meadow. Jake and Jasper, Daoshin's two hounds, ran swiftly to her side, wagging their tails. Not only was Daoshin amused by the change in her appearance, he acted like he had expected to see her this way.

"So," he greeted her, "you have decided to continue your quest? Will you leave today?"

Hanna'el felt very confused.

"How did you know . . . "

Daoshin cut her off, smiling. "Your scholar is home arguing with Maea, but I slipped away to greet you so the two of us might have a private talk. It is time we were plain."

Hanna'el, blushing furiously because of her shortened hair and confused by Daoshin's last remark, nodded. He saw her embarrassment and asked her to walk with him to the shady privacy of an oak. As Jake and Jasper stretched themselves at her feet, panting and scratching, Daoshin leaned against the trunk, his eyes half closed. She saw him search for the proper words. At last he spoke.

"I knew this morning that today was the day you'd decide to leave or stay. I promised Maea to do everything in my power to convince you to stay with us, and as long as you wavered I respected that promise, though in my heart I never expected you to remain here even this long."

Hanna'el, surprised by this confession, began to apologize, but Daoshin frowned. She saw that he already knew everything. There was no point dissembling; so instead, she asked if Daoshin could sell her two ponies, to help her on her way.

Daoshin hastily waved his hand. "Ponies? Of course. I'll *give* you all you need for your journey—as much as I can. But I don't want your money, not a coin. You still don't understand me very well if you have to ask me that, do you, *Hanna'el?*"

The strange accent he placed on her name surprised her, but before she could reply, Daoshin took from his pocket a small box made of walnut. He held it toward her, nodding that she should accept it.

"Take it," he said. "There's something inside that you will need. Open it; a friend told me to give it to you, if you ever decided to leave the El'ohyme."

"What friend?" she asked, suspiciously.

"Open the box," Daoshin repeated.

Inside, on a bed of purple velvet, lay a pearl. Hanna'el knew it was a pearl because her father, long ago, had shown her such a marvel. The pearl that he had shown her had been her mother's. Even though she had seen such a pearl years ago, she remembered it well. It had come from the shores of the far distant western ocean.

"I can't accept it," said Hanna'el, shaking her head with surprise. "It's much too precious . . . I have no need."

"You have greater needs than you can imagine," Daoshin said gently. "Do not be hasty, *Hanna'el.* Did you not undervalue and lose the Master's gift?"

Hanna'el startled when she heard Daoshin say this, for she had not told him anything of her dreams and visions, nor had she mentioned the shepherd's mysterious gift.

Again, the strange sensation overwhelmed her that she was not alone here with Daoshin. Two souls inhabited her, and the second observed her now. Hanna'el was suddenly very aware of that second presence, as though the stranger were visible here in front of her. She was someone much like herself, and yet, she was not—she was only a child . . . a child shy and frightened, and yet innocently resolved.

Daoshin watched her closely. "On the day that you first came here, I spoke to you of the Tree. At that time, you asked me no questions, nor have you asked me any since. Why haven't you asked me, Hanna'el?"

Hanna'el shook her head to clear her thoughts. And suddenly, as though someone else had spoken, she heard herself say: "Daoshin, are you the Master Walter?"

Daoshin laughed. "Ah, you are remembering. No, *Hannah*, I am not, though I have met that marvelous fish. But I have seen you in your garden, and I know what the Master told you. Do you remember that garden? You were alone there," he chided her, "once upon a time."

"Yes," she heard herself say, "but I thought I dreamed it. It was a place where no one lived, and I was alone."

Daoshin gently shook his head. "Not so," he corrected her. "Once people lived there, but now they are lost. The threads of remembrance that bound them to their world have weakened, frayed, and broken, for the Tree that sang their remembrance no longer sings. Slowly, inexorably, the stars are going out."

"Stars?" she repeated.

Daoshin smiled, stretching his legs and scratching Jake and Jasper behind their ears. The two dogs whined to be patted. "I call them stars," he said, "but others might call them memories just as well. Some call them worlds. It makes no difference how you name them, but it is a sign of their disappearance that you no longer can understand me very well. The dreams that trouble you—I have seen them . . . they are not imaginations; they are real: they are memories of those persons whom you are. Is that too confusing? Didn't Walter explain this to you once? Watch what I do."

Daoshin lifted the small white pearl from its walnut box and held it in his open palm. Suddenly, it seemed as though the pearl began to speak, although the words sounded only inside her head. Then, with a certainty whose source eluded her, she recalled that it was Walter who once had spoken those same words. He had spoken them to that girl she had seen inside the garden. The girl's name was Hannah. The name sounded much like her own.

Hannah, do you remember the pond where we met? Do you remember the Chinese Pavilion? The Tree of All Remembrance no longer sings, and because it is silent, worlds perish. These worlds do not fade all at once, nor does everyone notice their disappearance, but those who are

drawn to Elowyn feel it in their hearts. They know that the silence is
death. They feel that the Tree is dying, that the Tree of All Remembrance
does not sing. They feel this in their hearts as a sadness whose source
eludes them, or else they believe that their sadness is caused by lesser
things. Try though they might to cure their own disease, they are helpless;
they cannot recall their memories. And because they have lost
remembrance, they grow sick—as ill and withered and shrunken as the
Tree whose music eludes them.

Hanna'el stared at Daoshin, wondering how he could make
such words resound inside her head without speaking. Was it like
the trick the Singer had performed in front of Aeron, when her
father's voice had spoken from his harp?

Daoshin smiled.

"There are no tricks," he said. "There is only memory."

Before she could question, he spoke again. "It is not by chance
that you came here," Daoshin explained. "A part of you longed for
the safety of this farm. You long for it still. Indeed, you could do as
Maea wants: you could stay here. You could stay here *eternally,* if
you like. Time does not fret the El'ohyme. There really is no need
to leave."

But Hanna'el did not believe him. She had her memories,
after all, and she knew what they demanded.

"They will fade," said Daoshin. "And with them, time will
vanish. When time vanishes, you will vanish, too. Can you endure
that?"

He smiled.

"But what about my father?" she interrupted. "What about . . . "
and here she groped for words. " . . . what about *Walter?*"

Daoshin's dark eyes sparkled brightly. He seemed amused. "Walter is
one of the Masters, but he is not El'ohyme. His ways are not ours. Outside
this place, things change and alter, but here, life remains settled and serene.
Those dreams and memories that trouble you—many of which you barely
now can recall—you will forget them all, in time. That girl you saw in the
garden—that other self—she, too, will vanish—but here *you* will remain
forever *El'ohyme.*"

Hanna'el hesitated, feeling a tug of agreement and consent,

but she remembered Walter's words and touched the fresh-cut ends of her ragged hair. It felt so very tempting to agree to stay, and she knew that if she wavered for even a few more seconds, it would be impossible to leave.

Daoshin watched her, eyebrows raised. She saw that he had left the decision entirely up to her, and that in fact, whatever he had said to persuade her she had already said to herself. She had thought and felt this before. Daoshin's words were hers, whether she spoke them or not—and for that reason, she understood now exactly what she must do.

"I can't stay here. I've already decided. I want to continue my search for the Singing Tree."

Daoshin nodded. His expression did not change. He seemed as content with this decision as any other.

She had hoped that he would say something more encouraging, that he would somehow indicate that she had made the right and wisest choice. Instead, he returned the small white pearl to its box and closed the lid with a snap. "Well, then I've done all that I promised Maea—that and more. It's as I thought it would be. Here, take this pearl. It is my gift. Your father would want you to have it."

Wait, she wanted to say, *did I choose correctly?*

With a sense of irrevocable departure, Hanna'el accepted Daoshin's gift. But as she touched the wooden box, she momentarily remembered the old woman who had spoken to her so mournfully at Aeron's Caer. She still could not recall that woman's name, nor did she know why the thought of that encounter made her feel angry and sad.

But as she held Daoshin's gift, she felt stronger. The strange pearl, which reminded her surprisingly of her mother, gave her courage.

"I'll bring it back," she promised Daoshin. "Someday, I will return it. I promise."

The farmer smiled. "Act as you like, Hanna'el; you are free. Let's return and tell Maea. You and the scholar can leave at tomorrow's dawn."

BOOK SIX

The Road to Urd

DEPARTURE

The ancient road, known as the Crystal Highway, ran westward across the northern border of the El'ohyme. For three days, after leaving Daoshin and Maea, Hanna'el and Thomas plodded along that ruined highway, and, contrary to their fears and expectations, they met no other travelers. Hanna'el often thought of the friends she had left behind—in many ways, she had come to think of Daoshin and Maea as parents. The couple had prepared her for this journey as best they could: the ponies they had given her were stout and well suited for the hills that lay ahead; their packs were filled with provisions. Thomas and she each rode a pony, and they led behind them a third, which carried their ample supplies. In keeping with Daoshin's parting advice, Brother Thomas led the way, posing as an itinerant schoolmaster on route to a distant post. And Hanna'el, her hair cut short and her body well hidden by shapeless clothing, posed as a boy, Thomas' servant. They had decided to call her Jack. Daoshin had given Hanna'el a small bow and a quiver of arrows, and she wore this as she rode. But Thomas, though he had been urged several times to arm himself, had refused all weapons. "I'm too old for them," he protested.

On the first days of their travel, Hanna'el felt sad. Thomas, too, was very moody. The monotony of their pace recalled her earlier journey to Aeron's Caer, though she tried to force those painful memories from her mind. What had become of Bryhs, she wondered. Was the old chieftain dead? She had been told that most of her cohort had perished inside the Caer, but perhaps a few had become prisoners. She felt responsible for their fate and guilty that she had failed to protect them. She swore to herself that someday, were it possible, she would make amends for leading them to Aeron's Caer.

On the third day after their departure from the El'ohyme, the wind shifted to the north and storm clouds began to mass ominously. Thomas dourly predicted rain and, drawing out the map that Daoshin had made for them, he studied the shape of the road that lay ahead. "Daoshin mentioned an inn," he told her, shaking the map to make it unfold. "According to my estimate, we should come to it soon; I hope by nightfall. We'll be lucky to have some shelter against this storm."

Hanna'el wondered whether it was wise to present themselves at an inn. If Aeron had sent men to watch for them, those men would surely be on guard at such a place. But as the sky darkened and the wind blew harder, she changed her mind. Having ridden for three days and slept the past nights on the lumpy ground, a bed and a warm meal seemed very attractive. Besides, she reasoned, they could not avoid people forever. Eventually they would have to trust to their disguises.

Thomas' estimate of arrival was not far from the mark. They rode until late afternoon, and a fine drizzle had begun by the time they saw the smoke from the inn's cook fires rising above the trees. As they approached, Hanna'el noticed the inn's wooden sign swaying vigorously in the freshening wind. Something about that wooden sign as it swayed to and fro in the storm wind felt familiar, and she pointed the sign out to Thomas, who rode beside her. Thomas saw nothing unusual. The sign pictured a hunter with his club upraised and ready to strike a beast that appeared to be part lion, part reptile. The hunter was naked, except for a fur loincloth bound to his waist with a black, leather belt on which were visible three large, glistening jewels. A snarling black dog scampered at the hunter's heels, assisting his efforts.

"It is a depiction of the constellation Orion," Thomas commented. "Orion is the hunter. The dog at his heels is Sirius, the so-called dog star."

"It reminds me of something else," said Hanna'el.

Thomas shrugged.

"Is it only a feeling? Or can you say more precisely what you mean?"

But she could not.

The wind suddenly freshened, and Thomas drew his cloak tighter. He directed Hanna'el to press down her hat to conceal her face.

"Fall behind me," he said curtly. "You're my servant; don't forget the disguise. I'll do the talking. Be careful that you don't speak out of turn."

Hanna'el scowled at the tone of reprimand in the scholar's voice.

"And remember," he added. "Your name is *Jack*."

AT THE SIGN OF ORION

The inn that they approached was old in the service of the highway and, like the highway, had witnessed better days. A crumbling stone wall defined the border of the property: grounds that included a livery, courtyard, trough and tethering posts for horses. As they approached, Hanna'el noticed two men moving across the courtyard: one tall, the other short. The men paused to stare at them suspiciously and then hurried into the inn before Hanna'el could see their faces clearly. Already the rain had increased, so that her cloak had become heavy with moisture.

As they dismounted, Hanna'el had to resist the impulse to adjust her hat or touch her shortened hair. The many severed strands had been placed in a small box for safekeeping, and she kept the box in a saddle pack. Inside the box, bedded upon the hair and wrapped in a velvet cloth, lay the pearl that Daoshin had given her.

"Stay here with the horses," said Thomas. "I'll go inside to negotiate for rooms. Don't talk to anyone."

Hanna'el nodded, and her eyes scanned the inn's derelict courtyard. There was no one to whom she might talk.

Her attention moved back to sign of the hunter Orion that swayed more wildly in the wind. She knew that she had seen it before, or a sign much like it. *But where?*

"*Jack* . . . did you hear what I said?"

Hanna'el startled. "I'm sorry . . . What?"

Thomas frowned. "Pay attention. Stay alert. Remember what I told you. We cannot trust anyone."

"Yes," she nodded. "Of course. I'm sorry. I'll pay attention."

A strong gust of wind tore at her hat, and Hanna'el barely caught it in time. The first drops of rain splashed her face.

"See that you do," said Thomas sternly. And he plodded away.

The wind gusted again. As she struggled to keep the ponies calm, she noticed a lone figure standing at the edge of the inn's courtyard, about a hundred yards away, facing the wilderness. It appeared to be a man about the age of Brother Thomas, Hanna'el judged. The stranger stood with his back to her, and he leaned against the stone wall that looked out to the northwest, directly into the face of the storm that buffeted her. He was the only person in the courtyard beside herself.

Something about the stranger impressed her and held her attention, even though he stood quite a distance away. She could not see his face. His clothes were simple, just some leggings and an old farmer's cloak bound to his waist. Hardly enough protection in weather such as this, Hanna'el thought, but the stranger lounged indifferently. He carried no weapon except a staff; yet, something in his posture, even from behind, suggested an attitude of calm, stoic resolution. He was not very large, scarcely taller than she, and slightly heavier. His long gray and black hair had been gathered to his head in a careless topknot that the wind had begun to unravel. His paid it no mind. What made her most curious was the mood of relaxed ease that surrounded him, despite the threatening storm.

Suddenly, the stranger turned and looked directly at her. Their eyes met briefly, and Hanna'el, with a sudden tremor of embarrassment, felt a shock of self-consciousness spark through her entire body. It was as though a bolt of lightning had flashed from the stranger to her. Quickly, she recovered and looked away, pretending that the ponies needed attention.

At that moment, Brother Thomas returned from the inn. His face showed lines of disappointment. "It's bad timing on our part," he scowled. "The inn is small, and the owner claims all the rooms have been let for the night."

"How can there be so many travelers?" asked Hanna'el. "We saw no one on the road."

"I told you the journey would be hard," Thomas snapped. His angry response startled her.

"I'm sorry," he immediately added. "I did my best to make a bargain. I'm tired and worn out."

Confused, Hanna'el momentarily looked away from Brother Thomas to the stone wall where the stranger had observed her a moment earlier, but the man had vanished. She glanced quickly up and down the courtyard. Had he simply walked off into the outer storm?

"Did you hear what I said, *Jack?*"

She shook her head, confused. "Yes, of course . . . . " And then, "There was someone out there."

"Where?" said Thomas, alarmed by her distracted tone of voice. He scanned the courtyard.

"Over there, at the edge of the courtyard. A stranger."

Thomas looked concerned. He peered into the rainstorm. "Where? Did he speak to you? Did he recognize you? Was it someone from the Caer?"

"No . . . no, I don't think so."

She shook her head, troubled but unable to articulate the reason she felt disturbed. She remembered the brief intensity of the stranger's glance and the feeling that ran through her as their eyes had met. Even at a distance, it was as though a spark of recognition had passed between them.

"Are you sure he didn't know you?" said Thomas, alarmed by her distraction.

"No . . . I never saw him before."

"Was he armed? Was he someone from the Caer?"

She shook her head. "No, I don't think so. He did not have a weapon. He didn't know me."

Again, Thomas scanned the courtyard. "I'd just as soon ride on," he said nervously, "but the night's too grim. The storm is growing worse." He nodded at the inn. "The innkeeper's a liar and a thief, if you ask my opinion; nevertheless, I bargained for any shelter he might have. A soaking would do neither of us any good. He gave us what he had left: some space inside the stable. And we can have a meal. The inn is crowded with travelers. Stay alert. Don't say anything. Remember, you are my servant. We'll sit by ourselves. The room's shadowy; if you keep your hat on you'll go unnoticed. We'll eat as quickly as we can."

Hanna'el nodded, and they walked toward the stable where a grimy boy shuffled out to help them. He grunted a few sullen questions about the ponies, wiped at his nose, and otherwise paid them little courtesy or attention. All his preparations, Hanna'el noted, were done in a quick, haphazard fashion. Thomas gave him a coin when he was done, more to be rid of him than to pay for his help, and the boy hurried away with a scowl and not a word of thanks.

Disheartened, they looked about the stable, which thankfully felt secure against the storm. Thomas sniffed the moist, hay-scented air and scowled at the nearby animals in the stalls: two mules and an ancient mare. "At least we'll be alone," said Thomas dourly.

They took their most precious possessions with them to the inn and entered just as the innkeeper's wife dished up a pungent stew. The kitchen smelled of boiling cabbage and damp linen, and a large pot of laundry frothed inside a black, hissing pot. A baby squalled in a corner, its face streaked with applesauce and pork grease. The mother paid it no mind. She thrust a wooden bowl at Thomas almost before he had time to close the door. "It's all you get unless you buy seconds," she shouted above the screams of the wailing child. "There's water in the jug, or something stronger— for a price. Here's for your boy."

Hanna'el's bowl held far less than Thomas' portion, and, unlike the scholar, she received no wooden spoon. She accepted the fare and followed Thomas into the main room of the inn. The place was indeed shadowy and close, with air that reeked heavily of beer, sweaty wool, and tobacco. A large fire burned in an open pit, the smoke drifting lazily upward through an opening in the ceiling. Aside from this, no candles had been spared for illumination. Along the walls stood wooden benches, some split from age and wear. Hanna'el counted seven people, including the boy she had met at the stable. All seven sat near the fire; the benches along the wooden walls stood free.

Thomas' scholarly attire received a few curious glances, but no one paid much attention to Hanna'el, much to her relief. Undisturbed, they found a bench in the shadows and quietly began their meager meal. The stew was mostly water, a thin, greasy gruel overcooked and under salted, pocked with some nasty, nameless meat too gristly to chew. The stale chunks of rye bread tasted better, and Hanna'el contented herself with dipping these hard scraps into the stew to soften the crust. A dog, a mutt with a bald spot of mange on its back, whined for her attention, and after eating what she dared stomach Hanna'el quietly set down the bowl for the animal to finish off. Thomas, she noted, surreptitiously did the same.

They had just exchanged glances to leave the room when the innkeeper entered, shouting loudly. "Where's the scholar with those fine ponies?"

The innkeeper's bulk was as large as his voice. He moved like a ponderous bear.

Thomas stood up nervously and Hanna'el stiffened. Everyone looked their way.

"Sit down, sir, sit down," said the noisy innkeeper, stumbling forward and thrusting out his hand for a friendly clasp. "Don't let me trouble you. It's about your ponies. You didn't tell me you rode from the El'ohyme. Those are three fine animals you've got."

"What about our ponies?" said Thomas, ignoring the innkeeper's greeting.

The man wiped his hands on his leather apron. He smiled with yellowed teeth. "I admire them," he said to Thomas. "I haven't seen animals as fine as those for quite some time."

Now Hanna'el observed how a man in the opposite corner of the room tapped his companion's knee and leaned forward, plainly interested in this conversation. The two strangers began to whisper, and Hanna'el recognized them as the men she had seen crossing the courtyard when she and Thomas first arrived.

"What do you want?" said Brother Thomas, eager to be done with this conversation.

"The point of it is this," said the innkeeper, still smiling. "I admire those ponies. I'll make you a fine deal for one or all of them—a deal that will be worth your while, I assure you."

"I don't want to sell them," said Thomas. "Leave me alone."

"Now, now, wait until you've heard my offer."

Instead of retreating, the innkeeper sat down on the bench beside Thomas, pressing so close that the scholar shied away to the opposite wall.

"Boy," said the innkeeper to Hanna'el, "hop up and fetch us some ale!"

Hanna'el startled. She flushed and looked to Thomas, afraid to move.

"I don't drink," said Thomas testily. He looked at her sharply. "Stay where you are, *Jack*."

The innkeeper shook his head. "So tell me, my friend, where are you heading?" He appeared quite undisturbed by Thomas' refusal to drink, and he placed a familiar hand on Thomas' knee.

"West," said Thomas uneasily.

"Ah," said the garrulous innkeeper. "*West?* I thought so. West is a dangerous direction these days. This inn stands at a crossroads, and if I may advise you, I advise you to travel north. You're a scholar, aren't you? An educated man. I've helped men like you in recent times. We stand at the Pardish crossroad, and I advise you to travel north. The westward road is barely a road at all just two days from here. You should take the northern route. North, that's my advice. But let me tell you, those ponies will have a hard time of it either way, west or north. Mules are what you need, sturdy plodders. They'll serve you better, for the direction you're heading."

Thomas' face turned red. "And I suppose you have the very mules I need?"

The man laughed and slapped his knee. "The devil take you, I do! And I'll trade them honestly for those three ponies you've got in my stalls." Before Thomas could respond or remove himself from the trap into which he had stumbled, the innkeeper unloosened a cracked leather purse from his belt and took out three silver coins. He slapped the coins down on the scholar's knee.

"There! That's equal to the best price you'd get in a town market—three coins and the mules for those ponies. That's a fair profit in a country as wild as this. You'll not do any better."

"I'm not interested," said Thomas dryly, pulling away and pushing the coins back at the innkeeper.

The man ignored him. "Three coins—one for each animal. Three coins—plus the mules."

"I told you no. I don't want your mules."

Thomas tried to leave, but still the innkeeper blocked him.

"No so fast, my friend. Not so fast." He rubbed his chin, and his tone of voice shifted. Instead of outrage, he affected a mood of conspiracy. "All right, you drive a hard bargain. But this is what I'm prepared to do . . . "

"Don't you listen?" said Thomas angrily. "I told you, I don't want your money or your mules. We're going west to Urd and the Karakala. Now let me pass."

At the mention of Urd, the room became hushed.

The innkeeper lost his grin. "Urd?" he repeated. "Aye, then you're a stubborn fool. All the worse for you, I say. If you won't accept a profit, then take this advice. It's advice that will save your life. You've chosen a hard road through a country that's filled with murderers, brigands, and thieves. If you don't take my money, someone will take your life to have those ponies, you can be sure. Ask any man in this room if I am right. If you live to see the Karakala, count yourself a lucky man. Go north, if you wish to live."

"I've heard quite enough," said Thomas. "Thank you. I'm leaving. Let me pass."

And he and Hanna'el pushed past the angry innkeeper and went out into the stormy night.

The innkeeper let them pass. For a moment, he stood frowning, and then he grunted and rubbed his chin. He spoke as though to himself, but his voice was loud enough for anyone in the room to overhear. "It's the ponies I hate to see wasted," he muttered. "I'd pay a good price to have them—no questions asked—to anyone who offered to make the sale." Then he turned and entered the kitchen while the rest of the company sank back into conversation.

But the two men whom Hanna'el had observed briefly in the courtyard leaned closer to one another and began to talk.

"Tell me, Seth," said the one, "is this an opportunity? The scholar's a fool not to take the innkeeper's money, but it's all the same for us, if you take my meaning."

His companion nodded. He tapped the hilt of the dagger that hung at his side.

SETH AND SHEM

The rain pounded heavily on the roof and walls of the stable as Thomas and Hanna'el bed themselves down in the hay. Thomas, soured by the innkeeper's greedy argument, grumbled as he spread out his blanket. "Keep all your valuables close at hand," he cautioned Hanna'el. She had already done so, and she asked whether Thomas thought her disguise had been effective, for she recalled how she had frozen when the innkeeper ordered her to fetch beer. She felt certain that someone had noticed her embarrassment.

Thomas reassured her. "When the talk's about money, most men lose their attention for anything else. You can be sure that when the innkeeper opened his purse and took out those coins not a single person noticed you."

Hanna'el laughed and began to remove her floppy hat, but at that moment, the heavy barn door opened and two men entered. A gust of wet wind followed them, and the ponies neighed in their stalls.

Thomas froze.

The first of the strangers nodded. He was tall and thin, with a lean, hungry expression and eyes that darted nervously as he spoke. He walked with a slight stoop, as though his height were an embarrassment. His companion, a shorter man with curly, dark hair and a greasy leather vest that barely closed over his swelling stomach, followed behind. This shorter man watched Thomas closely, and he was the one who did the talking, smiling and bowing as he began. "Good evening, sir. I hope my brother and I haven't startled you. The fact is, we're your companions for the night. My name is Seth, and this is my brother Shem. We're travelers on the highway, just like you."

Hanna'el noted that as Seth, the short man, spoke, his gaze shifted cannily from Thomas to her, though he did not study her for long. He looked at her only long enough to take stock of her importance, Hanna'el judged.

"The innkeeper said we had this stable to ourselves," said Thomas indignantly.

Seth laughed. "Oh, did he? He told us the same. He's a filthy liar."

The two strangers shut the stable door.

Thomas began to protest. "Now just a moment! This won't do!"

Seth shrugged sympathetically. "The innkeeper's a liar and a cheat. You said so yourself. Pardon me, but I couldn't help overhearing what he offered for your ponies. Ridiculous! You were right not to trust him. Those ponies are worth more to you than mules. He had his nerve. Where are you heading, if I might ask? "

"That's our business."

"Indeed it is," the man grinned. He surveyed the barn, as his brother, Shem, stared silently at Thomas. "Well," said Seth, "it's a big stable for the four of us, don't you agree? Plenty of room."

He and his brother moved to a hay-filled corner and began to settle down.

"Good night to you, sir," said Seth. "I mean, as good a night as you can have in a place like this. We'll not disturb you any longer."

The two, however, kept talking as they laid out their bedding, taking no care to keep their conversation private. "A scholar," said the shorter man to his brother, Shem, who all this time had not ventured a single word. "Excuse me, sir," Seth suddenly questioned, "but did I hear the innkeeper say you were traveling west?"

Thomas grunted noncommittally, but the man named Seth took this for an answer. "Well, that's a coincidence, isn't it? My brother and I are heading west. Sir, don't believe a word of what that fat innkeeper told you about the road. It's passable enough, if you know the route. The innkeeper wants to scare you. A man meets the trouble he's born to encounter—don't you agree?—and worrying about misfortune never changed it. Am I right?"

Again, Thomas grunted, and Seth, undaunted, spoke again. "I'm glad you think so. Sir, I like your skeptical attitude. I like it very much. You stood up to the innkeeper better than I could have done. Why don't we travel together?"

"What!" sputtered Thomas. "Are you mad? We don't want your company."

"Now, now, not so hasty," said Seth, grinning. "You've every right to be wary—I'd be wary, too. But I can vouch for our good intentions. This offer will stand you in good stead. We know this country. Believe me, you don't want to chance it unprepared. You're a scholar, not a practical man. You're badly in need of two reliable guides. Why not us? We're going the same direction. It'll be no trouble."

"That's ridiculous," swore Thomas. "We don't need guides. Leave me alone."

The brothers had stretched out on the hay. And Seth's tone remained infuriatingly pleasant. "Good night to you, sir. Sleep on my offer. In the morning we'll all be better company."

So said, the one named Seth threw a blanket over himself, and his silent brother Shem did the same.

BETRAYED

The storm blew itself out during the night. Well before dawn, the sky had cleared.

With the change in weather, the air turned cool with a mountain freshness that woke Hanna'el early from her rest. Well before sunrise, she stirred and opened her eyes. Her sleep had been very fitful and filled with half-remembered dreams. As she lay in the dark, cold stable and awaited light, she could hear Thomas breathing heavily. The horses and ponies shifted in their stalls, while the two strangers, Seth and Shem, snored loudly in their corner of the barn.

Awake in the pre-dawn darkness, Hanna'el ran her hand through her recently cut hair. How strange it still felt to her, as though her head were bristling with an unfamiliar energy. She remembered the tiny, nervous figures that had danced about her at the river's edge and how several of them had vanished with every sharp snip of her scissors until at last only one or two remained. As she lay on the straw in the darkness of the stable, she tried to recall those tiny creatures. She could imagine their sounds and gestures, but the details of their features would not become clear. Their words and the tone of their speech still felt like a wistful farewell: *We've always been with you and always shall; no longer will you see us.*

Hanna'el stared upward to the stable's darkened rafters, observing the inward movement of her mood and thoughts. From somewhere deep inside, a question arose:

Walter, what is memory?

She startled, for the voice that spoke this question sounded so present and real. It was as if a child had whispered in her ear.

Instead of sitting up, she closed her eyes and continued to breathe calmly. Gradually, she could feel herself settle into a sphere of inward attention that hovered between sleep and wakefulness: a zone between memory and imagination.

As she relaxed into that point of balance, she could hear the patter of rain very clearly.

Startled, she opened her eyes, thinking that the outer storm had begun again. But the barn was silent. She lay silently for a moment, listening, then shut her eyes and willed herself to relax. Slowly, she found again that inner sphere of attention, which hovered between wakefulness and sleep. She called it a *sphere* of attention, but as she relaxed more completely, it became more difficult to distinguish where the boundaries of that sphere actually were.

Again, she heard rain.

She opened her eyes.

The battered wall of a ruined wooden shack surrounded her on every side. Outside, it was raining hard. From where she sat on the damp wooden floor, she could see through a missing plank in the wall the shore of a doleful pond.

A young man sat in front of her, and near to him, someone else. It was a child.

This young girl sat reading a journal-sized book.

With surprise, Hanna'el saw that it was the book she had found floating in the water at the bottom of the boat that had carried her from Aeron's Caer.

She remembered the words on its cover:

Operis Processio,
Multum Naturae Placet

And the strange sigil she had glimpsed inside.

The girl with the book sat reading very intently. She did not break her concentration for a moment, not even when Hanna'el tried to interrupt her, by touching her arm. The girl's lips slightly moved as she read whatever words were written in her book. Hanna'el saw that the girl still lived in that trembling borderland between childhood and early adulthood, and it was this borderland of change that gave such innocence and gravity to her expression. She felt a deep affinity for this young stranger, but she did not know why.

You will understand someday, when you reach the portal of the Three Sisters, a voice inside her said.

She looked at the young man who sat cross-legged in front of the child. Suddenly, she understood that *he* had spoken these words. As soon as she understood this, she could recognize him. She knew him as the shepherd who had confronted her in the grassy flatlands on the way to Aeron's Caer. He had given her a gift: a green and living twig. But she had lost it.

You know where it is, he told her. *It isn't lost. The twig will find you. Go forward, Hanna'el; follow the thief . . .*

Am I dreaming? she wondered.

Instead of answering, the young man reached forward slowly and touched her softly between her eyebrows with his forefinger. For a moment, the world rearranged itself, and she had the sensation that past, present, and future had collapsed.

Not dreaming . . . hovering . . . said the shepherd.

Hanna'el twitched with astonishment, and her sudden movements made the hay rustle loudly. Brother Thomas stirred from his sleep and sat up. The light of sunrise had begun to filter into the barn. Out in yard, a rooster crowed loudly. Brother Thomas rubbed his eyes and fought back a sneeze.

"Hanna'el, are you awake? Are you all right?"

He began to gather himself and inventory their possessions.

Scowling, he looked at the two brothers, Seth and Shem, still snoozing.

"Get ready," he said to her. "We mustn't linger."

But despite Brother Thomas' intentions, the brothers Seth and Shem were well awake by the time Thomas and she were ready to depart. They waited in the courtyard, grinning, as the fat innkeeper came out to make one more bid for the ponies and to collect a few coins that he claimed Thomas owed him as extra pay, since Hanna'el's supper had not been included in his price. Thomas grudgingly paid, glad to be quit of the fellow, and soon they had mounted and resumed their journey west. Shem and Seth fell in beside them, and there was nothing Thomas could do to drive them away. The two brothers walked behind, talking steadily.

"I'd sooner travel naked than have you yammering at my back," Thomas snapped at them. "If you know this road so well, come forward and lead the way."

"As you wish," said Seth, grinning. "Like I said, we're glad to help."

Thomas fell into a worried silence that grew more fretful with every step.

Now the road began to rise, threading through a forest that pressed closely on either side. The trees grew thicker and taller as the morning wore on, and the track became more uneven and harsh.

"Ho," shouted Shem after about an hour's steady plodding. "I need to rest."

They had come to a small clearing in the forest where the grass grew tall and sweet for the ponies to nibble. Thomas halted but did not dismount. "Why are you stopping?" he protested. "We can't rest here. We've barely started. Keep going. We've a long way to go."

But Seth set his hands on his hips, and his brother, like a menacing shadow, stood behind him. Seth grinned. "That's easy for you to say, sir—you're on a saddle. But my brother and I have to walk, and our feet are sore."

"Stay here if your feet are sore," said Thomas. "I didn't ask you to come with us. We don't need your company."

"Is that so?" said Seth, still grinning.

Something in the man's look made Hanna'el shiver. His brother, Shem, had not smiled at all. Shem watched them coldly.

Thomas began to bluster angrily, but before either brother could move closer or speak again, loud hoof beats sounded on the road behind them. Wheeling awkwardly on her nervous pony, Hanna'el saw an armed rider gallop toward them from the trees.

BRYHS

At first, she feared that Aeron's men had overtaken them, for the rider shouted her name as he drew near. Galloping masterfully, he notched an arrow to his bow and aimed at the startled brothers. Shem and Seth had retreated to the edge of the forest at first sight of the oncoming warrior, but they froze when he aimed his bow.

"Stay where you are!" the rider shouted.

Hanna'el nearly tumbled from her pony with surprise. "Bryhs!" she shouted.

Bryhs, the old warrior who had accompanied her from Arcatus to Aeron's Caer, did not shift his attention from the brothers, but he allowed his weathered face to beam with delight.

"Mistress! You're here! You're still alive! Praise the gods . . . I thought we'd never meet again. The devil take it—what happened to your hair?"

And when she told him that she had shorn her hair in an effort to disguise herself for their journey, Bryhs laughed. Still aiming his bow, he rode closer to Shem and Seth and forced them to sit in the center of the clearing, though they loudly protested their innocence and swore they meant no harm.

"Who are these scoundrels?" Bryhs demanded.

"Guides . . . " Hanna'el began, but Thomas cut her off.

"Thieves!" he exclaimed. "They were going to rob us. You stopped them just in time."

"That's not true!" Seth protested. "The scholar's lying. We were guiding them! We did nothing to harm them."

His brother, Shem, said nothing. He watched Bryhs steadily. But Bryhs did not lower his bow.

"Drive them away," Brother Thomas interrupted. "Shoot them."

Bryhs shook his head. "There are others on your trail. Men

from the Caer. They're right behind me. These two will betray you, if they go free."

"But we're innocent!" Seth protested. "The scholar's lying! We did nothing to harm anyone."

"You liar!" swore Thomas. "You wanted to rob us. I know what you were plotting."

Seth laughed. "Rob you? Sir, that's not true. That's ridiculous! Did either of us draw a weapon? Did we ever lay a hand on you? We were guiding you to Urd as a gesture of friendship. You *invited* us to come along."

"Liar! I did not such thing."

"Yes, you did, sir. In the barn, last night . . . I heard you plainly."

Bryhs turned to Hanna'el. "It's your decision, Mistress. What shall I do? I know men like this. I know what's in their hearts. They're evil scoundrels. If we drive them away, they'll betray us— you can be sure. The scholar is right. Your safety demands that we end the matter here."

But suddenly, as Bryhs spoke, Seth's face brightened with comprehension.

"You're a woman!" he exclaimed, turning to Hanna'el. He threw himself face down before her, in abject supplication. "Mistress, spare us! We meant no harm. Did either of us threaten you in any way? Did either of us harm you? We're innocent. Do you want the blood of innocent men upon your hands?"

"Don't listen to him, Hanna'el," Thomas warned her.

Bryhs looked at her for instructions. His arrow remained poised. Hanna'el knew that with but the slightest relaxation of his fingers, he could lodge the tip of that arrow in one of the brothers' throats. It only took the slightest nod of her head to loose that arrow.

"Put down your bow," said Hanna'el.

"No!" exclaimed Brother Thomas.

"Mistress, thank you, thank you . . . " Seth began to stammer. His brother, Shem, had not changed expression.

"Give Bryhs your weapons," she said to Shem and Seth.

And the brothers complied at once.

"Mistress," said Seth, "how can we repay you? Ask us anything. We can still be your guides . . . "

"Keep silent," she ordered him.

Thomas shook his head. "Hanna'el, you're making a bad mistake. These men will betray you."

"We cannot remain here," said Bryhs, glancing nervously at the trees. "The road is too dangerous. It's a miracle I found you. Why are you here? Are you following Carlon's trail? How did you escape the Caer?"

Hanna'el nodded, and her eyes passed to Shem and Seth, still guarded by Bryhs' menacing bow. Their fearful looks gave her an idea.

"These brothers know this country well. They offered to guide us." As she spoke, she looked directly at Seth. Now that she had reclaimed her identity, she no longer felt awkward or afraid to meet his eyes. She was glad that her deception had ended.

"Yes," Seth nodded eagerly. His brother, Shem, remained sullenly silent. "That's right, we can guide you. We know this forest. If enemies are in pursuit, leave the highway. We'll show you a path that they won't easily find. Where are you going?"

"To Urd," said Hanna'el, disregarding Thomas' angry glance.

Seth lost his smile. "To Urd? No one travels to Urd. The great bridge has fallen into the river; there's no other way to cross. Why would you wish to go there? The place is cursed."

"*Where* I go and *why* I go there is my own business," Hanna'el snapped. "I asked if you could guide us. Can you?"

Seth swallowed. He glanced at Bryhs.

"We can do it, Mistress," said his brother, Shem, suddenly, breaking his long silence. His words surprised everyone.

"No, Shem, listen . . . " Seth began.

"We can do it, Seth. Tell them. We agree."

Seth nodded. "Aye," he answered slowly. "Aye, we know the way. But it will cost you—you know you cannot force us to be your guides. Tell the rider to put down his bow."

"Don't lie to me," said Hanna'el. This time, she spoke to Shem.

"We can do it," Shem said to her. "We know the way. I've been there before. Several times."

Thomas scoffed.

"To Urd? That's impossible. You said yourself the bridge over the river has collapsed. No one can survive in Urd. Urd is a wasteland."

Shem looked at the scholar expressionlessly. "I have been there many times. I know the way. My brother does, too. We can guide you. I give you my word."

"Swear," said Hanna'el. "Swear on your life that you will guide us to the river and not try to do us harm."

"I swear," said Shem. "On my life."

"Swear as well," she said to Seth.

"I swear . . . " he stammered. "But . . . "

"But what?" growled Bryhs. He had kept his arrow aimed at Seth's throat.

Seth swallowed. "You must pay us to be your guides."

"Pay you!" exclaimed Thomas. "You lying thief!"

"Wait," said Hanna'el sternly. "I agree."

"You *agree?*" said Thomas.

"Yes." She stared at Seth and Shem. Seth grinned, but his brother Shem's expression had not changed. "I will pay them to guide us to the Karakala," said Hanna'el. "His request is fair. I will not be in their debt. They have not done us any harm. Bryhs, put down your bow."

"Thank you, mistress, thank you . . . " Seth stammered.

"Hanna'el," Thomas warned her, "this is wrong. It is a bad decision."

But Hanna'el cut him short.

"It's my decision."

"Mistress, you have made an excellent choice!" Seth exclaimed. "You are wise and merciful. You won't regret it. Shem and I can take you to the banks of Karakala. The river marks the easternmost border of Urd. It's a difficult journey through the forest, but we know the way. No enemy knows this country so well. How much will you pay us?"

"You impudent scoundrel," said Thomas. "You're lucky if we pay you with your lives."

Seth ignored him. He ignored Bryhs, too. He saw that only *she* was in control.

"How much do you want?" Hanna'el asked.

"Eight gold coins," said Seth at once. "Eight gold coins—one coin for each day's travel. It will take eight days to reach the Karakala."

"Eight!" exclaimed Bryhs. "Are you crazy! Mistress, this is absurd!"

"Hear him out," said Hanna'el.

Seth was emboldened. "Eight gold coins. And eight more for my brother. Eight for each of us. That's the price."

Shem said nothing. His expression had never changed. He sat cross-legged in dour silence, staring at her.

"Agreed," said Hanna'el. She met the eyes of both of them: first Seth, and then his brother. Seth grinned broadly, and his brother gave her a barely perceptible nod. "Pay them," she ordered Brother Thomas. "One coin per day, for each day's travel."

"Not fair!" exclaimed Seth. "All at once or not at all."

"One coin per day," said Hanna'el. "Those are my terms."

Shem made another scarcely perceptible nod.

"All right. Agreed," said Seth reluctantly.

"Pay them," said Hanna'el again.

"This is wrong," muttered Thomas. But he opened his purse and did as she asked.

"Now get going," she said. "Show us the trail."

Shem and Seth stood up. Seth pointed beyond the clearing where they had paused. "A bit farther," he said. "The path lies ahead. Follow us." He still clutched the coin that Hanna'el had given him. Seeing him so eager for his wage, she remembered the drover on the bridge, the young man who had defied her by hurling his reward into the stream. She had not thought of him until this moment, and the memory of that embarrassment upset her. Clearly, that young man's defiance had been a bad omen, prefiguring the disaster that had met her at the Caer. She turned to Bryhs and asked how closely they were followed.

The old warrior shrugged. "There are many enemies on your trail, but I am ahead of them. Your escape confused us. How did you do it? How did you travel so far and so fast? Aeron and Raemond sealed the valley, and their men were told to kill you on sight."

His questions confused her. "It's been months since I left the Caer," she explained to him. "We escaped by boat . . . " But here her voice faltered, for she felt confused by a swirl of memories. Instead she asked: "But how did you find us?"

Bryhs composed a thorough answer, as was his bent.

"Aeron's men overwhelmed us. Brother Thomas must have told you how Aeron broke the truce. His men captured me and put me in prison, alone and without any news. Over time, I gathered from the jailers that somehow you had eluded Aeron's trap. No one knew how. It was the news of your escape that sustained me. I had nothing else. I waited and prayed for your safety. After many weeks, an old man came to visit me. His name was Et'elred, and he told me that he had once been your father's friend."

As Bryhs spoke, they passed farther into the forest, leaving the highway. The path they followed was so narrow that Hanna'el and Bryhs could barely ride side by side. Thomas rode closely behind them, while the brothers, Seth and Shem, trudged silently ahead. Hanna'el had no doubt that Shem and Seth overheard every word Bryhs said, but she saw no way to prevent their spying.

Bryhs continued patiently.

"Et'elred told me how Aeron has not been seen since your escape, despite the return of his son, the lost Prince Raemond. It was the physician Azael who announced Raemond's return—and since that time the physician and Raemond were often seen together, as though Azael, not Aeron, cared most for the lad's return. It was as if the prince had become the physician's pupil. Et'elred believes that this physician has some evil power over Aeron's son, just as he had over Aeron. Aeron took ill shortly after Raemond's return, and Azael tended him night and day. Some whisper that Azael has enchanted both father and son—that he murdered Aeron's queen to gain this power. Et'elred believed that it was Azael who stole Raemond from the Caer when Raemond was a babe, and that it was Azael who kept Raemond in isolation, in ignorance of his identity, until such time as Azael might use Raemond to rule in Aeron's place."

"But how could Raemond be hidden for so many years?"

"As Et'elred told me, Raemond was raised as the foster child of a drover, one of the peasants who supply the Caer with beef and barley and cheese. Azael revealed Raemond's true identity only when the time came to supplant Aeron's rule. Et'elred believes, and I do also, that Aeron is more in thrall to this physician than anyone ever suspected—and now his son is, too."

Hanna'el trembled, for she suddenly recalled a detail from her earlier dream. She saw a child accompanied by a cat, which she knew to be the Singer's imp. Together, girl and cat walked toward a bank of midnight storm clouds, toward a towering pillar of rain. She remembered that this wall of storm had been called the *Zone of Night*.

She startled.

"Where is Raemond now?" she asked Bryhs suddenly.

"He hunts you to take revenge. Upon Azael's orders, Raemond left the Caer to track you down. I do not know the direction of his search, nor could Et'elred provide much help. Et'elred convinced me that you had escaped the Caer, and he argued that you would follow your father's footsteps to Urd. At first, I did not believe him—I thought that if you lived you would return to the safety of Arcatus—but Et'elred insisted that I travel west. He believed that the Tree has summoned you, just as it summoned Carlon, and that you would not return to Arcatus until that summons was fulfilled. Thankfully, he was right."

These words, too, caused Hanna'el much distress. "But hasn't the physician guessed my purpose also?"

"He may have guessed, but he cannot be certain. And Raemond, who serves Azael loyally, traveled first toward Arcatus, since that is your home. As I said, no one thought you would try something as daring as to follow the great highway westward to

Urd. And many weeks have passed since your escape. Where have you been all that time? Raemond's strength and cunning have been enhanced by Azael's art," Bryhs warned. "He will not tire, and by now, like me, he may have concluded where you are."

Hanna'el saw Seth and Shem exchange nervous glances. Thomas, too, looked at her to see how she took these words. "Perhaps the Tree summons Raemond also," she thought aloud. She did not know why this thought had entered her mind, and she saw that her words disturbed Brother Thomas greatly.

Bryhs lapsed into silence, for the path had become so narrow he could not follow at her side. As they rode, Hanna'el turned over what the old warrior had said. She kept her head low and allowed her thoughts to wander, though her thoughts seemed always to reach the same puzzling hub: the shepherd's hut where she had awakened from the first of her troubling dreams. Why had she asked Daoshin if his name was Walter, and what did the name Walter really mean?

"*Hannah . . .* " a voice seemed to whisper.

Once more, as though following the well-worn pathways of a maze, Hanna'el's attention turned to those half-remembered memories of the haggard woman she had met in the buried cell beneath the Caer. The woman's aged and sorrowful face flickered in and out of her remembrance, like a ghost. She could still hear the woman's parting words.

Find the Tree, Hanna'el. Find it, if you would be whole.

BOOK SEVEN

The Isle of Birch

ABOVE THE KARAKALA

For six days, the company continued through the forest, following a trail that at times became quite faint. Bryhs grumbled ceaselessly about the foolishness of Hanna'el's plan, but each time Hanna'el confronted Seth, he assured her that he and Shem knew exactly where they were going and that the forest would soon thin out. Seth had reckoned that they needed no more than eight days to reach the northern fork of the Karakala, the river that separated this forested country from the harsh and inhospitable land of Urd, though he doubted that they would be able to find a place to cross it safely.

His prediction proved correct. On the afternoon of the seventh day, they crested a hill and looked down on the distant river. The northern fork of the Karakala lay ahead, and beyond they saw the barren hills of Urd.

"We have arrived safely," Hanna'el said to Thomas.

Bryhs, overhearing this comment, frowned. Ever alert as they journeyed through the forest, he had several times made them halt as he examined the trail. "We are not safe anywhere in this country," Bryhs warned her.

That night, as they prepared the evening fire, Bryhs remained taciturn and withdrawn. He startled at the slightest noise and several times lost his temper with Seth and Shem. The brothers received these rebukes in sullen silence. As was their custom, they had placed their blankets as far from Bryhs as possible, and they kept their voices low.

"I've seen their kind before," Bryhs warned Hanna'el. "They'd sooner murder us in our sleep for a single copper coin than serve us eight days for an honest payment. Watch them closely. The one named Seth will divert you with his chatter while the silent one, Shem, misses nothing. I distrust them both. Even without their weapons they are dangerous."

As he spoke, an owl screeched from the branches of a nearby beech tree.

"The forest agrees," said Brother Thomas, who had overheard the warrior's words. "It was wrong to bring the thieves along, Hanna'el."

Tired of argument, Hanna'el only nodded.

Thomas invited Hanna'el and Bryhs to settle by the fire, where the stew he had prepared was ready to eat. As they sat, he raised his arm and pointed to the southwest sky, to where the slender crescent of a new, waxing moon shone visible. The sky was so clear that the dark portion of the moon could be glimpsed clearly in the horn of the lunar crescent, and the shape reminded Hanna'el of something she had seen before, though for a moment she could not recall what it was. As Bryhs and Thomas ate and shared conversation, she excused herself from their company. She wanted to view the sky from a vantage point near the trees.

Words that she had heard in Aeron's Caer again came to mind.

You have lost the shepherd's gift—another has claimed it. You will find your way much harder for its loss.

As she pondered this warning, she felt she understood why the moon had called her from the fire. She remembered the dream of the garden, and inside that dream, she remembered a book whose cover bore a strangely similar crescent shaped glyph.

And as soon as she recalled this, she saw that the crescent

moon, which shone in the sky above the Karakala, gleamed like a
heavenly inscription, a sign placed to guide her forward toward
the barren ruins of Urd.

For a moment she felt split in two, as though the two souls
that she had imagined to dwell inside her had each, suddenly,
come to a startled awareness of the other's presence. One was
Hanna'el, the young woman whose homeland lay far to the east in
the wide grassy steppes of Arcatus; but the other was only a child.

"Do not be afraid," she heard herself say, though no one stood
near to listen.

She spoke because of the child she could not see. And she felt
at once that the child had heard her and understood. She was not
so very young, Hanna'el realized.

Again, her gaze turned to the stars, and she saw the constellation
Orion, which had given its name to the inn where she had met
Seth and Shem. She knew that constellation very well, and others
beside it. As she contemplated those stars, she felt how, with just
the slightest effort, she might perhaps learn to read the hidden
script that the moon and the stars wrote upon the darkened sky.
These were secrets hidden from no one, Hanna'el thought, except
that she lacked the key to understand. That key must lie somewhere
deeply buried in her remembrance.

But how can I find it?

Momentarily, as she turned her gaze westward toward the
sparkling waters of the Karakala and toward the barren ruins of
Urd. She imagined that her spirit hung suspended between heaven
and earth.

An image of a hawk, flying high above her native homeland,
passed through her mind.

Other thoughts rose to remembrance as well, and briefly, she
heard a distant voice: *"The book writes and rewrites itself each time
you use it. The language is yours."* For just a moment, she felt that
the stars and she were not separate beings at all and that much
depended on her understanding of a kinship between the world
she saw outside her and the world she felt within. Nature and her
soul were one ever-changing, ever transforming script that wrote

and rewrote itself fluidly according to vast cycles of time, inspired by the rhythms of forgetfulness and recollection.

I am that key . . . *said a voice.*

She did not know who had spoken.

I am that key . . . *it said again.*

And then there was silence.

"Hanna'el, come back to the fire!"

Brother Thomas' voice broke the concentration of her reverie. Her mood of a moment earlier abruptly vanished, like a melody hushed by the slamming of a door.

"I'm here. I'm coming!" she shouted. They would worry if she did not answer soon.

But she did not go back. Instead, she faced the horizon. This time, however, she saw to her dismay that the moon was only the moon and the stars appeared as only points of light. The momentary sense of two souls within one body—one heavenly, the other earthly—had vanished also. And though she could *will* herself to think about the mood and feelings that had seized her a moment before, she could not conjure them forth with full intensity. She did not know how. Despite her best attempt, they remained only abstract, imageless thoughts that came to her randomly, for reasons hidden beyond her knowledge and control.

Will it always be that way?

"Hanna'el! Where are you?" Thomas, her guardian, shouted again.

She could see him rising at the campfire with Bryhs at his side.

"Coming," she shouted.

She glanced one final time at the sky.

And suddenly, like the scent of fading incense, a brief remembrance caught her attention.

Guard the twig. Guard the green and living twig and keep it sound.

Thomas approached nervously.

"Hanna'el. Why do you stand here? Is anything wrong?"

"No, nothing . . . " she answered, somewhat annoyed. "I told you I was here. Didn't you hear me? I'm coming. I need some time alone."

"Why?" he asked, peevishly. "Are you all right?"

"I'm fine. Just leave me for a minute. Please."

"It's not safe here alone. You should come to the fire."

"Please, just a moment."

Reluctantly, Thomas left her. But his presence had already changed her mood.

"Come back to the fire," he called to her again. "It's dangerous in the darkness."

Knowing it was no use to linger any longer, Hanna'el reluctantly turned toward the safety of the camp.

Conspiracy

Just before dawn, Shem awoke and poked his brother's side. "Wake up, you sluggard. It's time."

Prodded and pinched, Seth opened his eyes and yawned. He sniffed and began to cough, but Shem, with a quick movement, thrust his hand over his brother's mouth. He watched the other sleepers, but neither Thomas nor Bryhs had stirred.

"They sleep so soundly, you'd think they were home in their beds," Shem scoffed.

Seth gagged and pulled his brother's hand off his mouth. He had awakened enough to stifle his urge to cough, but he felt angry at being disturbed so early. Shem, who normally said scarcely half a dozen words at one time, calmed him with a whispered explanation. "I've watched the scholar closely and know where he keeps his money. He wears it in a belt beneath his tunic. You can see the bulge."

"So what?" said Seth, rubbing his eyes. He squinted at the starlit sky and angrily demanded sleep. But Shem would not be still. "Today's the last day of travel. She soon won't need us. The north fork of the Karakala is only a few miles ahead."

"Yes, so? Let me sleep."

"You fool. What do you think we've been doing?"

Seth wiped his eyes. He scoffed and said that Hanna'el would never dismiss them. Now, more than ever, she needed their services as guides, since both of them knew that the short-haired witch from Arcatus would find no safe passage to Urd. "And even if she does," Seth continued, scratching his stomach, "the ruins of Urd will drive her back. She'll soon discover her folly and beg us to lead her home. We'll earn more money. Now let me sleep."

But Shem angrily shook his head. "The time for sleep is over.

Pay attention. I've watched her; I've studied her; I understand what she intends to do. Even if the river's in full flood, she'll find a way to cross. She's determined to go on, and not even the cataracts of the Karakala will delay her. She'd rather die in the crossing than turn back."

"Then let her drown," said Seth impatiently. "I want to sleep." He squinted at the sky, perhaps judging how much sleep he still might get.

But his brother, Shem, had more to say. He poked Seth again. "All the more reason for us to act. Why be content with eight gold coins when we could have everything?"

"How?" demanded Seth. "Leave me alone. Do you want one of that warrior's arrows in your throat? Do you think you can take him by surprise? Let me sleep."

"You fool. Listen. I have a plan."

Seth stared at him for a moment, not certain whether Shem meant this as a taunt. "All right. What is it?" he asked at last, arching his brows.

Shem spoke patiently, without expression. "The old warrior is her only protection. Alone, she and her scholar are as helpless as babes. All we need do is to lure the old warrior away, then you or I can rob them of their money and those ponies."

Seth, curious, sat up. "How do we do that? It won't be so easy to lure him away. The warrior distrusts us."

But Shem, instead of answering, lay down with his hands behind his head. "I don't know yet how I will do it," he whispered thoughtfully, "but by afternoon I'll find a way. Watch me closely. The time is at hand. When I see a chance for us to strike I'll give you a signal."

"Aye, and get us killed."

But Shem, instead of arguing, only grinned. "Maybe. Maybe not. Just stay alert and watch for my signal."

And with that, he lapsed once more into his familiar silence. Despite insistence, Seth could not get another word from his brother's lips. Shem soon was asleep, but Seth, awakened now and excited, lay staring at the sky until dawn.

The Green Man

Anticipating their arrival at the river, Hanna'el woke early and urged them onward just after breakfast. The path had become broad and easy to follow, and Bryhs took the lead. Seth and Shem, grumbling, followed behind. "What's that sound?" asked Hanna'el, after they had traveled for an hour, and Seth, as was his custom, spoke at once. "Falls, cataracts, and rapids. Haven't you heard of them? The falls of the Karakala are famous."

Thomas, who knew geography well, nodded his head. "Surely you remember your geography lessons, Hanna'el."

"I do recall them," she said, though in fact she had forgotten this detail entirely. "If the falls are so huge, won't the current be too swift?"

"Deadly swift," Seth answered, grinning.

Bryhs spoke without slowing his pace. "I would give up the idea of crossing, Mistress. Even if a boat were at hand, the current is too rapid and forceful to navigate. Anyone who dares the river will be swept away like driftwood over the falls."

"But my father must have found a way to cross."

The old warrior frowned. Hanna'el knew from his expression just what he meant. He thought that her father was dead.

"Look there," said Thomas suddenly, pointing to a clearing just ahead.

The grass in the clearing had been trampled flat. The damage looked recent.

Bryhs dismounted to have a better look. He read the signs quickly.

"There's the track of a single rider, and he was here not more than an hour or two ago. Look at these saplings; they've each been cut by a single blow, perhaps with an axe."

Seth and Shem drew aside as Thomas dismounted to inspect the trees. He touched one of the severed stumps.

"These trees are too thick to cut with a single stroke," the scholar marveled.

Bryhs, too, shook his head. "Swordsmen have this custom, though seldom with targets as thick as these. When a blade is freshly honed, its owner tests its edge on a column of tightly bound straw. You can tell the mettle of the steel by the ease with which it cuts. Here, too, an axe man tested his blade."

Nervously, Hanna'el scanned the surrounding forest, searching for other signs of the mysterious warrior. "Could you cut such a tree?"

"Not I," Bryhs admitted. "And I'd not like to meet the man who could." He fell silent for a moment, pondering.

Thomas drew their attention to a flat and barren plot of ground. Hanna'el saw that the grass here had been burned away in a perfect circle, and in the midst of this ashen circle she saw a drawing that made her draw a quick breath.

"You know this symbol?" asked Bryhs, studying her expression.

But Seth and Shem interrupted before she could answer. The brothers had exchanged nervous glances.

"Sir, my brother and I need our weapons. Our knives are small protection, but if we're attacked it's better than being defenseless."

Bryhs refused, but Hanna'el heard some truth in Seth's request. She saw fear in the brothers' faces and did not want them harmed.

"They've served us honestly," she said to Bryhs. "Give them their knives; we're almost at the river. As soon as we reach it, they have fulfilled their task and can go. If there's danger they should be prepared."

Bryhs and Thomas complained, but Hanna'el looked again at the fallen trees and repeated her command in sterner tones. She recognized the glyph from Aeron's Caer and from her dreams. She knew that it had been drawn here as a challenge.

But by whom?

Shem's eyes glanced furtively at the woods.

"What do you see there?" Bryhs asked suddenly.

Shem denied seeing anything, but Bryhs' suspicions had been aroused. He cocked his head and listened to the breeze.

"I hear it, too," Seth whispered.

"Hear what?" asked Hanna'el.

"There, can't you tell?" said the thief. "A man is moaning."

Bryhs looked nervously from Seth to the shadowed wood. He glanced quickly at Hanna'el. "We're too exposed; this grove may be a trap."

"There," said Seth, "I hear it again! Someone's hurt!"

Bryhs did not wait for Hanna'el to give a command. He retrieved the brothers' daggers and handed them to Thomas. "Guard these," he told Thomas tersely. Then, turning to Seth, Bryhs ordered him to accompany him into the wood. "I'm not sure I heard anything, but it's wise to be certain."

"Yes," said Seth excitedly, "I'm sure you heard it. I hear it, too. Over there, beyond the glade. It's not so far. Someone's in danger. We need to hurry!"

Bryhs had expected Seth to protest when he forced him to come along unarmed, but the guide said nothing. He glanced at his brother and then departed into the brush, forging a path that Bryhs could follow. With every dozen steps, Bryhs halted to listen, and each time Seth insisted that he still heard the moan, claiming that the sound had grown much fainter, as though the person were losing strength. Confused, Bryhs pressed onward, pushing past Seth so that he could hack down the thick undergrowth that blocked their way. He knew that he made too much noise, but he had decided that secrecy was impossible. Whoever had cut the trees in the clearing did not care about discovery, so he reasoned that there was little danger of surprise attack.

But as they pressed deeper into the forest Bryhs grew nervous and perplexed. "Stop," he ordered, "we've come far enough. I hear nothing but the wind."

Just at that moment, a loud cry rose from behind them.

Bryhs spun round.

"Mistress!"

His sword flashed as Seth veered off the trail and darted into the trees.

"Stop!" shouted Bryhs. He was about to give pursuit when a second cry from Hanna'el sent him crashing back to the clearing. He charged with his sword ready to kill, terrified that he had made a deadly blunder.

But the danger had passed.

In the clearing, Bryhs found Thomas on the ground. The scholar sat bent over, clutching his side, while Hanna'el knelt beside him, her hands bloody from a wound in Thomas' arm. The ponies and Shem had disappeared.

"The money . . . " groaned Thomas weakly.

In breathless, halting words, Hanna'el said that Shem had attacked them shortly after Bryhs and Seth entered the wood. Seizing a knife, he had overpowered Thomas and stolen the scholar's money, their ponies, Bryhs' horse, and nearly all their supplies. In the struggle, he had wounded Thomas in the arm. The wound bled freely but was not deadly, though Thomas looked pale and ready to faint.

"All our possessions are gone," Hanna'el moaned, "except for one bag from my saddle. I had already taken it down when Shem attacked."

Bryhs shook his head in silent anger. He sheathed his sword and spat.

"It's all my fault," said Thomas. "If I had been more careful to watch the thief . . . ahh!"

Hanna'el pressed more forcefully on Thomas' wound and at last controlled the bleeding. "We must hurry to the river. We cannot stay here."

Bryhs nodded, grimly resigned.

*   *   *

With Thomas' gold securely in his hand, Shem rode from the clearing as fast as he could, driving the stolen ponies before him. When he thought that he had gone far enough to avoid capture, he reined and dismounted, allowing the loose ponies to calm and graze.

Shem threw himself down by an oak tree and sat with his back to the trunk. His plan had worked perfectly. With a wounded scholar to tend, Hanna'el and Bryhs would not make very fast progress. There was time to catch his breath and wait for Seth to meet him as they had agreed. In the meantime, he opened the scholar's purse.

To his surprise, the purse held far more wealth than he had dared imagine. He poured the golden contents over his fingers, laughing as the coins fell to the grass. His thoughts kept pace with his rapidly beating heart. "Why should I share this wealth with Seth?" he began to reason. "Whose idea was it to rob the scholar? If Seth had his way we'd still be plodding toward the river as their guides." He laughed once more at his plan's splendid success, and he dribbled a handful of coins over his hand like a stream of water. The sound of the metal delighted him.

Pulling off one of his boots, he hid a handful of the more valuable coins inside. In that way, there would be less to divide with Seth. Seth was too trusting to suspect he had been cheated, and besides, Shem decided, the plan had been his. Who should better be rewarded? Even a fifth of this wealth was enough to satisfy his stupid brother.

Shem pulled off his other boot and filled that with coins as well. He was about to start filling the inner pocket of his shirt when he heard a strange and persistent sound, a sound as regular as water turning a wheel—the sound of metal being sharpened on a stone.

The sound came from behind the oak tree where he sat.

Immediately he gathered his coins and poured them safely into the stolen purse. Crouching, he cautiously peered around the tree.

A warrior, clad entirely in green, stood amid the forest. He held an axe and whetted its edge on a stone.

Shem gasped and pulled away. He began to stagger to his feet, but the warrior had already seen him and started forward. The ponies, frightened by grim warrior's approach, shied from Shem's panicked grasp. They neighed and stomped nervously, their eyes gone white.

Shem staggered backwards until his foot snagged a root. As he fell, he dropped the scholar's purse, which opened and spilled its golden contents amid the leaves.

Frantically, Shem began to scoop up the coins, but the green warrior now stood above him, smiling at the thief's panicked haste. "Leave them," said the warrior, his face entirely hidden by a helmet and visor, green with a sprig of hemlock in the crown. He lifted the axe and tested its edge with his thumb. "Leave the coins where they lie," he repeated. "You'll have no more use for them."

The Letter

Because of Thomas' wound and their lack of horses, Hanna'el, Bryhs, and Thomas took until late afternoon to arrive at the river's shore. The path descended precipitously, so that Hanna'el and Bryhs had to steady the wounded scholar as they walked. The day was hot, and all of them sweated heavily by the time the river came into view. The sound of the famous falls roared in the distance, overwhelming their conversation.

As Bryhs had predicted, the water rushed rapidly by the shore, and Hanna'el saw at once that there was no hope of crossing at this place. Even if they had a boat, a dozen strong rowers would not have been able to fight that current.

Hanna'el shielded her eyes and examined the opposite bank, tree-lined and green. The path to the river passed through a grove of cottonwood, whose leaves swayed in the breeze that blew downriver toward the falls. In the center of the broad river, white and green like the shore she stood upon, rose a narrow island of stunted birch trees.

Though the falls were loud, the mood along the shore was peaceful and soothing in the shade of the cottonwood grove. Thomas rested while Bryhs and Hanna'el fetched water. They drank greedily, exhausted by their trek. Thomas' wound no longer bled freely, but he felt too weak to walk. Hanna'el saw that they would have to spend the night here.

They had no way to cross the raging stream.

Bryhs squinted at the roaring river. "What now?" he asked her, but Hanna'el had no answer. She felt as though she had done as much as she could. They had no food, and the only possession she had saved from Shem's attack was a small wooden box that contained Daoshin's pearl and some lengths of her severed hair. Though Bryhs had repeatedly warned her that the river could not be crossed, she had always expected to prove him wrong. She had received so much help and had come so far that it seemed impossible for her journey to end so abruptly. "Perhaps if we travel upstream we'll find a crossing," she suggested. But Bryhs shook his head. "Unlikely, Mistress," he told her dourly. "We'd have to travel miles to find such a spot, and even then, we'd need a boat. You can't expect to swim. The current's too wild."

Hanna'el had no answer. She felt exhausted and told Bryhs she needed time to think things over, time to herself.

After making sure that Thomas lay comfortably, she excused herself.

"Don't wander far," Bryhs warned her.

Hanna'el walked upstream and faced the water. To her left she could hear the constant rumble of the falls and could see in that distant spume the weaving colors of a rainbow. To her right, the river stretched like a silvery border.

She glanced at the woods behind her and wondered if she and her small company could find their way back to the highway without the aid of Shem or Seth, or how they would feed themselves, now that their food supplies had been stolen. Would she have to return to Arcatus after all, and what would she find there? Perhaps there was no place left for her to go.

Had her father come this way also?

Pondering still, she followed the rise of the bank to the shadowed woodland, hoping that Bryhs would have the good sense not to disturb her. She saw near the trees a piled mound of river stones that stood nearly as tall as herself, and she wondered if someone had placed them there as a sign. The stones lay far enough from the river that unless the water rose in an exceptional flood the stones might remain secure and undisturbed for many years.

She recalled what she had learned of Urd, that ancient land of ruins that called itself the cradle of civilization. Here, along the Karakala, the landscape looked pleasant enough, but farther west nature became barren, treeless, and hot. Because of the high mountains that separated Urd from the western ocean, little rain fell on that land. All the water came from the northern fork of the Karakala. The river's yearly flooding accounted for what little green the land still enjoyed.

Some said that the ancient Guir had come from Urd, driven out centuries ago by the harsh conditions of their homeland. It was said that those few who had stayed behind dwelt amid the haunted ruins of their ancient civilization—a furtive, legendary race—a misshapen remnant of their former glory. Sun and sand and time's ceaseless pressure had effaced almost all of their once magnificent temples, as well as the roads and cities that had been the achievements of their proud and powerful civilization. All of it had vanished.

As she stood there pondering this fate, a fish leaped high in the flowing river, its golden scales catching the light of the western sun. It splashed in the water just in front of her.

Hanna'el saw the fish only briefly, its darting sleekness silhouetted against the pale birch trees that grew on the river's central island. But that single sighting roused her from her reverie like a summons.

Walter!

For a moment she felt on the verge of remembering something vastly important, though only for the barest moment did this feeling persist. The leaping fish might have been only a trick of the waning sunlight, for it vanished before she could be certain it was there. She sighed and leaned against the mound of river stone beside her, feeling the stones' stolid coldness, so smooth and worn and hard. Her touch, gentle though it was, dislodged the delicate balance of the mound, which perhaps had been waiting for this disturbance, and several stones fell with a noisy clatter. Before she could move aside, the entire stone column began to shift, tumbling into a heap in front of her. One of the stones struck her calf, and she cried out loudly.

Then, as she stood and rubbed her bruise, she saw that the mound had crumbled to reveal a metal box.

She lifted it up, surprised at its lightness, and saw that it bore no lock, though the lid fit very snugly. Age had rusted the metal, so that at first she doubted whether she could get the box open at all. She thought of returning to Bryhs and Thomas, but before she could make up her mind, the box slipped out her hand and struck the stones. The blow loosened the lid and spilled the contents at her feet: a single sheet of blue paper, closely written in black ink.

Hanna'el stooped to read it. The paper was thin but not so old that time had made it brittle. The metal box had sealed itself so tightly that no water had rotted the page. Strange, she thought, that this was so, since the lid had sprung apart so readily.

The writing on the paper was like none that she had ever seen. She studied it closely, unable to decipher the curious script, yet feeling ever so oddly disturbed by the wavering lines. She felt that she had seen such a script before—though where and how, she had no idea. Surely, if Thomas had tutored her in such lore, she would have remembered this alphabet, and she wondered if the scholar could help her read it.

"*Hannah*," said a gentle voice behind her.

She gasped and turned around.

A young man had stepped from the forest—a young man with tousled, brown hair that fell loose to his shoulders. He smiled at her knowingly.

Hanna'el staggered back, for she recognized him at once as the shepherd who had given her the green twig months ago.

"You . . . " she began.

"Give me the letter," he told her, extending his hand. "I will read it. I know how."

As though moving within a dream, Hanna'el saw her arm stretch forth. She felt the stranger's touch. Carefully, he smoothed the paper, holding it reverently, as though it were a precious text. "I will read you this letter," he told her. "You were meant to find it. Walter made certain that you did. Mistress, you are in great danger, but if you use the El'ohyme's gift, you may yet cross the river into Urd. Listen closely; I cannot stay long. This letter is from your father, Charles."

"But my father's name is *Carlon . . .* "

The young man, the shepherd, smiled and shook his head. "*Charles*, the world explorer, wrote this letter. He left it for his only daughter, knowing that one day she would stand upon this shore. He has gone beyond the Karakala, into the barren lands of Urd. Many years have passed since he crossed over."

Hanna'el's legs became weak, and she sat upon the mound of fallen stones heavily. The young man—she was certain that he was the shepherd who had given her the twig—watched her and waited, smiling vaguely. He began to read.

> Dearest Hannah:
>
> I know that you will find this letter, though I am told that when you read it you will not remember who I am. I know this because I have conversed with the Master of Memory, Walter—and Walter told me that he spoke to you and that he knows you very well. I am glad to hear this, my darling daughter, though I find it hard to imagine you have followed me this far. There are few who can. I shall leave this letter by the river as Walter, the Master of Memory, has instructed me to do. It is all that I can give you as remembrance and advice, for I cannot remain here very long and have nothing else to offer. Even as I write, a boat draws near to ferry me across the Karakala, to the Isle of Birch and then, if I am ready, to the ancient land of Urd. Remember me when you read this—I hope you can!—for years and years shall

have passed since last we spoke . . . and you were then so young! To you those years may seem like time that never was. I shall do all in my power to complete my journey to Elowyn, for I cannot abandon my quest for the Singing Tree, but Walter has already warned me that the chances of success are very slim. In case I do not return, I have asked Walter to send you a green and living twig that grows from the Tree. There are so few left in the world, but if only one person can return one twig to the roots that bore it, the Tree shall live and sing. You must try your best to guard it—

I must go—I cannot write more—the Singer's boat draws near. All my love to you, Hannah. Remember me in Elowyn—and remember to speak my name if you reach your goal. I hope that we shall meet beneath those boughs.

Your loving father, Charles

Hanna'el, blinking, heard the shepherd's voice as though he spoke to her from a very great distance. His words sounded clear and familiar, and yet they were also impossible and strange. One part of the letter especially disturbed her.

"Who is Walter and what has happened to the green and living twig?" she heard herself ask.

The stranger looked at her as though she were just a silly child. "Didn't you see Walter, leaping above the river? As for the twig, you will soon see where you have sent it."

Just as he spoke, Hanna'el heard a cry from the distant grove of cottonwood where she had left Thomas and Bryhs. She turned to see Bryhs running toward the forest, his sword drawn for combat. Before him, emerging from the trees, stood a warrior clad in green armor. The warrior stood ready for combat, and he wielded a mighty axe.

THE SHADOW WARRIOR

Before Hanna'el could move from the crumbled mound of stone, Bryhs and the green warrior met in combat. Bryhs was no match for the strength of that encounter. The first blow broke his sword; the second caught the old warrior's side. Bryhs screamed and staggered backwards, as Hanna'el ran shouting from the mound of stones.

The green warrior turned to meet her, and he threw aside his helmet.

Hanna'el gasped when she saw her opponent's face: he was the young drover who had defied her on the bridge below the Caer— the same intemperate youth who had cursed her and thrown her coins into the raging stream.

This recognition stopped her, but in the next moment, she saw something more terrible. About the drover's neck, hanging from a golden string, was the green and living twig that the shepherd had given her, the twig that she had been urged to cherish and protect.

As though in a flash of recognition or remembrance, she understood how the twig had been lost. Thomas had left it in her room the night of Aeron's feast, and somehow this drover had found it. The scene at the bridge rose before her in a single vivid scene; she heard the drover's taunts and saw him throw the coins into the stream. His name, she remembered, was Kit. No doubt, he had followed her to the Caer and had somehow found his way to her chamber. He had stolen the twig that the shepherd had given her as a precious gift. But how had he tracked her here, and why did he wish to harm her?

Kit grinned, clearly enjoying her confusion, grief, and panic. "Hanna'el of Arcatus, at last we meet as equals face to face. *Sister*, you were foolish to run away."

He advanced toward her, allowing his axe to hang with its cutting edge down. His eyes, bright and piercing, bored into her like sharpened nails. "Sister, don't you know me? I am Raemond, your half-brother. Raemond, the son of Carlon and At'theira, Aeron's Queen. Surely you recall me—now I am the Lord of the Caar`oq Hyme."

The roaring of the river receded behind her like a dream. The world narrowed to just this moment of encounter. She saw again the sorrowful woman she had met in Aeron's Caer, and she heard that woman's mournful voice.

Carlon loved me—and I loved him. I love him still! Child, were it possible, he would have married me, and you would then be my stepdaughter.

As though emerging from a darkened cave into full sunlight, Hanna'el gasped as memories of Queen At'theira flashed before her. She recalled in a single flood of recollection every detail of her encounter with that lost woman.

Raemond laughed, enjoying this moment of power. He touched the green and living twig that hung from his neck—the gift he had stolen. "You're as great a fool as our father. The physician Azael showed me the rightful use for this twig—Azael knows its powers. Stupid girl, you tossed it away! You ignored it. Now it is mine. This twig is a talisman of strength; he who wears it draws might and sustenance from every green and living thing. With this above my heart, I am invincible."

As Raemond spoke, he raised his glistening axe. He stood so close that his bulk eclipsed the sun.

"Carlon left the Caer because he was weak, because he could not protect my mother from Aeron's wrath. He abandoned me, but I have grown strong in the care of the good physician. Azael has given back to me the memories of who I am—he has made me invincible."

Hanna'el cringed as her brother's axe fell in swift descent. A scream rent the air, and metal struck stone only a hand's breadth from where she crouched.

Raemond staggered to his knees in front of her. The shaft of an arrow protruded from his neck. In another moment, he collapsed.

The scholar Thomas had shot him. He had used Bryh's fallen bow. Weak and frightened, he had somehow summoned the courage to come to her aid.

Raemond gasped and clutched at the bloody shaft. Hanna'el, unable to speak or move, stared at him with horror.

"Look!" cried Thomas, pointing to the river.

A boat had set forth from the Isle of Birch, and it kept a perfect course against the river's swift, inexorable current.

The boat carried two passengers: one was the Singer she had met at Aeron's Caer; the second, the Singer's imp.

THE SINGER RETURNS

As soon as the boat touched shore, the Singer stilled the music of his harp. It was the harp's music that had piloted the boat across the Karakala from the Isle of Birch. The Singer leaped to the shoreline gravel, cradling the magic harp beneath his arm. His imp scampered beside him.

"Hanna'el, do you remember me?"

The Singer's eyes flashed merrily, and his streaming black hair danced in the lively wind. His silver harp strings caught the glint of the late afternoon sunlight.

Before she could answer, the Singer had knelt by Bryhs and her wounded brother.

Prince Raemond could not speak; his breath rasped weakly through his bloody lips. His eyes were wild and unfocussed—wide open, so that he appeared to be staring vaguely at the cloudless sky.

"Your friend Bryhs is dead, and your brother, too, is dying," said the Singer. "I will guide their spirits if I can, but my powers are weak on this side of the river. We must ferry them to the Isle of Birch. You and the scholar must come with me. The Tree that you are seeking lies in that direction."

Having told her this much, the Singer's attention shifted to his imp, which had transformed itself into an affectionate beagle and leaped at him, barking delightedly and wagging its tail.

"Be still," said the Singer sternly, but the imp would not or could rest. It was not in his nature.

In another moment, the imp had transformed again, this time becoming a chattering monkey that climbed upon the Singer's shoulder and howled.

But the dark-haired Singer knew what to do. Reaching into a pouch that he wore at his side, he removed a small, gray amulet fashioned from lead. This he hung about the chattering monkey's neck, and immediately the creature leaped to the ground. The imp's shape changed once more, and it took the form of a rather dull-witted five year-old child. The child squatted on the stones and picked its nose, the leaden amulet dangling loosely from its neck.

"There now, be still," said the Singer.

The imp's eyes turned inward, vacant and abstracted. It grinned at them stupidly.

"Give me Daoshin's pearl," the Singer said to her. "Find it quickly. Prince Raemond is your brother. If he dies under the physician's care, you will be much to blame. Can you bear that consequence?"

"But he tried to kill me," she protested.

The Singer watched her carefully. She felt that he weighed her soul. At last he spoke. "Raemond suffers under the power of Aeron's cruel physician. If he dies with that curse upon his soul, it will be very difficult for him in the land of spirit. The physician's art will bind him to the earth and to memories of his former lifetime. You remember Aeron's queen—the woman you discovered in the Caer? She roamed between two worlds, neither dead nor living. The same fate will be his. Those who can help him, must. If not, they must bear the consequences."

Hanna'el shuddered. She could not wish Queen At'theira's doom on anyone. Nevertheless, she hesitated.

"Please," said the Singer. "Do this for your father's sake and for his quest. Fetch me Daoshin's pearl."

His words seemed to light up a panorama of brilliant images inside her. For one brief moment, those bright pictures showed her how all her actions and deeds—those done and yet to come—were linked in unity like a single artwork. She gasped; this startling vista of images was vast in its scope and complexity.

The Singer's voice drew her back. "*Hannah*," he said to her sharply, "this is a only a glimpse of what lies ahead. Do not turn back now. Fetch me Daoshin's gift."

The Singer's sharp tone of voice startled her. She had left the small treasure inside the grove of cottonwood where Thomas and Bryhs had rested, and she ran to get it. By the time she found it and returned, the sun had slipped lower and the shadows had grown dark on the western shore.

"Open the box," said the Singer. "Remove the pearl and hold it against your dying brother's chest. Only you can do this. What happens next must happen because you will it to be so."

She saw Brother Thomas watching her intently. He had not heard Raemond's confession and did not understand why the Singer had called Prince Raemond her brother. He knew nothing of what Raemond or Queen At'theira had said.

"Don't do it!" he warned her.

But Hanna'el knelt down, moving as though her will were outside her own body. She felt dull and distant from herself, her emotions numb.

Following the Singer's instructions, she took the pearl from its casket and placed it on Raemond's heaving chest. He moaned as he felt her touch, and Hanna'el nearly drew back her hand.

"Have courage," said the Singer gently but firmly.

Raemond blinked, and his eyes suddenly focused. He looked directly into her face. For a moment, hatred and jealousy flashed in his expression and it seemed that he meant to strike her. Hanna'el gasped and nearly drew back in fear. But the hatred, like a distorting shadow, passed swiftly. Raemond sighed, and his features relaxed. He became more childlike.

"*Sister*," he exhaled. The word, for once, was spoken with no malice, anger, or self-pity.

Daoshin's pearl had grown warm in her hand, like a heated stone. She kept it in place on Raemond's chest, above his heart, as the Singer instructed. She met her brother's gaze; she did not look away. But at the periphery of her vision, she saw what appeared to be a hideous shadow rise like a subtle vapor from her brother's chest. The shadow had the shape and contour of Raemond's body; it belonged to him, but its face was a distorted mask of rage—a demonic caricature of Raemond's features. The evil shadow darted at her angrily, and she nearly fell back in fright, but the Singer, moving swiftly, held her hand in place. He kept her steady. In another moment, the monstrous shadow had dissolved, and now, when she looked upon her brother, his face had lost all lines of hatred and tension. A fresh and childlike innocence shone in his expression. "Sister," he said once more, and this time his tone held only affection, weariness, and sorrow. Hanna'el felt Daoshin's pearl burn like a glowing ember against her palm.

"Good," said the Singer. "Continue."

Raemond shut his eyes and sighed profoundly.

His body trembled and then completely relaxed. He was dead.

Hanna'el gasped and opened her fist to shake loose the heated pearl. To her horror, the jewel had been transformed. No longer snowy white, it had become a lump of blackened charcoal.

The Thief Returns Also

At first she could say nothing; her hand trembled and her head throbbed and ached. She stared at the blackened pearl as though it were some terrible scarab beetle that had crawled upon her flesh. She wanted to hurl it away, for she continued to see the hideous shadow that had risen from Raemond's chest. The face of that demonic shadow mocked and tormented her.

Are such monstrous things part of me as well?

"Watch," said the Singer.

Momentarily, Hanna'el felt the black stone increase in size, and she saw that the blackness of the pearl swirled like angry storm clouds. She saw within those thunderclouds a flash of golden light whose shape reminded her of a dragon. Darkness and light intermingled, transforming in the chaos of the storm. Then darkness gave way to the bright gold of dragon's fire; the stone clarified, contracted, and became once more the smooth and perfect pearl that it first had been, without a trace of discoloration.

The Singer looked to sky. In the deepening twilight, Hanna'el saw the planets Venus and Mars.

"It is finished," said the Singer. "Now let us bear the bodies to the Isle of Birch. Take the precious twig from your brother's neck. Keep it safely in your possession, always." He helped her by removing the string that held the twig, for Hanna'el's hand trembled too much to perform the deed.

Suddenly, Thomas raised himself with his elbows and pointed downstream. "Look there, the thief! He's come back!"

Hanna'el saw Seth stagger from the trees.

"That man stole our money and our ponies," said Thomas angrily. "He must be punished!"

"Let him approach," the Singer said calmly.

As Seth came closer, Hanna'el felt more in possession of herself. The thief's reappearance was like a dash of cold water in her face.

"You dog!" Thomas shouted.

But Seth ignored the scholar. He glanced from the bodies to the Singer and his imp, and then, breathing heavily, dropped to his knees before Hanna'el, clasping his hands together as though in prayer. He began to kiss her feet. "Oh mistress, dear lady, it wasn't my fault! My brother Shem—he's the one who plotted to rob you. I didn't know what he planned to do. I heard your cries for help and came as fast as I could, but the old chieftain, Bryhs—he lies there dead—the spirits bless him!—he never believed I meant to help you. Bryhs chased me away before I could explain, and I was afraid to approach while he was alive. Ah mistress, I saw everything. Thank god, you survived! My brother Shem is dead—I found him—he was beheaded."

But Thomas had no pity for Seth's complaint.

"Where's my gold, you evil scoundrel? Get up; stop kissing her feet! Where are the ponies? What have you done with our supplies, you black-hearted traitor!"

"Gone, all gone," Seth moaned, rolling his eyes. He did not release Hanna'el calves. "My brother took them, but he's dead and all that he stole disappeared. Even the supplies he kept for *me*— those, too, are missing. All I found is his headless body in the woods. The evil one had hung him upside down."

Thomas fell back, wincing and exhausted. "You blackguard," he muttered. But the Singer stood apart and observed Seth's pleas without expression.

"Take me with you," Seth pleaded to Hanna'el. "I never meant to betray you, Mistress—I swear! Who guided you to this river? Who advised you? Shem's the one who wished you harm, but Shem is dead. Spare me; spare me, Mistress, please. Take me with you! I can be useful to you still; I know this country. I've been to Urd."

But the Singer had heard enough. He silenced Seth with a wave of his arm. "Hanna'el, we must go quickly—the night is at hand. These bodies must be carried to the boat. I cannot move them by myself. If this thief wishes to join you, let him help by doing the heavy work. Make him bear the corpses. Otherwise, I advise you to drive him away."

"Don't trust him, Hanna'el" urged Thomas, his voice hoarse with pain and fatigue. "He betrayed us twice. He'll betray you again."

But in fact, thought Hanna'el, she had not seen Seth do anything wrong. Shem was the one who had attacked them. And Shem alone had wounded Thomas and stolen the horses and supplies.

She looked at the Singer, hoping that he might tell her what to do, but the Singer kept silent and waited for her decision. Seth, on his knees, pleaded mightily and clutched at her feet. Embarrassed, angry, and perplexed, she tried to step backwards, but the thief would not release his grip.

Disgusted, yet moved to pity, she told him to keep still.

"You heard what Singer told us," she answered him brusquely. "If you want to help us, bear those corpses to the boat. If not, go away from here. You are free to decide your own fate."

Seth nodded eagerly. "Mistress, I'll do anything! I'll do whatever you command. Please don't leave me behind! Whoever killed my brother will kill me, too, if you leave me here all alone. I have no weapons or supplies. I'm completely helpless."

"Hurry," said the Singer to Hanna'el, "you alone must decide what we must do. Once the last gleam of sunlight vanishes, it will be too late to make our crossing. We must reach the Isle of Birch while there is twilight."

Hanna'el nodded, remembering the conversation she had once shared with Bryhs. If the Tree summoned her to Urd, perhaps it summoned the thief as well. Why had Seth returned to the river? What could he hope to gain by joining them? And how could he betray her once they crossed the Karakala? She saw no way that he might profit from deceit.

"Seth, the decision's yours. You may leave or come along. If you join us, do what the Singer asks."

"Gladly!" the thief agreed. He stood up happily.

Thomas protested, but in his weakened state, he could not argue.

"All right, quickly then," said the Singer. "We must go."

Together, Seth and the Singer bore the bodies of Raemond and Bryhs to the boat, and the imp slouched chattering at their heels.

"Follow me, get in," said the Singer, once they were done. He raised his harp.

Hanna'el and Thomas entered the craft and crouched as the imp shoved the boat into the current. For a moment, the swift river seized them and bore them downstream toward the thundering falls. Then the Singer touched his strings, and his harp resounded with startling clarity. Seized by the sudden enchantment of the music, the small craft shuddered and changed course for the Isle of Birch.

The Isle of Birch

They began their journey across the Karakala to the Isle of Birch as the last fading light of sunset glowed on the distant hills. Hanna'el feared that they might not have enough time to make the crossing, but the boat, once seized by the spell of the Singer's harp, moved swiftly against the current; it did not falter. By the time they neared the shore of the middle island, Hanna'el saw the crescent of the waxing moon. The sky had darkened, and the last traces of day bled thin across the horizon. A breeze blew southward along the river, cool from the northern mountains, and the wind swayed the slender birch trees that lined the shore. Their leaves seemed to whisper. As the wind waved the birches to and fro, Hanna'el imagined that the trees had assembled to welcome them and that they swayed to the enchanted music of the Singer's harp. She had heard many times, and now she could believe it, that of all trees, birches were those most inclined to speak to human beings, and especially when they were questioned about the dead.

Hanna'el, still dressed in the servant's clothing that she had worn as her disguise, raised the hood of her jacket to keep the wind off the back of her neck. She hunched low in the boat as the Singer, without word or movement, guided the craft with his music toward a silvery, sandy beach. She shivered, feeling the exhaustion of recent events. Bryhs and Raemond lay stretched before her, their bodies covered by blankets that the Singer, thankfully, had provided. She did not feel strong enough to look upon them now. Thomas sat beside her, but he kept his face turned downwards to the water, and his eyes were ancient and withdrawn. She thought that he, too, had suddenly felt the weariness of their journey, or else that his wound distressed him. He did not meet her glance.

As the boat came closer to the island's shore, Hanna'el raised her head to better hear the Singer's music. His fingers kept a delicate, constant rhythm upon the strings while his throat hummed a threnody shared by the wind and the churning, frothy water at their wake. His hair blew wildly to the left side of his face, and his dark eyes gazed straight ahead, never moving until the boat had beached. Beside him, the melancholy imp hunched like a dull-witted idiot or devoted servant, while Seth, who had confessed upon departure that he could not swim, fretted at the boat's prow, blinking his eyes in fear and scarcely hidden terror as now and then the wind sprayed water upon his face. Hanna'el saw Seth glance frequently toward the sound of the roaring waterfall to their left. He bit his lip and clutched the gunwale tightly.

As the boat scraped the shore of the island, Seth was the first one out. Moving gracefully, the Singer then stepped ashore, his harp silenced, and after him came the imp, leaping from the bow so as not to wet his feet in the shallow water. Hanna'el came next, supporting Thomas, and then the Singer ordered Seth to drag the boat ashore. "Here we may keep our vigil while I sing."

Already it was dark. Seth drew the boat securely ashore and searched for a spot of soft ground on which to rest. They needed fire and food, but before Hanna'el could speak, the Singer touched the strings of his magical harp. His voice tuned to the instrument's subtle chords, and though the wind had increased, Hanna'el heard every word and note clearly.

"I am not permitted to remain with you for long," the Singer said. "In the time that is given to us, I will make a song that will assist the fallen warriors on their journeys, a song that may also illumine your path. I beg you to be patient and to listen."

He began before she could speak, and the music at once had power to silence any questions. The flow of the Singer's melody felt as powerful as the current of the river, and it soothed her like a powerful draught of wine. Hanna'el saw Seth and Thomas nod with exhaustion, and soon their heads had lowered in heavy slumber. She, too, felt stone-weary and sore, though she struggled mightily to stay awake. The imp alone looked sprightly and gay, enraptured by the wind that rustled the birch trees, by the water that stirred constantly at the shore, by the shimmer of moonlight upon the swiftly flowing river.

The Singer's music continued.

At first Hanna'el followed carefully the rise and fall of every note, but the more determined she became to find the inner meaning of this music, the more she felt drawn toward sleep. Her eyelids fluttered in sweet exhaustion, unable to resist fatigue, until at last the need to rest thrust her down like an overpowering opponent. Then, as she hovered in that realm between sleep and wakefulness— her consciousness weak as a wind-blown candle—she heard in the lilting tones of the Singer's melody the stern whisper of Bryhs' phlegmatic voice.

"Hanna'el," the dead warrior said to her slowly, "*do not fall asleep*. Follow the Singer's music. You must learn to *hover*."

And yet, despite this admonition, she felt her awareness drowning in the song, as though the great tide of night rose inexorably inside her, washing over her like waves overlapping a shore, drawing her downward into its velvet, soothing depths. The thread of her self-awareness felt drawn to a limitless length, thinner than the finest gossamer.

And then it snapped.

Hanna'el awoke.

Before her in the boat lay the bodies of Bryhs and Raemond, peaceful and composed, as though asleep. The hour seemed late into the night. The moon, which had shown as a waxing crescent, had slipped below the horizon. The clear night sky shone entirely filled with stars. She could see the constellation called Orion, and beside it the hunter's companion: Sirius, the dog star. The cool wind that had chilled her had subsided, and the silvery leaves of the birch trees were dark and still.

The Singer had ceased his singing, though his fingers still played lightly upon the strings. He watched the bodies of Bryhs and Raemond and turned when he felt her awaken.

Hanna'el could barely stifle a yawn. "I slept," she confessed, feeling sheepish. "The song was too powerful."

The Singer nodded. He glanced at Seth and Thomas, sleeping still, and his lips curved with the slightest smile. "Did you follow the course of your dreams? Could you read their script?"

She realized she had not. Nor could she recall dreaming. She asked him how long she had slept.

"Soon it will be dawn. When the sun rises, we must launch Bryhs and Raemond into the river. The current will carry them over the falls. Watch now—what can you see?"

Hanna'el turned to the small boat that held Bryhs and Raemond, but she could see nothing unusual or new. The gentle notes of the harp continued to fill the quiet air, and the music sounded even sweeter and more poignant. It filled her with painful nostalgia for her home, for the vast and waving grasslands of Arcatus.

No more words were spoken until the first rays of the sun illumined the sky. Only when the full sunlight shone upon them did the Singer cease to play. He put down his harp and, assisted by the imp, launched the boat into the current. Hanna'el stood in silence as the river bore the bodies of Bryhs and Raemond toward the falls, which were arched by a brilliant rainbow. The Singer stood beside her and gently spoke. "Could you follow the course of my singing? Did you listen as I asked you to do? That which you search for, the Singing Tree, was present with the dawn. Its branches receive the dead. It has joined their memories to its singing."

Hanna'el said nothing, but her expression bore witness to her confusion and shame.

"I saw nothing . . . " she admitted guiltily.

She feared that the Singer would be angry, but instead he merely nodded and summoned the imp.

"Then it is a sign that you must continue into Urd. See, the others are stirring. Stand up and help them prepare. I will tell you what you must know."

"Depart?" said Hanna'el, alarmed by his words. "How can I leave this island? Where shall I go?"

"To Elowyn," said the Singer. "You must follow the northern fork of the Karakala deeper into Urd. There you must confront the one who awaits you."

THE THIEF HAS A FRIEND

Thomas awoke, yawning and stretching, while Seth slumbered on as soundly as a child. "Ah," said Thomas as he stood and shook the sleep from his limbs, "that was a better rest than I have had for many months. What hour is it? I don't think I stirred all night."

"The sun has risen three times since you closed your eyes in slumber," said the Singer, laughing brightly. And when Thomas and Hanna'el refused to believe they had slept so long, he only shrugged. "Believe me or not, it is the truth. Tonight when the moon rises, you will see by its size that I am right. Look how the one named Seth slumbers still. Wake him, for if you don't he'll likely sleep through a fourth day."

Thomas gave Seth a poke with his foot, and the thief groaned and rolled to his side. "The devil take you!" he cried, slapping at Thomas. "I'll not be kicked awake by anyone."

"Peace," said the Singer. "You have slumbered long enough. It is time to leave this island. The bodies of Bryhs and Raemond have been sent over the Karakala Falls."

Seth stood up at once when he heard this news. "Over the falls? How will we leave the island without a boat? And where could we go if we had one?"

"To Urd," said the Singer in an even tone of voice.

Seth swore with disbelief. "Are you mad? Why should we go *there*? That land is cursed."

Thomas groaned with exasperation. "You see," he complained to Hanna'el, "I told you we should have left him behind."

Seth flushed when he heard the scholar. "Shut up," he growled. "Your opinion isn't wanted. I know this country better than you. I made my choice. I swore to her. Who are you to doubt me all the time?"

But his words only made Thomas angrier. "Ungrateful wretch! No one cares for your opinion. You stole our supplies, and now you think you can treat us as your equals."

Seth laughed at the scholar's taunts, and his laughter made Thomas even angrier. He was about to speak another insult when the Singer intervened.

"Hanna'el," he said, stepping between Seth and Thomas, "perhaps it is wise to heed the scholar. I can ferry Seth across the river, and once across he can find his way through the forest back to his home."

"No!" Seth exclaimed, glancing nervously at the swift current that separated him from the shore they had left behind. "I'll not be sent back to starve and die alone. I won't lose my head like Shem. I merely spoke my opinion honestly—you wouldn't want me to lie, would you? You asked me to guide you and give advice. Well, I have. I did. And I will! It is folly to enter Urd. Only the dying may go there."

Hanna'el's head throbbed from this argument. She wished that she could be alone. "We must continue," she repeated, though she thought that her voice sounded more eager to convince herself than Seth. "If you don't want to come, stay behind."

The thief stepped forward to plead his disappointment, but just as he moved, the imp, who had done almost nothing since the leaden amulet had fixed his shape to that of an idiot child, walked to Seth's side and silently took his hand. Seth, not noticing the imp's approach, was so unnerved by the contact that he shrieked and jerked away. The imp pursued him, its face split wide with a silly grin. The closer the imp approached, the more frightened Seth became, but his discomfort only made the imp more affectionate. "Call him off," shouted Seth, dancing back and shaking his arm as though fire ants crawled over it. "Keep him back—don't let him touch me."

Hanna'el and the Singer, observing this strange pursuit, laughed. "Come to me," ordered the Singer.

At once, the imp turned from Seth and settled itself at the Singer's feet, as obedient as a melancholy hound.

Hanna'el, seeing Seth's panic, suddenly knew what she wanted to do. "If Seth will follow us to Urd, let him do so. If he will not cross the river to Urd, then send him back to the forest after we are gone. In any event, that's where I am going. Seth, you may come with us or not."

Her tone left no doubt that her decision could not be argued, and Seth, still panting from the imp's pursuit, nodded in agreement. "Of course, Mistress, I'll do whatever you want."

"Do as *you* want," she reprimanded him. "You're free to decide."

"Free?" he scoffed. "Free to do what? Free to die if I turn back? Free to die if I don't? What kind of freedom is that? Hear me out, Mistress. I mean no disrespect. Your idea of freedom and mine are very different. But you can put yourself at ease. Mistress, I surrender my freedom. You can have it. I give it to you . . . freely! My life is yours. Only, don't make me go back across the river and die like my brother Shem."

"Very well, then," Hanna'el scowled.

Thomas groaned. "You're making a terrible mistake, Hanna'el," he warned her.

But the Singer nodded. "Good, it is settled. If this is your decision, then let my imp accompany you as well. He knows the way, and he has helped you. The thief will not harm you as long as my imp remains at your side."

"What!" said Seth. "Never! You can't put me near that ugly beast."

And Hanna'el, seeing Seth's distress, could not restrain a laugh.

The imp scampered near and took the thief's hand.

"Ah!" Seth exclaimed, "get him off me! Call him back!"

"Those are the terms," said the Singer sternly. "The imp must go, too. The decision's made. Let us get ready. Seth, help us prepare."

THE SINGER'S ADVICE

While Thomas and Seth readied themselves for the journey, Hanna'el and the Singer withdrew to a quiet knoll beneath the trees. The Singer handed his harp to the imp, who cradled it fondly as he sat by his master.

Now that they were alone, Hanna'el wanted to ask what was foremost in her mind: how had the Singer found her in this place—who was the child that she had dreamt of so often—*who was Walter*, and what was the meaning of the twig that she had removed from her brother's neck after he died?

The Singer understood her before she spoke.

"I am not Walter, though you are right to ask that question. Singers are the messengers of those whom you call Masters of Memory. Walter is such a Master; there are seven in all. I was sent here to meet you, for Walter foresaw your progress and what would happen when you arrived. As for the child you remember from your dreams, that child is you. She carries the answer to your destiny. Summon your memories, Hanna'el. Did Walter not show you memory and allow you to swim in its currents? Do you recall that experience?"

The Singer's words resonated deeply inside her.

Hanna'el could indeed recall a conversation from long ago. Was it imagined? She had been in a small room with Walter, who was a fish, and she had asked him a simple question: *"Walter, what is memory?"* But, instead of answering, he had shown her the river time. She had swum inside that stream of remembrance and had heard the weaving melodies of its infinite, crystalline spheres.

"Why can't I go home?" she suddenly asked. It surprised her to hear this question, for the words seemed to come from someone else.

And as soon as she thought this, a wave of nostalgia overcame her. She wished that she had never left her garden. She wished that her father had never gone to discover the last unknown country in the world. She wished that her father had lived in that garden with her and Uncle Joseph forever, or at least, for as long as their lives would permit, and she wished that she could sit in that garden now and see Joseph stumble in from his daily chores, covered with dirt, for a noonday snack and a peek at one of his old books of philosophy. She wished that she would find one of his books of philosophy half read upon the breakfast table, sticky with marmalade jam. She wished that she could meet the Seven Friedrichs—or even just the Privy Counselor—and that she would find them all quite sensible and fully in charge. *I don't want to be in charge* . . . she heard someone say. *Not any longer.* She wanted someone else to bear that burden. *Oh, why did I dare to enter the Zone of Night?*

This sudden feeling of homesickness made her pale, and she shivered as the Singer reached out to reassure her.

"You have never left that garden," the Singer said, touching her trembling hand and speaking gently. His eyes had a curious light, as though the irises, like flakes of gold, sparkled in the sun. His voice rang low and barely audible above the river's steady current and the sound of the enormous falls, but Hanna'el heard every word.

"You cannot return, for you have never left, and the child you remember is with you even now. Home is not a place; it is remembrance. But because your powers of recollection are so weak—because the sacred Tree has grown so ill—you cannot recall the truths of those many selves. Only she who has heard the Tree sing in its strongest blossoming can withstand the full power of recollection. I can do so, but I am at the end of a process that for you has only begun. My imp can also live as many selves, but in him, the power of remembrance has run wild. Just as you need the Tree to restore your remembrance, my imp needs the Tree to restore in him the power to forget. Forgetting and remembrance must abide in continual balance, like the balance of waking and sleep, like inhalation and exhalation, like night and day. These currents of uprising and descent are tended by the Masters, but for some those currents run wild. My imp recalls too much; he is a victim of memory. He cannot retain a constant form."

As though to demonstrate, the Singer called the imp to his side and removed the leaden amulet from the imp's neck. Immediately the creature leaped high into the air, spun gaily, and took the shape of a peregrine falcon. Hanna'el gasped as the imp flew high above her and darted away to the west.

"Don't worry," said the Singer, "I can recall him whenever I want. The amulet will hold him again. As long as the leaden amulet is on his neck, my imp cannot alter his shape. The spell of the amulet has power to subdue him. With the amulet on his neck, he will serve you faithfully, although his actions lack intelligence. He has no self—no "I," no ego, to center him. You must be firm and exact in your commands. Treat him like the child he appears to be. Above all, do not remove the amulet, for if you do he will succumb to the swirl of memory and lose his shape. He will become whatever he looks upon, or else whatever his fancy happens to recall."

"But how do you get him to return?" She remembered her dream of the garden and the black tomcat who had accompanied her to the *Zone of Night*.

Were they the same?

The Singer smiled. "My imp will always return. He must return, because he loves me, and I love him. He loves me because I sing to him and because he, too, was once a Singer—a far greater Singer than I will ever become. So great was his talent, he could hold nature spellbound by his art. Greater and greater became his powers until one day, intoxicated by his art, he dared to test his strength against the sun. But the sun overcame him with hardly a notice of his singing, and he lost the balance of his recollection— the balance we call forgetting and recall. The power of his art, run wild within him—unchecked by the power to forget—transforms him to an imp with no fixed shape. He is all and nothing. He can assume the appearance of anything in this world, but he lacks the greater blessing of self-knowledge." He paused for a moment as

Hanna'el pondered his words. And then he said: "Take out the green and living twig that Walter gave you. Now is the time to learn what it is for."

As soon as Hanna'el touched the twig, she again felt the presence of that child she had dreamt of in the garden, and she recalled the letter that she had found in the mound of stones. That letter had been written to *Hannah*, a name that was so much like her own.

The Singer said: "Walter gave you this twig to aid you in your quest; you must take it to the roots of the dying Tree. The twig is meant for you and you alone. Your half-brother, Raemond, stole it—you gave him that chance. But in him, the twig's fierce power ran wild. It enflamed the ambition and anger that already preyed upon Raemond's soul and made him the helpless victim of Aeron's physician. The physician is but the shadow of a greater power; he serves a Master whose name I cannot speak. Someday you may learn of him. In the cycles of remembrance, that Master's time is nigh."

The Singer stood.

"Come, we must get ready for your departure. I will show you one more thing."

"Wait," said Hanna'el, "not yet. Tell me more. Tell me about the Tree. Did my father find it?"

"He did," said the Singer gravely. "But he could not return. Urd has has claimed him, as it claims all things and beings that are forsaken, lost, or forgotten. It would claim you as well, were it not for Walter's twig. You must set your father free—he and all the others, who are a part of you."

"But how can I do that?"

"Do as Walter said. Carry the twig to Elowyn and plant it at the root of the dying Tree. If you do, even though your gesture is very small, you will have done enough. Take the twig, and take the pearl that Daoshin gave you; carry them to Urd. There you will find a portal through which you may cross to Elowyn, if you succeed. The portal is in the care of a derelict singer named Azael. He will challenge you."

Hanna'el startled. "I know that name. The Queen, Raemond's mother, foretold I would meet him . . . in the place where the two become one." She touched the slender twig that rested near her heart. "Aeron's cruel physician . . . "

"Bears the same name," the Singer nodded. "Azael was once a Singer like me, but he coveted the appearance of humanity and longed to possess your human freedom. He will meet you in whatever shape you grant him. Do not be afraid. Fear gives him strength. You must meet his challenge."

"But how will I find him? How will I know the way?"

"You already know the way. You have been following it for many years, for many lifetimes. Your question leads you. Your question is your path."

What is my question? Hanna'el wanted to say. For she suddenly felt that she had never known or understood it.

This Singer expects too much!

He spoke again. "The ancient folk of Urd will assist you. When the time is at hand, you will know what to ask them and what you must do."

THE SINGER'S HARP

Having said this much, the Singer rose and fetched his harp from where the imp had placed it on the ground. He looked to the river, where Thomas and Seth still argued loudly with one another. Before Hanna'el could ask him anything else, he raised his hand to summon Seth and Thomas.

"The morning has come. It is time that you left. In the tall reeds farther up the shore, you will find a boat. Seth must fetch it. You will use that boat to travel into Urd."

Seth grumbled but obeyed, cowed by the Singer's authority. As he walked up the beach, he glanced nervously at the sky, for he had seen the imp transform, and he worried that the annoying creature might wing down upon his head.

While Seth busied himself with his task, the Singer inspected Thomas' wound and applied a fresh dressing. He told Hanna'el that the scholar's injury would heal as long as he did not strain himself too much.

"How can I not strain myself?" Thomas asked peevishly. "We have a long journey ahead of us. Every step I take strains my wound."

"You must not enter Urd on foot," the Singer replied. "The soil of Urd is too potent and wearisome for human travelers. Here the land looks green and inviting, but only a short distance from the river the country changes. No human can travel through Urd without succumbing to despair, for the ruins work an enchantment that overwhelms the hardiest traveler. Urd needs no stronger magic than this to guard its borders from trespass. The only way forward is by water; for the ruins have less power over the flowing world. You must follow the river downstream to the mighty falls. There, almost at the point where the waters fall thunderously into a misty abyss, a lesser stream that flows from Urd joins the broad Karakala.

Follow that lesser stream against its current. You may stop at night to rest, but do not linger ashore beyond the hour of sunrise. The power of those dread ruins waxes with the daylight. Even in darkness, you must beware and not succumb to the temptation to wander far from the river's edge."

"But how will we avoid the falls? And how can we travel against the current? How will I find my way?"

"Take my harp. I will teach you to play it so that its music will give you power over the flowing world. The music will also aid you inside Urd. The ruins and those who haunt them have a weakness for music, human memories and human speech. Such envy will work to your advantage; but use that advantage wisely. Beware, Hanna'el. Urd is a dead kingdom abandoned to the desert, but a misshapen remnant of its ancient folk still linger amid the ruins. My harp is your defense; those creatures love music. Use music to persuade them. The Urdish folk will help you find Azael if you tempt them with the harp's sweet music. You will need their help, but take care—the Urdish folk will strike a hard bargain. Do not believe everything they tell you. Their form is contemptible, but they are clever. Do not try to outwit them; no human can equal their intelligence. Trust in my harp, and in the purity of your quest; that is your best strategy. Watch now, I shall summon my imp."

The Singer raised his harp and repeatedly struck some chords. Suddenly, from the western horizon, a falcon appeared in rapid flight. It flew straight at them, winging swiftly from the sky. As it neared the ground it tumbled and landed with a thump beside the Singer, its shape now that of a sad-faced, idiot child. Reaching in his leather pouch, the Singer quickly drew forth the leaden amulet and hung it around the imp's neck.

"There," he said. "My imp will remain in that shape as long as he wears the amulet. The power of lead stills his restless fancy; he cannot remove the amulet by himself, for he lacks volition, nor will he do much of anything unless you command him. As I told you, speak to him exactly and do not confuse him by asking him to think for himself. He cannot reason; he has no inner constancy.

He must rely entirely on you for self-control. You will see that his powers of imitation are not entirely tamed by this leaden charm. Despite the magic, he may mimic you or someone else, but he will not be able to change his shape. Beware lest the amulet fall from his neck, for his unfixed spirit will abandon you, and then you will be entirely alone."

Seth interrupted from the river shore. He had fetched the boat from the reeds and stood uncertainly, holding the prow against the current. The Singer handed his harp to Hanna'el and showed her how to play the proper chords.

"Go now; peace be with you. There is nothing more I can tell you. The rest depends on you."

Hanna'el turned and walked to the boat, taking the imp with her. The imp moaned like a sad child to see the Singer stay behind, but he did not abandon Hanna'el.

"Dare we trust ourselves to the magic of the harp?" Thomas asked, eying the river anxiously. Even here, the sound of the waterfall was loud.

Seth overheard the scholar's remark. "You mean we have to leave without the Singer?" He retreated from the boat, too terrified to approach the river. "We'll drown if we set out alone."

Hanna'el stepped into the boat and told Thomas to launch it. The imp clambered to her side. "Stay here if you like," she answered Seth. "The Singer will transport you across the river."

Not waiting for the thief to make up his mind, Hanna'el struck the chords that the Singer had shown her, and although her music was faint and tentative, the boat at once trembled and began to move. Because she floated with the current, she at first could not tell if the music had worked a proper spell. She had to trust the Singer's words.

"Wait!" cried Seth, as the boat floated from the shore. He splashed through the water and nearly capsized them as he climbed aboard.

They moved quickly once underway, and the sound of the waterfall grew louder. Soon they could see the spume from its cascade, rainbowed in the sunlight like the arch of a cathedral built of light, and the current increased in relentless strength. Hanna'el scanned the shore, searching for the stream that the Singer had mentioned. Seth, white-faced and shivering, clutched the gunwale and stared at the approaching cataract whose vast spumes rose through the rainbowed arches just ahead, while Thomas pursed his lips in stoic composure. The imp alone sat untroubled. He stared at Hanna'el with round, adoring eyes.

"Play the harp again," said Thomas, eying nervously the cliffs that reared higher and more confining as they neared the precipitous falls. "I cannot see any passage."

Hanna'el feared that her nervous fingers would be unable to play the harp adequately, but as soon as she touched the strings, the boat changed course, moving now to starboard as though directed by an unseen helmsman. Despite the strong current, their craft moved easily. It was plain even to Seth that they would not wash over the falls. Instead, they made for a tributary that fed into this river about a quarter mile from the cataract. And though this lesser river flowed quite swiftly, the music of the harp maintained their steady course upstream.

BOOK EIGHT

The Ruins of Hkaar

URD

The roaring falls of the Karakala soon subsided in the distance, and the travelers found themselves in a hot river canyon whose reddish cliffs towered several hundred feet above them, blocking the sky. The silent canyon felt oppressive. No one spoke, not even Seth, who grimaced and hunkered down in the boat's narrow prow, afraid that any moment the Singer's magic would falter and the boat, like helpless driftwood, would be borne by the swift current back downstream to its destruction. But the magic did not fail, and with time the cliffs began to diminish as the canyon gave way to the flat, sandy, barren plains of Urd.

The sun stood well past its zenith by the time they emerged from this canyon entirely. During the last miles of their travel, Hanna'el saw what looked to be caves dotting the sheer vertical cliffs of the canyon walls. She saw no way to reach those entrances, for the cliffs fell perpendicularly to the river.

Thomas, who knew some of the history of Urd, told her that long ago those caves had served as cells for pious hermits. Once sequestered, the monks remained in those cells for decades, receiving food at periodic intervals in baskets dangled from above. But this practice, he told her, had occurred only during the last waning days of the Urdish kingdom, after the older mystery rites of Urd had fallen into decadence. The anchorites and holy men who had dwelt in these canyon caves had not come from Urd; they were foreigners drawn to this barren land for meditation and penance. At that time, Thomas told her, the enchantment that lay upon the ruined kingdom had not yet extended to the Karakala. Though the ruined temples and cities were inaccessible, men could still visit outlying regions, such as the cliffs, and the borderland of Urd became a refuge for madmen, criminals, and saints.

At one point as Hanna'el gazed upward at the cliffs, she saw before one of the cave entrances what looked to be a sun-bleached human skeleton. After this, she asked no more questions, and when at last the cliffs diminished, she felt a great relief. Ahead, the once fertile plains of Urd stretched to the west, north, and south. These plains had become a vast, unpopulated desert lacking any sign of human life. Again, Thomas could recall enough history to explain the lay of the land. He told her that this tributary river divided Urd into two halves. Northward and west lay the temples past which they must travel, the fabled ruins of the memory palaces of Hkaar. Southward stood the ruins of once great cities, Katesh, Mor'el, Horem—and others, whose names he had forgotten. The desert plains that stretched to either side had been lush farmland, famous for grain. Now it was all a wasteland, he added sadly. Hanna'el could only wonder what evil misfortune had transformed this once fertile landscape into the barren desert she saw now.

The country that they entered became ever more a place of rock and thorn. The boat moved steadily against the current, never slowing, while the sun, no longer softened by clouds or any green and living thing, shone down unmercifully.

The boat navigated every obstacle and chose the deepest water as though guided by a canny helmsman. Seth, who sat in panicked silence as the boat passed through the river canyon, grew nervous with boredom as the cliffs gave way to the open plains. He complained loudly of the journey, so loudly that Thomas lost patience and insulted him. This only caused an argument that

Hanna'el felt in no temper to endure. She was about to shout them both into silence, when the imp, who had squatted quietly all the while, moved closer to Seth and placed his hand fondly on the thief's knee. Seth recoiled at once, but the imp would not be put off. It moved so close that Seth had no choice but to accept its friendship or tumble out of the boat. Whenever Seth grew angry or began to complain, the imp smiled stupidly and placed its hand affectionately on Seth's leg. In this way, to Hanna'el's amusement, they soon had peace, for Seth felt too disturbed by the imp's devoted attention to argue with the scholar. Thomas chuckled at the unlikely partnership of imp and thief, while Hanna'el gave herself over to the rhythm of their travel and turned her attention inward.

With each passing hour on the river, she felt more distant from herself, and though she tried to remain confident and brave, she could not escape feeling that she had entered a landscape from which she would not return. She did not know if Thomas shared her anxiety, nor did she trouble him with her thoughts. She waited, but as the day lengthened, she felt as though the bonds of hope and sympathy that joined her to her past and to her future had been severed by her recent experiences. She traveled into a region where human emotion and memory could not thrive—a land of unvaried sunlight and remorseless clarity, dead to its past and lacking any promise—doomed to a sterile present that banished life and hope.

She recalled the Singer's words, and, even more troubling, she recalled the girl, the child known as *Hannah*, the child she had once imagined in a garden unlike any she had ever known. No longer did she feel so very distant from that vision or that child. She felt that the child was with her. She could feel her presence alive and conscious inside her, and she could hold to this awareness while at the same time she remembered her identity as *Hanna'el*. She felt as well that the child depended on her, though why or for what reason Hanna'el could not say.

Strangely, the remembrance of that child increased with each passing hour of travel. Perhaps the twig made this possible, the green and living twig that she wore above her heart. She touched it often and wished that she could explain her feelings to Thomas, but she did not want to speak in front of Seth. Instead, she dwelt upon her memories until, with each passing hour, she could no longer swear with certainty who was real: *Hanna'el of Arcatus* or *Hannah*, the child whose father had left her to discover the last unknown country in the world. *Or were they one and the same?* Certainly, she recalled her own departure from Arcatus, her journey to the Caer, her confrontation with Aeron, and all that had happened since . . . and her mind teemed with memories of a childhood spent on the steppes, in the grassy, hilly country she called Arcatus, her distant homeland. But what of that other place—her garden, that *other* home? As they traveled slowly upriver, she could remember more and more of that second home—its odors, its tastes, the flowers and the vegetables planted by the man she called Uncle Joseph—but were those images true memories or only the mere enchantments of her imagination?—mere longings for a world that could never be? She could not tell. And she felt dizzy with the confusion of these thoughts, as though trapped in an infinite regression of opposing mirrors, an endless vista of cascading selves and lost identities. She had always thought that somewhere—hidden deeply perhaps inside her—dwelled a self who was truly *Hanna'el*, an inviolable center whose identity felt as real and palpable as the pearl Daoshin had given her as a gift from the El'ohyme—as real as the earth. This is what she believed and what she had been taught, but her experiences since leaving her homeland had made her doubt everything. As she traveled upriver, her doubts steadily increased. Instead of a fixed center—sovereign and inviolable—perhaps this sense of self emerged from an oftentimes chaotic swirl of imagination, memory, and desire, a dynamic and ever-transforming flux that demanded constant change and alteration, which demanded always to die and to be reborn. Yet, to contemplate such endless currents of transformation and becoming felt terrifying—and the freedom that it promised felt more like a sickness she feared she could not endure. Where was the center . . . *where am I*—or was there no center . . . merely a flux of possibilities, each of whose currents could become a different story, a different *I, another self?* Her identity might be a tale that changed itself endlessly.

Again, she touched the twig above her heart. *Who am I really and why was I chosen for this quest?* If the Singing Tree existed, why had it summoned *her?* Why didn't it summon someone more capable, someone older—a person like Bryhs? Why not her step-brother Kit? The Singer had said that the Tree had summoned her father but that her father lacked the strength to pass through Urd. Which father had the Singer meant?—Carlon of Arcatus or that other person, *Charles* . . . the father who had left his daughter a letter concealed in a mound of stones? Clearly, that letter had been written to *Hannah*, not to Hanna'el. If so, then why had she found it, even though she could not read its foreign script?

Were these the currents of her past or of her future?

As they traveled farther upstream into Urd and as the outer landscape became more hardened, barren, and dry, Hanna'el felt how her inner world of remembrance became more fluid, as though all solid certainty slowly, inexorably dissolved. Surely the settled boundary between imagination and memory blurred, allowing contradictions to mingle in an alchemy of contending opposites, a swirl of remembrance and imagination that made her doubt and question everything.

She recalled the Singer's story concerning the imp: how the imp had lost the power of self-remembrance and how for this reason he was condemned to hover, to be everything and nothing at once. *Will something similar happen to me?*

The image of Bryhs and Raemond rose up before her, and she heard the Singer's words: *That which you seek was present—the Tree with all its branches reached down to receive the warrior's memories . . .*

And behind these thoughts, there loomed another question, perhaps the greatest—but one that she still lacked the courage to face.

SORGA

All day the travelers floated upstream. Sustained by the supplies that the Singer had placed in the boat, they watched the Urdish landscape grow more barren and inhospitable. At last, the fading sunlight allowed them to seek refuge for the night. Hanna'el played the chords that the Singer had taught her, and the boat immediately changed direction. It struck a course for the shore, toward a spot where they could land with little difficulty.

They had traveled so far that what once had been open farmland gave way to ruined buildings. She guessed that the first temples stood near. As the shore drew closer, she saw against the fading sky the silhouette of broken walls and severed columns.

The imp leaped out first, running up and down the small, pebble-strewn beach like a happy puppy. When Seth clambered out and began to pull the boat from the water, the imp stood beside him and delightedly mimicked his motions. Nothing Seth could say or do would drive the creature off; indeed, observed Hanna'el, the imp appeared to have conceived a great fondness for Seth.

Now Hanna'el recognized the wisdom behind the Singer's decision to send the imp along. The imp's imitative zeal made him closer to Seth than the thief's own shadow. Such companionship guarded Seth better than a dozen well-armed men.

As she watched them together, Hanna'el felt puzzled by the imp's unrestrained joy. The expression on the his face as he hounded Seth about their campsite looked as close to love and devotion as Hanna'el could imagine, though Seth saw only malice and mischief in the imp's unwavering pursuit.

That night they took shelter beside a crumbling wall of one of the ancient ruins. Seth barely had time to collect some meager brush and scraps of dead wood for the evening's fire before the light grew too dim for them to forage. There was little they could burn, for almost nothing grew in this country.

Seth wanted to search amid the stones for relics, but Hanna'el reminded him of the danger: only by night could they rest on Urdish soil, and even now, she felt a heavy weariness. She soon observed from their movements and conversation that Seth and Thomas felt such weariness as well.

The three prepared their meal quickly and ate in silence. Then Seth withdrew to rest sullenly against the boat, the imp beside him, while Thomas moved close to Hanna'el so that the two might converse privately. The moon shone in the sky, and Thomas observed it keenly, understanding its message.

"So it *was* a three-day sleep," he mused aloud. "The Singer's spell was very powerful." He paused for a moment, perhaps waiting for Hanna'el to volunteer some of the knowledge she had gained from the Singer's company. But when Hanna'el remained silent, he spoke again. "I dreamt while I slept, a troubling dream that will not leave me in peace. May I share it? You might find it meaningful."

Thomas' voice had lost its pedantic certainty, and he spoke as much to himself as to Hanna'el. She felt surprised by the change in him.

"I dreamed of Carlon, your father," he began slowly. "Carlon appeared as last I'd seen him, before he left Arcatus on his quest. It is difficult to recall the dream clearly, but I believe that I saw him standing close to the ocean's shore. Why that should be so, I cannot answer—I have never been to an ocean, nor had he, as far as I know. In the dream, we saw each other clearly. I did not speak, or if I did, he could not answer, yet I felt his joy to see me again. I dreamed that it was sunset when we met."

This description roused Hanna'el's full attention. She recalled that the Singer had asked her what she had witnessed while she slept, but she had seen or remembered nothing. "Go on," she urged him.

"Hanna'el, what do you remember of your mother?"

Hanna'el startled. Seldom, if ever, had Thomas mentioned her mother. Why did he do so now? "My mother died in the plague shortly after my birth. I remember nothing."

"Think back," Thomas urged her. "I would not ask you to do this if the dream had not prompted me to speak."

"What has my mother to do with your dream?"

Thomas sighed. "I do not know. It is confusing. Yet, in my dream, I felt that Carlon wished to say something about your mother, if only he could speak. Somehow, he could not find the words. I remember his sorrow—a sorrow deep as the ocean near which we stood. I wish I had asked the Singer what this dream meant, but I forgot it until now."

Hanna'el stood up restlessly. "Stay here and observe the thief. I need to walk."

"Wait, where are you going? It's dangerous to wander in the dark."

"I remember the Singer's warning," she told him brusquely. "I won't go far."

Head down and withdrawn, Hanna'el walked until the darkness of the silent ruins enfolded her. Alone now, she settled herself on a rock and waited until her thoughts and feelings had settled. After many minutes, she took out the Singer's harp. She had carried it with her for safekeeping, wrapped in a cloth. The harp's silver strings caught the light of the waxing moon. Delicately and carefully, she plucked them.

At once, the harp's clear, pellucid tones shimmered in the darkness like the gleam of distant stars. Again, she plucked the strings, allowing her fingers to caress them, and the tones rose clear and lovely in the dry desert air.

At first, she thought that the harp's magic would not work.

Then, from all around her in the darkness she heard the rustle of stone and sand, as though many tiny bodies were in movement. She gasped and stood, ready to bolt, but a voice called out from the darkness and begged her to stay. The voice's harsh accent told her immediately what she had done. Just as the Singer had foretold, the harp's silvery notes had summoned the Urdish folk. They had come to hear her music.

"Play," said the voice. "Play for us the Singer's harp."

Hanna'el touched the strings again, and when she finished, she heard an even greater movement of sand and stone. She could see no bodies.

Once again, in harsh, throaty accents, the voice begged her to play, but Hanna'el, more composed now and recalling the Singer's advice, knew better than to agree. "No," she answered firmly. "I will not. Not until you help me."

At once, she heard curses and grumbles, and the sand shifted noisily.

"Play," said the same, harsh-sounding voice. "Play, and we will reward you with precious stones."

"I don't want your wealth," said Hanna'el.

The night air filled with angry whispers and sudden movements.

"Play," urged the voice. "Play, and we will reward you with rare metals and costly jewels."

Hanna'el hesitated, knowing the risk she was about to take. "I do not want your metals or your jewels. I do not want anything you possess," she answered boldly. "I will only play if you assist me with my journey."

These words stirred a hornet's nest of angry whispers. She heard harsh discussion within the darkness and feared that she had dared to say too much. But in a moment, the bargainer spoke again. His tone, though edged with impatience, was guarded and canny. "How much?" he asked her. "What is your price?"

"Come forward if you wish to bargain."

Then followed a long silence, a silence so lengthy that Hanna'el feared that the unseen creatures had vanished. Perhaps the Urdish folk meant to test her. If so, she had no choice but to bluff. She wrapped the Singer's harp inside its protective cloth and turned away as though ready to retreat to the safety of the river.

"Wait," said the voice, much closer now, eager and tense. "What is your price?"

The speaker stepped from the darkness, appearing quite unexpectedly at her feet.

The creature she beheld stood no more than a cubit tall and was gnarled in limb and feature like some sun-blasted, weathered desert stump. To Hanna'el, the Urdish creature looked like a grotesque marriage of human and crab, with a hard carapace from which several bony, stunted limbs extended clumsily. Two leathery, black, vestigial wings lay curled to its back. Crab-like, it moved with a jerky, mechanical motion sideways across the ground. Its head, in comparison to its torso, was disproportionately large, so large that she wondered how the creature found strength to support it. Because of its size, the head appeared weirdly independent of the creature's torso, as though all the creature's vital forces had been gathered up and concentrated in this one dominant part of its anatomy, to the detriment of everything else. It seemed to float above the creature's body, attached by a slender neck. The creature's dark eyes gleamed with cunning brightness, and its skin, where visible beneath its carapace, hung pocked and leathery as a lizard's scaly hide.

"My name is Sorga. I speak for my kin."

She nodded. "My name is Hanna'el of Arcatus. I come from beyond the Karakala. This harp belongs to a Singer. I am traveling with his imp."

The other unseen Urdish folk whispered excitedly. Their peculiar speech sounded like stones grating in a mill.

"Hanna'el," said Sorga, expelling her name harshly. "Why do you disturb us? We do not tolerate humans in this land."

"Whether you do or not is unimportant," said Hanna'el. "I need your help and am ready to bargain. Do you wish to discuss my terms?"

Her bold reply brought another wave of whispered discussion. Hanna'el realized that the harp must exert a very strong appeal

upon these folk, for, by the sound of the conversations, their number
had increased.

"Speak," said Sorga guardedly, "tell us what you want."

This was the moment she had anticipated. This was the parting
of the ways. Hanna'el knew that she had a choice: she could wrap
up the Singer's harp and remain silent, and tomorrow, when the
sun rose, allow the current to carry her away from this sun-cursed
land. Or, she could bargain for their help.

She knew that once she decided, there would be no turning
back.

Hanna'el spoke with as much courage as she could summon. "I
seek a Singer named Azael who dwells in your country. I must travel
to him. Aid me in my quest, help me find him, and I will pay you."

Contrary to her expectation, Sorga looked confused by her
demand. His stunted limbs twitched, and he eyed her with what
she thought to be even greater suspicion, cocking his ponderous
head like a lizard. His wings unfurled and fluttered uselessly.

"Azael? Why do you seek *him?* We have greater wealth than
Azael—Azael is nothing! Play, and we shall reward you beyond
your dreams. These ruins contain vast treasures, relics of an ancient
race whose knowledge and power shall never be equaled. Is it wealth
you covet? We can bestow the wealth of many kingdoms. Is it
wisdom? These ruins guard the wisdom of countless lost generations
of initiates, prophets, and seers. Is it beauty, immortal life, pleasure,
power? All of these and more, we can bestow, for we are the ancient
remnants of Urd and nothing above the earth or under it lies hidden
from us. Play, and we shall grant whatever you desire—that and
more. Do not be deceived. Azael has no secrets; he is only a derelict
Singer who can offer you nothing but the poisonous music of his
imprisonment."

For a moment, Hanna'el felt confused by Sorga's response. Then
she recalled the Singer's warning that the Urdish folk were very sly,
and she spoke again. "Nevertheless, I seek Azael. I require your
knowledge and help to find him."

"We have much knowledge," said Sorga, twitching nervously.
"Much knowledge, much power, much wealth."

"Then state your terms."

"A song each night, for as long as you remain in our country."

"Agreed."

"And a tale of your childhood, told to us at once," Sorga added. "One tale, one song, for every day you trespass our realm."

This second demand surprised her. Perhaps the Singer had misjudged these creatures' appetites. Or perhaps they planned some deceit. Nevertheless, she agreed. It seemed a favorable bargain.

Sorga smiled, if indeed that sorry grimace meant pleasure. "We have made our deal, Hanna'el of Arcatus. You are bound by your oath. Now ask me what you wish to know."

"Azael's weakness and habits . . . Where does he dwell?"

As soon as she stated her wishes, the Urdish folk began to laugh. The laughter was like the sound of splintering ice. Their black wings beat the air. The rapid motion made a sound like buzzing insects. "Azael's habits? What a foolish, useless request! Azael lives among us and serves us, though he thinks himself to be grand. He hoards whatever thoughtless humans like you allow him to collect. From such miserable castoffs, he makes his bitter songs, but his music is far inferior to yours. Azael is contemptible. Why do you seek him? You would do better to learn from us."

"Is Azael a Master of Memory?"

Sorga eyes grew wide with surprise. Again, loud laughter rang from the dark. "He may pretend to be so," Sorga scoffed. "Who told you these fantastic tales? Azael is a derelict Singer, an embittered, lonely hermit filled with self-loathing and hate. He hates everyone and everything, even himself. That is why his music is so powerless. He is a liar consumed by ambition. I doubt he will even see you. Azael knows only two emotions: hatred and fear. And he fears and hates his own reflection most of all. He is a poisonous snake, but his poison works chiefly on himself. He wraps himself in rags like a leper. Hs temple is a pit of rot and misfortune. No human can abide it. What evil destiny leads you to this misfortune?"

"I must find him," said Hanna'el.

Sorga laughed. "Azael will destroy you. By naming him, you give him power. By thinking of him, you make him part of yourself.

The more you contemplate Azael, the stronger his evil becomes—the more it becomes part of you. Flee, while you have that harp to protect you."

But Hanna'el remembered what she had seen and heard on the Isle of Birch, and she knew that her father's path had gone this way. She had to follow him.

Again, she felt the keen attention of that other self inside her, the child whom she had come to name Hannah.

"Does Azael guard the Tree?"

"What tree?" scoffed Sorga. "There are no trees in Urd. Open your eyes. Urd is a wasteland. Nothing grows or lives in Azael's temple. He guards the giant stones known as the Three Sisters, but that is all you find there—except your death. Now play for us," Sorga ordered, "for that is our bargain."

And though she had planned to ask more questions, the forcefulness of Sorga's request made her obey.

Hanna'el cradled the Singer's harp.

Tentatively, she played a simple melody from her childhood, a song that Sylvia, her childhood nurse, had taught her, for that was all that her untrained fingers could pluck. Yet, it was enough. As soon as her notes sounded, they vanished, consumed as though swallowed by an endless, soundproof vault.

"Now speak," said Sorga greedily. "Tell us a story from your childhood. That is our price."

Wearily, she told them a story from Arcatus, how her father once had taken her to ride upon his horse when she was so young that a day lasted forever and a ride with her father held more wonder than a whole lifetime could contain. To her surprise, she found herself speaking with great feeling, and the flow of her recollections made her speak much longer than she had planned. She saw and felt and smelled every detail of that cherished memory, and she could hear her father's noble laughter ringing loudly above her as she recalled the joy of that ride. She felt embraced and protected by her father's love. It had happened long ago, in a golden age.

"Well," she asked at last, when she had finished, "are you satisfied?"

But Sorga eyed her harshly and did not show any gratitude or joy. His body swayed mechanically to and fro.

"Tomorrow another melody and recollection—and each day after that another and another, for as long as you trespass our realm. Follow the river upstream, as you have done. When the time comes, we will help you find Azael."

Thus spoken, Sorga moved with an awkward, jerky, mechanical motion sideways into the shadows of the rocks.

No sooner was he gone than suddenly Hanna'el felt a great burden of exhaustion, as though he body had grown heavier. She exhaled a great sigh. With trembling hands, she wrapped the Singer's harp inside its cloth and returned to the light of the campfire.

Thomas gasped when he saw her face. "Hanna'el, what happened? Are you ill? You look so much older!"

Before she could answer, he gave her a small mirror.

"Thomas, what's happened to me!"

Her own reflection shocked her. In the course of only an hour, she had aged many years. The faint aura of girlhood that had lingered in her features had vanished entirely. Instead, the lines of her face lay more deeply etched, and her eyes had an expression of care, sorrow, and maturity.

Now she realized the full extent of the bargain she had struck with the creatures of Urd. Each childhood memory that she shared with these crab-like creatures departed from her forever, and the loss of that living memory shortened her life.

THE PACT

Well before dawn, after a night of fitful, shallow sleep, and in keeping with the Singer's instructions, the travelers launched their boat upon the stream and continued their journey, propelled by the constant magic of the harp. No one spoke, and even Seth had fallen uncharacteristically silent. The change in Hanna'el's features, her sudden aging, had shocked him. Seth hunched at the prow of the boat, the imp crouching by his side, and did not argue as he had done so often the day before. Hanna'el caught him often staring at her, and she read the fear in his expression.

When the sun rose behind them in the east, they saw the first of the many ruins that Thomas called the temples of Hkaar. These ruins stretched for miles in front of them.

Even from the middle of the river, Hanna'el could feel how the size and mass of these vast temples weighted her spirit to the earth. The grandeur of their construction, even centuries after they had fallen, expressed indifference and a serene but inhuman fortitude to the weathering passage of time. Thomas told her that the ancient priests of Urd had built these temples according to prophecies read in the stars. So great, said Thomas, had been the knowledge and skill of those ancient priests that they could shape the pattern of their own successive lifetimes, thus achieving a constancy and profundity of knowledge that no culture had equaled since. The secrets of that knowledge were preserved in the dimensions and proportions of their stones. In future ages, Thomas told her, those priests would be reborn to find their wisdom hidden in these ruins.

"Why did they vanish?" Hanna'el asked.

But the scholar had no answer. He only shrugged.

A feeling of gloom and depression settled more heavily on Hanna'el as she listened to Thomas talk, and she hoped that the Singer's magic would continue to protect them. Combined with this melancholy, she also felt a morbid longing to investigate those sublime ruins on either side of them. As the day wore on and became hotter, she felt this urge increase. The sun shone so remorselessly upon the river that their improvised awning gave little relief. All three lay panting in the boat, and Seth complained bitterly, urging her to relent and play the harp to bring them to shore so that they might find more cooling shelter among the stones. "No," she told him, "I must not."

That day felt longer than any day she had ever experienced. By mid-afternoon her vision began to blur. Twice she found herself holding the Singer's harp, her hand ready to play the music that would turn the boat landward. Thomas lay unconscious, while Seth had stripped nearly naked, using a rag to drip water on his brow. "Play the harp," he urged her. Somehow, she found the strength to resist, though she doubted she could endure another day of torment.

She had never felt so grateful to see the sunset. As soon as the great reddish disk of the sun disappeared below the western horizon, she struck the chords that turned the boat toward land. They had traveled many miles upstream, yet the ruins continued onward, vast and serene. They had become even grander in size, with immense statues of men and animals decorating the abandoned forecourts and avenues.

They landed at a sandy beach just in front of a causeway that led through a forest of columns and enormous sculpted figures to the ruins of several temple halls behind which, glimmering in the fading sunlight, rose a complex of stepped pyramids.

At once Seth rushed forward into the shadowy stones, determined to find something of value before the sunlight vanished entirely.

Hanna'el called him back, but he would not listen. The imp set off in pursuit, but remembering the Singer's instructions, she commanded it sternly to stop, and it did, looking sad and abandoned because the thief had gone.

Thomas could barely raise himself from the boat. His face was sunburned, with parched lips and reddened eyes, and his wound pained him constantly. Hanna'el realized that another day of travel might prove too much for the old scholar and perhaps for her as well. Her emotions wearied her as much as the strenuous heat of the sun. She bathed herself in the river to revive, then shared some food with Thomas and refreshed the cool rags on his brow. Gradually, as the twilight deepened, he felt stronger and able to move about.

While enough light yet remained, Thomas asked her to accompany him to the ruins.

Seth still had not returned from foraging, so Hanna'el took the harp and ordered the imp to remain steadfastly at the boat and to guard it. Then she and Thomas lit a torch and passed slowly down the colonnade until they came to an archway of a temple. Here they halted, for the light had nearly failed.

The enormous blocks used in the temple's construction dwarfed the architecture of Aeron's Caer and made that fortress appear like a primitive cave. Thomas paced the length of a typical stone at twenty feet—in height it was twice his size and just as thick—and there were many of greater girth, each block faultlessly dressed and fitted seamlessly into place, despite the irregular outlines. The surface of the archway had been carved with the ancient script of Urd. Thomas ran his hand across the stones, longing to read them, for the ancient language of Urd had been lost for centuries.

While Thomas pondered this mystery, Hanna'el walked away, following an avenue filled with sand and debris, on either side of which rows of identically carved sphinxes gazed stoically into the distance. She found she could not wander far, for even at night the power of these ruins felt immense and she dared not succumb to their magic.

"How far do you think we need to travel?" Thomas asked.

She could not say.

"I cannot endure this heat," he told her frankly. "Why can't we travel now?"

Hanna'el nodded. His suggestion made sense. In the coolness of the night, they could progress many miles upstream.

"Let's find the thief and launch the boat. There is no reason to delay our journey," Thomas argued. "Whether we sleep here or on the river, it makes no difference."

Much as she would have liked to explore these ruins more, Hanna'el agreed.

As they turned toward the river, she pressed the scholar's hand. She could not bring herself to admit what lay most heavily on her heart: that she feared she would never return from this barren country.

Hanna'el and Thomas hurried back to the river, but the thief had not yet appeared.

"Damn his greedy soul," Thomas swore. He shouted loudly, but all that he heard in response was the echo of his voice amid the ruins.

Hanna'el glanced at the stones, now swathed in darkness, and at the imp who squatted patiently at the boat. Perhaps the imp could find Seth, but she felt uncertain how much she could trust it. If only it could talk. Maybe if she removed its leaden amulet it would change into a creature capable of speech. But she recalled the Singer's warning and dared not try.

"I don't like this," said Thomas nervously. "We're wasting valuable time. Perhaps he deserted us—I wouldn't put it past him. I say we go on without him. He'd betray us in a moment, if he had the chance."

But Hanna'el refused. Having agreed to travel with Seth, she did not feel she could abandon him. He had gone into the ruins expecting to find them when he returned, and she couldn't just leave him behind.

"Remain with the imp," she instructed Thomas. "I'll call him from the colonnade. If he returns while I am searching, shout loudly. In the meantime, prepare us some food."

Thomas protested, but there was nothing he could do to change her mind. Taking the Singer's harp for protection, Hanna'el walked back amid the columns, finding her way by the light of the rising moon. Twice she stopped to shout the thief's name, but no one answered. She hoped he hadn't injured himself or gotten lost. In that case, they might never see him again.

She paused, realizing she had gone in a different direction than before and sensing danger if she continued blindly. The moon cast a silvery glow on the temple wall just ahead; it allowed her to see carved on the archway a symbol that she recognized at once. The sight of that sigil made the hair prickle on the back of her neck.

Suddenly, from all around her came the sound of hurried footsteps.

"Hanna'el of Arcatus, keep your bargain," came a voice from the ruins. "Another day has passed; you remain in Urd. Play the Singer's harp and tell us your tale. That is our price."

Hanna'el sighed with weariness and sat upon a fallen block of granite. The Urdish folk hovered invisible in front of her in the darkness, and she felt their eager presence. Slowly, she unwrapped the Singer's harp. Touching the strings hesitantly, she began to play a simple tune, and once again, the lovely notes vanished as soon as she plucked them. She forced herself to play until the song was over.

"Now the story," demanded Sorga.

Again, in conformance with her bargain, she told a tale from her childhood, a story of her early days in Arcatus. She spoke of a time she had spent with her nurse, her kind old Sylvia. Hanna'el's voice grew slow and heavy as she remembered this good woman, and by the time she reached the end of her remembrance, she felt even more exhausted and depressed.

"A poor excuse for a tale," Sorga taunted. "You must speak and play with more enthusiasm if you wish to receive our help. Make sure you do better next time."

Hanna'el felt too weary to argue, but she answered that Sorga must keep his share of the bargain, too.

"Done," he gloated harshly. "Return to the river. It is not much farther that you will see to your left a lesser stream. Turn and follow it into the hills. Where the stream begins, you will find a path. It is clearly marked. We made certain you would find it. Follow that path into the hills. The distance is not far. At the end of that path, you will find what you seek. May you endure it. Azael dwells amid the ruins of his miserable temple. He awaits you; he knows you are coming. Speak with him as you like—that is your business. But remember, tomorrow you must meet us, and the next day, and the next day after that . . . for as long as you sojourn in our country."

He laughed as he said this, a cold cruel laughter that mocked her.

Suddenly, Hanna'el heard Thomas summon her from the shore. The thief had returned.

Sorga's laughter grew fainter in the darkness.

"Wait," she recalled him, "tell me more about this place. What do these temples mean? What happened to the people who built them?"

For a moment, it seemed that Sorga had vanished, but then she heard him behind her, near the arch on which she had seen the mysterious glyph. His black wings fluttered.

"What is there to tell? These are the fallen temples of Hkaar, where once the mysteries of my people were celebrated. Here we preserved the wisdom of our culture, a civilization greater and older and wiser than any before or since."

"Why did this happen? Where are your people? Why did these temples fall?"

Sorga laughed. "Ask Azael those questions. He will instruct you. He is your master. He loves to teach. In the ruins of his shrine, he has gathered many relics of ancient Urd. Nothing is lost to him. Long ago we traded him our knowledge in exchange for the freedom we now enjoy."

Hanna'el startled at these words, for she saw nothing free in this creature's miserable existence, and his words appeared to contradict what he had told her earlier: that Azael was a singer whose powers were very weak. Had Sorga lied?

Sorga laughed, sensing her perplexity. "These matters are beyond your understanding, Hanna'el. You are *human;* that is your weakness and your strength. As human, you are bound to the law of genesis, the laws of arising and descent. You cannot escape the cycles of remembrance and forgetting, and for this reason you feel so strongly the power and despair of these ruins, which remind you of your fate. Do not confuse what you see with what you are. Once my people suffered like you, prisoners on an ever-turning wheel of change and becoming, but we found a way to break free, and now we exist in an unchanging realm of spirit." He laughed again, more harshly. His wings unfurled. "I know what you are thinking, Hanna'el. My body disgusts you. How can *spirit* inhabit a body as hideous and misshapen as mine? After you have lived many lifetimes, you will understand. These hideous bodies are not as we once were. They are only shells for our earthly convenience; they are moved about and inhabited by spirits that neither perish nor alter nor despair. To achieve such godlike freedom, what price would you pay? These ruins are our testament, Hanna'el. We struck a bargain long ago—in exchange for wisdom, immortality. Azael can offer this to you as well, if he finds you worthy. And well he might, for you have something precious that he covets, something unique that he lacks. We have seen it in you and heard it, Hanna'el. Azael has seen it, too. He has scavenged the worlds for rarities, but this precious something that you possess has always eluded him. He cannot steal it; it must be given to him freely. And now you bring it to his lair. For this reason, you will be a great temptation for Azael." Once more, Sorga laughed. "Oh yes, a very great temptation. Know this, and bargain wisely."

As Hanna'el rose in horror from the stone on which she sat, her foot struck something hollow and brittle. Looking down, she saw the shell of an Urdish creature. Dried and withered, this black, crab-like body had been abandoned to the sand. It shattered to dust as she touched it.

"And yet you need my memories . . . " she whispered, horrified.

"Need? We *need* nothing," Sorga scoffed. "Examine your heart. It is *you* who need us. *You* summoned us. *You* struck the bargain for our aid. *Your* needs are greater, unknown though they may be, even to you."

Refusing to hear more, Hanna'el staggered back toward the river.

Thomas met her at the edge of the ruins. "Thank god, you're back," he exclaimed, "I thought you'd been hurt or lost."

"Leave me alone," said Hanna'el. She did not want Thomas to see her. She did not want to speak.

But the thief had kindled a fire at the shore, and in the flickering light of the flames, Thomas saw what had happened.

"You met them again!"

"I had to," Hanna'el confessed, "it was our bargain."

She saw the horror on the scholar's face and realized what had happened. Rushing to the boat, she found his mirror and beheld her reflection in the glass. She now looked like a woman well past forty.

The Arrival

They ate a hurried meal and launched the boat. Hanna'el had expected Seth to complain about her decision to travel at night, but the thief did not argue. He had suffered in the heat as much as they, and he had found nothing that he valued in the ruins.

For a long time no one spoke. Hanna'el felt Thomas' silent concern, but she did not have the strength or interest to talk to him. Her thoughts lingered on her journey, and at last, she dozed off.

The sun awoke her. It already had risen high. The others lay like dead men in the bottom of the boat, except for the Singer's imp, who squatted at the prow, alert and resourceful as ever.

Panicked that she had missed the passage that Sorga had mentioned, Hanna'el scanned the shore. She saw that they had passed beyond the precinct of the temple ruins and had come to a hilly country. She did not know how far behind them the ruins lay.

Just as she considered waking Thomas and asking his advice, the imp began to tap excitedly on the boat. His tapping woke Thomas and Seth.

"What the devil is he doing?" the thief complained. The imp tapped loudly right next to his head.

"I think he means to tell us we've come to the turn," said Thomas, rubbing his eyes.

Hanna'el soon saw that he was right.

At a bend in the riverbank, a stream came into view. Though she had no way to be certain, she guessed it was the stream that

Sorga had meant. Before the others could argue, she raised the Singer's harp and touched the strings, and the boat changed direction.

"What are you doing?" demanded Seth.

"The Urdish folk advised me to take this stream. It will lead us to Azael. I must go there to complete my journey."

Seth's eyes widened.

"You spoke to the Urdish folk? What did they tell you? The Urdish folk are rich. They know where the tombs are hidden. Those ancient tombs contain the wealth of Urd. Did you question them? Will they help us?"

"I'm not interested in treasure," said Hanna'el.

"You foolish woman," said Seth. It was the first time she had heard such a sharp tone of anger and disgust in his voice. "Look at yourself—aged and ugly. Why did you come here, if not to find those tombs? Look where you are. Open your eyes. Urd is a landscape of ghosts and skeletons. Were it not for the wealth in those tombs, no one would ever trespass this godforsaken desert. We have an opportunity. Give me the harp. We must go back to the ruins and ask the Urdish folk to help us."

He reached suddenly for the Singer's harp. Hanna'el jerked away.

Seth looked ready to challenge her, but the imp intervened. He put his hand on Seth's arm, and his mere touch was enough to make the thief shudder.

"Sit down," said Thomas. "We gave you a choice. You could have stayed behind."

Seth looked back toward the river. Grumbling and cursing, he hunkered down in the boat, as far from the Singer's imp as he could move himself. "You're both mad," he muttered.

Soon, the banks of this tributary stream pressed close on either side. They traveled between hills covered with rocks and thorns. Often she saw snakes and lizards.

The day that dawned proved just as hot as the day before. Slowly the stream grew more narrow and shallow. Just past noon, the boat began to scrape the rocky bottom. Though it continued to magically navigate through the shallows for several miles, they eventually were able go no farther.

The sun had but recently passed its zenith when they ran aground for good.

"What now?" asked Thomas. "We must go back. The stream has ended. If we leave the water, the curse on this place will poison us. Remember the Singer's warning? He told us to remain on water and to touch shore only at nightfall."

"We must disembark," said Hanna'el, scanning the barren hills for signs of the path that Sorga had promised. "I know what the Singer told us, but we have no choice. There is no other way forward. The Urdish folk promised that I would find a path when the stream came to an end. The path leads into the hills. It will take us to Azael. We must follow it. If we wait until dark, we will not be able to find the way."

"Are you mad?" exclaimed Seth. "You can't be serious? How long can we last if we leave the water?"

"We will see," said Hanna'el.

Again, Seth cursed. "Did the Urdish folk advise you to do this? They are liars, cheaters, thieves. I'll tell you what they want. They want that harp. They know that if you leave the water during daylight you will quickly weaken and die. Once you're dead, they'll take it."

Hanna'el shook her head. "We have no choice. We must go on foot. At night the path will be invisible."

"Then I'm staying here," Seth said, crossing his arms.

But Hanna'el did not trust him to remain alone with their boat. "You're coming, too. That was your bargain."

And the imp, seeming to understand this argument, laid his head affectionately against Seth's shoulder.

"Bah," he exclaimed, shaking the creature away. "You'll kill us all."

It did not take her long to discover a cairn of stones, and beyond this modest marker she saw others that outlined a meandering trail into the barren hills. Sorga had kept his bargain.

"What's this?" said Thomas, as he stepped from the boat to the gravel.

Hanna'el saw a glint of metal just ahead of where the boat had run aground. When she brushed away the dirt, she discovered that the metal was the blade of a small knife. She lifted the knife out of the sand and looked at it carefully.

The design was unlike any she had ever seen. On one side of the four-inch blade, someone had carved the initials CK. On the other side, she saw the initials RC. She knew no one whose name matched those letters. The metal was pitted and weathered, and the leather on the knife's hilt had begun to decompose.

"Someone's been this way," said Thomas. "Was it Carlon? Your father? Hanna'el, do you recognize this blade?"

Hanna'el shook her head. The knife did not resemble any of the weapons she ever had seen in Arcatus. And it was too small to be an effective weapon.

And yet, the discovery thrilled her.

"I know this from somewhere," she whispered. "I can almost remember it . . . "

"Perhaps it will bring us luck," said Thomas. He inspected it again, but the workmanship was unfamiliar.

Unable to learn anything more, Hanna'el wrapped the small knife in a cloth for safekeeping and gave it to the scholar.

Then, gathering their meager supplies and taking as much water as they could carry, they began their trek inland.

The way proved hard, for not only had the Urdish folk marked this rocky, steep path poorly but the evil nature of Urd quickly attacked their spirits as the Singer had warned them. It grew increasingly difficult for Hanna'el to concentrate or remain mindful of her goal and purpose. Even to keep her attention fixed on Sorga's markings was a daunting task. Often she had to double back to rediscover the faint, meandering trail that led ever upwards into the reddish, rocky hills. Each time this happened, Thomas complained of exhaustion and the thief criticized her incompetence. The hot sun and the curse that lay on that dead landscape added to their fatigue. Hanna'el could feel the weight of that curse with every step, and it took all her inner discipline and attention to keep her thoughts from sliding into a black pit of self-absorbed melancholy.

She saw that Thomas and Seth suffered, too, but each in a different way, each according to his temperament and personality. In Seth, the curse worked strongly on his anger. He grumbled foully. The hate, greed, and envy that that he had worked so hard to conceal from her came more and more to expression as they struggled deeper into the hills. In Thomas, on the other hand, a mood of resigned apathy began to hold sway. He began to lose whatever tentative hope or optimism he once had been able to summon, and he complained incessantly of his wound, his age, and their prospects of success. "We'll never leave this place alive," Thomas muttered. Hanna'el knew that this was only an exaggeration of their individual faults and weaknesses, but she saw that unless they reached their goal quickly, the dark emotions that were welling up in each of them would soon overpower them entirely.

Only the imp was gay. He scampered ahead so quickly that Hanna'el, Seth, and Thomas could hardly keep up. Remembering the Singer's advice, Hanna'el sternly commanded the imp not to run ahead, and though the creature obeyed her at first, it could not contain itself for long. Its will and hers were in a constant tug of war. But in a way, this tension helped her. Whenever Hanna'el felt like surrendering to exhaustion, the imp's energetic disobedience roused her from her torpor and teased her onward.

In this way they soldiered on until the sun at last went down and the landscape became shadowy and vague in the deepening twilight.

Almost at once she could feel their moods lighten.

"Stop," Hanna'el ordered as the imp ran briskly up a hill. The imp paused at the crest, watched her, and waved its arms. She felt too weary to pursue him, but the imp appeared so excited that she forced herself to climb that final rise.

She had expected him to scamper ahead. But the imp waited patiently and stared down the slope toward a place where the hills formed a natural amphitheater.

"What is it?" asked Thomas, breathing heavily as he reached her side.

Suddenly, she knew why the imp had stopped. She had reached the goal of her journey.

"Azael," she responded to Thomas' question.

And her voice sounded tired, flat, and lost.

Azael's Lair

The travelers stood upon the hill and looked down at the stones below them. The twilight had spread a rust-red glow across the landscape, and the moon, only a few days lacking in fullness, shone upon them through the haze of the southeast sky. On the horizon, a single red planet rose visible, while the wind blew down from the distant northern mountains, sounding its lonely trill among the dry and wavering stalks of yarrow and star thistle that clung to the stony soil.

The path to Azael's dwelling wound downward, narrow and strewn with rubble, and the landscape reminded Hanna'el of an open pit mine. Only a yew tree (the first tree she had seen since entering Urd) grew at the bottom of this pit—its stunted, sun-dried branches hung with charms and talismans, bone and bits of shredded cloth. At the base of this blasted yew, on stones piled high on either side of the trail, lay fragments of skeletons—human and animal. More whitened bones lay scattered nearby, while at the exact center of this natural amphitheater, upright, stood three tremendous stones, roughly hewn and rectangular, each more than the height of a man.

Hanna'el walked forward to the edge and shouted loudly. Three times she shouted, but her shouts went unanswered in the dusk.

"Ah," said Thomas, shivering, "this wind grows cold. We must find shelter for the night."

Seth glanced nervously down the hill, and his teeth chattered. "There's nothing here to burn but that dead tree. There's no shelter anywhere."

"Be still," said Hanna'el.

Then, from all around in the dry brush of the windswept hillside, she heard the scamper and scuttle of many feet. Seth and Thomas startled, fearing attack, but Hanna'el knew who had come.

"Hanna'el of Arcatus, keep your bargain," hissed a voice from the surrounding rocks. "Another day has passed; you remain in Urd. Play the Singer's harp and tell us your tale. That was our price."

"Who's that?" exclaimed Seth excitedly. "Are those the creatures of Urd? Where are they? Have they brought their gold and jewels?"

"They've brought us nothing," said Hanna'el wearily. "Stay here with Thomas. I must speak to them alone."

"Alone! Why? To make a trade?"

Once more Sorga's voice sounded loudly from the darkness. "Hanna'el of Arcatus, keep your bargain. The time has come to play the harp and share your memories. That was our price."

"I must go to them," said Hanna'el.

But Seth would not relent. He grabbed her roughly.

"Why do they like the Singer's harp? What was your bargain? Have you worked some secret trade? The Urdish folk are rich. Everyone knows that. Give them the Singer's harp and let's escape. If we trade the harp, we'll be wealthy for the rest of our lives. We can pilot the boat downriver. I know the way."

"Let me go," she told him angrily. "I have business here. I must take care of it."

She wrenched herself free and walked into the darkness. When Seth tried to follow, the imp blocked him.

"Trade the harp," Seth shouted at her. "Give them whatever they want! Don't be a fool!"

Hanna'el walked until she could no longer hear the thief's complaints. She seated herself cross-legged on the ground and unwrapped the Singer's harp. She began to play at once, without preparation or forethought. It was another song from her distant childhood, a simple lullaby . . . and then, as soon as she finished, she began a story from her youth, a memory of distant Arcatus.

She spoke far longer than she had intended, lost in recollection. Her memories seemed very alive to her and rich. So much so, that she spoke much longer than she had planned, finding new recollections that unfolded, each from the other, until her entire life seemed spread in front of her, like a richly woven fabric.

When she completed this reminiscence, her face had dampened with tears.

The hill was weirdly silent for many minutes.

At last Sorga spoke.

"Better," he whispered. His voice sounded strangely satisfied, almost content. "You have done much better, Hanna'el. You are learning to sing. Is there anything now that you wish to ask us? It was our bargain. I pledged to speak."

Hanna'el shook her head. She had no questions. She felt terribly exhausted, as though a part of her were dying.

"Then go," said Sorga proudly. "Soon you will see the one you have traveled so long to confront. Return to the hilltop. Azael will find you. But tomorrow you must meet us again."

He laughed as he said this, a cold, cruel laughter that mocked her.

Hanna'el felt greatly aged. Her body ached in ways she had never felt it ache before, and she moved from the stones unsteadily.

"Is this what it means to grow old?" she thought with horror. And though she had thought of death before, always it had seemed a threat so far in the distant future that she had thought that by the time her death arrived she would be ready for it, having lived a full and satisfied life without regret.

How blind and young and stupid I have been!

As she staggered back to the others, she heard Thomas begin to shout. Just as Sorga had predicted, Azael had come forth, lured by the gentle tones of the Singer's harp.

THE ENCOUNTER

Azael, veiled in rags, cursed and breathed heavily as he climbed the winding trail that led from the bottom of his pit. He moved with the stiffness of great age.

"Who plays a Singer's harp? Who is foolish enough to enter this land of Urd? Speak, stand forth and greet me. I am Azael, keeper of this shrine. Great is my mastery and art."

Azael's words had a cold, inhuman, metallic ring much like the speech of the Urdish folk. His voice easily overcame the sighing wind.

Hanna'el answered as loudly as she could force herself. "It is I, Hanna'el of Arcatus, who played the Singer's harp. I have come to find my father, Carlon of Arcatus, who went in search of the Singing Tree. I have come to bring him home."

"The Tree!" Azael shouted, hobbling up the slope. "How dare you speak of the Tree amid my temple? Who are those others who are with you? Name them, I demand it."

Brother Thomas promptly shouted his identity, but Seth had to be coaxed. The imp said nothing, nor could Hanna'el tell if the imp paid notice to Azael at all. He appeared quite relaxed and self-distracted. Nor did Azael seem aware of him. The evil magic of this place appeared to have no effect on him.

Azael moved farther up the hillside. His body remained concealed in swaths of tattered cloth. "What will you give me, Hanna'el of Arcatus, to keep me from killing you outright and scattering all your bones across these hills? I am not one of those miserable Urdish creatures whose fancy can be bought with pretty lies and pretty songs. Come forward, old woman, and let me see you."

"Don't do it, Hanna'el," Thomas urged.

But Hanna'el knew she had to obey.

Moving carefully on the loose stones and slippery soil, she advanced down the barren hillside. The imp tried to follow, but Hanna'el ordered him back.

Azael waited, a looming shadow. She could hear the sound of his breath as it wheezed through his gaping mouth, fluttering the rotted rags that concealed his face. Because of those rags, she could see nothing of his features. She recalled Sorga's warning that Azael's evil countenance was poisonous, even to himself, and she summoned all her courage.

"Azael, I have come very far to speak with you. My father came before me. He sought the Singing Tree. I seek it also . . . but first I must find my father, and for that I need your help. A Singer gave me this harp that I might pass through ruined kingdom of Urd. And its music has led me to you. Help me, I beg you. I can go no farther on my own. I need your help."

"Old woman, follow me," Azael muttered darkly.

He began to descend the hill, moving slowly toward the three giant stones that formed the center of his ruined temple, past the blasted yew tree hung with relics and bones.

"Wait!" cried Brother Thomas somewhere above her. "Hanna'el, come back!"

But she would not.

Steadfastly, she kept her attention centered on Azael as the ragged, ancient hermit staggered back down the slope of his miserable pit.

When they reached the bottom, Hanna'el saw that each of the rough, rectangular stones that Azael guarded was as thick as she was tall. Azael paused in front of them and beckoned her closer.

"First you must show me the Singer's harp."

And Hanna'el, not knowing any better strategy, unwrapped the harp from its protective cloth. The harp's silvery strings shimmered in the moonlight like costly pearls.

Azael drew a covetous breath. His voice became softer.

"A Singer's harp . . . " he muttered. "Let me touch it!"

"No," said Hanna'el, quickly drawing the harp away. "Not unless you help me."

Azael laughed harshly.

"Foolish woman, do you think I am one of those miserable Urdish folk with whom you can bargain? Do not believe their lies. I know you, Hanna'el. I know where you come from and where you wish to go. I know your father. I know your dreams and hopes and everything you once knew but have forgotten—I know these things more intimately than you can know yourself. I know of your father's quest and what became of him. And I know what will soon become of you. How much would you give to learn my secrets? How much would you give to be young forever instead of old? How dearly do you long to find the Singing Tree? Your father—do you wish to see him? *Your father is here.*"

Hanna'el froze. She stared at Azael's ragged outline and at the three enormous granite stones that stood behind him like monstrous shadows. She did not know whether to believe his words or not.

"Show me proof," she demanded, "prove that you aren't lying."

Without another word, Azael raised his ragged arm.

Hanna'el gasped and cringed, afraid that the hermit meant to draw aside the tattered rags that hid his features. But Azael only reached into the folds of his cloak and withdrew a small piece of metal fastened to a long string of human hair. He dangled the object in front of her, until she saw that it was half of a golden ring.

At once, she remembered that she, too, possessed such a broken ring. Queen At'theira, Raemond's mother, her own step-mother, had given her this gift in Aeron's Caer.

With trembling hands, Hanna'el took out At'theira's severed ring and compared its broken fragment to the piece that Azael held before her. The two halves joined perfectly and made a whole.

"Now do you believe me, Hanna'el?" Azael taunted her.

"Where did you get this? How?"

"How else, but from your father, when he came to me long ago. Didn't you know that? All travelers who seek the Tree must find their way at last to me. I am the keeper of that passage; I am the shepherd of the boughs."

He gave her no time to ponder this riddle but quickly spoke again in his reedy, raspy voice. "Be attentive, Hanna'el, be mindful of my warning. I can show you the Tree and reunite you with your father, but my price is the Singer's harp and the green and living twig that Walter gave you long ago. I know you have the twig—I can sense it. *It is I who inspired you to bring it to this place.* It is I who guided your journey."

"You're lying. That can't be true. I came of my own free will. And if you want these things so badly and are so powerful, why don't you just take them?"

"Foolish woman, do you think I cannot? I can imprison you inside these stones forever—just as I imprisoned your father. If I merely show you my face, your memories are mine. But that is not my pleasure—no, not yet. I wish to help you complete your journey. Prove to yourself that you have come here freely and not because I recalled you. Give me the harp and the green and living twig as gifts of your free will, and in return I shall restore your father and allow you both safe passage to the place you most desire to go. Is that not what you want? Is that not what you long for? If you doubt my words, come forward and touch this stone. Let your own senses confirm what I have told you, and then decide."

Azael moved backward as he said this, inviting Hanna'el near. The stone he meant her to touch was the tallest of the three megaliths.

She saw no reason not to try.

Tentatively, Hanna'el placed her fingers on the first stone's rough, unpolished surface, and immediately she heard the sound of cascading waves and smelled the salt air of the ocean. She drew back her hand in surprise.

"Once more," said Azael. "Now touch the second stone."

Hanna'el obeyed. This time, she smelled no ocean and heard no waves. For a moment Azael and his wretched temple disappeared, and before her stretched an endless, sun-drenched grassland. A cold fresh wind stirred her hair, and she saw white clouds on a flat horizon. The soil smelled green and alive, and its potent scent mingled with the smell of horses, damp wool, leather, smoke from simmering cook fires and pungent stews. She saw that she had returned to Arcatus. The yurt where she had lived stood before her. The sweet-smelling plains of endless grass grew as tall as her chin. She staggered forward as the yurt's entrance blanket drew back. Her father looked out. He smiled and laughed at her. She saw him and raised her arms. Now he came close to sweep her up; but she knew what would happen next, and she turned away with resolution. She knew she must not dwell in this remembrance.

"No," she cried, withdrawing her hand from the second stone, "it isn't *real*... I will not see it. *Don't make him leave me again.*"

"These are memories, living memories," said Azael. "Nothing is lost to me. I shepherd them all. Now, touch the third stone," he commanded her.

And though she knew she should not listen, she felt helpless and forced to obey.

Darkness. Only darkness... and somewhere in that darkness the distant rustle of a wind that blew ceaselessly at night through a starlit grassland.

Wind and cold and darkness. Endless time and space, and I am alone.

She lay in her childhood bed and listened. She could not move her limbs. She could not stand. Someone leaned over her, watching and waiting. She felt so alone and abandoned. She wanted to scream.

Suddenly, she understood that this, too, was a remembrance from her distant past. Her father had left her to begin his quest, and she had remained in Arcatus, abandoned and alone. She had no one in the world to protect her, except the scholar, Brother Thomas, and her old nurse Sylvia.

She heard someone crying, and she knew that it was she.

Azael laughed, extending his ragged arm. "Now you have seen, Hanna'el. Now you can understand me. This temple is the portal to Elowyn—*Elowyn is you.* That is why you have come to me. You've known this truth in your heart ever since you began your journey. With every step, you've felt it more and more. But now you have journeyed as far as your weakened powers can help you go. Only with *my* help can you proceed. That is why you need me. That is why you are here. You know this in your heart. Give me the Singer's harp and Walter's twig. If you do, I shall not harm you; I shall let you pass. Indeed, I shall restore to you whole and undiminished every memory to which you were ever bound—that and more. You shall gain the Tree and all that the Singing Tree can bestow. The power of all remembrance will be yours. No longer will you fear the passage of time, the sting of death, the anguish of separation, the pangs of disappointment, sorrow, or loss. You shall possess all time and all remembrance and dwell like a goddess in your perfection, a being of splendor no longer bound to earthly time. This I can grant and give to you—*I alone*—if you will agree."

Hanna'el felt that the giant, standing stones pulled her toward them like powerful magnets. Azael's voice beat inside her like a drum.

"I cannot," she muttered. "No, not yet . . . I can't."

"Is your desire for the Tree so weak that you hesitate now, at this last moment? Foolish woman, don't tempt my patience. Go and consider my offer. I shall hear your answer soon."

DISASTER

Cautiously and slowly, Hanna'el picked her way up the barren, darkened hillside of the singer's pit. She breathed heavily, and her aged body had barely the strength to climb the slope.

Thomas and Seth stood waiting when she returned. Thomas, who had not seen her clearly since she spoke to the Urdish folk, was shocked by her aged appearance.

"Hanna'el, is it you? Dear child, what has happened? You look even older than me. Oh Hanna'el, let me help you! We must leave this evil place."

But Seth demanded to know if she had struck a bargain.

When she found her voice and told them of Azael's offer, the thief grew frantic.

"Give Azael the harp and the twig and let's be gone from this hellhole. We're lucky we're still alive."

She shook her head. But inside, she could feel her resolve weakening. Seth's words made sense.

Confused and weary, Hanna'el allowed Brother Thomas to steady her. Her limbs felt heavier than lead.

"Lie down, Hanna'el," he urged her. "Rest here. I will keep watch."

Gratefully, she gave in to his advice. "Watch for me," she said to him, as she stretched out on the sand and closed her eyes. "Do not let me sleep. I need only a moment to rest. Just one moment."

She tugged at her collar, breathing quickly. Her head throbbed wickedly, and she could not quiet her thoughts. Retreat was impossible, and yet, she knew that she must not surrender Walter's twig. She clutched it tightly. The youth-destroying power of the

Urdish folk and the enchantment of Azael's temple had nearly overwhelmed her.

"Watch for me," she pleaded with Thomas again. "I just need a moment, only a moment . . . Please keep watch for me . . . "

Something had shifted. She could feel that shift deeply inside her, like a great slumbering dragon stirred to wakefulness in its cave.

Suddenly, she knew in one tortured gasp of awareness that for years she had struggled to hold back an annihilating rage. This inner rage rose up now and seized her like a black, irresistible storm, and she gave herself to its fury. She raged at herself and at her father and at all the years that had passed since his departure— she raged at the silence and solitude and loneliness that his departure had left behind, and at the sense of guilt and betrayal he had seeded in her heart. Self-pity, rage, and frustration overcame her like a crashing ocean wave, and she felt herself swept over, under, and down.

She had never felt so abandoned and alone.

"Go back," said a voice. "Give Azael the harp. Give him the Master's twig. Surrender, and you will be able to rest."

She shook her head. "No, not yet, I can't."

"But why not, Hanna'el? What is stopping you?"

The voice was Azael's. She could not answer him. She could find no reason in her exhausted heart not to do as he wanted.

But then she remembered the child. The child, whose name was Hannah, stood apart. She listened and watched and observed her.

"What must I do?" Hanna'el asked her.

But child did not speak. Perhaps she was not able, or perhaps she did not know what to say.

I must decide, thought Hanna'el. *It is my decision; it is my sacrifice.*

She saw herself as though observing a stranger: an old woman who wandered orphaned in a dry, hilly landscape, condemned to follow a Singer's speechless imp. She imagined that this imp was a cat, and that the cat's silly name was Fritz. And then she saw her garden, but the house that she had lived in had begun to shake itself to bits.

How can this be?

The day was still a sunny May 2. She looked out at her pleasant garden, aware that something was wrong.

I'm wrong, she understood.

Right or wrong or indifferent, the whole garden had begun to shake itself to bits. Her home, her world, her childhood was becoming unmade. This unmaking chaos swirled like the dragon rage and anger that howled from the pit of her memory. Bits and pieces of a roof from the house that stood behind her flew off in every direction as she watched. The gutters broke free; the porch furniture overturned; the windows popped. A water pipe burst in a hectic fountain.

Was this dream, imagination, or remembrance? She couldn't tell. The cat alone looked perfectly unconcerned. It sat and serenely cleaned its fur, purring softly.

Fritz . . .

"Where are you going?" it said to her.

"Nowhere and everywhere," she answered. "Always toward home."

"Correct," it smiled, contentedly. "Now you understand. Now you are *hovering*. It certainly took a long time."

Then, like an eagle, she surveyed the vast and silent ruins of Hkaar. Those ancient memory temples were also collapsing, just like the house behind her that blew to bits. She soared above those ruins and looked down. Amid the rock and sand, the black, crab-like creatures that called themselves the remnants of Urd scuttled between the falling stones, their black wings beating the air like untrimmed sails. Some of those miserable, ancient creatures lay crushed beneath the fallen columns; others writhed and circled like machinery run amok. They did not care if they lived or if they perished; they cared nothing for their earthly bodies, Hanna'el saw. They laughed, as the barren temples broke apart. Already they had abandoned this perishing world. They enjoyed such chaos.

"Join us!" they screamed at her gleefully.

She turned away in horror, but the ground heaved up beneath her and she felt herself fall.

Earthquake, some small, reasoning part of herself pronounced. And yet, that was impossible. There were no earthquakes where she lived.

No earthquake? Then you're dead . . .

And perhaps it was so. She felt as though a wind roared through her brain, as though a great equinoctial storm had swept her up. This raging rainstorm wanted to blot her out, to scatter her thoughts and memories like pieces of straw. It wanted to destroy her.

Hanna'el's hand clutched reflexively at her neck. It searched for the green and living twig that hung above her heart.

The twig was not there.

"Hanna'el, wake up!"

She struggled to remember who she was.

"Hannah! Hanna'el!"

Brother Thomas shook her awake. Blinking, she saw that the old scholar's face was bruised and dirty; his robe was torn. "Wake up, wake up!" he shouted. A terrible shrieking music filled the air. The shrill music wrenched at her skull; it seemed to come directly from the earth: discordant, harsh, and deafening.

"What is it, Thomas? What's wrong?"

"The thief betrayed us! He overcame me. He took the harp to Azael!"

THE RECKONING

Hanna'el searched for the shepherd's twig, feeling inside her shirt in case it had fallen. The twig was gone! She couldn't find it, and she was certain she had worn it before she slept. She remembered clutching it tightly.

"Oh Hanna'el, forgive me! I tried my best!" the scholar moaned.

With tears in his eyes, Thomas stammered his account of the thief's attack, but Hanna'el could scarcely hear his words. "It's my fault! I tried to stand watch, but I was exhausted. Seth waited until I slept, and then he struck. Let me bear the blame. Seth stole the harp. He stole the twig. He wants to strike a bargain with Azael."

"Stay here," shouted Hanna'el, "I must speak to the Urdish folk. Thomas, it's not your fault. I was the one who brought Seth into this country."

But Thomas was already running away from her to the edge of Azael's pit.

"I'll find him," he shouted. "I'll make him come back!"

"Thomas, wait!"

But the scholar had already dropped out of sight.

Hanna'el staggered forward. Running to the path that led downward to Azael's temple, she saw her old companion sliding down the hill. "Thomas!" she cried, "come back! Don't leave me!" But the scholar could not or would not return.

Before Hanna'el could start down the hillside after him, the imp came bounding to her side. He had been waiting on the hilltop, idly watching and scratching his nose as the earth heaved and shook. Azael's terrible music had no effect on him. Quite at odds with the chaos all around, the imp looked serene, untroubled, and at peace.

"Help me!" she shouted desperately. "Do something!"

But the imp just grinned at her stupidly.

Suddenly the world became still. The earth ceased to tremble and the air grew heavy and dense, edged with an odor of sulfur.

Quickly, Hanna'el stumbled down the trail, the imp bounding faithfully beside her, like a spaniel. Breathless and terrified and ignoring the many scratches and bruises she received as she rushed forward, she staggered to the three gigantic stones.

Azael awaited her, the Singer's harp cradled in his arm. The green and living twig, the shepherd's gift, hung from a slender string about his neck.

She shuddered when she saw it.

"Where is Brother Thomas! What have you done to him?"

"Inside the stones," said Azael, stretching forth his ragged arm. "And that is where you shall go, too. Blessings on you, Hanna'el! You have brought me a gift most desired above all else. See what the thief, your companion, has fetched for me. This twig was the last of its kind to leave Elowyn, the last that I could not claim. Now you have brought it. It is mine, and with it, I have gained the power to leave this cursed existence. That is why I summoned you, Hanna'el. Old woman, do you think that you came here of your own free will, out of love for your father? The truth is otherwise: *I guided you.* I am the one who inspired your longing; I am the one who directed your steps. Your father never loved you; had he loved you, he never would have abandoned you as a child. I found you in your sleep; I worked upon your memories; I inspired your dreams. I sang you here; I led you—and now you have brought me the only object I was powerless to fetch myself. With this I can become a Master of Memory—in time, a greater Master than the others. So it has been written in the stars."

Hanna'el felt Fritz press tightly against her side, but Azael ignored the imp. Perhaps, since the imp was not human, Azael took no interest in him. His attention centered only on her.

Azael slowly raised his arm. "Look upon me, Hanna'el; behold my countenance. It is my gift. I shall show you what few humans have yet seen, though many shall. You and all your memories are mine. Behold what you have long desired."

Hanna'el staggered backward, shielding her face, but Azael only laughed more harshly. With a quick gesture, he tore loose his heavy wrapping, exposing his naked, horrible features. At the same moment, he reached out to pluck at her eyes.

Hanna'el cringed with horror. She felt abjectly frozen to the depths of her soul, as though a dagger of ice had pierced her heart. She realized she could do nothing and that all her struggles had led her to this pit and to this moment. The rage and anger that the three standing stones had torn from her memory—the rage and anger and loneliness that she had buried so deeply inside herself—were chains that held her fast to Azael's lair. She could not defeat him. She was helpless against him. The two were one.

But just as the Master's wrappings fell free, she recalled the words spoken by the Urdish folk. *Azael fears everything, even his own reflection—he fears his own reflection most of all.* And with this remembrance, she felt empowered to make one final effort of defiance.

Do not confuse what you see with what you are.

With trembling hands, Hanna'el reached down to the Singer's imp, and with a cry of exhausted anguish tore from its neck the leaden amulet that fixed the imp's shape, the amulet that the Singer had told her never to remove.

And the imp, whose attention centered raptly upon Azael, immediately transformed and became a perfect reflection of what it beheld.

The Singer's imp became a reflection of Azael.

Azael screamed to behold his own image and fell backward against the tallest of the giant stones. As he fell, the imp rushed forward. Reaching out swiftly, it plucked the precious twig from Azael's neck.

Azael screamed again. He hurled the Singer's stolen harp at the imp, who caught it deftly and hurled it back. With a terrible crack, the stone behind Azael split apart as the Singer's harp struck it. The harp released a cascade of hectic chords.

And then, like a gaping vacuum, the fissure sucked Azael into its depths.

Just as Azael disappeared, Hanna'el dared to open her eyes. She forced herself to do this. Knowing what it meant, she made herself look down into the splintered megalith into which Azael plummeted. Their eyes met, and she followed him into the darkness.

As she did, the sun rose over the edge of Azael's pit, and its golden light shot like a swiftly hurled lance or diving kestrel into the granite opening, illuminating entirely the face of the evil she most feared.

Hanna'el did not flinch.

As Azael fell backward into the splintered stone, she beheld his naked countenance fully and completely in every line of its detail. She forced herself to fix that horrid visage in her gaze, and to know it. She did not look away but held to that vision steadfastly, even though she knew this final deed would destroy her.

And then, it was done.

As though from a distance, Hanna'el saw her aged body collapse. She exhaled a great, rasping sigh, and her spirit sprang free like a bird let loose from a narrow cage. For a moment this spirit trembled, startled by its newfound freedom between earth and sky—poised to soar or fall as she decided. She had that choice.

She felt herself longing to plunge into the gaping fissure of the megalith in which Azael had vanished; she felt herself sucked downward by Azael's swift descent, still bound to his horrible countenance. But it was fear, she realized, her own fear and anger that drew her toward him. Fear and anger bound them, and she let those emotions go. As soon as she did, a dark, heavy cloud flowed out of her dying body and followed the derelict Singer into the stone, a dark cloud that bore a distorted resemblance to her features but yet was not herself.

Purged of that shadow, Hanna'el felt light and eager and free. There was no reason to remain here, she understood. And yet, she paused a moment still. Looking down, she saw her dying body. Surprised by that sight, she felt even more surprised that she no longer felt any sympathy for that tired, old woman's body that lay crumpled in the sand—nor did she feel any longing or remorse. That body—*her* body—appeared so unneeded and so worn out; it appeared so very much older than she knew herself to be. She could feel how already this body had begun to mingle its particles of matter with the earth, as though celebrating a joyful reunion after years of long exile. She saw that she could stop that reunion and force that tired body to live again, but she thought she would not. No, she no longer felt that need. Her time here was done. She had finished her journey, and it was time for her to move on. She had done all that she could. Only one thing still troubled her: the child who had come with her, whose presence she increasingly had felt . . . *Where had she gone? What would she do? What would become of her?*

Must I leave her all alone?

This thought made Hanna'el sad. For the child's sake, she wished to linger, but she felt there was little more that she could accomplish as Hanna'el. She had sacrificed herself so that the child, whose name was Hannah, could continue, and now she must trust that this child would know what to do.

And as this understanding arose in her, all her memories blossomed in a warm pulse of streaming light. She saw these many memories sweep before her like a landscape opened wide before her soul.

She had found her passage to Elowyn . . .

BOOK NINE

The Singing Tree

HANNAH RETURNS

Hannah raised her head and stared into the face of a large black tomcat. The cat looked at her as though surprised that she could sleep so long and well. She felt bruised and exhausted, and her ears rang wickedly. Slowly she sat up, surprised by her barren surroundings, surprised that she was not all soaking wet from the *Zone of Night*.

How did I get here?

She remembered she had entered the terrible *Zone*. The Privy Counselor had sent her. Fritz the cat had come along. She had lost her yellow raincoat in the storm—but so what, she decided, it wasn't raining. It was actually quite sunny here, and hot. A bit like the Mojave desert, Hannah observed.

She blinked and looked about.

She saw that she had fallen into some kind of steep, gravelly pit. Three gigantic black stones stood before her, and one of them, the tallest, had cracked wide open from bottom to top. A thin stream of smoke drifted out through this dark opening, though how could there be smoke inside a rock? She held her nose. Fritz the cat walked close to the opening and sniffed disdainfully.

To her surprise, she saw that she held some kind of necklace in her hand. The necklace had a pendant made of lead. It wasn't very special, so she dropped it. The smoking stone seemed much more interesting. Fritz meowed loudly and swished his bushy tail, and she saw him batting something with his paw, as though he had caught a mouse. Walking closer, she saw that he had found Walter's twig, the green and living twig that Walter had given her—*Walter's gift.*

"Get away," she scolded Fritz.

She picked up the twig and squinted at it, relieved that she had recovered the precious talisman at last. She vowed that she would never lose the thing again.

"Come here, kitty," she said to Fritz.

Holding the cat to her chest, she peered into the gaping stone, but all she could see was darkness, and the smoke had a terrible stench. The only other object of interest in this pit was a small wooden harp with broken strings. She did not know how to play it, but she plucked a few strings anyway just to hear how it sounded. *Sweet, but out of tune,* she decided. She put it down, and as she did so, the cat jumped out of her arms and into the smoking rock.

"Oh, drat! Come back!" but as soon as he passed through the fissure, Fritz completely disappeared.

Alarmed that she might lose him again, Hannah leaned close to the broken stone.

"Kitty kitty kitty," she shouted loudly, but the cat did not return.

Worried, she leaned even closer to the stone and peered inside. *Nada.*

Nothing.

Nix.

She threw in a pebble to discover what might happen, but the pebble, if it fell anywhere, fell very quietly and very deeply.

"Fritz! Can you hear me? Come out!"

Finally, not knowing what else to try, Hannah stuck her arm into the megalith. Her arm entered the darkness and disappeared entirely from view.

She pulled it out. Everything looked okay—nothing injured. But the cat had not returned.

She stuck in her arm again, farther this time, calling "kitty kitty kitty," and she kept her hand inside the stone much longer, noting how the air inside felt warm.

Well, she decided, if the cat could do it, so could *she*. Entering this megalith could not be much worse than entering the *Zone of Night*, Hannah considered.

And anyway, a world explorer has to be resolved . . .

Rolling up her sleeves and biting her lip for courage—and still calling *kitty kitty kitty* in case that helped—Hannah took a step and entered the smoking megalith. She thought that the smoke would choke her, but once past the opening she hardly noticed the smoke at all.

Very little changed. She could see the sunlight through the entrance threshold, but she could not see farther inside. The entrance seemed very far away, but this sensation, at least, was quite familiar, for it reminded her of walking toward the *Zone of Night*: things became more distant one way but closer the next.

Perhaps the *Zone* had dried and become a rock.

Stranger things had happened, Hannah thought. But the important thing was to go farther, because she needed to fetch her cat.

"Kitty kitty kitty!"

Hannah walked onward, watching her step. Once her eyes adjusted, she found that she could see quite well inside the rock. To her surprise, she saw that she wasn't in a volcano *or* a megalith. In fact, the place looked rather ordinary; in fact, she saw that she was walking on a city street. She could tell it was a city because the buildings were city-size shapes: giant warehouses, one after another, *huge* windowless structures made of glass and concrete whose purpose she could not discern. She walked on and stared at the sights, and with every step, the megalith's entrance grew smaller and farther away. *Don't go too far*, she warned herself, for she knew she would have to go back.

Now she could tell the reason for the smoke. The smoke rose as vapor from the ground on which these building stood. A dense, powdery ash had settled on the streets and pavements, and the ash clung to her sneakers. The ash muffled the sound of her footsteps as though her feet had been swaddled with cloths, and it rose as a fine dust wherever she stepped. *Moon dust*, she decided. Fritz wouldn't like this dirt a bit.

Actually, this ash-gray, burned-out city reminded her of something else, though for a moment she couldn't quite tell what it was. When the answer finally came, she stood stock-still surprised. This dead and smoking city reminded her of the junkyard where Walter, the Fish of Wisdom, had once decided to hide. *Worldwide Dismantlers*, it had been called. Was the fish still swimming in his tank? She wished that Walter were with her to answer her questions, for right now she had many questions to ask. This whole world, which appeared to be a city, was really an enormous pile of junk. She knelt and sifted the ash, brushing it aside from where she stood. Just as she had suspected: the ash did not cover the ground; it covered rooftops. This city, vast and empty, stood piled on top of another city: a city, she suspected, older than the first. Like cars piled one on top the other, each city had been compressed. She realized that this whole shadowy vault was just a giant yard for storing junk.

Curious, she entered one of the buildings—not a special building, but one just like the others that she saw. She passed through the revolving door into a coldly air-conditioned interior brightly lit by unseen florescent bulbs. And because the floor had been made of some transparent substance such as glass, she saw that the enormous building went downward into the ground to the same distance that it went up. It felt like an enormous library. Shelves and metal racks filled it completely from bottom to top, and these shelves were crammed with files, books, folders, photographs, and piles of paper. She walked a bit farther, following a catwalk suspended from the walls. Ahead she heard an electric hum. She came to a platform from which she could look down into the cells and cubicles of an enormous office building in which people sat busy and studious at quiet tasks. "Hello!" she shouted, but no one looked up. She realized they were zealously transcribing vast heaps of printed information. They all looked very efficient. Equidistant from every cubicle, suspended so that everyone could see, hung bright color broadcast screens—each screen broadcasting the same program with the sound turned off.

She walked even farther and came to a railing that marked the perimeter of a circular shaft. The shaft rose through the center of the building and descended into the ground to a furious depth. Its opposite side was so far away that the people who worked there looked like miniatures in a dollhouse. Gazing downward into the shaft, Hannah felt dizzy, as she had felt once long ago when Uncle Joseph had coaxed her to stand at the edge of Niagara Falls. At regular intervals, bands of light marked the descending floors. These bands of light sparkled like reflections from innumerable Milky Ways, and at the very bottom of the shaft, far far below, she saw heaped up in one enormous pile the shards of countless broken mirrors, shimmering like a frozen lake of shattered ice. The most remarkable feature of this shaft was at its center, for from here a stream of cold air blew strongly upwards from the pile of broken mirrors and whistled in the shaft. This air carried on its currents pages and pages of paper, and it reminded Hannah of a white tornado. The paper rustled loudly as it rose and disappeared from view, sucked toward the invisible apex of this building. There was something indescribably sad and wistful about that sound, Hannah thought. She could almost imagine that she heard human whispers and not the rustle of endless pages, as though bodiless, homeless spirits or melancholy angels circulated continually up and down this shaft, trapped in this current of cold wind. In every building, she imagined there must be similar shafts with similar whispering pages, empty of life. A page broke free from this swirling vortex and fluttered like a feather to her feet. She picked it up, surprised to see that it showed a childish scrawl done in blue crayon, a misshapen stick figure of a human being such as a child might have drawn. Someone had written the word *Hannah* in the same unformed and childish hand, using a red crayon and pressing hard. On the opposite side of this paper she saw another stick figure— apparently a man, for its face had a crude dark beard. This person stood alone beneath a tree. A Christmas tree, it looked like.

The word beneath it said: *Dad.*

Almost she could recall what this picture meant, but she released it to the wind of the bottomless shaft.

As the picture left her hand, she heard a voice

Hannah, do not remain here. Leave at once. In the dirt outside you will find the Singer's harp. Return to the boat and use the harp to guide you down the river. You will find the entrance to Elowyn over the falls.

She waited, hoping for something more, not quite understanding what the voice had said.

"Who are you? Where are you?"

But the voice remained silent, and for all her shouting, nothing changed. She walked away from the shaft and looked down on the busy offices. The activity below continued without interruption. She saw piles and piles of books and manuscripts being wheeled toward busy clerks. Everyone did his part without fuss or bother. They did not need breaks. It all had an air of tremendous, supernatural, and customer-friendly efficiency. As soon as someone completed transcribing the written words, the pages on which the words were written were whisked away by neatly attired assistants pushing carts. These carts dumped their contents into openings along the walls. Hannah guessed that from here the discarded pages fell into the enormous shaft, were seized by the ceaseless wind, and were uplifted.

She did not know what happened to them after that.

She felt a soft pressure against her leg. Looking down, she saw Fritz, the kitty cat, covered with ash.

"Bad kitty," she told him, picking him up and rubbing his ears.

Fritz purred. He did not bite her. Now that she had found him, she wanted out. As quickly as she could, she left this deadly building and walked back to the entrance of the stone. She emerged into the bright sunlight of the outer world, blinking furiously, and saw that she was completely covered with ash. The harp lay just where she had seen it on the ground. Curious now, she picked it up. Three of the harp's seven silver strings had snapped, but the rest of the instrument felt sound enough. She tucked it under her arm and called to the cat to follow. She did not think a boat could be near, but at least she would look. She followed a narrow path upwards out of the pit, and once she was free, the trail, to her surprise, looked vaguely familiar, as though she had come this way before. She followed it doggedly, and as she continued, the feeling of familiarity increased. Now and then, she felt Walter's twig, which hung from a string about her neck. Its presence was very reassuring.

Even before she came to the end of the trail, she knew she would find a stream and a boat waiting ready on a beach. She saw footsteps in the sand all around this wooden boat, and these, too, did not surprise her, though she could not recall how they had been made. Even the harp felt more familiar to her now. She entered the boat and plucked a tentative chord, knowing that this was the music she would need and feeling not at all surprised when the boat, as though propelled by unseen oarsmen, drifted away from the shore. Fritz meowed for attention, so she picked him up and held him in her lap.

Moving swiftly with the current, the boat found safe passage down the stream. She did not have to guide it, nor did she worry that the boat, misdirected, might hit a rock and sink. She felt certain that the harp would keep her safe. Perhaps in a dream she had done all this before, though she thought that in the dream she had gone in the other direction, and she did not think she had been alone that other time.

Patiently, she watched as a desolate landscape, filled with ruins, drifted by monotonously until at last the shadows lengthened and night came upon this barren world. She saw the moon rise full above the horizon, cool and comforting in its icy roundness, and the cat began to purr. It had left her lap to settle like a sphinx in the prow of the boat. Onward they traveled. She slept and woke and slept again, and still the night persisted.

At last, she heard a sound that she thought to be the *Zone of Night*, a roar and a rumble, as though a mighty thunderstorm distantly raged. She peered downriver, hoping to see the approaching clouds, and as she looked, a golden fish leaped high above the moonlit stream, delighting in its movement.

"Walter!"

Walter, the Fish of Wisdom, swam to the side of her boat, moving swiftly just inches beneath the surface of the river. She could hear his words clearly inside her head.

"Drop the Singer's harp. Return it to me. You will not need its magic any longer."

Although she had a hundred questions she wanted to ask, she obeyed at once.

"Ahead are the falls of the Karakala," Walter said. "You must pass over the falls. Do not be afraid; I shall guide you and swim beside you. Hold the twig that I gave you long ago. Your journey will soon be at its end."

Now the sound of falling water became so loud that she could no longer hear Walter nor see the fish in the frothy waves. She stared at the approaching cataract, which roared like a screaming vortex inside the *Zone of Night*. She had no time to speak or flinch or scream. Clutching the twig tightly, she reached for Fritz just as the boat swept them over the thunderous falls.

Operis Finis

When at last Hannah came to her senses, the full moon had completed half its journey across the dome of night. The air tasted sweet and salty, and in the distance, she heard the sound of breaking waves.

Hannah rose from where she had fallen against the side of her tiny craft and gazed over the boat's gunwale to behold a limitless ocean. She saw that she had drifted toward a moonlit, sandy beach. To either side of her, waves rolled gently toward the shore, while ahead stood a bank of sand dunes. She heard laughter and voices and saw, as she scanned the wide beach before her, that seven adults had gathered in a semi-circle upon the sand. These strangers faced the water and watched as her boat drifted near. She had the feeling that she knew them, every one, though in the moonlight she could not see their faces very clearly. All of these adults were men, except for one woman, and as the boat drew near the woman left the group and walked into the rolling waves. There she waited with her body half in water. As soon as she could, the woman seized the bow of Hannah's boat and with firm, surprising strength pulled it ashore. She stood with her hand outstretched for Hannah's balance. "Come," she smiled at her shyly, "my child, you have returned."

Hannah saw that the woman's skin was the color of the moonlit beach and that her hair was a shade of auburn like her own. The woman wore a simple dress made from cotton, fastened to her waist with a woven belt. Hannah wondered if she had met her long ago.

"Are you a friend of Walter's?" Hannah asked.

The woman smiled with a loving and chaste expression, and her eyes looked momentarily toward the open water. "I am," she admitted shyly.

Hannah stepped from the boat, cheered by this answer, and she allowed the woman to steady her as she jumped. The stranger's touch felt warm and encouraging, and her eyes seemed to wish her only well. "Come to the shore. The waves and the wind told us you would come. At first, I did not believe them, I was afraid. "

"Afraid of what?" asked Hannah. But the woman again looked away, her eyes blinking as though the wind had blown them with sand.

"Hannah, don't you know me?"

And when Hannah said no, the woman's thoughtful face grew very sad. She asked to see Walter's gift, the tiny twig that Hannah wore about her neck, and at once Hannah recalled the fish's words. "Is this Elowyn?" she asked. The woman nodded. And then, to her amazement, the strange and beautiful woman bent down and kissed her.

"My child," she whispered, "I know it was wrong to greet you, but how could I have foreseen what you would recall? Take the green and living twig that Walter gave you and carry it to the roots of the Singing Tree. There you will remember who I am."

Surprised, Hannah saw the woman gesture toward the dunes. But she saw no Tree: only sand, sky, ocean, and silver moonlight.

The other six adults stood watching them at a distance in a circle.

The woman stepped away toward the open water, wading up to her hips in the rolling waves. "Where are you going?" asked Hannah, growing alarmed.

"I must return to the waves; they will not harm me. It is only for this moment that we may meet. Go now; continue your journey. You have not yet pursued it to its end."

"But I have," said Hannah, "you said so yourself. Isn't this the unknown country?"

But the woman made no answer to this question.

Confused, Hannah saw the woman wade farther into the waves, while along the shore the strange adults rose and waded into the water also, submerging one by one beneath the waves as though they were creatures of that element. At last they all vanished.

Now the ocean had claimed the woman's breasts. In another moment, her face would disappear beneath the water, Hannah saw. A panicked doubt gripped her heart and made her speak. She did not want the woman to go away.

"Who are you?" Hannah shouted. "What's your name?"

As her cry sounded over the water, Hannah saw the woman hesitate, and the waves swirled and washed her auburn hair. Seeing that the strange woman meant to submerge herself, Hannah splashed into the rolling, moonlit ocean, too. But the woman moved farther back, and now the ceaseless waters lapped her chin.

"Hannah, do not follow, keep away. This ocean will not harm me. It was a mistake to have met you—Walter warned me not to come. But how could I resist—*you are my daughter!* Hannah, I am your mother—and this, the land of Elowyn, is my home."

Her words took all the strength from Hannah's legs. She floundered and nearly fell. A wave of lost remembrance overcame her, overpowering her with a sudden, wrenching sense of numbing loss. She staggered and cried out with a strangled voice, but her mother's face had nearly passed from view.

"Daughter, go back! I cannot stay here. One day we shall meet in a place that neither can yet recall. It will happen if you do as Walter asked. Take the twig that Walter gave you and plant it at the root of the dying Tree. Do this, my daughter, hurry! Do this if you would be whole."

Now the waves washed higher, plunging her mother's head into the sea. Hannah thrashed forward, but a greater wave rolled down on her and threw her back. It crashed and overcame her, turning her over and over like a piece of driftwood. Sand and saltwater stung her nose and eyes. And all the while, she called her mother's name.

"Always toward home . . . "

Hannah lay on the beach until the great orb of the moon had nearly set. Her mother's parting words had filled her with a deep, inexpressible sorrow. She had seen into the heart of her remembrance and had met the memory most lost and distant to herself. The pain of that meeting throbbed like an open wound that the salt water cleansed. That pain would stay with her long after the wound had healed.

She no longer knew the way forward, nor did she care where her path might lead. Moving numbly, as though from habit, she left the shore and walked toward the dunes that bordered this endless ocean. When she reached the dunes, she turned and looked once more toward the ocean waves, toward the spot where her mother had last appeared. She held tightly in her hand the twig that Walter had given her, the green and living twig that the Seventh Friedrich and the Privy Counselor had urged her to guard, though now she scarcely felt its slender weight.

"Hannah," said a voice from close behind her. "Hannah, your journey is nearly over. It is time to recall your way home."

She turned, surprised to hear herself addressed in just this way and feeling for a moment very dizzy and unsettled.

Before her stood a man with snow-white hair. He was dressed like a humble gardener, with long blue overalls and black rubber boots caked with mud. His hair rose wild and unruly from his scalp like a porcupine's quills, as though he had cut it himself and had never bothered to use a comb. And his eyes were the most brilliant shade of gold.

He smiled at her warmly, and Hannah felt that she had known him for a very long time.

"You're Walter," she said without surprise.

The old gardener nodded.

His eyes flashed as he smiled, much like the golden shimmer of a fish.

"Yes," he replied, "I am Walter. I swam long and hard to keep up with you, Hannah, and now I have come to bring you home."

"Home?" asked Hannah in wonder as the smiling Master of Memory reached to brush her forehead gently between her eyes. Her whole body felt warmed by the Master's touch.

Walter spoke to her firmly, like the fish he had always been. "We have one last moment to share in this distant place. Take what you have received here, the gifts of your remembrance and your striving, and carry those possessions in your heart. In another time and place, you will recall them, and then they will yield their ripened fruit. But for now, dear Hannah, look behind me to the east. The sun has risen. Look within its aura—there you will behold the Tree you sought."

Hannah turned in the direction Walter pointed. Before her, resplendent in the weaving colors of the dawn, grew a Tree from earth to heaven and from heaven again to earth. From its leaves and sweeping branches, in harmonious and gentle ordering, radiant human voices resounded in song, their clear tones rising and falling in the constant glowing halo of the boughs.

"Look closer, Hannah," she heard the Master instruct.

A person had appeared. Walking closer, Hannah saw that this person was a woman, though not any woman she had ever met. The woman—many, many years older than herself—came toward her slowly with a look of startled curiosity and surprise. Hannah saw that her face was much like her own, though greatly aged and seasoned by care and sorrow, as though the person were herself in later years. The woman's raven hair, well streaked with gray, had been clipped close and carelessly to her head, so that, except for her figure and the maternal, wise maturity of her face, one might have thought that she was an ancient man.

Hannah stood for a moment in silence, beholding this stranger and wondering what this meeting could mean, and then the silent woman took her hand. As soon as their fingers touched, a flood of images overwhelmed Hannah in cascade, as though the portals of her memory had opened. She saw the strange woman's eyes grow wide with the same revelation, and in that moment she understood that she and the old woman were the same. The two were one. They had arrived, each in the rhythm of her season, and in time the others would arrive here, too.

"Hurry," said Hannah, "we must go forward. Walter told me to plant the twig."

Hand in hand, Hannah and the old woman approached the Singing Tree, although to Hannah it seemed as though the Tree merely drew them toward its boughs. When she came beneath the canopy of its branches, she knelt and began to turn the soil, and the woman knelt beside her and lent a hand. Hannah knew this soil at once—it was soil from *her* garden, Uncle Joseph's garden— damp and dark and alive as she remembered it—and the air smelled sweet like all the forests she had ever loved.

Together, they placed the twig in the ground that was its home and patted the soil in place to cover it gently.

"I found you at last," said the woman, her eyes shining, though Hannah was not certain whether the woman spoke to her or the fabled Tree.

Then Hannah felt the woman release her hand, and in that same moment, she heard Walter call her name a third and final time. She turned to find him but saw, instead of Walter, the garden she had known and loved so well. Only few steps were needed to cross to that distant lawn.

She saw her backdoor, which suddenly opened. A stranger stepped out. She thought it was a stranger, but in another moment, behind him, she saw her Uncle Joseph, too. "Hannah!" the stranger shouted excitedly, laughing loudly with sheer delight. And suddenly she recognized who it was. Her father, Charles, had returned at last from his long journey to discover the last unknown country in the world. He had come home, and he held out his arms to receive her.

Overjoyed, Hannah waved. She turned one last time to bid farewell to Walter and to the woman who had met her at the Singing Tree, but the strangely familiar woman had withdrawn, and Walter also. Hannah could just barely glimpse the woman's outline as she strode beneath the Tree's high swaying boughs. "Good bye," Hannah shouted loudly, though the distant woman did not respond. *Perhaps*, thought Hannah, *she could not.* Perhaps this strange woman heard nothing but the singing of the Tree she had sought so long. *Was she glad to journey onward all alone?*

This question made Hannah hesitate, but she did not tarry long. Her father's laughing voice called to her again, and she turned in joy to greet him. With every step, she felt infused by a warming radiance whose source was the Tree she had found. She saw the *Zone of Night* and then beyond it, appearing through a shimmering veil of rain, she saw the two adults whom she loved most in the entire world.

Her father and Uncle Joseph—*what would they say when she returned?*—waved and called her on. Fritz sat purring at their feet.

Hearing their joyful greeting, Hannah broke into a run. She knew she could trust the good Master to guide her home.

Completum est quod dixi de operatione Solis.

The End

BIOGRAPHY

Bruce Donehower is the author of several novels including *ICE (Xlibris)* and *Miko, Little Hunter of the North* (Farrar, Straus and Giroux). He holds a Ph.D. in English and M.A. in German from the University of California, Davis, where he lectures part-time. He and his wife Marion are co-founders of the *Novalis / Tieck Group for Fairy Tale, Mythology, and Culture,* an initiative for the furtherance of the humanities in the spirit of Rudolf Steiner's Anthroposophy. The *Group* sponsors a variety of workshops, seminars, and publications. Interested persons should contact the *Group* at www.novalis.info.

Printed in the United States
16179LVS00002B/193